# FLIGHTS

# FLIGHTS

## OLGA TOKARCZUK

*Translated by Jennifer Croft*

RIVERHEAD BOOKS

NEW YORK

2018

RIVERHEAD BOOKS
An imprint of Penguin Random House LLC
375 Hudson Street
New York, New York 10014

Copyright © 2018 by Olga Tokarczuk
English translation © 2017 by Jennifer Croft
Originally published in Polish as *Bieguni* by Wydawnictwo Literackie, Kraków
English-language edition first published in Great Britain by Fitzcarraldo Editions, London
First American edition published by Riverhead Books, 2018
Penguin supports copyright. Copyright fuels creativity, encourages diverse voices,
promotes free speech, and creates a vibrant culture. Thank you for buying an authorized
edition of this book and for complying with copyright laws by not reproducing, scanning,
or distributing any part of it in any form without permission. You are supporting
writers and allowing Penguin to continue to publish books for every reader.

Portions of this book appeared in *Asymptote*, *BOMB*,
*The Brooklyn Rail*, *Exchanges*, and *n+1*.

Library of Congress Cataloging-in-Publication Data

Names: Tokarczuk, Olga, author. | Croft, Jennifer (Translator), translator.
Title: Flights / Olga Tokarczuk ; translated by Jennifer Croft.
Other titles: Bieguni. English
Description: First American edition. | New York : Riverhead Books, 2018.
Identifiers: LCCN 2017039765| ISBN 9780525534198 (hardcover) |
ISBN 9780525534211 (ebook)
Classification: LCC PG7179.O37 B5413 2018 | DDC 891.8/537—dc23
LC record available at https://lccn.loc.gov/2017039765
p.    cm.

International edition ISBN: 9780525541264

Printed in the United States of America
3   5   7   9   10   8   6   4

BOOK DESIGN BY MEIGHAN CAVANAUGH

# FLIGHTS

# HERE I AM

I'm a few years old. I'm sitting on the windowsill, surrounded by strewn toys and toppled-over block towers and dolls with bulging eyes. It's dark in the house, and the air in the rooms slowly cools, dims. There's no one else here; they've left, they're gone, though you can still hear their voices dying down, that shuffling, the echoes of their footsteps, some distant laughter. Out the window the court-yard is empty. Darkness spreads softly from the sky, settling on everything like black dew.

The worst part is the stillness, visible, dense—a chilly dusk and the sodium-vapor lamps' frail light already mired in darkness just a few feet from its source.

Nothing happens—the march of darkness halts at the door to the house, and all the clamor of fading falls silent, makes a thick skin like on hot milk cooling. The contours of the buildings against the backdrop of the sky stretch out into infinity, slowly lose their sharp angles, corners, edges. The dimming light takes the air with it—there's nothing left to breathe. Now the dark soaks into my skin. Sounds have curled up inside themselves, withdrawn their snail's eyes; the orchestra of the world has departed, vanishing into the park.

That evening is the limit of the world, and I've just happened upon it, by accident, while playing, not in search of anything. I've discovered it because I was left unsupervised for a bit. I realize I've fallen into a trap here now, realize I'm stuck. I'm a few years old, I'm sitting on the windowsill, and I'm looking out onto the chilled courtyard. The lights in the school's kitchen are extinguished; everyone has left. All the doors are closed, the hatches down, shades lowered. I'd like to leave, but there's nowhere to go. My own presence is the only thing with a distinct outline now, an outline that quivers and undulates, and in so doing, hurts. And all of a sudden I know: there's nothing for it now, here I am.

## THE WORLD IN YOUR HEAD

The first trip I ever took was across the fields, on foot. It took them a long time to notice I was gone, which meant I was able to make it quite some distance. I covered the whole park and even— going down dirt roads, through the corn and the damp meadows teeming with cowslip flowers, sectioned into squares by ditches— reached the river. Though of course the river was ubiquitous in that valley, soaking up under the ground cover and lapping at the fields.

Clambering up onto the embankment, I could see an undulating ribbon, a road that kept flowing outside of the frame, outside of the world. If you were lucky, you might catch sight of a boat there, one of those great flat boats gliding over the river in either direction, oblivious to the shores, to the trees, to the people who stand on the embankment, unreliable landmarks, perhaps, not worth remarking, just an audience to the boats' own motion, so full of grace. I dreamed of working on a boat like that when I grew up—or even better, of becoming one of those boats.

It wasn't a big river, only the Oder, but I, too, was little then. It had its place in the hierarchy of rivers, which I later checked on the maps—a minor one, but present, nonetheless, a kind of country viscountess at the court of the Amazon queen. But it was more than enough for me. It seemed enormous. It flowed as it liked, essentially unimpeded, prone to flooding, unpredictable.

Occasionally along the banks it would catch on some underwater obstacle, and eddies would develop. But the river flowed on, parading, concerned only with its hidden aims beyond the horizon, somewhere far off to the north. Your eyes couldn't keep focused on the water, which pulled your gaze along up past the horizon, so that you'd lose your balance.

To me, of course, the river paid no attention, caring only for itself, those changing, roving waters into which—as I later learned—you can never step twice.

Every year it charged a steep price to bear the weight of those boats—because each year someone drowned in the river, whether a child taking a dip on a hot summer's day or some drunk who somehow wound up on the bridge and, in spite of the railing, still fell into the water. The search for the drowned always took place with great pomp and circumstance, with everyone in the vicinity waiting with bated breath. They'd bring in divers and army boats. According to adults' accounts we overheard, the recovered bodies were swollen and pale—the water had rinsed all the life out of them, blurring their facial features to such an extent that their loved ones would have a hard time identifying their corpses.

Standing there on the embankment, staring into the current, I realized that—in spite of all the risks involved—a thing in motion will always be better than a thing at rest; that change will always be a nobler thing than permanence; that that which is static will degenerate and decay, turn to ash, while that which is in motion is able to last for all eternity. From then on, the river was like a needle inserted into my formerly safe and stable surroundings, the landscape composed of the park, the greenhouses with their vegetables that grew in sad little rows, and the sidewalk with its concrete slabs where we would go to play hopscotch. This needle went all the way through, marking a vertical third dimension; so pierced, the landscape of my childhood world turned out to be nothing more than a toy made of rubber from which all the air was escaping, with a hiss.

My parents were not fully the settling kind. They moved from place to place, time and time again, until finally they paused for longer near a country school, far from any proper road or a train station. Then traveling simply became crossing the unplowed ridge between the furrows, going into the little town nearby, doing the shopping, filing paperwork at the district office. The hairdresser on the main square by the Town Hall was always there in the same apron, washed and bleached in vain because the clients' hair dye left stains like calligraphy, like Chinese characters. My mom would have her hair dyed, and my father would wait for her at the New Café, at one of the two little tables set up outside. He'd read the local paper, where the most interesting section was always the one with the police reports, gherkins and jam jars stolen out of cellars.

And then the vacations, their timid tourism, their Škoda packed to the gills. Endlessly prepared for, planned in the evenings in the early

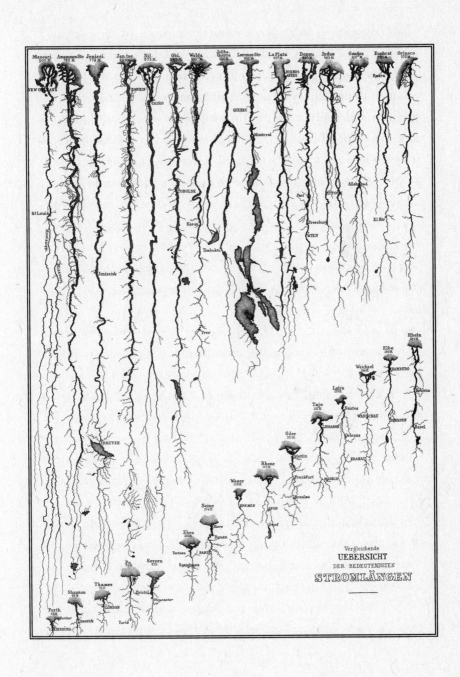

spring when the snow had all but stopped, though the ground had yet to come back to its senses; you had to wait until it finally gave itself to plow and hoe, when you could plant in it again, and from that moment forward it would take up all their time, from morning to eve.

Theirs was the generation of motor homes, of tugging along behind them a whole surrogate household. A gas stove, little folding tables and chairs. A plastic cord to hang laundry up to dry when they stopped and some wooden clothespins. Waterproof tablecloths. A ready-made picnic set: colored plastic plates, utensils, salt and pepper shakers, and glasses.

Somewhere along the way, at one of the flea markets that he and my mother particularly loved to visit (since they were not interested, for instance, in having their pictures taken at churches or monuments), my father had purchased an army kettle—a brass device, a vessel with a tube in the middle that you would fill up with tinder you lit on fire. Though you could get electricity at the campsites, he would heat up water in that smoking, spluttering pot. He'd kneel down over the hot kettle, taking no small pride in the gurgle of the boiling water he'd then pour over our tea bags—a true nomad.

They'd set up in the designated areas, at campsites where they were always in the company of others just like them, having lively conversations with their neighbors, surrounded by socks drying on tent cords. The itineraries for these trips would be determined with the aid of guidebooks that painstakingly highlighted all the attractions. In the morning a swim in the sea or the lake, and in the afternoon an excursion into the city's history, capped off by dinner, most often out of glass jars: goulash, meatballs in tomato sauce. You just had to cook the pasta or the rice. Costs were always being cut, the

Polish zloty was weak—penny of the world. There was the search for a place where you could get electricity and then the reluctant decamping after, although all journeys remained within the same metaphysical orbit of home. They weren't real travelers: they left in order to return. And they were relieved when they got back, with a sense of having fulfilled an obligation. They returned to collect the letters and bills that stacked up on the chest of drawers. To do a big wash. To bore their friends to death by showing pictures as everyone attempted to conceal their yawns. This is us in Carcassonne. Here's my wife with the Acropolis in the background.

Then they would lead a settled life for the next year, going back every morning to the same thing they had left in the evening, their clothes permeated by the scent of their own flat, their feet tirelessly wearing down a path in the carpet.

That life is not for me. Clearly I did not inherit whatever gene it is that makes it so that when you linger in a place you start to put down roots. I've tried, a number of times, but my roots have always been shallow; the littlest breeze could always blow me right over. I don't know how to germinate, I'm simply not in possession of that vegetable capacity. I can't extract nutrition from the ground, I am the anti-Antaeus. My energy derives from movement—from the shuddering of buses, the rumble of planes, trains' and ferries' rocking.

I have a practical build. I'm petite, compact. My stomach is tight, small, undemanding. My lungs and my shoulders are strong. I'm not on any prescriptions—not even the pill—and I don't wear glasses. I cut my hair with clippers, once every three months, and I use almost no makeup. My teeth are healthy, perhaps a bit uneven, but intact, and I have just one old filling, which I believe is located in my lower left canine. My liver function is within the normal range. As is my pancreas. Both my right and left kidneys are in great shape. My abdominal aorta is normal. My bladder works. Hemoglobin 12.7. Leukocytes 4.5. Hematocrit 41.6. Platelets 228. Cholesterol 204. Creatinine 1.0. Bilirubin 4.2. And so on. My IQ— if you put any stock in that kind of thing—is 121; it's passable. My spatial reasoning is particularly advanced, almost eidetic, though my laterality is lousy. Personality unstable, or not entirely reliable. Age all in your mind. Gender grammatical. I actually buy my books in paperback, so that I can leave them without remorse on the platform, for someone else to find. I don't collect anything.

I completed my degree, but I never really mastered any trade, which I do regret; my great-grandfather was a weaver, bleaching woven cloth by laying it out along the hillside, baring it to the sun's hot rays. I would have been well suited to the intermingling of warp and weft, but there's no such thing as a portable loom. Weaving is an art of sedentary tribes. When I'm traveling I knit. Sadly, in recent times some airlines have banned the use of knitting needles and crochet hooks on board. I never learned, as I say, any particular line of work, and yet in spite of what my parents always used to tell me, I've been able to get by, working different jobs as I go, staying afloat.

When my parents went back to the city after their twenty-year experiment, when they had finally tired of the droughts and the frosts, healthy food that ailed all winter in the cellar, the wool from their own sheep assiduously stuffed inside the gaping mouths of comforters and pillows, they gave me a little bit of money, and I set off on my first trip.

I took odd jobs wherever I happened to be. In an international factory on the outskirts of a large metropolis I assembled antennas for high-end yachts. There were a lot of people like me there. We were paid under the table and never questioned about where we came from or what our plans were for the future. Every Friday we got our money, and whoever didn't feel like it anymore simply didn't come back on Monday. There were high school graduates taking a break before applying to university. Immigrants still en route to that fair, idyllic country they were sure was somewhere in the West, where people are brothers and sisters, and a strong state plays the role of parent; fugitives from their families—from their wives, their husbands, their parents; the unhappily in love, the confused, the melancholic, those who were always cold. Those running from the law because they couldn't pay off their debts. Wanderers, vagabonds. Crazy people who'd wind up in the hospital the next time they fell ill again, and from there they'd get deported back to their countries of origin on the basis of rules and regulations shrouded in mystery.

Just one person worked there permanently, an Indian man who had been there for years, though in reality his situation was no different from ours. He didn't have insurance or paid vacation. He worked in silence, patiently, on an even keel. He was never late. He never found any need to take time off. I tried to talk some people into setting up a trade union—these were the days of Solidarity—if only for him, but he didn't want to. Touched by the interest I'd taken in him, however, he began to share with me the spicy curry he brought in a lunch box every day. I no longer remember what his name was.

I was a waitress, a maid in an upscale hotel, and a nanny. I sold books. I sold tickets. I was employed in a small theater for one season to work in wardrobe, making it through that long winter ensconced backstage amidst heavy costumes, satin capes, and wigs. Once I'd finished my studies, I also worked as a teacher, as a rehab counselor, and—most recently—in a library. Whenever I managed to save any money, I would be on my way again.

## YOUR HEAD IN THE WORLD

I studied psychology in a big, gloomy communist city. My department was located in a building that had been the headquarters of an SS unit during the war. That part of the city had been built up on the ruins of the ghetto, which you could tell if you took a good look— that whole neighborhood stood about three feet higher than the rest of the town. Three feet of rubble. I never felt comfortable there; between the new communist buildings and the wretched squares, there was always a wind, and the frosty air was particularly bitter, stinging you in the face. Ultimately it was a place that, despite reconstruction, still belonged to the dead. I still have dreams about the building where my classes were—its broad hallways that looked like they'd been carved into stone, smoothed down by people's feet; the worn edges of the stairs; the handrails polished by people's hands, traces imprinted in space. Maybe that was why we were haunted by those ghosts.

When we'd put rats in a maze, there was always one whose behavior would contradict the theory, who couldn't have cared less about our clever hypotheses. It would stand up on its little hind legs, absolutely indifferent to the reward at the end of our experimental route; disdaining the perks of Pavlovian conditioning, it would simply take one good look at us and then turn around, or turn to an unhurried exploration of the maze. It would look for something in the lateral corridors, trying to attract our attention. It would squeak, disoriented, until the girls would break the rules, remove it from the maze and hold it in their hands.

The muscles of a dead, splayed frog would flex and straighten to the rhythm of electrical pulses, but in a way that had not yet been described in our textbooks—it would gesture to us, its limbs clearly making menacing and mocking signs, thereby contradicting our hallowed faith in the mechanical innocence of physiological reflexes.

Here we were taught that the world could be described, and even explained, by means of simple answers to intelligent questions. That in its essence the world was inert and dead, governed by fairly simple laws that needed to be explained and made public—if possible with the aid of diagrams. We were required to do experiments. To formulate hypotheses. To verify. We were inducted into the mysteries of statistics, taught to believe that equipped with such a tool we would be able to perfectly describe all the workings of the world—that ninety percent is more significant than five.

But if there's one thing I know now, it's that anyone looking for order ought to steer clear of psychology altogether. Go for physiology or theology instead, where at least you'll have solid backing—either in matter or in spirit—instead of psychology's slippery terrain. The psyche is quite a tenuous object of study.

It turned out it was true what some people said about psychology being a degree you choose not because of the job you want, or out of curiosity or a vocation to help others, but rather for another very simple reason. I think all of us had some sort of deeply hidden defect, although we no doubt all gave the impression of intelligent, healthy young people—the defect was masked,

skillfully camouflaged during our entrance exams. A ball of tautly
tangled emotions breaking down, like those strange tumors that
turn up sometimes in the human body and that can be seen in any
self-respecting museum of pathological anatomy. Although what
if our examiners were the same sort of people, who knew exactly
what they were doing in selecting us? In that case, we would
be their direct heirs. When, in our second year, we discussed the
function of defense mechanisms and found that we were humbled
by the power of that portion of our psyche, we began to understand that if it weren't for rationalization, sublimation, denial—all
the little tricks we let ourselves perform—if instead we simply saw
the world as it was, with nothing to protect us, honestly and cou-
rageously, it would break our hearts.

What we learned at university was that we are made up of de-
fenses, of shields and armor, that we are cities whose architecture
essentially comes down to walls, ramparts, strongholds: bunker
states.

Every test, questionnaire, and study we also conducted on each
other, so that by the time we got through our third year I had a
name for what was wrong with me; it was like discovering my own
secret name, the name that summons one to an initiation.

I didn't exercise the trade for which I'd trained for very long. During
one of my expeditions, when I had gotten stuck in a big city with no
money and was working as a maid, I started writing a book. It was
a story for travelers, meant to be read on the train—what I would
write for myself to read. A bite-sized snack of a book, that you
could swallow whole.

I was able to concentrate and became for some time a sort of gargantuan ear that listened to murmurs and echoes and whispers, far-off voices that filtered through the walls. But I never became a real writer. Life always managed to elude me. I'd only ever find its tracks, the skin it sloughed off. By the time I had determined its location, it had already gone somewhere else. And all I'd find were signs that it had been there, like those scrawlings on the trunks of trees in parks that merely mark a person's passing presence. In my writing, life would turn into incomplete stories, dreamlike tales, would show up from afar in odd dislocated panoramas, or in cross sections—and so it would be almost impossible to reach any conclusions as to the whole.

Anyone who has ever tried to write a novel knows what an arduous task it is, undoubtedly one of the worst ways of occupying oneself. You have to remain within yourself all the time, in solitary confinement. It's a controlled psychosis, an obsessive paranoia manacled to work, completely lacking in the feather pens and bustles and Venetian masks we would ordinarily associate with it, clothed instead in a butcher's apron and rubber boots, eviscerating knife in hand. You can only barely see from that writerly cellar the feet of passersby, hear the rapping of their heels. Every so often someone stops and bends down and glances in through the window, and then you get a glimpse of a human face, maybe even exchange a few words. But ultimately the mind is so occupied with its own act, a play staged by the self for the self in a hasty, makeshift cabinet of curiosities peopled by author and character, narrator and reader, the person describing and the person being described, that feet, shoes, heels, and faces become, sooner or later, mere components of that act.

I don't regret developing a taste for this odd occupation: I would not have made a good psychologist. I never knew how to explain, how to call forth family photos from the depths of someone's thoughts. And the confessions of others more often than not simply bored me, though it does pain me to admit it. But to be honest, it was often the case that I would have preferred to reverse the relationship and start talking to them about me. I had to watch myself to keep from suddenly grabbing the patient by her sleeve and interrupting her mid-sentence: "I can't believe you! I have a completely different reaction! Well, you won't believe the dream that I just had!" Or: "What do you know about insomnia, sir? And that's what you call a panic attack? Surely you're joking. The panic attack I had not too long ago, on the other hand . . ."

I didn't know how to listen. I didn't observe boundaries; I'd slip into transference. I didn't believe in statistics or verifying theories. The postulate of one personality to one person always struck me as overly minimalist. I had a tendency to blur what seemed clear and to question irrefutable arguments—it was a habit I had, a perverse mental yoga, the subtle pleasure of experiencing internal motion. I would examine with suspicion every judgment, turn each one over in my mouth, until finally I figured out what I'd expected: not a single one of them was right, they were all fakes, knockoffs. I didn't want to have set opinions, which were just excess baggage. In debates, I'd be on one side one time and the other the next—which I know never endeared me to my interlocutors. I was witness to a strange phenomenon that occurred in my mind: the more I would find arguments for something, the more arguments against it would occur to me, too, and the more I grew attached to those arguments in favor, the more alluring the opposition became.

How was I supposed to analyze others when it was hard enough for me to get through all those tests? Personality diagnostics, surveys, multiple columns of multiple-choice questions all struck me as too hard. I noticed this handicap of mine right away, which is why at university, whenever we were analyzing each other for practice, I would give all of my answers at random, whatever happened to occur to me. I'd wind up with the strangest personality profiles—curves on a coordinate axis. "Do you believe that the best decision is also the decision that is easiest to change?" Do I believe? What kind of decision? Change? When? Easiest how? "When you walk into a room, do you tend to head for the middle or the edges?" What room? And when? Is the room empty, or are there plush red couches in it? What about the windows? What kind of view do they have? The book question: Would I rather read one than go to a party, or does it also depend on what kind of book it is and what kind of party?

What a methodology! It is tacitly assumed that people don't know themselves, but that if you furnish them with questions that are smart enough, they'll be able to figure themselves out. They pose themselves a question, and they give themselves an answer. And they'll inadvertently reveal to themselves that secret they knew nothing of till now.

And there is that other assumption, which is terribly dangerous—that we are constant, and that our reactions can be predicted.

## SYNDROME

The chronicles of my travels would in fact be chronicles of an ailment. I suffer from a syndrome that can easily be found in any atlas of clinical syndromes and that—at least according to the literature—occurs with greater and greater frequency. We had better take a peek at this old edition (published in the seventies) of the *Clinical Syndromes*, which is an encyclopedia of syndromes of sorts. For me, it is also an endless source of inspiration. Is there anyone else who would dare to describe people as totalities, both objectively and generally? Who would employ with such conviction the notion of personality? Who would build up to a convincing typology of it? I don't think so. The idea of the syndrome fits travel psychology like a glove. A syndrome is small, portable, not weighed down by theory, episodic. You can explain something with it and then discard it. A disposable instrument of cognition.

Mine is called Recurrent Detoxification Syndrome. Without the bells and whistles, its description boils down to the insistence of one's consciousness on returning to certain images, or even the compulsive search for them. It is a variant of the Mean World Syndrome, which has been described fairly exhaustively in neuropsychological studies as a particular type of infection caused by the media. It's quite a bourgeois ailment, I suppose. Patients spend long hours in front of the TV, thumbing at their remote controls through all the channels till they find the ones with the most horrendous news: wars, epidemics, and disasters. Then, fascinated by what they're seeing, they can't tear themselves away.

The symptoms themselves are not dangerous, allowing one to lead a normal life as long as one is able to maintain some emotional distance. This unfortunate syndrome cannot be cured; science is reduced in its case to the regretful constatation of its existence. When, sufficiently alarmed by their own behavior, patients end up in the offices of psychiatrists, they'll be told to try healthier living—

giving up coffee and alcohol, sleeping in a well-ventilated room, gardening, weaving or knitting.

My set of symptoms revolves around my being drawn to all things spoiled, flawed, defective, broken. I'm interested in whatever shape this may take, mistakes in the making of the thing, dead ends. What was supposed to develop but for some reason didn't; or vice versa, what outstretched the design. Anything that deviates from the norm, that is too small or too big, overgrown or incomplete, monstrous and disgusting. Shapes that don't heed symmetry, that grow exponentially, brim over, bud, or on the contrary, that scale back to the single unit. I'm not interested in the patterns so scrutinized by statistics that everyone celebrates with a familiar, satisfied smile on their faces. My weakness is for teratology and for freaks. I believe, unswervingly, agonizingly, that it is in freaks that Being breaks through to the surface and reveals its true nature. A sudden fluke disclosure. An embarrassing oops, the seam of one's underwear from beneath a perfectly pleated skirt. The hideous metal skeleton that suddenly pops out from the velvet upholstery; the eruption of a spring from within a cushioned armchair that shamelessly debunks any illusion of softness.

## CABINET OF CURIOSITIES

I've never been a big fan of art museums, which I would happily exchange for cabinets of curiosities, where collections encompass the rare, the unique, the bizarre, the freakish. The things that exist in the shadows of consciousness, and that, when you do take a look, dart out of your field of vision. Yes, I definitely have this unfortunate syndrome. I'm not drawn to centrally located collections, but rather to the smaller places near hospitals, frequently moved down to basements, since they're deemed unworthy of prized exhibition spots, and since they suggest the questionable tastes of their original collectors. A salamander with two tails, faceup in an oblong jar, awaiting its Judgment Day—for all the specimens in the world will be resurrected in the end. A dolphin's kidney in formaldehyde. A sheep's skull, a total anomaly, with double sets of eyes and ears and mouths, pretty as the figure of an ancient god with a dual nature. A human fetus draped in beads and a label in careful calligraphy saying *"Fetus aethiopis 5 mensium."* Collected over the years, these freaks of nature, two-headed and no-headed, unborn, float lazily in formaldehyde solution. Or take the case of the *"Cephalothoracopagus monosymetro,"* exhibited to this day in a museum in Pennsylvania, where the pathological morphology of a fetus with one head and two bodies calls into question the foundations of logic by asserting that $1 = 2$. And finally a moving culinary specimen: apples from 1848, resting in alcohol, each of them odd, abnormally shaped. Evidently there was someone who recognized that these freaks of nature were owed immortality, and that only what is different will survive.

It's this kind of thing I make my way toward on my travels, slowly but surely, trailing the errors and blunders of creation.

I've learned to write on trains and in hotels and waiting rooms. On the tray tables on planes. I take notes at lunch, under the table, or in the bathroom. I write in museum stairwells, in cafés, in the car on the shoulder of the motorway. I jot things down on scraps of paper, in notebooks, on postcards, on my other hand, on napkins, in the margins of books. Usually they're short sentences, little images, but sometimes I copy out quotes from the papers. Sometimes a figure carves itself out of the crowd, and then I deviate from my itinerary to follow it for a moment, start on its story. It's a good method; I excel at it. With the years, time has become my ally, as it does for every woman—I've become invisible, see-through. I am able to move around like a ghost, look over people's shoulders, listen in on their arguments and watch them sleep with their heads on their backpacks or talking to themselves, unaware of my presence, moving just their lips, forming words that I will soon pronounce for them.

## SEEING IS KNOWING

Each of my pilgrimages aims at some other pilgrim. In this case the pilgrim is in pieces, broken down.

Here, for instance, is a collection of bones—but only bones that have something wrong with them: curved spines and ribs in ribbons, taken out of what must have been equally deformed bodies, treated, desiccated, and even varnished. There is a little number by each bone to help the viewer locate a description of the illness in a directory that has long since ceased to exist. What kind of durability, after all, does paper have in comparison with bone? They should have written right along the spine.

And here you have a femur that some curious person sawed open lengthwise, in order to take a peek at what was hidden inside. Said person must have been disappointed with the result, because they then tied the two halves together with hemp string and put the femur back in the showcase, their mind already elsewhere.

The showcase holds several dozen people with no relation to one another, separated by space and time—now in such a beautiful resting place, spacious and dry, well lit, and condemned to eternity in a museum. They must be the envy of those bones that got stuck in eternal wrestling matches with the earth. But aren't there some among them—the bones of Catholics, perhaps—that worry as to how they will get found on Judgment Day, as to how, dispersed as they are, they'll be able to build back those bodies that committed sins and did good deeds?

Skulls with growths of all conceivable structures, with bullet holes and other holes, or atrophied. Hand bones wrecked by arthritis. An arm with multiple breaks that then healed naturally, randomly: petrified long-term pain.

Long bones that are too short and short bones that are too long, tubercular, covered in patterns of alterations; you might think they'd been eaten by bark beetles. Poor human skulls, backlit in Victorian showcases, where they bare their teeth in big grins. This one, for instance, has a big hole in the middle of the forehead, but nice teeth. Who knows if that hole was lethal. Not necessarily. There was a man once, a railway engineer, whose brain was run clean through by a metal rod, but he lived for many more years with that wound; needless to say, this came in quite handy for neuropsychology, as it proclaimed to all and sundry that we exist primarily through our brains. He didn't die, but he changed completely. He became a different person, as the expression goes. Since who we are is dependent on our brains, let us proceed directly to our left, down the hall of brains. Here they are! Cream-colored anemones in solution, large and small, some brilliant and others that couldn't count to two.

Next comes the designated section for fetuses, miniature munchkins. Here are the little dolls, the smallest specimens—everything in miniature, so that a whole person will fit in a little jar. These youngest ones, the embryos, which you can barely even see at all, are like little fish, little frogs, suspended from a horse's hair, floating in an expanse of formaldehyde. These bigger ones display the order of the human body, its marvelous packaging. Little not-yet-human crumbs, semi-hominid young, whose lives never crossed the magic border of potentiality. They have the right shape, but they never grew into souls—perhaps the presence of a soul is somehow connected with the size of the shape. In them matter had begun, with somnolent obstinacy, to gear up to live, to accumulate tissue and get organs going and systems running; work on the eyes was already under way, and the lungs were being readied, though to light and air there still remained a ways.

The next row holds the same organs, but now fully grown, pleased to have been allowed by circumstances to attain their full dimensions. Their full dimensions? How did they know how big they were supposed to get, when to stop? Some of them didn't: these intestines grew and grew, and it was hard for our professors to find a jar that would contain them. It's even harder to imagine how they would have fit into the stomach of this man who figures on the label as a pair of initials.

The heart. All its mystery has been conclusively revealed—for it's that unshapely lump the size of a fist, its color a dirty light brown. Please note that that is, in fact, the color of our bodies: grayish brown, ugly. We would not want to have walls in our houses or a car that color. It's the color of insides, of darkness, of places light can't reach, where matter hides in moisture from others' gazes, and there isn't any point in its showing off. The only extravagance able to be afforded went to blood: blood is a warning, its redness an alarm that the casing of the body has been breached. That the continuity of the tissue has been broken. In reality, on the inside we have no color. When the heart pumps out blood as it's supposed to, blood looks just like snot.

## SEVEN YEARS OF TRIPS

"Every year we take a trip, we've been doing it for seven years, ever since we got married," said the young man on the train. He was wearing a long, elegant black overcoat, and he was carrying a stiff briefcase that looked a little like a fancy container for a set of cutlery.

"We have tons of pictures," he was saying, "and we keep them organized. The South of France, Tunisia, Turkey, Italy, Crete, Croatia—even Scandinavia." He said they usually looked at the pictures several times: first with their families, then at the office, and then with their friends, and after that the photographs got safely tucked away in plastic folders, like evidence in a detective's cabinet—evidence that they had been there.

Lost in thought, he gazed out the window at the landscape that seemed to hurry off somewhere. Didn't he ever think: What does "We were there" really even mean? Where did those two weeks in France go? Those weeks that today can squeeze into just a couple of memories—the sudden onset of hunger by the city's medieval walls and the twinkling of evening at a café where the roof was covered in grapevines. What happened to Norway? All that's left is the chill of the water in the lake that endless day, and then the delight of the beer bought just before the shop shut, or the arresting first glimpse of the fjord.

"The things I've seen are mine now," the young man, suddenly revived, concluded, slapping his palm down on his thigh.

## GUIDANCE FROM CIORAN

Another man—gentle, shy—always took a book of Cioran with him when he traveled for work, one of the ones made up of very short texts. At hotels, he'd keep it on his bedside table, and every morning on waking he would open it at random and find his guiding principle for the day to come. He believed that hotels in Europe ought to replace all their copies of the Bible with books by Cioran as soon as possible. From Romania all the way to France. That for the purposes of predicting the future, the Bible was no longer any good. What use is the following verse, for example, come upon at random one April Friday or December Wednesday: "All the other articles used in the service of the tabernacle, whatever their function, including all the tent pegs for it and those for the courtyard, are to be of bronze" (Exodus 27:19)? How are we supposed to take that? In any case, he said it didn't necessarily have to be Cioran. There was a challenge in his eyes as he continued: "Feel free to suggest something else."

Nothing came to my mind. He took from his backpack a worn, slender volume, which he opened to a random page. His face lit up.

"Instead of paying attention to the faces of people passing by, I watched their feet, and all these busy types were reduced to hurrying steps—toward what? And it was clear to me that our mission was to graze the dust in search of a mystery stripped of anything serious."*

---

*Emil Cioran, *Anathemas and Admirations*, translated by Richard Howard.

## KUNICKI: WATER (I)

It's midmorning, he doesn't know exactly what the time is—he hasn't looked at his watch—but he hasn't been waiting, he doesn't think, for longer than fifteen minutes. He leans back into his seat and shuts his eyes halfway; the silence is as piercing as a shrill relentless noise. He can't collect his thoughts. He still hasn't realized that what it sounds like is an alarm. He moves his seat back from the steering wheel and stretches out his legs. His head is heavy, and it drags his body down with it into the white-hot air. He's not going to move. He'll just wait.

He must have smoked a cigarette, and maybe even two. After a few minutes he gets out of the car to go and pee into a ditch. He doesn't think anybody else has gone by, although now he's not sure. Then he gets back in and takes a big drink of water from a plastic bottle. He's finally beginning to get impatient. He honks the horn, hard, and the deafening sound precipitates the flash of rage that draws him back down to earth. Deflated, he now sees everything much more clearly, and he gets back out of the car again and sets off after them, imagining absentmindedly the words he's about to pronounce: "What the hell have you been doing all this time? What were you thinking?"

It's an olive grove, bone dry. The grass crunches underfoot. There are wild blackberry bushes in between the gnarled olive trees; new sprouts attempt to slip out onto the path and seize him by the leg. There is trash everywhere: Kleenexes, those disgusting pads, human excrement populated by flies. Other people also stop alongside the road to relieve themselves. They don't bother to go any farther into the thicket; they're in a hurry, even here.

There's no wind. There's no sun. The motionless white sky looks like the canopy of a tent. It's muggy, and particles of water jostle up against one another in the air, and everywhere there is the smell of the sea—of electricity, of ozone, of fish.

Something moves, but not over there amidst the spindly trees— right here, beneath his feet. An enormous black beetle emerges onto the path; palpating the air for a moment with its antennae, it pauses, evidently aware of a human presence. The white sky is reflected in the beetle's flawless carapace as a milky blot, and for a moment Kunicki feels as though he's being watched by an odd eye on the ground not belonging to any body, detached and disinterested. Kunicki nudges the earth slightly with the tip of his sandal. The beetle scurries across the narrow path, rustling in the desiccated grass. It disappears into the blackberries. That's it.

She had said: "Stop the car." When he'd stopped, she had gotten out and opened the back door. She'd unfastened their son from his car seat, taken him by the hand, and led him off. Kunicki had had no desire to get out—he'd felt sleepy, tired, although they had come only a couple of miles so far. He'd barely even glanced at them out of the corner of his eye; he hadn't known he was supposed to be watching. Now he tries to call back up that blurred image, make it sharper, bring it up closer—keep it still. He watches them walk away from him, down the crackling path. He seems to think she's wearing light-colored linen trousers and a black T-shirt. Their son is wearing a tricot tee with an elephant on it, which he actually knows for sure because he was the one who put it on him that morning.

As they walk, they talk to each other, but he can't hear them: he hadn't known he was supposed to be listening. Then they vanish into the olive trees. He doesn't know how long all of this takes, but it's not long. A quarter of an hour, maybe a little more. He loses track of time. He hadn't looked at his watch. He hadn't known he was supposed to keep track of the time.

He hated when she asked him what he was thinking about. He would always answer "Nothing," but she never believed him. She said you couldn't not think. She'd grow indignant. But he can—and here Kunicki feels something like satisfaction—not think about anything. He knows how.

But then suddenly he stops in the middle of the blackberry brush, stands still, as though his body, straining toward the blackberry rhizome, has inadvertently discovered a new equilibrium point. The quiet is accompanied by flies' buzzing and by the roar of his thoughts. For a moment he can see himself from above: a man wearing ordinary cargo pants with a white T-shirt and a little bald spot on the back of his head, among the clumps of the thicket, an intruder, a guest in someone else's home. A man under fire, dropped into the epicenter of a momentary cease-fire in a battle involving both the blazing sky and the chapped earth. He panics; he would like to hide now, run back to the car, but his body ignores him—he can't move his foot, can't force himself back into motion. Can't force himself to take a step. The links have been severed. His foot in its sandal is an anchor that keeps him stuck to the ground. Consciously, trying hard, surprised at himself, he does force it forward again. There is no other way out from that hot, boundless space.

They came on August 14. The ferry from Split was full of people—lots of tourists, though mostly locals. The locals carried shopping bags; everything was cheaper on the mainland. Islands spawn parsimony. It was easy to tell the tourists apart, because when the sun began its inevitable descent into the sea, they crossed over to starboard and pointed their cameras at it. The ferry slowly passed by scattered islands, and then it was as though it had emerged into open sea. A disagreeable sensation, a fleeting, frivolous moment of panic.

They had no trouble finding the guesthouse where they were staying, called Poseidon. It was owned by a bearded man named Branko wearing a T-shirt with a shell on it. He insisted they be on a first-name basis and patted Kunicki familiarly on the back as he led them through the narrow stone house and up the stairs to their apartment, which he showed them with evident pride. They'd have two bedrooms and a corner kitchenette with the traditional furnishings, pantries made of laminated fiberboard. Its windows looked out on the beach and open sea. There was an agave in full bloom at one window—the flower, sitting atop its strong stem, rose triumphantly up above the water.

He pulls out a map of the islands and considers the options. She might have gotten disoriented and simply rejoined the road in a different spot. She was probably just standing somewhere else now. Maybe she would even flag down a car and go—where? According to the map, the road drew a winding line across the whole of the island, so that you could travel all the way around without ever getting down to the sea. Which was how they had gone to the town of Vis a few days earlier.

He puts the map on her seat, on top of her purse, and starts driving. He goes slowly, looking for them among the olive trees. But at some point the landscape changes: the olive grove makes way for rocky wastelands overgrown with dry grass and blackberries. White limestone's bared like giant teeth fallen from the mouth of some wild beast. He turns around after a few kilometers. Now to his right he sees stunningly green vineyards, and within them, every so often, little stone toolsheds, bleak and empty. The best-case scenario is for her to have gotten lost, but what if she has become unwell, she or their son—it's so stuffy, so hot. Maybe they need urgent care, and instead of doing anything, he's just driving up and down the road. What an idiot, he thinks—how had he not thought of this before? His heart starts striking sooner. What if she had sunstroke? What if she broke her leg?

He goes back and honks the horn a few times. Two German cars go by. He checks the time; it's already been about an hour and a half, which means the ferry will have gone. White, commanding, it will have swallowed up the cars, shut its rear doors, and set off across the sea. Minute by minute, ever broader tracts of indifferent sea will separate them. Kunicki has a sense of foreboding that dries his mouth out, a sense of something that has some connection to the trash by the road, the flies and the human waste. He gets it. They're gone. They're both gone. He knows they're not among the olive trees, and yet he runs down the dry path and calls out for them, knowing they won't respond.

It is the hour of postprandial siestas on the island of Vis, and the little town is almost empty. On the beach, right by the road, there are three women flying a light blue kite. He takes a good look at them once he's parked. One of them is wearing cream-colored trousers stretched skintight over her big buttocks.

He finds Branko sitting at a little café, sharing a table with three other men. They're drinking wormwood liqueur like whiskey, with ice. Branko smiles in surprise when he sees him.

"Did you forget something?" he asks.

They offer him a chair, but he doesn't sit. He wants to tell them everything in an orderly manner, and he switches over into English while at the same time wondering in some other part of his brain, as though this were a film, what one does in a situation like this. He says they're gone—Jagoda and his son. He explains when, and where. He says he looked and couldn't find them. Then Branko asks:

"Did you have a fight?"

He says no, which is true. The other two men toss back their liqueur. He wouldn't mind some of that himself. He can taste it, sweet and sour, on his tongue. Branko slowly takes a pack of cigarettes and a lighter from the table. The others get up, as well, reluctantly, as though preparing themselves for a battle—or maybe they'd rather stay here, in the shade of this awning. They're all going, but Kunicki insists that they have to let the police know first. Branko hesitates. His black beard is shot through with rays of gray hairs. On his yellow T-shirt, the drawing of the shell and the inscription "Shell" begin to redden.

"Maybe she went down to the water?"

Maybe she did. They come to an agreement: Branko and Kunicki will return to that spot on the road while the other two go to the police station to call down to the town of Vis; Branko explains that Komiža itself has only one policeman. Glasses holding melting ice still stand on the table.

Kunicki has no trouble recognizing the place where they'd pulled off, where he had been parked before. It feels like ages ago. Time is passing differently, thick and acrid, sequenced. The sun appears from behind the white clouds, and suddenly it is hot.

"Horn," says Branko, and Kunicki applies pressure to the horn.

The sound is long, mournful, like the voice of an animal. Then it stops, shattered into cicadas' small echoes. They move through the olive brush, bellowing out from time to time. They don't run into one another again until the vineyard, and then after a brief talk they decide to inspect that entire area. They scour rows half in shadow, calling out for the missing woman: "Jagoda, Jagoda!" It occurs to Kunicki that his wife's name means "berry" in their native Polish. It is such a common name that he had forgotten about that until now. Suddenly it seems to him that he is taking part in some sort of ancient ritual, blurry, grotesque. From the bushes there hang grapes in swollen, deep violet bunches, perverse, multiplied nipples, and he wanders the leafy labyrinths, shouting, "Jagoda! Jagoda!" Who is he saying that to? Who is he looking for?

He has to stop for a second. He has a stitch in his side. He doubles over between the rows of plants. He buries his head in the shadowy cool, Branko's voice muffled by the foliage till it finally falls silent, and now Kunicki can hear the flies buzzing—quiet's familiar warp.

Past the vineyard there's another, separated from this one by just a narrow path. They stop, and Branko calls someone on his mobile. He repeats the words "wife" and "child" in Croatian—those are the only words that sound enough like Polish for Kunicki to be able to understand. The sun grows orange; great, swollen, it weakens before their eyes. Soon they'll be able to look at it directly. The vineyards, meanwhile, take on an intensely dark green color. Two small human figures stand helplessly in that green-striped sea.

. . .

By dusk, there are already some cars and a small cluster of men on the road. Kunicki is sitting in a car that has "Police" written on it, and with Branko's help, he responds to the haphazard—it seems to him—questions he is being asked by a big, sweaty cop. He tries to speak simple English: "We stopped. She went out with child. They went right, here"—he points—"and then I waited, we can say, fifteen minutes. Then I decide go and look for them. I can't find them. I don't know what have happen." He is given lukewarm mineral water, which he drinks in desperate gulps. "They are lost." And then he adds again: "Lost." The officer dials somebody on his phone. "It is impossible to be lost here, my friend," he tells him, while he waits for them to pick up. Kunicki is struck by that "my friend." The officer's walkie-talkie says something. It is another hour before they set out, in loose line formation, for the island's heart.

In that time, the puffy sun sinks down around the vineyards, and by the time they've gotten all the way to the top, it's already reached the sea. Like it or not, they view the operatic drawing out of its setting. Finally they switch on flashlights. In the dark now, they climb down the island's steep shore, which is full of little inlets, two of which they check; each has little stone houses inhabited by the more eccentric tourists who don't like hotels and prefer to pay more to not have running water or electricity. People use stone stoves to cook or bring gas tanks with them. They catch fish, which travel straight from the sea to the grill. No, no one has seen a woman with a child. They're about to eat dinner—on the table are bread, cheeses, olives, and the poor fish that only this afternoon had been fully absorbed in their mindless exercises in the sea. Every so often Branko calls the hotel in Komiža—at Kunicki's request, since he figures perhaps she got lost but ended up getting back by a different route. But Branko just pats him on the back after each call.

Around midnight the pack of men disbands. Among them are the two Kunicki had seen at Branko's table in Komiža. Now, as they take their leave, they introduce themselves: Drago and Roman. They walk together to the car. Kunicki is grateful to them for the help, he doesn't know how to show it, he's forgotten how to say "thank you" in Croatian; it must be similar to the Polish *dziękuję*, something like *dyakuyu* or *dyakuye*, but he doesn't know. With a bit of goodwill they really ought to be able to work up some sort of Slavic koine, a set of similar, handy Slavic words, to be used without grammar, rather than falling into a stiff and simplified version of English.

That night a boat comes up by his house. They have to evacuate—there's a flood. The water has already reached the second floors of some buildings. In the kitchen it forces its way in through the joints between the tiles on the floor, flowing out in warm streams from the electrical outlets. Books bulge with moisture. He opens one up and sees that the letters run off like makeup, leaving empty, blurry pages. Then he realizes that everyone else has gone already, taken by an earlier boat, and that he is the only one left.

In his sleep he hears drops of water trickling lazily down from the sky, about to become a violent, short-lived downpour.

## BENEDICTUS, QUI VENIT

April on the motorway, the sun's red streaks across the asphalt, the world all delicately decorated with a glaze from the recent rain—an Easter cake. I'm driving on Good Friday, at dusk, from the

Netherlands to Belgium—I don't know which country I'm in now, since the border has vanished; unused, it's been expunged. They're playing a requiem on the radio. At the Benedictus, the lights come on along the motorway, as though reinforcing the blessing I'm getting involuntarily from the radio.

But in reality it could not have meant anything other than that I'd made it to Belgium, where, happily for travelers, all the motorways are well lit.


## PANOPTICON

The panopticon and the Wunderkammer, as I learned from a museum guide, are a rather venerable duo whose existence precedes that of museums. They exhibited collections of all types of curiosities that their owners had brought back from journeys to places near and far.

Nor should it be forgotten that Bentham chose "panopticon" as the name for his brilliant system of prison surveillance; his goal was to construct a space that would ensure that every prisoner could be ceaselessly seen.


## KUNICKI: WATER (II)

"The island's not that big," says Branko's wife, Djurdjica, as she fills his cup with thick, strong coffee.

Everyone says this over and over like a kind of mantra. Kunicki gets the message—he wouldn't have needed to be told, anyway, that the island is too small for anyone to disappear on it. It's just over ten kilometers across, with only two real towns, Vis and Komiža. Every inch of it is searchable. It's like rifling through a drawer. Plus everyone knows each other, in both towns. And then the nights are warm, the grapes in full flourish on the vines, the figs nearly ripe. Even if they had gotten lost somehow, they would have been fine—they wouldn't have frozen or starved to death, and they could hardly have been devoured by wild beasts, either. They would simply have spent a warm night on sunburned grass, beneath an olive tree, with the sea's sleepy rumble in the backdrop. It can't be more than three or four kilometers to the road from any place. Little stone buildings housing wine barrels and presses stand at intervals in the fields, some equipped with provisions, candles. For breakfast they'd have juicy grapes, or a normal meal with the tourists in the inlets.

They go down to the hotel, where a policeman awaits them. It's a different one, a younger one, and for a moment Kunicki feels hopeful of getting good news, but then he is asked for his passport. The youthful officer takes down Kunicki's information, carefully, meticulously, telling him as he does so that they've decided to expand their search to the mainland, too—to Split, and to the neighboring islands.

"She could have made it to the ferry along the shore," he explains.

"She didn't have any money," Kunicki says, in Polish, and then in English, "No money. Here, everything." He displays her purse to the policeman, pulling out her red wallet, embroidered with little beads. He opens it and holds it out. The policeman shrugs and writes down their address in Poland.

"And the kid was how old?"

"Three," says Kunicki.

. . .

They drive down the serpentine road back to the same place, the day promising to be hot and bright, everything overexposed like in a picture. By noon all images will have been drained from it. Kunicki wonders whether they couldn't do the search from on high, from a helicopter, given that the island is almost completely bare. Then he wonders about those chips they can put in animals, migrating birds, storks and cranes, and yet here they don't have enough for people. Everyone should have one of those chips, for their own safety; then you could track every human movement on the internet—roads, rest stops, when people start to get lost. How many lives could be saved! He can just see the computer screen with its color-coded lines that mean people, uninterrupted traces, signs. Circles and ellipses, labyrinths. Maybe, too, incomplete figure eights, maybe unsuccessful spirals cut short suddenly.

There's a dog, a black shepherd; they hand him her sweater from the backseat. The dog sniffs around the car and then sets off into the olive grove. Kunicki feels a rush: it's all about to be cleared up, now. They run after the dog. It stops at a spot where they must have peed, although there's no trace of them. It looks pleased with itself—but come on, dog, that isn't it! Where are the people? Where did they go? The dog doesn't understand what they want from him, but reluctantly it sets back off again, off to one side now, down the road, away from the vineyards.

So she went down the main road, thinks Kunicki. She must have been confused. She could have kept going and waited for him a few hundred meters from here. Hadn't she heard him honking? And then what? Maybe someone had given them a ride, but since they hadn't turned up yet, where could that someone have taken them? Someone. A vague, out-of-focus, broad-shouldered figure. Broad neck. A kidnapping. Would he have knocked them out and shoved them into the trunk? He would have taken them aboard the ferry, to the mainland, and now they'd be in Zagreb or Munich, or wherever. Although how would he have crossed the border with two unconscious people in his trunk?

But the dog turns now into the empty ravine running diagonally off the road, into the deep, stony breach, running down along those stones into its depths. You can see an untended little vineyard down there, and within the vineyard, a stone hut that looks like a kiosk covered in rusted corrugated steel sheets. A heap of dried grapevine stalks lies in front of its door, probably for a fire. The dog meanders around the house, circling and circling and then returning to the door. But the door is padlocked. It takes them a moment to take this in. The wind has scattered sticks across the threshold. There's obviously no way anyone could have gotten in there. The police officer looks in through the grime on the windows and then starts to beat at it, harder and harder, until he finally batters it down. Everyone looks in then, struck in unison by the all-encompassing smell of must and sea.

The walkie-talkie crackles, they give the dog something to drink, and then they have him smell the sweater again. Now he circles the hut three times, goes back to the road, and then, after some hesitation, continues in the same direction toward bare rocks, only occasionally grown over by dry grass. The sea is visible from the cliffs. The search party stands assembled, facing the water.

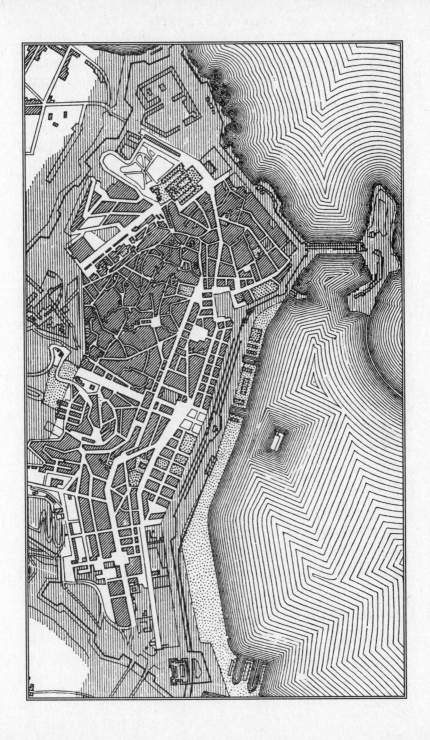

The dog loses the trail, turns around, lies down in the middle of the path.

*"To je zato jer je po noči padala kiša,"* somebody says, and Kunicki, parsing the Croatian through his own Polish, understands that they're discussing the fact that it rained last night.

Branko comes and takes him for a late lunch. The police stay there while Branko and Kunicki go down to Komiža. They hardly speak. Kunicki thinks Branko must not know what to say to him, and in a foreign language besides. So fine, let him not talk. They order fried fish at a restaurant right on the water; it's not even a restaurant, just a place belonging to some of Branko's friends. He knows everyone here. They're all sort of similar-looking, too, with sharp features, sort of windblown, a tribe of sea wolves. Branko pours him some wine and talks him into drinking it all. He downs his own, too. Then he doesn't let him pay for anything.

Branko receives a phone call. "Police," he then explains. "They manage to get helicopter, also airplane."

They work out a plan of attack, deciding to take Branko's boat along the island's shores. Kunicki calls his parents back in Poland. He hears his father's familiar raspy voice. He tells him they have to stay another three days. He will not tell him the truth. Everything's fine, they just need to stay. And he calls in to work, says he's run into this minor issue, asks if he can have three more days of vacation. He doesn't know why he says three days.

He awaits Branko at the dock. Branko shows up wearing that same T-shirt with the red shell symbol, but then Kunicki sees it's a different one, fresh, clean—he must have a bunch of them. They find the little fishing boat among the many moored vessels. Blue letters written ineptly across its side proclaim its name: *Neptune*. Suddenly Kunicki remembers that the ferry they'd taken to get here had been called *Poseidon*. And a lot of things, a lot of bars, a lot of shops, a lot of boats, are called Poseidon. Or Neptune. The sea must spit these two names out like outgrown shells. How do you obtain copyright from a god? Kunicki wonders. What would you have to pay for it?

They settle into the fishing boat, small, cramped, actually a motorboat with a little cabin cobbled together out of wood planks. Here Branko keeps a store of water bottles, both empty and full. Some of them contain wine from his vineyard—white, good, strong. Everyone here has their own vineyard and their own wine. The boat's motor is kept in the cabin, too, but now Branko hoists it out and attaches it to the stern. It starts on the third try. Now in order to talk they have to scream at each other. The motor's roar is deafening, and yet after just a moment the brain grows accustomed, as it does in the winter to thick clothing that separates the body from the rest of the world. That noise slowly submerges the view of the diminishing inlet and the port. Kunicki catches a glimpse of the apartment they were staying in, the kitchen window with its agave flower desperately shooting off into the sky like a frozen firework, a triumphant ejaculation.

He sees everything shrink and blend: the houses into a dark, irregular line; the port into a white blot traversed by the little marks of masts; meanwhile, above the town the towering hills, bare, gray, mottled with the green of the vineyards. They increase in size until they become enormous. From within, from the road, the island seemed small, but now its power is made manifest: solid rock shaped into a kind of monumental cone, a fist hurled out of the water.

When they turn left, leaving the bay for the open sea, the island's shore seems vertiginous, dangerous.

They are carried along by the white crests of the waves that strike the rocks and the birds disturbed by the presence of the boat. When they turn the engine on again, the birds take fright and take wing. There is also the vertical line of the jet that tears the sky into two sheets. The plane is flying south.

They are moving. Branko lights two cigarettes and gives one to Kunicki. It's hard to smoke: tiny little droplets of water splash up from beneath the bow and land on everything.

"Look at the water," shouts Branko. "At everything swimming."

As they near a bay with a cave, they see a helicopter, flying the other way. Branko stands up in the center of the boat and waves. Kunicki looks at the chopper, almost happy. The island isn't big, he thinks for the hundredth time; from above there isn't anything that can be hidden from the sight of that great mechanical dragonfly, it would all be as obvious as the nose on your face.

"Let's go to *Poseidon*," he shouts to Branko, but Branko seems unconvinced.

"There's no way through there," he shouts back.

But the boat turns and slows. They enter the cove between the rocks with the engine off.

This part of the island should also be called Poseidon, thinks Kunicki, just like everything else. The god had built himself cathedrals here: naves, caves, columns, and choirs. Their forms were unpredictable, their rhythm off and uneven. Black igneous rocks sparkle damply as though coated in some rare dark metal. Now, at dusk, the structures are all devastatingly sad—this was quintessential abandonment: no one ever prayed here. Kunicki suddenly has the sense that he is seeing the prototypes of man-made churches, that all the tours should be brought here before they're taken to Reims or to Chartres. He wants to share this discovery with Branko, but the ruckus from the engine is too much for them to talk. He sees another, larger boat with the words "Police, Split" written on it. It's traveling down the steep coastline. The boats convene, and Branko talks with the policemen. There are no signs of them, nothing. Or so Kunicki judges, at least, because the mechanical cacophony drowns out their conversation. They must be reading each other's lips, and interpreting the gentle, helpless raising of their shoulders, which doesn't suit their white police shirts with their epaulets. They indicate they ought to head back, because it will be dark soon. That's all Kunicki can hear: "Go back." Branko steps on the gas, and it sounds like an explosion. The water stiffens; little waves like goose bumps spread across the sea.

Hitting the island now is completely different than it is by day. The first thing they see are glittering lights that become increasingly distinct from one another by the second, forming rows. They increase in the gathering darkness, becoming separate, different— the lights of yachts arriving at the waterfront are not the same as those in people's windows; the illumination of signs and shop fronts are not the same as shifting headlights. A safe view of a tamed world.

Finally Branko turns the engine off, and the boat sidles up to the shore. Suddenly they scrape along stone—they've come up onto the little town beach, right by the hotel, a long way away from the marina. Now Kunicki sees why. By the ramp, right at the beach, there is a police car, and there are two men in white shirts who have clearly been waiting for them.

"They must want to talk to you," says Branko, tying up the boat. Kunicki's forces fail him—he is scared of what he may be about to hear. That they found the bodies. That's what he's scared of. He walks up to them with his knees weak.

But thank God, it's just an ordinary interrogation. No, there's nothing new. But so much time has passed now that the matter has become serious. They take him down the same—the only—road to Vis, to the police station. It's completely dark now, but they obviously know the road well because they don't even slow down at the bends. They quickly pass that place where he lost them.

There are new men now at the station, awaiting his arrival. A translator, a tall, handsome man who speaks—why beat around the bush—poor Polish, though he was brought in especially from Split, and an officer. They ask some routine questions, almost involuntarily, and he gradually becomes aware that he has become a suspect.

They give him a lift right up to the hotel. He gets out and makes as if to enter. But he only pretends to go in. He waits in the dark little passageway until they drive off, till the rumble of the car's engine dies out, and then he walks out into the street. He walks toward the largest concentration of lights, toward the boulevard by the marina where all the cafés and restaurants are. But it's late now, and although it's Friday, there isn't much of a crowd there anymore; it must be one or two in the morning by now. He looks around for Branko among the few customers seated at the tables, but he doesn't find him there, doesn't see that seashell T-shirt. There are some Italians, a whole family, who are finishing up their meal, and he also sees two older people, who are drinking something out of a straw and staring at the noisy Italian family. There are two women with fair hair, intimately turned toward each other, shoulders touching, absorbed in their conversation. Local men, fishermen, this couple. What a relief that no one pays him any mind. He walks along the edge of a shadow, right on the waterfront, and he can smell fish and feel the warm, salty breeze off the sea. He feels like turning and going up along one of the little backstreets that go toward Branko's house, but he can't bring himself to really do it—they must be asleep. So he sits down at a little table at the edge of the patio. The waiter ignores him.

He watches the men who converge around the table next to his. They bring over an extra chair—there are five of them—and sit down. Even before the waiter comes, before they've ordered anything to drink, they are already connected by an invisible, unspoken pact.

They are different ages, two of them with thick beards, and yet all of their differences are about to disappear into the circle they've already automatically created. They talk, but it doesn't matter what they're saying—it almost looks like they're rehearsing for a song they'll sing together, trying out their voices. Their laughter fills up the space inside the circle—jokes, even hackneyed ones, are completely appropriate, even called for. It's a low, vibrating laughter that conquers the space and makes the tourists at the next table over be quiet—middle-aged women suddenly startled. It attracts curious gazes.

They're preparing their audience. The appearance of the waiter with a tray of drinks becomes an overture, while the waiter, just a kid, becomes their unwitting MC, announcing the dance, the opera. They liven up when they see him; someone's hand goes up and shows him where to put things—here. There is a moment of silence, and now glass rims are raised to lips. Some of them—especially the impatient ones—are unable to resist shutting their eyes, exactly like in church when the priest solemnly places the white wafer on the outstretched tongue. The world is ready to be overturned— it's only a convention that the floor is beneath our feet, while the ceiling is overhead, the body no longer belongs just to itself, but is instead a part of a live chain, a section of a living circle. Now, too, glasses travel to lips, the moment of their emptying practically invisible, taking place in rapid-fire focus, with momentary gravity. From here on out the men will hold on to them—the glasses. The bodies seated around the table will begin to describe their rings, tops of heads indicating circles in the air, first smaller ones, then larger ones. They will overlap, tracing new chords. In the end, hands will come up, first testing their own strength on the air, in gestures to illustrate their words, and then they will roam to companions' arms, to their backs and shoulders, patting and encouraging them. These will in fact be gestures of love. This fraternizing by way of hands and backs is not intrusive; it's a kind of dance.

Kunicki looks on with envy. He'd like to leave the shadows and join in with them. He's never experienced that intensity. He is more familiar with the north, where masculine society is shyer. But here in the south, where wine and sunshine open bodies up faster and more shamelessly, this dance becomes really real. After only an hour the first body pushes back from the table and holds on to the armrests of the chair.

Kunicki's back is slapped by the warm paw of the nighttime breeze, which pushes him toward the tables as though urging him on: "Come on, come on now." He would like to join in, wherever it is they are going. He would like for them to take him along.

He goes back down the unlit side of the boulevard to his little hotel, making sure not to cross the line of darkness. Before entering the stuffy, narrow stairwell, he takes in some air and stands still for a moment. Then he climbs the stairs, feeling out for each step in the darkness, and he falls instantly into bed with all his clothes on, on his stomach, with his arms thrown out to either side, as though someone had shot him in the back, as though for a moment he had contemplated that bullet, and then died.

He gets up after a few hours—two, three, because it's still dark—and blindly he goes back down to the car. The alarm whoops, and the car flashes understandingly, like it's been lonely. Kunicki takes their bags out of the trunk at random. He carries their suitcases up the stairs and tosses them onto the floor in the kitchen and the bedroom. Two suitcases and a ton of packages, bags, baskets, including the one with their food for the road, a set of flippers in a plastic sack, masks, an umbrella, beach mats, and a box with the wines they had bought on the island, and ajvar, that spread made of red pepper they'd liked so much, and then some jars of olive oil. He turns on all the lights and sits now in this mess. Then he takes her purse and delicately empties out its contents onto the kitchen table. He sits there and takes in that pile of pathetic things as though this were a complicated game of pickup sticks and his was the next move—extracting one stick without moving any of the others. After a moment's hesitation, he picks up a lipstick and removes its cap. Dark red, almost new. She hadn't used it often. He smells it. It has a nice aroma, hard to say of what exactly. He becomes bolder, taking every single object and putting it aside. Her passport, old, with the blue cover—she's much younger in the picture, with long hair, loose, and bangs. Her signature on the last page is blurry—they often get held up at the border. A little black notebook, shut with a rubber band. He opens it and flips through—notes, a drawing of a jacket, a column of numbers, the card for a bistro in Polanica, in the back a phone number, a lock of hair, of dark hair, not even a lock, just a few dozen individual hairs. He puts it aside. Then he examines it all more closely. A cosmetics bag made of exotic Indian fabric, containing a dark green pencil, a compact almost out of powder, waterproof green mascara, a plastic pencil sharpener, lip gloss, tweezers, a blackened little torn-off chain. He also comes upon a ticket to a museum in Trogir, and on the back of it a foreign word; he brings the little piece of paper up to his eyes and manages to make out καιρός, which he thinks is K-A-I-R-O-S, although he's not sure, and he doesn't know what that would be. It's full of sand at the bottom.

There's her mobile phone, which is almost dead. He checks her recent call log—his own number comes up, mostly, but there are others, too, he doesn't know who they would be, two or three of them. There's only one text in her inbox—from him, from when they'd gotten lost in Trogir. *I'm by the fountain on the main square.* Her sent messages folder is empty. He returns to the main menu, and a kind of pattern lights up for a moment on the screen and then goes out.

There's an open pack of sanitary napkins. A pencil, two pens, one a yellow Bic and the other with "Hotel Mercure" written on the side. Pocket change, Polish and euro cents. Her wallet, with Croatian bills in it—not many—and ten Polish zlotys. Her Visa card. A little orange notepad, dirtied at the edges. A copper pin with some antique-looking pattern, seemingly broken. Two Kopiko candies. A camera, digital, with a black case. A peg. A white paper clip. A golden gum wrapper. Crumbs. Sand.

He lays it all neatly on the black matte countertop, every thing equidistant from every other thing. He goes up to the sink and drinks some water. He goes back to the table and lights a cigarette. Then he starts taking pictures with her camera, each object on its own. He photographs slowly, solemnly, zooming in as much as possible, with flash. His only regret is that the little camera can't take a picture of itself. It is also evidence, after all. Then he moves into the hallway where the bags and suitcases are standing, and he snaps one image of each of them. But he doesn't stop there, he unpacks the suitcases and starts photographing every article of clothing, every pair of shoes, every lotion and book. The kid's toys. He even empties out the dirty clothes from their plastic bag and takes a picture of that shapeless pile as well.

He comes across a small bottle of rakia and drinks it down in a single gulp, with the camera in his hand still, and then he takes a picture of the empty bottle.

It's already light out when he sets off in his car for Vis. He has the dried-out sandwiches she'd made for the road. The butter had all melted in the heat, soaking into the bread, leaving a glistening layer of oil, and the cheese was hard now and half transparent like plastic. He eats two of them as he leaves Komiža; he wipes his hands off on his trousers. He goes slowly, carefully, keeping track of either side of the road, of everything he drives by, keeping in mind he has alcohol in his blood. But he feels dependable as a machine, strong as an engine. He doesn't look back, although he knows that behind him the ocean is growing, meter by meter. The air is so pure that you can probably see all the way to Italy from the highest point on the island. For now he stops in the coves and scans their surroundings, every scrap of paper, every piece of trash. He also has Branko's binoculars—that way he surveys the slopes. He sees rocky rises covered in scorched mulch, faded grass; he sees immortal blackberry bushes, darkened by the sun, clinging to the rocks with their long shoots. Spent, wild olive trees with twisted-up trunks, little stone walls from before the vineyards were abandoned.

After an hour or so he heads up into Vis, slow, like a police patrol. He passes the little supermarket where they'd gotten their groceries—mostly wine—and then he's in town.

The ferry has already docked at the quay. It's huge, as big as a building, a floating block. *Poseidon*. Its great doors are agape already, and a line of cars and people half asleep has formed and is about to begin to advance. Kunicki stands by the rail and checks out the people buying tickets. Some of them are backpackers, including a pretty girl in a brightly colored turban; he looks at her because he can't look away. Standing next to her there is a tall guy with Scandinavian handsomeness. There are women with children, probably locals, no luggage; a guy in a suit with a briefcase. There's a couple—she is nestled up into his chest, eyes closed, like she's trying to top off an interrupted night's sleep. And several cars—one of them loaded up to the gills, with German plates, and two Italian ones. And the island's vans, going off for bread, vegetables, mail. The island must survive somehow. Kunicki peeks discreetly into the cars.

The line begins to move, the ferry swallowing up people and cars, no one protesting, like a herd of calves. A group of French people on motorbikes pulls up, five of them, and they're the last on, disappearing with the same submissiveness into the jaws of the *Poseidon*.

Kunicki waits until the doors shut with that mechanical groan. The man selling tickets slams down his window and steps outside to smoke a cigarette. Both men are witnesses to the ferry's sudden fuss and distancing from the shore.

He says he's looking for a woman and a child, takes her passport out and sticks it in his face.

The ticket seller squints down at the picture in the passport. He says something in Croatian along the lines of: "The police already asked us about her. Nobody saw her here." He takes a drag off his cigarette and adds, "It's not a big island, we'd remember."

Suddenly he claps Kunicki on the shoulder as though they were old pals.

"Coffee?" And he nods at the little café that's just opened by the port.

Sure, coffee. Why not?

Kunicki sits at the little table, and in a moment the ticket seller comes up again with a double espresso. They drink in silence.

"Don't worry," says the ticket seller. "There's no way to lose somebody here." He says something more and holds his hands out, fingers splayed, palms furrowed with thick lines, as Kunicki slowly translates his Croatian into Polish: "We all stand out like sore thumbs," or something like it.

The ticket seller brings Kunicki a roll with a cutlet and some lettuce. He walks off, leaving Kunicki alone with his unfinished coffee. Once he's gone, a short sob escapes Kunicki; it's like a big bite of bread, and he swallows it. It tastes like nothing.

The image of the sore thumb lingers in his mind. To whom do we stand out? Who is it that's supposed to be looking at them, at this island in the sea, following the threads of paved roads from port to port, at the couple of thousand people, locals and tourists, melting in the heat, staying in motion? Satellite images flash through his mind—they say you can make out the writing on a matchbox with them. Is that possible? Then you must also be able to tell from up there that he's beginning to go bald. The great cool sky filled with the movable eyes of restless satellites.

He goes back to the car via the small cemetery near the church. All the graves face the sea, like in an amphitheater, so the dead observe the slow, repetitive rhythm of the port. Perhaps the white ferry cheers them, perhaps they even take it for an archangel escorting souls in that passage through the air.

Kunicki notices a few names that crop up again and again. The people here must be like the local cats, keeping to themselves, circulating among a couple of families and rarely leaving that circle. He stops only once—he sees a small gravestone with just two rows of letters:

ZORKA 9 II 21—17 II 54
SREČAN 29 I 54—17 VII 5

For a moment he searches these dates for an algebraic order, they look like a cipher. A mother and a son. A tragedy captured in dates, written out in stages. A relay.

And here is the end of the city already. He is tired, the heat has reached its zenith, and now sweat floods his eyes. As he climbs back up into the heart of the island in the car, he sees how the sharp sun transforms it into the most inhospitable place on earth. The heat ticks like a time bomb.

At the police station he is offered beer, as though the officers hope to hide their helplessness beneath that white foam. "No one's seen them," says a massive man, politely turning the fan in Kunicki's direction.

"What do we do now?" Kunicki asks, standing in the doorway.

"You ought to get some rest," says the officer.

But Kunicki remains at the station and eavesdrops on all their phone calls, on all the crackling of their walkie-talkies, so full of hidden meanings, until finally Branko comes for him and takes him to lunch. They barely speak. Then he asks to be dropped off at the hotel. He is weak and lies down in bed fully dressed. He smells his own sweat, the hideous scent of fear.

He lies there on his back, in his clothes, among the things dumped out of her purse. His eyes attentively probe their constellations, positionings, the directions they point in, the shapes they make. It could all be an omen. There's a letter to him, in regard to his wife and child, but above all in regard to him. He doesn't recognize the writing, doesn't recognize these symbols—it was not a human hand that wrote them, of that he is certain. Their connection to him is obvious, the very fact that he is looking at them important, the fact that he sees them a great mystery: the mystery that he can look, and see—the mystery that he exists.

## EVERYWHERE AND NOWHERE

Whenever I set off on any sort of journey I fall off the radar. No one knows where I am. At the point I departed from? Or at the point I'm headed to? Can there be an in-between? Am I like that lost day when you fly east, and that regained night that comes from going west? Am I subject to that much-lauded law of quantum physics that states that a particle may exist in two places at once? Or to a different law that hasn't been demonstrated and that we haven't even thought of yet that says that you can doubly not exist in the same place?

I think there are a lot of people like me. Who aren't around, who've disappeared. They show up all of a sudden in the arrivals terminal and start to exist when the immigration officers stamp their passports, or when the polite receptionist at whatever hotel hands over their keys. By now they must have become aware of their own instability and dependence upon places, times of day, on language or on a city and its atmosphere. Fluidity, mobility, illusoriness—these are precisely the qualities that make us civilized. Barbarians don't travel. They simply go to destinations or conduct raids.

This opinion is shared by the woman offering me herbal tea from a thermos while we both wait for the bus from the train station to the airport; her hands are hennaed in a complex design made less legible by each passing day. Once we're on the bus, she sets out her theory of time. She says that sedentary peoples, farmers, prefer the pleasures of circular time, in which every object and event must return to its own beginning, curl back up into an embryo and repeat the process of maturation and death. But nomads and merchants, as they set off on journeys, had to think up a different type of time for themselves, one that would better respond to the needs of their travels. That time is linear time, more practical because it was able to measure progress toward a goal or destination, rises in percentages. Every moment is unique; no moment can ever be repeated. This idea favors risk-taking, living life to the fullest, seizing the day. And yet the innovation is a profoundly bitter one: when change over time is irreversible, loss and mourning become daily things. This is why you'll never hear them utter words like "futile" or "empty."

"Futile effort, empty account," laughs the woman, placing her painted hand on her head. She says the only way to survive in that sort of extended, linear time is to keep your distance, a kind of dance that consists in approaching and retreating, one step forward, one step back, one step to the left, one to the right—easy enough steps to remember. And the bigger the world gets, the more distance you can dance out this way, immigrating out across seven seas, two languages, an entire faith.

But I take a different view of time. Every traveler's time is a lot of times in one, quite a wide array. It is island time, archipelagos of order in an ocean of chaos; it is the time produced by the clocks in train stations, everywhere varying; conventional time, mean time, which no one ought to take too seriously. Hours disappear on an airplane aloft, dawn issues fast with afternoon and evening already on its heels. The hectic time of big cities you're in for just a bit, wanting to fall into the clutches of its evening, and the lazy time of uninhabited prairies seen from the air.

I also think that the world will fit within, into a groove of the brain, into the pineal gland—it could well be just a lump in the throat, this globe. In fact, you could cough it right up and spit it out.

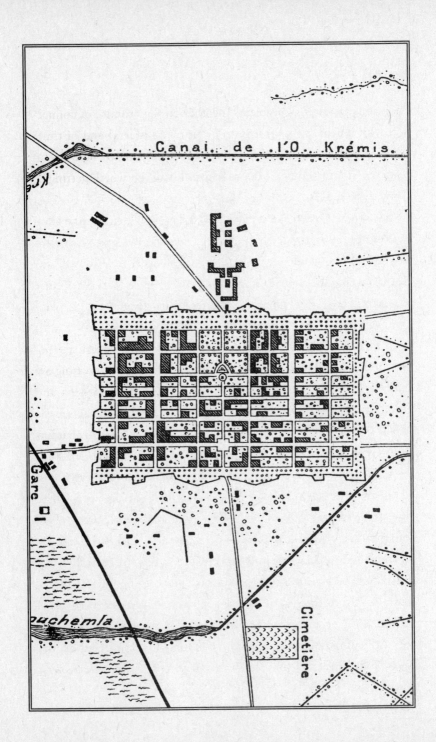

## AIRPORTS

Enormous airports assemble us together on the promise of connection with our next flight; it is an order of transferral and of timetables in the service of motion. But even if we had nowhere else to go in the coming couple of days, it would still be worth getting to know these spaces.

Once they were in the outskirts, supplementing cities, like train stations. But now airports have emancipated themselves, so that today they have a whole identity of their own. Soon we may well say that it's the cities that supplement the airports, as workplaces and places to sleep. It is widely known, after all, that real life takes place in movement.

In what possible way could airports be considered inferior to actual cities, nowadays? They hold conference centers, interesting art exhibits, festivals, and product launches. They have gardens and promenades; they instruct: at Amsterdam's Schiphol you can see excellent copies of Rembrandt, and there is an airport in Asia that has a museum of religion—a fabulous idea. We have access to good hotels and a wide variety of restaurants and bars from inside airports. There are little shops and supermarkets and shopping malls where you can stock up not only on provisions for the road, but also on souvenirs, in advance, so as to not waste any time once you get where you are going. There are gyms, places that offer both traditional and Eastern massage, hairstylists and customer service representatives from banks and mobile phone companies. And after satisfying the needs of our bodies, we can move on to spiritual succor at the numerous chapels and meditation spaces offered by airports. Sometimes they host readings and book signings for travelers.

Somewhere in my backpack I still have the program from one such event: "The History and Foundations of Travel Psychology," "The Development of Seventeenth-Century Anatomy."

Everything is well lit; moving walkways facilitate the migration of travelers from one terminal to another so they may go, in turn, from one airport to another (sometimes at a distance of some sixteen hours of flight!) while a discreet staff ensures the flawlessness of this great mechanism's workings.

They are more than travel hubs: this is a special category of city-state, with a stable location, but citizens in flux. They are airport-republics, members of a World Airport Union, and while they aren't yet represented at the UN, it is only a matter of time. They are an example of a system where internal politics matter less than ties with other airport members of the Union—for only these provide them with their raison d'être. An example of an extroverted system, where the constitution is spelled out on every ticket, and where one's boarding pass is one's only identification as a citizen.

The number of inhabitants here always varies quite a bit. Interestingly, the population increases in fogs and storms. Citizens, so as to feel comfortable anywhere, must not be too eye-catching. Sometimes, as one is going down a moving walkway, one passes one's brothers- and sisters-in-travel, who may give the impression of having been preserved in formaldehyde—as though everyone is peering out at everyone else from inside bell jars. In the airport-republic, your address is your seat on the plane: 7D, let's say, or 16A. Those great moving belts whisk us away in opposite directions, some voyagers in cloaks and hats, others in shorts and Hawaiian shirts, eyes blurred by snow or skin darkened by the sun, seeped in the damp of the north, the scent of rotting leaves and softened earth, or bearing desert sand in the recesses of their sandals. Some bronzed or tanned or burned, others blindingly, fluorescently white. People who shave their heads and those who never get a haircut. The big and tall, like that man, and the delicate and petite, like that woman who reaches up only to his waist.

Airports also have a sound track, a symphony of airplane engines, a couple of simple sounds that extend into a space devoid of rhythm, an Orthodox twin-engine choir, gloomy minor, infrared, infrablack, largo, based on a single chord that bores even itself. A requiem that opens with the potent introitus of takeoff and closes with an amen descending into landing.

## RETURNING TO ONE'S ROOTS

Hostels ought to be sued for ageism: for some reason, they offer accommodation only to the young. The acceptable age range is determined on a hostel-by-hostel basis, but nowhere will a forty-year-old make the cut. Why should the young receive such special treatment? Are they not, even aside from this, showered with the privileges of biology itself?

Let us take as an example those backpackers who constitute the vast majority of hostel-goers: they are strong and tall—both the men and the women—with clear, glowing skin, and they rarely smoke, if at all, let alone take drugs, or at most a joint from time to time. They travel by ecologically friendly means—in other words, by land: overnight trains, packed long-distance buses. In some countries they even hitchhike. They get to their hostels at night, and as they dine they all begin to ask one another the Three Travel Questions: Where are you from? Where are you coming in from? Where are you going? The first question determines the vertical axis, while the next two establish two horizontal axes. Thus these backpackers are able to create something like a coordinates system; when they have all situated one another on that map, they drift peaceably off to sleep.

The guy I met on the train was traveling, like so many of them, in search of his roots. His was a complicated journey: his grandmother on his mother's side was a Russian Jew, his grandfather a Pole from Vilnius (now Lithuania); they left Russia with General Anders's army and immigrated to Canada after the war. On his father's side, meanwhile, his grandfather was Spanish, and his grandmother a Native American whose tribe I can't recall the name of.

He was at the beginning of his trip, and he seemed rather overwhelmed.

## TRAVEL SIZES

These days, any self-respecting pharmacy offers its customers a special range of travel-sized toiletries. Some places even set aside whole aisles. Here, one can obtain anything and everything one might want on a trip: shampoo, a tube of liquid soap to wash your underwear in the sink at the hotel, toothbrushes you can fold in half, sunscreen, insect repellant, shoe polish wipes (the whole gamut of colors is available), sets of feminine hygiene products, foot cream, hand cream. The defining characteristic of all of these items is their size—they are miniatures, tiny tubes and jarlets, itsy-bitsy bottles the size of one's thumb: the smallest sewing kit fits three needles, five mini-skeins of different-colored thread, each three meters in length, and two white emergency buttons and a safety pin. Of particular usefulness is the travel-sized hairspray, whose miniature container measures no more than a woman's palm.

It is as if the cosmetics industry sees the phenomenon of travel as mirroring sedentary life, but in miniature, a cute little baby version of the same.

## MANO DI GIOVANNI BATTISTA

There's too much in the world. It would be wiser to reduce it, rather than expanding or enlarging it. We'd be better off stuffing it back into its little can—a portable panopticon we'd be allowed to peek inside only on Saturday afternoons, once our daily tasks had been completed, once we'd made sure there was clean underwear to wear, ironed shirts taut over armrests, floors scrubbed, coffee cake cooling on the windowsill. We could peer inside it through a tiny little hole like at the Fotoplastikon in Warsaw, marveling over its every detail.

But I fear it may already be too late.

We have no choice now but to learn how to endlessly select. Learn how to be like a fellow traveler I once met on a night train who told me that every so often he goes back to the Louvre just to see the one painting he considers to be worthwhile, of John the Baptist. He just stands there before it, beholding it, gazing up at the saint's raised finger.

## THE ORIGINAL AND THE COPY

A guy in the cafeteria of this one museum said that nothing gives him such great satisfaction as being in the presence of an original artwork. He also insisted that the more copies there are in the world, the greater the power of the original becomes, a power sometimes approaching the great might of a holy relic. For what is singular is significant, what with the threat of destruction hanging over as it does. Confirmation of these words came in the form of a nearby cluster of tourists who, with fervent focus, stood worshipping a painting by Leonardo da Vinci. Just occasionally, when one of them couldn't take it anymore, there came the clearly audible click of a camera, sounding like an "Amen" spoken in a new, digital language.

## TRAINS FOR COWARDS

There are trains that are designed to be slept on. They are made up, in their entirety, of sleeping compartments and a single café car, not even a restaurant car, because a café car is enough. This type of train runs, for example, from Szczecin to Wrocław. It leaves at 10:30 at night and gets in at 7:00 in the morning, although the trip itself is not that long, only about two hundred miles, and you could make it in five hours. But the point isn't always to get there faster: the company cares about its passengers' comfort. The train stops in fields and stands in their nocturnal fogs, a quiet hotel on wheels. There's no sense in trying to race the night.

There's a very good train from Berlin to Paris. And from Budapest to Belgrade. And from Bucharest to Zurich. I feel as though these trains were just invented for people with a fear of flying. They're a little embarrassing—it's better not to admit that you take them. And they're not really advertised that much. They're trains for long-standing customers, for that unfortunate percentage of the population that has a heart attack over every takeoff and every landing. For those with sweaty hands who wad up Kleenex after Kleenex in despair, and for those who grasp on to the flight attendants' sleeves.

This sort of train stands humbly on the side track, keeping a low profile. (For example, the one from Hamburg to Krakow at Altona, where it is concealed by billboards and other advertising.) People taking one for the first time wander around the station for a while before they find it. Boarding is carried out discreetly. In the outer pockets of suitcases there are pajamas and slippers, toiletry cases, earplugs. Clothing is hung carefully on special hooks, and at the minuscule washbasins closed off in closets the tools for teeth-brushing are arrayed. Soon the conductor will take breakfast orders. Coffee or tea? That's the closest to freedom the railway gets. Had these passengers just got one of those cheap flights, they would have been there in an hour, and it would have cost them less money, too. They would have had a night in the arms of their longing lovers, breakfast at one of the restaurants on rue je-ne-sais-quoi, where oysters are served. An evening Mozart concert at a cathedral. A walk along the riverbanks. Instead they must fully surrender to the time taken by rail travel, must personally traverse every kilometer according to the age-old custom of their ancestors, go over every bridge and through each viaduct and tunnel on this voyage over land. Nothing can be skipped, nothing bypassed. Every millimeter of the way will be touched by the wheel, will for an instant be part of its tangent, and this will be an unrepeatable configuration for all time—of the wheel and the rail, of the time and place, unique throughout the cosmos.

As soon as this train for cowards sets off into the night—practically without warning—the bar begins to fill up with people. Drawn in are men in suits who come for a couple of quick ones or for a pint to help them sleep, elegant gay men whose eyes dart around like castanets; forlorn football fans, separated from their friends—who'd flown—as insecure as sheep parted from their flocks; female friends over the age of forty who have left their boring husbands in search of some excitement. Slowly there begins to be less and less space, and passengers behave as though they are at a big party, and sometimes the amiable waiters will introduce them to one another: "This fellow travels with us every week"; "Ted, who says he won't go to bed but is actually always the first one snoring"; "The passenger who travels every week to see his wife—he must really love her"; "Mrs. I'm Never Traveling on This Train Again."

In the middle of the night, as the train creeps along the plains of Belgium or Lubusz, as the nighttime mist thickens and blurs everything, the café car is host to a second round of visitors: exhausted, insomniac passengers who are not ashamed of the slippers on their unstockinged feet. They join in with the rest as though putting themselves in fate's hands—whatever will be, will be.

But it seems to me that the only things that can happen to them are the things that are for the best. After all, they are now in a place that is mobile, that moves through black space; they are borne by the night. Not knowing anyone and being recognized by no one. Escaping their own lives, and then being safely escorted right back to them.

## ABANDONED APARTMENT

The apartment doesn't understand what's happened. The apartment thinks its owner has died. Ever since the door slammed shut, since the key grated around in the lock, all sounds are muffled, their shades and edges absent, as in indistinct stains. Space condenses, unused, undisturbed by any draft, any ruffling of the curtains, and in this motionlessness, trial forms tentatively begin to crystallize, forms suspended for a moment between the floor and ceiling of the entryway.

Of course no new thing comes into being now—how could it? These are only imitations of familiar shapes, melding into bubbly, blistery clumps, maintaining their outlines just for a second. These are individual episodes, isolated gestures, like a footprint on a soft carpet that is made endlessly and always in the same exact spot and then vanishes. Or a hand over a table, going through the motions of writing, although the motions are incomprehensible because they occur without a pen, without paper, without writing, without even the rest of the body.

## THE BOOK OF INFAMY

She was not my friend. I met her at the Stockholm airport, the only one in the world with wood floors: a pretty, dark oak parquet with carefully matched slats—a low estimate would put it at about ten acres of northern woods.

She was sitting next to me. She stretched out her legs and rested them on a black backpack. She wasn't reading, she wasn't listening to music—she just had her hands folded over her stomach and was

staring straight ahead. I liked how peaceful she was, completely resigned to waiting. As I stared at her more openly, her gaze slid away
from mine and down onto that polished floor. Blurting out the first
thing I could think of, I said it was a waste of the woods to use them
for flooring in an airport.

"They say that you have to sacrifice some living being when you
build an airport," she replied. "To ward off catastrophe."

The flight attendants were having some sort of problem at the gate.
It turned out—they announced to those waiting—that our plane
was overbooked. By some fluke in the system, there were simply too
many people on the passenger list. A computer error, such was the
guise of fate these days. They'd give two people two hundred euros,
a night at the airport hotel, and a dinner voucher if they'd be willing
to leave the following day instead.

People glanced nervously around. Someone said, let's draw
straws for it! Someone laughed, and then an uncomfortable silence
descended. Nobody would want to stay, and understandably
enough: we don't live in a vacuum, we have places to be, we have to
see the dentist tomorrow, we have invited friends over for dinner.

I looked down at my shoes. I wasn't in a hurry. I never have to be
in any particular place at any particular time. Let time watch me,
not me it. And besides—there are different ways of making a living,
but here a whole other dimension of employment opened up, perhaps the employment of the future, the kind of thing that would
guard against joblessness and the production of excessive waste.
Stand aside, get your day's wages just by staying at a hotel, have
some coffee in the morning and a buffet breakfast, take advantage
of the smorgasbord's wide range of different yogurts. Why not? I

stood up and headed over to the jittery flight attendants. Then the woman who'd been sitting beside me stood and came up, too.

"Why not?" she said.

Unfortunately, our bags flew without us. An empty shuttle took us to the hotel, where we were given comfortable little adjoining rooms. There was nothing to unpack, just a toothbrush and a pair of clean underwear—we were down to iron rations. Plus face cream and a big book, a page-turner. And a notepad. There would be time to note down everything, to describe the woman: She is tall, with a good body, her hips quite wide, her hands delicate. Her thick, curly hair is tied back in a ponytail, but it's unruly, and strands float above her head like a kind of silver halo—she is completely gray. But she has a young, bright, freckled face. She must be Swedish. Swedish women tend not to dye their hair.

We arranged to meet downstairs, at the bar, that evening, after a luxurious shower and a look through the various channels on the TV.

We ordered white wine, and after the polite preliminaries, including the Three Basic Travel Questions, we moved on to matters of greater substance. I started off by telling her a bit about my peregrinations, but as I was speaking I got the impression she was listening only to be polite. This made me lose momentum, for I figured she must have a more interesting story to tell, until finally I gave her the floor.

She was collecting evidence, she said, she had even gotten a grant for it from the European Union, although it still didn't cover her travels, so she had had to borrow money from her dad—who had since passed away. She swept a little coil of gray hair from her forehead (I decided for sure then that she couldn't be over forty-five), and we ordered salads in exchange for our airline vouchers; the only option with the voucher was the Niçoise. She narrowed her eyes when she talked, which lent her words a slightly ironic undertone, which was probably why for the first few minutes I couldn't tell if she was being serious. She said that at first glance the world seems so diverse. Wherever you go you find all sorts of different people, different cultures, cities constructed according to local custom, using different materials. Different roofs and different windows and different courtyards. Here she speared a piece of feta on her fork and traced circles with it in the air.

"But don't let yourself be taken in by the diversity—it's superficial," she said. "It's all smoke and mirrors. In reality, everywhere is the same. In terms of animals. In terms of how we interact with animals."

Calmly, as though reiterating a lecture she knew by heart, she began to enumerate: dogs strain against chains in the sweltering sun, just desperately hoping for water—these puppies are chained up so tight that by the time they're two months old they can't even walk; ewes give birth in the fields, in the winter, in the snow, and all the farmers do is arrange large vehicles to cart off the frozen lambs; lobsters are kept in restaurant aquariums so that the customer may sentence them, with the rap of an index finger, to death by boiling, while other restaurants breed dogs in their storerooms—dog meat restores virility, after all; hens in cages are defined by the number of eggs they lay, rushed by chemicals through their brief lives; people put on dogfights; primates are injected with diseases; cosmetics are tested on rabbits; fur coats are made of sheep fetuses—and she said all of this unfazed, inserting olives into her mouth.

"No, no," I said, "I can't listen to this."

So she took her bag, which was made of rags, from the back of her chair, and she took out from inside it a folder of laminated pages in black Xeroxed print. She handed it to me across the little table. I reluctantly flipped through the darkened pages, the text in two columns, like in an encyclopedia or in the Bible. Small print, footnotes. "Reports on Infamy," and the address of her website. I took a look and knew instantly I wasn't going to read any of it. But still I tucked the material away inside my backpack.

"That's what I do," she said.

Then, over our second bottle of wine, she told me about the time she had gotten altitude sickness on a trip to Tibet and almost died. She was healed by some local woman who beat a drum and mixed her herbal tinctures.

Our talk was free that evening, our tongues—which had yearned for long sentences and stories—well lubricated by white wine, and we went to bed late.

The next morning over breakfast in our hotel, Aleksandra—that was this angry woman's name—leaned in over the croissants and said:

"The true God is an animal. He's in animals, so close that we don't notice. Every day God sacrifices Himself for us, dying over and over, feeding us with His body, clothing us in His skin, allowing us to test our medicines on Him so that we might live longer and better. Thus does He show his affection, bestow on us His friendship and love."

I froze, staring at her mouth, shaken not so much by this revelation as by the tone in which she said it—so serene. And by the knife that glinted as it spread layers of butter over the fluffy insides of her croissant, back and forth, methodical, relentless.

"You can find the proof in Ghent."

She extracted a postcard from her hodgepodge bag and tossed it onto my plate.

I picked it up and tried to glean some meaning in the proliferation of details; I would have needed a magnifying glass to do that, though.

"Anyone can see it," said Aleksandra. "In the middle of the city there's a cathedral, and there, on the altar, you'll see an enormous, beautiful painting. In it there are fields, a green plain somewhere outside of the city, and in that meadow there is an ordinary elevation. Right here," and she pointed with the tip of her knife, "here is the Animal in the form of a white lamb, exalted."

I did recognize the painting. I'd seen it a number of times in different reproductions. *Adoration of the Mystic Lamb.*

"His true identity was discovered—His bright luminous figure draws the gaze, causes heads to bow before his divine majesty," she said, pointing at the lamb with her knife. "And you can see how from just about everywhere there is a procession flowing toward Him—those are all these people coming to pay tribute to Him, to gaze upon this humblest, humiliated God. Here, look at how the rulers of countries are making their way up toward Him, emperors and kings, churches, parliaments, political parties, guilds; there are mothers and children, elderly folk and teenage girls . . ."

"Why do you do this?" I asked.

"For obvious reasons," she replied. "I want to write an exhaustive volume that leaves out no crime, from the dawn of the world to our time. It will be humanity's confessions."

She had already gathered the excerpts from ancient Greek literature.

## GUIDEBOOKS

Description is akin to overuse—it destroys; the colors wear off, the corners lose their definition, and in the end what's been described begins to fade, to disappear. This applies most of all to places. Enormous damage has been done by travel literature—a veritable scourge, an epidemic. Guidebooks have conclusively ruined the greater part of the planet; published in editions numbering in the millions, in many languages, they have debilitated places, pinning them down and naming them, blurring their contours. Even I, in my youthful naiveté, once took a shot at the description of places. But when I would go back to those descriptions later, when I'd try to take a deep breath and allow their intense presence to choke me up all over again, when I'd try to listen in on their murmurings, I was always in for a shock. The truth is terrible: describing is destroying.

Which is why you have to be very careful. It's better not to use names: avoid, conceal, take great caution in giving out addresses, so as not to encourage anyone to make their own pilgrimage. After all, what would they find there? A dead place, dust, like the dried-out core of an apple. The *Clinical Syndromes* (aforementioned) also includes the so-called Paris Syndrome, which largely ails Japanese tourists who visit Paris. It is characterized by shock and by a number of physical symptoms like shortness of breath, heart palpitations, sweating, and arousal. Occasionally there are hallucinations. Then sedatives are administered, and a retreat to the home is recommended. Such disturbances can be explained by the discrepancy between the pilgrims' expectations and the reality of Paris, which bears no resemblance to the city described in guidebooks, films, and television.

## NEW ATHENS

No book ages quite so quickly as a guidebook, which is in fact quite the blessing for the guidebook industry. In my own travels I have remained faithful to two books which I refer to above all others, in spite of their age, because they were written with real passion, and a genuine desire to portray the world.

The first was written in Poland in the early eighteenth century. Around the same time, other essays written in the Enlightenment West may have been more successful, but none possesses as much charm as this one. Its author was a Catholic priest named Benedykt Chmielowski, who hailed from Volhynia (a region now shared by Poland, Ukraine, and Belarus). He was a kind of Josephus cloaked in a provincial fog, a Herodotus on the outermost outskirts of the world. I suspect he might have suffered from the same syndrome I did, although unlike me, he never actually left his home.

In a chapter with the lengthy title of "On other strange and wonderful persons of the world: That is, Anacephalus, alias Headless, or Cynocephalus, alias Dog-Headed; and on other persons of curious form," he writes:

> There is a Nation known as Blemij, which Isidorus calls Lemnios, where men have the figure and the symmetry of our ilk, yet whole heads they have not, rather only faces in the center of their breasts . . . Pliny the Elder, meanwhile,

that great researcher of the natural world, not only confirms the selfsame sentiment *de Acephalis*, alias of headless persons, but also situates their close relatives, the
Troglodytes, in Ethiopia, a Swart Country. Much of this
knowledge these Authors derive from the *Momentum* of
Saint Augustine, *oculatis Testis* [that is, eyewitness], regarding peregrinations in that Country (being Bishop of
African Hippo not overly removed thence) and sowing the
*semina* [seeds] of the Holy Christian faith, as he mentions
directly in his Sermon in Eremo [in the Desert] to the Au-
gustinian Brotherhood, which he had founded himself: ". . . I was already Bishop of Hippo, when I went into
Ethiopia with some servants of Christ there to preach the
Gospel. In this country we saw many men and women
without heads, who had two great eyes in their breasts;
while the rest of their appendages were akin to our
own . . ." Solinus, that Author invoked so many times already, writes that in the Indian mountains there are people
with dogs' heads and voices, alias barking. Marco Polo,
who surveyed India, asserts that on the Isle of Angamen
there are people with dogs' heads and dogs' teeth; this is
corroborated by Odoricus Aelianus (*lib.* 10), who situates
such people in the deserts and the Forests of Egypt. These
human monsters Pliny calls Cynanalogos, while Aulus
Gellius and Isidonus call them Cynocephalus, i.e., canine
heads. . . . Prince Mikołay Radziwiłł in his *Peregrinations*
(Third Epistle) admits that he had with him two Cyno-
cephali, that is, persons with canine heads, and that he
further imported them to Europe.

*Tandem oritur questio* [This ultimately raises the question]: Are such monstrous Persons capaces [able] to be saved? Saint Augustine, Oraculum of Hippo, responds thus, that man, wherever he may be born, so long as he be good, and wise, having wisdom in his soul, even diverging from us in form, color, voice, bearing, has inevitably descended from the first human forebear, Adam, and is thus capax for salvation.

The other one is Melville's *Moby-Dick*.

Though if you can just check Wikipedia from time to time, that's also perfectly sufficient.

## WIKIPEDIA

As far as I can tell, this is mankind's most honest cognitive project. It is frank about the fact that all the information we have about the world comes straight out of our own heads, like Athena out of Zeus's. People bring to Wikipedia everything they know. If the project succeeds, then this encyclopedia undergoing perpetual renewal will be the greatest wonder of the world. It has everything we know in it—every thing, definition, event, and problem our brains have worked on; we shall cite sources, provide links. And so we will start to stitch together our version of the world, be able to bundle up the globe in our own story. It will hold everything. Let's get to work! Let everyone write even just a sentence on whatever it is they know best.

Sometimes I start to doubt that it will work. After all, what it has in it can only be what we can put into words—what we have words for. And in that sense, it wouldn't be able to hold everything at all.

We should have some other collection of knowledge, then, to balance that one out—its inverse, its inner lining, everything we don't know, all the things that can't be captured in any index, can't be handled by any search engine. For the vastness of these contents cannot be traversed from word to word—you have to step in between the words, into the unfathomable abysses between ideas. With every step we'll slip and fall.

It would appear the only option is to get in even deeper.

Matter and anti-matter.

Information and anti-information.

## CITIZENS OF THE WORLD, PICK UP YOUR PENS!

Jasmine, the nice Muslim woman I'd spent the whole evening talking to, was telling me about her project: she wanted to encourage everyone in her country to write books. She had noticed that you don't need very much in order to write a book—a bit of free time after work, not even a computer. Any such intrepid person might end up writing a bestseller—then their efforts would be rewarded by social advancement. It's the best way of getting out of poverty, she said. If only we all read each other's books, she sighed. She'd founded a forum on the internet. Apparently it already had several hundred members.

I love the idea of reading books as a brotherly, sisterly moral obligation to one's people.

# TRAVEL PSYCHOLOGY: LECTIO BREVIS I

At airports over the past few months I've come across some scholars who, amidst the din of travel, between departure announcements and boarding calls, organize little lectures. One of them explained to me that it was part of a worldwide (or perhaps EU-wide) educational outreach program. So at some point I decided to linger in view of the screen in the waiting area and the small group of curious listeners.

"Ladies and gentlemen," began a young woman, nervously adjusting her colorful scarf while her companion, a man in a tweed jacket with leather patches on the elbows, prepared the screen that was hanging on the wall. "Travel psychology studies people in transit, persons in motion, and thus situates itself in opposition to traditional psychology, which has always investigated the human being in a fixed context, in stability and stillness—for example, through the prism of his or her biological constitution, family relationships, social situations, and so forth. In travel psychology, these factors are of secondary, not primary, importance.

"If we wish to catalog humankind in a convincing way, we can do so only by placing people in some sort of motion, moving from one place toward another. The fact of the repeated emergence of so many unconvincing descriptions of the stable, fixed person appears to call into question the existence of a self, understood nonrelationally. This has meant that for some time in travel psychology there have been certain prevailing voices claiming that there can be no other psychology besides travel psychology."

The little cluster of listeners shuffled restlessly. A vociferous group of tall men distinguished by their sports team's colorful scarves—a clan of fans—had just passed by. At the same time, there were still people coming up to us, intrigued by the screen on the wall and by the two rows of chairs set out. They would sit down for a moment on their way between gates or in between wandering around the airport shops. Evident on many of their faces was exhaustion and disorientation in time: you could tell they'd be glad to take just a little nap, and they must not have been aware that around the next corner there was a comfortable waiting room with armchairs you could sleep in. Several travelers had stood up when the woman began talking. A very young couple was standing locked in an embrace, listening with rapt attention as they tenderly stroked each other's back.

The woman paused briefly, then started up again: "A fundamental concept in travel psychology is desire, which is what lends movement and direction to human beings as well as arousing in them an inclination toward something. Desire in itself is empty, in other words it merely indicates direction, but never destination; destinations, in any case, always remain phantasmagoric and unclear; the closer we get to them, the more enigmatic they become. By no means is it possible to ever actually attain a given destination, nor, in so doing, appease desire. This process of striving is best encapsulated in the preposition 'toward.' Toward what?"

Here the woman glanced out over her glasses and cast her pointed gaze about the audience, as though awaiting any form of confirmation that she was addressing the right group of people. This was not to the liking of the couple with two children in a stroller, who exchanged a look and pushed their luggage onward, moving down to take a gander at the imitation Rembrandt.

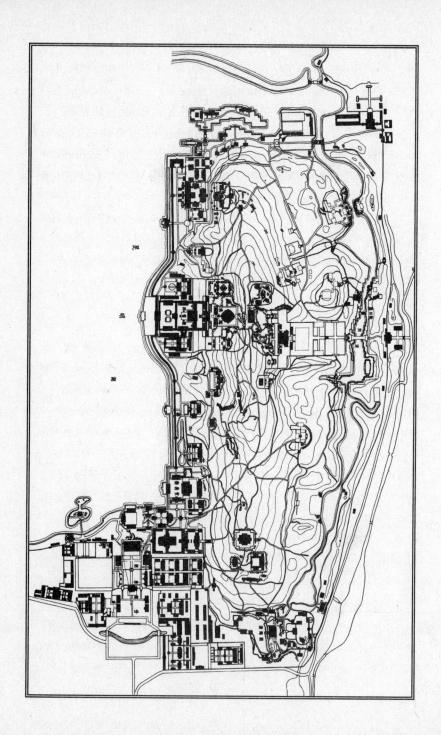

"Travel psychology has not cut all ties with psychoanalysis . . ." the woman continued, and I suddenly felt sorry for these young lecturers. They were talking to people who had wound up here by accident and who did not look particularly interested. I went over to the vending machine to get myself a cup of coffee, added a couple of sugar cubes, trying to revive myself, and by the time I returned, it was the man speaking instead.

". . . foundational idea," he was saying, "is constellationality, and right away the first claim of travel psychology: in life, unlike in studies (though in fact in scholarship, too, much gets overtaxed for the sake of order), there exists no philosophical primum. That means that it is impossible to build a consistent cause-and-effect course of argument or a narrative with events that succeed each other casuistically and follow from each other. That would merely be an approximation, in the same way that an approximation of the earth gives us a grid of latitude and longitude. When in reality, in order to reflect our experience more accurately, it would be necessary instead to assemble a whole, out of pieces of more or less the same size, placed concentrically on the same surface. Constellation, not sequencing, carries truth. This is why travel psychology envisions man in equivalently weighted situations, without trying to lend his life any—even approximate—continuity. Life is made up of situations. There is, of course, a certain inclination toward the repetition of behaviors. This repetition does not, however, mean that we should succumb in our imaginations to the appearance of any sort of consistent whole."

The man looked out over his glasses at his listeners, uneasy, no doubt wanting to ascertain whether they were actually listening. We were listening, attentively.

At that moment a group of travelers with children ran past; they must have been late for their connecting flight. This unfocused us a little, we looked for a moment at their flushed red faces, their straw hats and souvenir drums and masks and shell necklaces. The man cleared his throat a few times to bring us back to order, gathering air into his lungs, but then, looking back at us, he let it out again and fell silent. He flipped through a few pages of his notes and finally said:

"The history. Now a few sentences on the history of the field. It developed in the postwar years (in the fifties) out of airline psychology, which arose in conjunction with the growing number of airplane passengers. At first it dealt with the particular problems connected with passenger movement—the functions of task forces in emergency situations, the psychological dynamics of flight—then it expanded its area of interest in the direction of the organization of airports and hotels, the appropriation of new spaces, the multicultural aspects of travel. In time it branched out into distinct specializations, like psychogeography, psychotopology. Clinical branches came about . . ."

I stopped listening. The lecture was too long. They ought to dispense this education in smaller doses.

Instead I observed a man, poorly dressed, all rumpled, no doubt in the middle of a long journey. He had found someone's black umbrella and proceeded to inspect it. But it turned out that the umbrella was unusable. Its wires were broken, and the black covering couldn't be extended. Then, to my surprise, the man began to meticulously detach the umbrella's covering from the rods and end pieces, which took him some time. He did it fully concentrated, standing still amidst the flow of crowds of travelers. When he had finished, he folded up the material into a cube, placed it in his pocket, then disappeared into the stream of people.

I turned then, and went on my way as well.

## THE RIGHT TIME AND PLACE

Many people believe that there exists in the world's coordinate system a perfect point where time and space reach an agreement. This may even be why these people travel, leaving their homes behind, hoping that even by moving around in a chaotic fashion they will increase their likelihood of happening upon this point. Landing at the right time in the right place—seizing the opportunity, grabbing the moment and not letting go—would mean the code to the safe had been cracked, the combination revealed, the truth exposed. No more being passed by, no more surfing coincidences, accidents, and turns of fate. You don't have to do anything—you just have to show up, sign in at that one single configuration of time and place. There you will find your great love, happiness, a winning lottery ticket or the revelation of the mystery everyone's been killing themselves over in vain for all these years, or death. Sometimes in the morning one even has the impression that this moment is close by, that today might be the day it will arrive.

## INSTRUCTIONS

I dreamed I was leafing through an American magazine with photographs of ponds and pools. I saw everything, detail by detail. The letters *A*, *B*, and *C* described precisely every component part of the plans and outlines. I eagerly began reading an article titled "How to Build an Ocean: Instructions."

## ASH WEDNESDAY FEAST

"You can call me Eryk," he would announce in lieu of a greeting as he walked into the little bar, which at that time of year was heated only by the wood in the fireplace, and everyone would smile in a friendly way to him, some even beckoning him over with a wave that meant simply "Pull up a seat." All things considered, he was a good companion and—in spite of his eccentricities—was well liked. To begin with, before he'd had enough to drink, he would sit in the corner looking gruff, at a remove from the warmth of the fireplace. He could afford to do so—he had a powerful build, was resistant to cold, could keep himself warm.

"An island," he'd start, seeming to be sighing to himself but loud enough so that the others would hear, provoking them as he ordered his first giant beer. "What a miserable state of mind. Asshole of the world."

The others at the bar didn't really understand him, it seemed, but they would chuckle knowingly.

"Hey, Eryk, when are you going on your whale hunt?" they would holler, their faces flushed from the fire and alcohol.

In response Eryk would curse baroquely, pure poetry, like no one else—this was a part of the nightly ritual. For every day went ahead like a ferry on its cables, from one shore to the other, passing on its route those same red buoys tasked with breaking up the water's monopoly on vastness, making it measurable, and in so doing, giving a false impression of control.

After another beer Eryk would be ready to sit with the others, and he usually did so, although lately as he drank his mood tended to turn sour. He'd sit there grimacing, sarcastic. He no longer spun his yarns of distant seas—if you had known him long enough you knew he never repeated any tales, or at least they differed from one another significantly in the details. But now, more and more often he simply attacked the others rather than telling any stories. Angry Eryk.

There were also evenings when he'd fall into a kind of trance, and at these times he'd become unbearable. More than once Hendrik, the owner of the small bar, had had to intervene.

"Consider yourselves enlisted," Eryk would shout, pointing his finger at each person in the room in turn.

"To the last man. And I am to set sail with such a heathen crew that have small touch of human mothers in them! Whelped somewhere by the sharkish sea! Oh, life! 'tis in an hour like this, with soul beat down and held to knowledge—as wild, untutored things are forced to feed."

Hendrik would amiably pull him aside and give him a friendly pat on the back, while the younger clientele would guffaw at his strange speech.

"Give it a rest, Eryk. You don't want to make trouble, do you?" the older ones, who knew him well, would say to try to calm him down, but Eryk would not allow himself to be calmed down.

"Talk not to me of blasphemy. I'd strike the sun if it insulted me."

When this happened the only thing to be done was pray he didn't offend some visiting guest, since the locals didn't take offense at Eryk. What could you expect of him, now that he looked out at the bar as though through a milky plastic curtain; his absent gaze revealed that he was traveling the seas within himself now, his stay-sail up. Now the only thing that could be done was to mercifully send him home.

"Listen, then, hard-hearted man," Eryk kept babbling, planting his finger on somebody's chest, "I'm talking to you, too."

"Come on, Eryk. Let's go."

"Ye've shipped, have you? Names down on the papers? Well, well, what's signed is signed; and what's to be will be; and then again, perhaps it won't be, after all . . ." he mumbled and went back from the door to the counter, demanding a last round, "a draft of a draft," as he said, even though no one knew what that meant.

He'd continue making a fuss until someone seized the perfect moment to tug him out by the tail of his uniform and sit him back down until his taxi came.

But he wasn't always so belligerent. More often than not he left before he reached this state, since he still had to walk four kilometers—and he found this march home, he noted, most loath-some. The route was monotonous, along a road that ran between old pastures overgrown with weeds and looming dwarf pines. Sometimes, when the night was clear, he could make out in the distance the outline of a windmill, long since inactive, serving only as a backdrop for tourists as they photographed themselves and one another.

The heating would kick in about an hour before he got back—he had it set that way to save on electricity—so clouds of cold—damp, soaked through with sea salt—still hovered in the darkness of both rooms.

He sustained himself on the same single basic dish, the only thing he hadn't tired of yet: thin-sliced potatoes, interlaid with strips of bacon and onion, cooked in a cast-iron pot. Sprinkled with marjoram and pepper, liberally salted. The perfect meal, nutritional proportions perfectly preserved: fats, carbohydrates, starch, protein, and vitamin C. With dinner he'd turn on the television, but then, since he hated TV most of all, he'd always open a bottle of vodka in the end and drink it dry, before finally going to sleep.

What a godforsaken place, this island. Shoved up into the north as into a dark drawer; windy and wet. For some reason people still lived here and had no intention whatsoever of moving to bright, warm cities. They just hunkered down in their tiny wooden homes arranged along a road that rose with each new asphalt coating, condemning them to eternal diminishment.

You can all go down along the shoulder of that road, toward the small port, which is made up of several seedy buildings, a plastic hut that sells the ferry tickets and a lousy marina—largely abandoned at this time of year. Perhaps in the summer a few yachts will come in bearing some eccentric tourists who have tired of all the racket around southern waters, rivieras, azures, and sweltering beaches. And then people like us—restless people, ever ravenous for new adventures, backpacks brimming with cheap ramen—might wind up in this sad place by accident. What will you see here? The very edge of the world, where time, reflected off the empty waterfront, turns around disappointed and heads toward land and pitilessly leaves this place to its perpetual enduring. For how is 1946 different from 1976 here, or 1976 from 2000?

Eryk got marooned here after an array of adventures and misadventures. In the beginning, long ago, he fled his country, one of those bland, flat communist lands, and as a young immigrant got hired to work on a whaling ship. At that time, he had only a few English words under his belt, intermittent pinpoints between "yes" and "no," just exactly enough to answer the simple grunts the guys on the ship would exchange among themselves. "Take," "pull," "cut." "Fast" and "hard." "Catch" and "tie." "Fuck." It sufficed at first. And it sufficed, too, to change his name to a simple, widely known one: Eryk. To get rid of that dragging corpse that no one knew how to pronounce correctly. And to toss into the ocean the folders of papers, school certificates, diplomas, transcripts from additional studies, and records of vaccines—those would never come in handy here; if anything, they'd just humiliate the other sailors, whose entire résumés consisted of a few long voyages and some escapades in portside pubs.

Life aboard a ship is immersion not in salt water, not in the rains over the northern seas, nor even in sunshine, but rather in adrenaline. There is no time to think, no meditation over spilled milk. The country Eryk came from was far away and not particularly seafaring, having only sparing access to the ocean. Its ports were an embarrassment. It favored towns situated on safe rivers bound by bridges. Eryk didn't miss it at all, greatly preferring it here in the north. He'd thought he would sail for a few years, save up some money, then build himself a wooden home, marry a flaxen-haired Emma or Ingrid with whom he would have children, for whom he'd make floats for float fishing, with whom he'd clean sea trout. Someday he would write his memoirs, when his adventures had arranged themselves into a suitably attractive package. He couldn't say how it had happened that the years had raced by as they had, taking some shortcut through his life—lightweight, fleeting, leaving no traces.

At most they left a record on his body, his liver in particular. But that was later. In the beginning, after his first voyage, it so happened that he ended up in jail—for more than three years—when the evil captain framed his whole crew for smuggling cigarettes and a large packet of cocaine. But even in prison in a distant land Eryk stayed in the dominion of the ocean and whales. In the prison library there was only one book in English, left no doubt by some other prisoner years earlier. It was an old edition, from the turn of the century, with brittle pages, yellowed, bearing the traces of daily life.

And so for over three years (which in any case was not so severe a sentence, given that under the laws in effect at a remove of just a hundred nautical miles, the punishment for the same offense was death by hanging) Eryk secured himself free language lessons in advanced English, a course in literature and whaling and psychology and travel all in a single textbook. A good method, not inviting of distractions. In just five months he was able to recite the adventures of Ishmael in passages he knew by heart, and to speak in the voice of Ahab, which brought him special pleasure, for this was the manner of expression most organic to Eryk, fitting him like comfortable clothing; who cared if it was strange and old-fashioned. And what a stroke of luck that such a book had fallen into the hands of such a person in such a place. A phenomenon known to travel psychologists by the name of synchronicity, evidence of the world making sense. Evidence that throughout this beautiful chaos threads of meaning spread in every direction, networks of strange logic, all bearing, if one were to believe in God, the contorted imprints of His fingers. Which is how Eryk saw it.

Soon, then, in that distant, exotic prison, where in the evenings it was hard to breathe because of the tropical humidity, where anxiety and longing rankled the mind, Eryk would immerse himself in reading, becoming a bookmark, being happy. In fact, he would not have made it through his time in prison without that novel. His cellmates—smugglers, too—often heard him reading aloud and quickly succumbed to the charm of the whalers' adventures. It would not have been at all surprising if they had tried, after being released, to educate themselves further in the history of whaling, writing dissertations on harpoons and nautical equipment. The most gifted among them might have attained a higher degree of initiation: a specialization in clinical psychology in the field of perseverance in the face of any obstacle. And so the Sailor from the Azores, the Portuguese Sailor, and Eryk began to speak to one another in a prison slang all their own. They even managed to discuss in this manner the little Asian guards:

"By Jove! For isn't he a jolly fellow!" would cry the Sailor from the Azores when, for example, one of the guards would smuggle a pack of damp cigarettes into their cell.

"Upon my word, I am of more or less the same sentiment. Let us give him our blessing."

This was good for them, since each newly imprisoned cellmate understood little at the start, becoming their foreigner, necessary for them to be able to conduct any semblance of a social life.

Each of them had his favorite lines, which he'd read aloud each evening, the others finishing his sentences in a chorus.

But the main topics of their conversations in their increasingly refined language were the sea, their travels, and getting offshore, entrusting themselves to the water, which—as they determined after several days' worth of discussion worthy of the pre-Socratics—was the most important element on earth. They were already planning the routes they'd take to sail home, readying themselves for the views they'd see en route, composing in their minds the tele-grams they'd send their families. How would they earn a living? They argued about the best ideas, but they always ended up circling back around to the same theme, having caught (though they didn't know it yet) the fever, been infected with it; deeply unsettled by the mere possibility of the existence of something like a white whale. They knew there were still countries that fished for whales, and although that work was less romantic than how Ishmael described it, it was hard to come up with anything better, given their current circumstances. They'd heard Japan needed men for whaling, and switching from cod and herring to whales was like moving from crafts to fine art . . .

Thirty-eight months was long enough to work out the details of their future lives; to minutely, point by point, discuss them with their colleagues. There were no serious disputes.

"Merchant service be damned. I'll take that leg away from thy stern, if ever thou talkest of the merchant service to me again. Flukes! Man, what makes thee want to go a-whaling, eh?" roared Eryk.

"What have you seen of the world?" the Portuguese Sailor would cry.

"The Baltic is no stranger to me, and I have traveled the length and breadth of the North Sea. I know the currents of the Atlantic like my own veins . . ."

"You are very certain of yourself, my dear fellow." They had to say *something* to each other.

Ten years—that's how long it took Eryk to get home again—and no doubt he had it better in this sense than his comrades. He took a circuitous route back, through peripheral seas, the narrowest straits and widest bays. Just when estuaries started to blend into the open waters of the seas, just when he'd enlist for a ship heading home, suddenly some new opportunity would arise, more often than not in the exact opposite direction, and if he did hesitate for a moment, he would usually come to the conclusion that the truest argument was an old one—the earth is round, let us not be too attached, then, to directions. And this was understandable—to someone from nowhere, every movement turns into a return, since nothing exerts such a draw as emptiness.

During those years he worked under the flags of Panama, Australia, and Indonesia. On a Chilean freighter he transported Japanese cars to the United States. On a South African tanker he survived a wreck off the coast of Liberia. He transported workers from Java to Singapore. He got hepatitis and was hospitalized in Cairo. After having his arm broken in a drunken brawl in Marseille, he quit drinking for a few months, only to then drink himself into a stupor in Málaga and break the other arm.

We won't dwell on the details. The twists and turns of Eryk's fates on the high seas are not what interest us here. Let us skip to the moment he finally came ashore on that island he later came to hate, getting hired to work the small, primitive ferry that ran between the islands. Working that job—humiliating, he called it— Eryk lost weight and became a little paler. The dark tan he'd had before disappeared forever from his face, leaving behind dark splotches. His hair grayed at his temples, and wrinkles made his gaze more penetrating, sharper. After this initiation, which was a powerful blow to his pride, he got transferred to a route with more responsibility—now his ferry connected island to mainland, and no cable imprisoned him. His wide deck could accommodate sixteen people's cars. The job provided him a steady wage, health insurance, and a peaceful life on that northern island.

He'd get up every morning, wash his face with cold water, and arrange his gray beard with his fingers. Then he'd put on the dark green uniform of the United Northern Ferry Company and go on foot to the port where he had docked the previous evening. Shortly thereafter someone from the ground service, Robert or Adam, would open the gate, and straightaway the first cars would get in line to drive up the iron ramp and onto Eryk's ferry. There was always enough room for everyone, and it also happened sometimes that the ferry was empty, clear, light as a daydream. Then Eryk would sit in his cabin, suspended on high in his glassed-in stork's nest, and that other shore would seem so close. Wouldn't it be better to build a bridge than make people go back and forth and pester him this way?

It was a question of states of mind. Each day he could choose between two. One was sensitive, quick to take offense—he would be sure he wasn't as good as anybody, that he was lacking what everyone else had, that he was a deviant of some sort who didn't even know, for God's sake, what was wrong with him. He'd feel isolated, lonely, like a child sent to his room looking out the window at his peers as they played happily. That fate had intended him for a small supporting role in these chaotic human peregrinations across land and sea, and now, since settling on this island, this episode had turned out to be a minor one, as well.

The other state of mind strengthened his conviction that actually he was better, unique, exceptional. That he was the only one who sensed and understood the truth, that only he was capable of being exceptional. And he sometimes managed to spend a number of hours in this elevated self-esteem, and even days, when he felt, let's say, somehow happy. But then it faded, like intoxication. And by way of a hangover there appeared the terrifying thought that in order to seem like a person worthy of respect, he had to continually fake it in these two ways and that—worst of all—someday the truth would come out; it would be revealed that he was no one.

He was sitting in his glassed-in cabin observing the loading of the first morning ferry. He saw people he'd known a long time from the little town. Here was the R. family in their gray Opel—the father worked at the port, the mother in the library, while the children, a boy and a girl, were still in school. Here were four teenagers, schoolkids, who would take their bus on the other side. And here was Eliza, the nursery school teacher, with her little daughter, whom she was of course taking with her to work. The little girl's father had disappeared all of a sudden two years earlier and had never been heard from since. Eryk suspected he must be fishing for whales somewhere. Here was old S., who had something wrong with his kidneys; twice a week he had to take the ferry to go to the hospital for dialysis. He and his wife were trying to sell their little dwarf-like wooden house and move closer to the hospital, but for some reason or other they hadn't managed to do so. The truck from Organic Foods was going to stock up on products on the mainland. Some black foreign car, probably guests of the director. The yellow van that belonged to the brothers Alfred and Albrecht, two stubborn old bachelors who continued to raise sheep on the island. A couple of cyclists, numb with cold. The delivery vehicle from the car shop—must have been going for parts. Edwin waved to Eryk. You could recognize him on any island of the world—he always wore checkered shirts lined with artificial fur. Eryk knew them all, even the ones he was seeing for the first time—he knew why they had come here, and knowing the aim of a journey, you know enough about a person.

There were three reasons for coming to the island. Reason One, because you simply lived here; Reason Two, because you were a guest of the director; and Reason Three, because of the windmill, to have a picture of yourself taken with it in the background.

The ferry took twenty minutes. In that time some of the passengers got out of their cars and lit a cigarette, even though they weren't allowed to. Others stood at the railing and just looked out at the water, until their rocking vision finally hooked on to the other shore. Soon, excited by the smells of the mainland, with all their incredibly important tasks and obligations, they would disappear onto the little streets by the waterfront, ebbing away like the ninth wave that reaches furthest and soaks into the ground and never returns to sea. Others would come to take their places. The veterinarian in his elegant pickup; he earned his living by spaying and neutering cats. A field trip to investigate the flora and fauna of the island for a class on the natural world. A delivery of bananas and kiwis. A television crew coming to interview the director. The G. family, returning from a visit to the grandmother. Another suntanned couple of cyclists would replace the first.

During loading and unloading, which took almost an hour, Eryk would smoke a few cigarettes and try hard not to give in to despair. Then the ferry would return to the island. And so it would go eight times, with a two-hour break for lunch, which Eryk always ate in the same little place. One of three places around there. After work he'd buy potatoes, onions, and bacon. Cigarettes and alcohol. He'd try not to drink until noon, but by the sixth trip he would already be smashed.

Straight lines—how humiliating they were. How they destroyed the mind. What perfidious geometry, how it makes us into idiots—there and back, a parody of travel. Going forth merely in order to return again. Speeding up just to put on the brakes.

So it was, too, with Eryk's marriage, which had been brief and turbulent. Maria, a divorcée, worked in a shop and had a young son who went to a boarding school in the city. Eryk moved in with her, into her nice, cozy little house with its enormous television. She had a slim figure, with somewhat generous contours, light-colored skin, and tight-fitting leggings. She soon learned to serve his potatoes with bacon and started adding marjoram and nutmeg to them, while he threw himself into chopping wood for their fireplace on his days off. It lasted a year and a half; after a while the never-ending noise of the television started to wear him down, its gaudy illumination, the rag by the mat where you had to leave your muddy boots, and that nutmeg. After he got drunk a few times and swore at her like a sailor, finger raised, she threw him out of the house, and shortly thereafter she moved to the mainland, to be near her son.

/////

Today was March 1, Ash Wednesday. When he opened his eyes, Eryk saw the gray light and the sleet falling, which would leave blurred tracks on the windows. He thought of his old name. He'd almost forgotten it. He said it out loud, and it sounded as though he were being called by some stranger. He felt the familiar pressure in his head after yesterday's drinking.

Because it must be noted that Chinese people have two names: one given by their families, used to summon the child, scold and punish him, but also the basis for affectionate nicknames. But when the child goes out into the world, he or she takes another name, an outside name, a world name, a personage name. Donned like a uniform, a surplice, a prison jumpsuit, an outfit for a formal cocktail party. This outside name is useful and easy to remember. From here on out it will corroborate its person. Best if it's worldly, universal, recognizable to everyone; down with the locality of our names. Down with Oldrzich, Sung Yin, Kazimierz, and Jyrek; down with Błażen, Liu, and Milica. Long live Michael, Judith, Anna, Jan, Samuel, and Eryk!

But today Eryk answered the call of his old name: I'm here.

No one knew that name, so I won't say it, either.

The man named Eryk donned his green uniform with the logo of the United Northern Ferry Company, ran his fingers through his beard, turned off the heating in his little dwarf-like house, and set out along the asphalt. Then, as he waited in his aquarium for the ferry to be loaded and the sun to finally come out, he had a can of beer and lit his first cigarette. He waved from on high to Eliza and her little daughter, friendly, as though wanting to reward them for the fact that today they wouldn't make it to nursery school.

After the ferry had left the shore and was already halfway between the two marinas, suddenly it stalled, then set out for open sea.

Not everyone realized what was happening at first. Some, so accustomed to the routine of the straight line, looked at the disappearing shore indifferently, numbed, which would no doubt have confirmed Eryk's drunken theories about the fact that traveling by ferry flattens out the brain's coils. Others realized only after a long while.

"Eryk, what are you doing? Turn around right now," Alfred shouted at him, and Eliza joined in with her high-pitched, squeaky voice: "People will be late for work . . ."

Alfred tried to get up to where Eryk was, but Eryk had thought to close the gate and lock his cabin.

From above he saw everyone simultaneously take out their phones and place calls, talking indignantly into empty space, gesticulating anxiously. He could imagine what they were saying. That they'd be late to work, that they wanted to know who would cover the punitive damages in question, that drunks like Eryk shouldn't be allowed, that they always knew things would end up like this, that they don't have enough jobs for their own people and here they were, hiring immigrants; who knew how they learned the language so well, but in any case there was always . . .

Eryk couldn't have cared less. He was pleased to see that after some time they settled down and looked out at the sky getting lighter and distributing beautiful beams of light down between the clouds. Only one thing worried him—the light blue coat of Eliza's daughter, which (as every sea wolf knows) was a bad omen aboard a ship. But Eryk closed his eyes and soon forgot about it. He headed for the ocean and went down to his passengers with a box of fizzy drinks and chocolate bars that he'd prepared for this occasion long ago. These refreshments did them a world of good, he saw: the kids quieted down as they gazed at the shore of the island fading into the distance, and the adults evinced increasing interest in their journey.

"Where are we headed?" asked the younger of the brothers T., matter-of-factly, then burping from the fizzy drink.

"How long before we reach the open seas?" Eliza, the nursery school teacher, wanted to know.

"Did you make sure you have enough fuel?" asked old S., the one with the kidney problems.

Or at least it seemed to him that they were saying these things, rather than others. He tried not to look at them and not to care. He'd already steadied his eyes on the line of the horizon, its reflection slicing straight across his pupils, the top half lighter from the sky, the bottom half darker, from the water. And his passengers were calm now, too. They'd pressed their caps snug onto their heads, pulled their scarves around their necks a little tighter. It might be said they sailed in silence, until their peace was pierced by the helicopter's rumble and the wail of police motorboats.

//////////////

There are things that happen of their own accord, journeys that begin and end in dreams. And there are travelers who simply answer the chaotic call of their own unease. One of these stands before you now . . ." So Eryk's defense embarked upon his short-lived trial. Unfortunately, not even this moving defense could keep our hero from another prison sentence. I hope spending another spell inside worked out to his advantage. Life for someone like Eryk is made of inevitable highs and lows, similar to the rhythmic rocking of the waves and the sea's inexplicable ebbs and flows.

But this is no longer our concern.

If, however, at the conclusion of this story someone wanted to ask me, wanting to dispel any last doubts regarding truth and nothing but the truth, if I were seized by the arm and shaken impatiently and shouted at: "Tell me, I beg you, if in keeping with your innermost conviction this story and its contents are completely true. Kindly forgive me if I press too much." I would forgive them, and I'd respond: "So help me God, I swear on my honor that the story I have told you, ladies and gentlemen, is in its contents and general terms true. I know this for a fact: it happened on our globe; I myself was on the deck of that ferry."

## NORTH POLE EXPEDITIONS

I'm reminded of something that Borges was once reminded of, something he had read somewhere: apparently, in the days when the Dutch were constructing their empire, ministers announced in Danish churches that those who took part in North Pole expeditions would be practically guaranteed salvation of their souls. When nevertheless there were few volunteers, the ministers acknowledged that the expedition was a long and arduous one, certainly not for everyone—only, in fact, for the very bravest. But still few came forward. So to avoid losing face, the ministers finally simplified their proclamation: actually, they said, any voyage could be considered an expedition to the North Pole, even a little trip, even just a ride in a public carriage.

I suppose these days even the subway would have to count.

## THE PSYCHOLOGY OF AN ISLAND

According to travel psychology, the island represents our earliest, most primal state prior to socialization, when the ego has already individualized enough to attain a certain level of self-awareness, but without yet having entered into complete, fulfilling relationships with its surroundings. The island state is a state of remaining within one's own boundaries, undisturbed by any external influence; it resembles a kind of narcissism or even autism. One satisfies all one's needs on one's own. Only the self seems real; the other is but a vague specter, a Flying Dutchman just darting over a distant horizon. In fact, one can't be altogether certain it was not a figment of one's imagination, an adornment by an eye accustomed to a straight line that splits the field of view cleanly into an up and a down.

## PURGING THE MAP

If something hurts me, I erase it from my mental map. Places where I stumbled, fell, where I was struck down, cut to the quick, where things were painful—such places are simply not there any longer.

This means I've gotten rid of several big cities and one whole province. Maybe someday I'll eliminate a country. The maps don't mind—in fact, otherwise they miss those blank patches, the shape of their happy childhood.

Whenever I have had to visit one of these nonexistent places (I try not to bear grudges), I've become an eye that moves like a specter in a ghost town. If I could fully focus, I would be able to slip my hand right inside the tightest blocks of concrete and traverse the jam-packed streets, making my way through backed-up traffic un-fazed, incurring no damages, and making no fuss.

But I have not done that. I've played by the rules as established by the people who live there. And I've tried not to betray to them the phantom nature of these places where they're still stuck, poor things, all erased. I simply smile at them and nod at everything they say. I wouldn't want to confuse them with the knowledge that they don't exist.

## IN PURSUIT OF NIGHT

It's hard for me to get a good night's sleep when I stay in a place for just one night. Now the city was slowly cooling off, calming down. My hotel was one run by the airlines and included in the price of my ticket. I was supposed to wait in it until tomorrow.

On the bedside table there was a light blue pack of condoms. Right by the bed there was a Bible and the Teachings of the Buddha. Unfortunately, the plug for my electric kettle didn't fit into the socket—so I would have to do without tea. Although perhaps it was coffee I should be drinking at this hour? My body was in no state to interpret the numbers on the clock built into the radio on the bed-side table, although it would appear that numerals are interna-tional, despite being known as Arabic. Was the yellow glow out the window the onset of dawn, or was it a dusk that had already largely condensed into night? It was hard to determine whether this part of the world—over which the sun was about to appear or else had just vanished—was the East or the West. I concentrated on counting up the hours I'd spent on the plane, employing as an aid an image I'd once seen on the internet of a globe with a nocturnal bar that moves from east to west like a giant mouth that systematically devours the world.

The square in front of the hotel was deserted, just stray dogs skirmishing around its closed stalls. I finally decided it must be the middle of the night, and without tea or a bath I went to bed. Although on my time, on the time I was carting around on my mobile phone, it was early afternoon. So I could not naively count on drifting off to sleep.

What you do is get under the covers and turn on the TV—volume down, let it grumble, flicker, whine. You hold the remote out like a weapon, and you take shots at the very center of the screen. Each shot kills one channel, but then another follows directly on its heels. My game this time, though, was to pursue the night, to choose only those channels that were broadcast from places where it was currently dark. To picture the globe and the dark scar running down its gentle curvature, evidence of some past attack—disfigurement after an audacious operation to separate light and dark, those conjoined twins.

Night never ends. Its dominion always spans some section of the world. And you can keep up with it with your remote, look exclusively for stations that fall within the shadowy purview of that dark, concave hand that upholds the earth, and in this way you can continue westward country by country, hour by hour. You will encounter an interesting phenomenon if you do.

The first shot I fired at the smooth, mindless forehead of the television produced Channel 348, the Holy God Channel. Here I beheld a crucifixion scene—some movie from the sixties. The Virgin

Mary had perfectly plucked eyebrows. Mary Magdalene must have had a corset on underneath her peasant dress, which was a dingy blue—you could tell it was a black-and-white movie that had been inexpertly colored later on. Her massive breasts, cone-shaped, protruding absurdly; her tiny waist. As the unattractive soldiers cackled and divided the outer garments, the filmmakers interspersed images of every cataclysm imaginable, footage that appeared to have been ripped right out of nature programs and inserted here without alteration. Now there were clouds gathering at an accelerated rate, lightning bolts, sky, funnel pointing down at the ground, whirlwind, finger of God—which would next sketch a series of flourishes on the earth's surface. Now furious waves pounding a shore, some sailboats, some cheap-looking dummies blown to pieces by that riled water. Volcanoes erupting, a fiery ejaculation that might well have inseminated the sky—but it was a nonstarter; the lava slid inertly down the volcanoes' sides. Thus was ecstasy unignited, demoted to plain old nocturnal emission.

Enough. I took another shot. Channel 350, Blue Line TV. A woman masturbating, her fingertips disappearing between her slim thighs. The woman was talking to someone in Italian, speaking into a microphone that was clipped to her ear and reminiscent of a long thin tongue licking each of those Italian words right off her lips, every *sì*, *sì*, and *prego*.

Channel 354, Sex Satellite 1: this time it was two girls masturbating, both bored—they must have been finishing up their shift, unable to hide their tiredness. One of them ran the camera that recorded them with her own remote control, so in that sense they were entirely self-sufficient. Every so often a kind of grimace would surface on their faces, as though they suddenly remembered what they were doing—eyes closed, mouth half open—but it would evaporate again in a flash, and tiredness and distraction would set in in its place. No one was calling them, despite what I presumed were alluring words in Arabic at the bottom of the screen.

And suddenly Cyrillic—I'd taken another shot at the screen—Genesis in Cyrillic. The words that scrolled along the bottom of the screen were no doubt illustrious ones, illustrated in fact by images of mountains, of the sea, of clouds, plants, and animals. On 358 they were showing the best scenes by an apparent pornographic sensation whose name was Rocco. I paused here for a moment, noting a drop of sweat on his brow. As he executed his pelvic thrusts into anonymous buttocks, the porn star put one hand on his hip, and you might have mistaken him for someone concentrating on the practice of some samba move, or salsa move: one-two, one-two.

On 288, Oman TV, they were reading verses from the Koran. So I supposed, anyway. A lovely and utterly unintelligible pattern of Arabic script floated placidly across the screen. It made me want to reach out and catch them first, hold them awhile before trying to decipher their meaning. Tease out those intricate flourishes, pull them out into a simple, soothing line.

Another shot and there was a black minister and an audience eagerly rejoining hallelujahs.

Night, then, quieted the raucous and aggressive news and weather and film channels, setting to one side the daytime ruckus of the world, bringing in instead the relief of the simple coordinate system of sex and religion. The body and the divine. Physiology and theology.

## SANITARY PADS

Each of the wrappers from the pads I'd picked up at the pharmacy
had entertaining little facts on them:

> The word "lethologica" describes the state of being unable
> to recall the word you're looking for.
> Ropography is a painting term for the attention the artist
> pays to trifles and details.
> Rhyparography is the painting of decaying and disgusting
> things.
> Scissors were invented by Leonardo da Vinci.

In the bathroom, where I unwrapped the entire box of these pads
with their curious teachings, it hit me like a revelation that this was yet
another part of the project of the great encyclopedia now coming into
being, the encyclopedia that would encompass all things. So I went
back to the pharmacy and scoured the shelves in search of the name of
this strange company that had determined to unite necessity with usefulness. For what sense could it ever possibly make to wrap pads in
paper that had flowers and strawberries on it? Paper was created to be
the bearer of ideas. Paper packaging is wasteful and should be banned.
But if you really do have to package something, then you ought to be
able to do it only in novels and poems, and always in such a way that
what is contained and what contains it have some connection.

> Starting at the age of thirty, humans begin to slowly shrink.
> Each year more people are killed by kicks from donkeys than
> by plane crashes.

If you wind up at the bottom of a well, you'll be able to see
   the stars even during the day.
Did you know that your birthday is shared by nine million
   people around the world?
The shortest war in history was waged between Zanzibar
   and England in 1896, lasting thirty-eight minutes.
If the earth's axis were tilted just one degree more, the planet
   would be uninhabitable, because the regions around the
   equator would be too hot and the poles too cold.
Due to the earth's rotation, throwing something westward
   will send it flying farther than if it's going east.
The average human body contains enough sulfur to kill
   a dog.
Arachibutyrophobia is the fear of getting peanut butter stuck
   to your palate.

But the one I was most struck by was this:
The strongest muscle in the human body is the tongue.

## RELICS: PEREGRINATIO AD LOCA SANCTA

In Prague in the year 1677 you could go to Saint Vitus Cathedral to
see: the breasts of Saint Anne, totally intact, kept in a glass jar; the
head of Saint Stephen the Martyr; the head of John the Baptist. The
nuns of Saint Teresa would show interested visitors a sister deceased
some three hundred years earlier, sitting behind bars, very well preserved. The Jesuits, meanwhile, had the head of Saint Ursula and
the hat and finger of Saint Francis Xavier.

. . .

A hundred years earlier a Pole had wound up in La Valletta on Malta, whence he wrote that a local priest took him around the city and showed him: "*palmam dextram integram* (the whole right hand) of Saint John the Baptist, perfectly fresh, as though he'd just cut it off the body, and having opened its crystal case, he gave it to my unworthy lips to kiss, the which being the greatest glory this sinner has ever known, blessed be the Lord. He also permitted me to kiss a snippet of that saint's nose, the whole leg of Saint Lazarus Quadriduanus, the fingers of Saint Magdalene, a portion of the head of Saint Ursula (this striking me as strange, for in Cologne, on the Rhine, I also saw the whole head, and touched my unworthy lips to it)."

## BELLY DANCE

After the food the waiter hurriedly brought me a coffee, then retreated into the back of the room, behind the counter; he would watch, as well.

We lowered our voices because we were forced to do so, because the lights went out softly, and in between the tables came the young woman I had seen a few minutes earlier smoking a cigarette outside. Now she stood among the seated people and shook her loose black hair. Her eyes were heavily painted; her fitted top, embroidered with sequins around her breasts, shimmering brightly, all the colors at once, would have pleased any child, any girl. The bracelets on her arms clanged and clattered. Her long skirt flowed down from her hips to her bare feet. A very pretty girl, her teeth shone an impossible white, her eyes casting intrepid glances under which it was impossible to sit still: you wanted to move, stand up, smoke. The woman was dancing to the rhythm of the drums as her hips showed off, challenging to a duel anyone who might so much as dream of underestimating their power.

Finally a guy responded to this call and boldly ventured up to dance; he was a tourist, wearing shorts, not particularly suited to her sequins, but he was trying, shaking his hips excitedly, while his friends at his table stomped and whistled. And now two young girls set forth to dance; in jeans, thin as rails.

This dance in our cheap pub was holy. That was how we felt about it—I and my companion, another woman.

When the lights came back on we discovered our eyes were filled with tears, and that we were rushing to wipe our eyes with napkins, embarrassed. Men—worked up into a kind of frenzy—made fun of us. But I was certain that our being moved by this dance was a quicker route to grasping it than the men's excitement.

## MERIDIANS

A woman named Ingibjörg was traveling along the prime meridian. She was from Iceland, and she began her journey in the Shetland Islands. She complained that it was, of course, impossible to travel in a straight line, since she was totally dependent upon roads and ship routes and train tracks. But she was trying to stick to her guns, continuing south, maneuvering along the line as best she could, in a zigzag.

She talked about it so vividly and so enthusiastically that I didn't have the courage to ask her why she was doing it. Although the answer to that kind of question is more or less always: Why not?

As she spoke, I saw in my mind's eye the image of a drop sliding down the surface of a globe.

And yet I find the idea unsettling to this very day. Meridians don't exist, after all. Not really.

## UNUS MUNDUS

I have a poet friend who, unfortunately, was never able to live off her poetry. Is there anyone who lives off poetry? So she started working at this travel agency, and since she spoke excellent English, she ended up becoming a tour guide for American groups. She was great at it, and she kept getting recommended for even the most exacting guests. She would pick them up in Madrid, fly with them to Málaga, and then they'd sail to Tunis. Normally it was a small group, around ten people.

She enjoyed these assignments, and she had on average two per month. She liked to relax then in the finest hotels, taking the opportunity to sleep in. Because she was responsible for leading her groups around the various landmarks, she read a lot in those days in preparation. On the sly she also wrote. When some especially interesting idea came to mind—a phrase, an association—she knew she had to write it down right away, because if not, it would be gone forever. Memory falters with age, gets spottier. So she'd get up and go to the bathroom and write it down, sitting on the toilet. Sometimes she would write on her hands, just letters, mnemotechnics.

She was not a specialist in Arab countries and their cultures— she had studied literature and linguistics—but she consoled herself with the fact that her tourists weren't, either.

"Let's not kid ourselves," she'd say. "It's just one world."

. . .

You didn't need to be a specialist; you just had to have an imagination. Sometimes when there would be some interruption in their travel, when they'd have to sit for hours in strange shadow, in the middle of nowhere, because a cable in their Jeep just snapped, she would have to entertain her clients somehow. That was when she started telling stories. They expected her to. She took some from Borges and embellished them a little, dramatized them. Others came from the *Thousand and One Nights*, although even then she always added a little something of her own. She said you had to find stories that hadn't been made into films yet, and it turned out in fact there were quite a few of them. To everything she lent some Arab color, holding forth on details of dress, cuisine, camel varietals. They must not have listened to her too attentively, because on the occasions when she would mix up some historical fact, no one ever pointed it out to her, until in the end she simply stopped bothering about the facts.

## HAREM (MENCHU'S TALE)

Words won't do justice to the harem's labyrinth. So picture perhaps the cells of a honeycomb, the curved arrangement of intestines, the insides of a body, the canals of an ear; spirals, dead ends, appendixes, soft rounded tunnels that finish just here, at the entrance to a secret chamber.

The center is hidden deep, as in an ant's nest, these are the sultan's mother's chambers, lined with a uterine matrix of carpets, censed with myrrh, cooled by water that makes the parapets into streaming

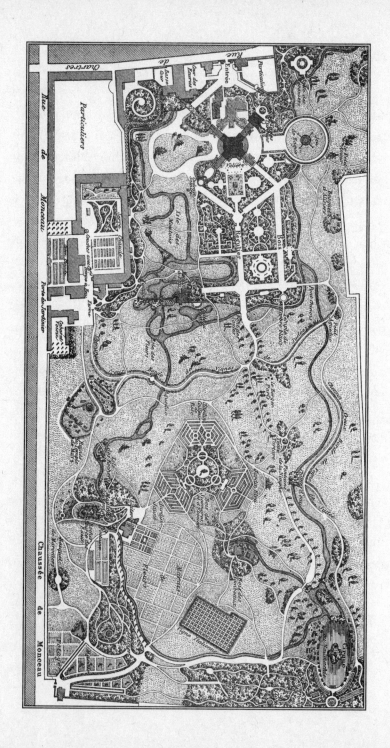

riverbeds. Around this extend the rooms of sons not yet of age; they, too, are women, after a fashion, enveloped in the feminine element until initiation cleaves by sword their pearly amniotic sac. Past these internal courtyards a complex hierarchy of cells for concubines opens up: the least desirable women are transferred upward, as though their bodies, forgotten by men, were undergoing a mysterious process of angelification; the eldest live right beneath the roof—soon their souls will float away, off into the heavens, while their bodies, once so alluring, will dry out in imitation of ginger root.

Among these myriad corridors, atria, secret alcoves, cloisters, and courtyards the young ruler himself has his bedrooms, each paired with a royal lavatory, where in stately luxury he indulges in tranquil royal defecation.

Every morning he's released from the clutches of the mothers into the world, like an oversized child learning to walk a tad too late. Clad in his ceremonial caftan, he plays his role—then in the evening returns with relief to the body, to his own intestines, to the soft vaginas of his concubines.

He returns from the chambers of the elders, where he governs his desert country—receiving delegations and administering the politics of a collapsing little local kingdom, politics in vain. For the news is frightful. The bloody clashes of the three great powers leave no doubts: they have to place a bet on a color, like in roulette, come down on one of the sides. What is unclear is how to make this decision— based on where he was educated? An affinity for the culture? The sound of the language? This uncertainty's fueled further by his guests, whom he receives each morning. They are businessmen, merchants, consuls, whispering advisers. They arrange themselves before him on ornate pillows, wiping the sweat off their foreheads, which, perpetually covered with pith helmets, remain a surprising white, reminiscent of the shade of rhizomes underground—stigma of these people with infernal origins.

Others are in turbans and torses, pawing at or chewing on their long beards, unaware of the fact that this gesture can be associated only with lies and deceptions. They all have matters to discuss with him, wish to commend to him their services as negotiators, try to talk him into the one right choice. This gives him headaches. The kingdom isn't large—all told a few dozen settlements in the oases of the rocky desert, of all the possible resources of nature it has only open-pit salt mines. It has no access to the sea, no ports, strategic capes or straits. The women who reside in this small country raise chickpeas, sesame, and saffron. Their husbands transport travelers and merchants in caravans across the desert to the south.

The young ruler has never been drawn to politics, doesn't understand in the least what others find so fascinating about it, how his great father could have dedicated his whole life to it. But then he bears not the slightest resemblance to his father, who over the course of decades of fighting with the nomads in the desert built up this modest kingdom. From among his many brothers he was selected as his father's successor solely because his mother was the eldest of the wives, an ambitious person. His mother assured him the power that for biological reasons she could not have for herself. The brother who would have been a serious rival to him met an unfortunate end, stung by a scorpion. His sisters don't count, he doesn't even really know them. When he looks at women, he always remembers that each could have been his sister, and, in some strange way, this fills him with peace.

On the council of elders, that grim group of bearded men, he has no friends. When he appears in the meeting room, they suddenly fall silent, which always makes him feel as though they are conspiring against him. No doubt they are. Then, after a series of ritual greetings, they discuss matters and cast glances at him that only barely hide their contempt and aversion, though they are supposed exclusively to seek approval. Sometimes it seems to him—unfortunately, more and more often—that these fleeting glances contain an enmity that's gotten rather tangible, sharp as a knife—that ultimately they don't care if he ends up saying "yes" or "no," they judge only whether or not he should even continue to occupy this place in the center of the room, this privileged position, and if this time he will manage to make any sound at all.

What do they expect of him? He is incapable of following their shouting over one another, so impassioned, the logic of their arguments. He focuses instead on the beautiful saffron turban worn by one of them, who happens to be the minister of fresh water resources, or on the exceptionally poor appearance of another; it's difficult not to notice the sickly pallor of his face framed by that gray and massive beard. He must be ill; he'll no doubt die soon.

"Die"—the word fills the young ruler with overwhelming disgust; it isn't good he's thought of it, already he can feel saliva flood his mouth, his throat contracting—perverse inversion of orgasm. And he knows he must get out.

This is why he knows already what he's going to do, though he keeps it all a secret from his mother.

She comes to him late that evening, nonetheless, although even she must first announce herself to his two trusted guards, eunuchs, black as ebony: Gog and Magog. She visits her son as he's enjoying

his time in the arms of his little friends. She sits at his feet on a beautifully woven pillow, her bracelets clanking. Every time she moves,
she sets off waves of the spicy fragrance of the oils in which she
coats her aged body. She says she knows about everything, and that
she'll help him to set out, just so long as he promises to take her
with him. Does he realize that by leaving her here he would be condemning her to death?

"We have devoted kin in the desert who will certainly receive us.
I already sent a man to them with our news. We will wait out the
worst time there, and then in disguise, taking what is ours, jewels
and gold, we shall set out for the West, for the ports, and escape
from there and not return. We shall settle in Europe, but not too
far, so that in good weather we'll be able to glimpse Africa's shores.
I will still care for your children, son," she says, and it is clear she
does believe in this flight of theirs, but it is just as clear that in those
grandchildren she can no longer—certainly not.

What can he say? He pets their silken heads, consents.

But in the hive there are no secrets, word spreads hexagonally, cell
by cell, through the fireplaces, the restrooms, corridors, and courtyards. It spreads with the hot air off cast-iron pans that burn char-
coal so as to make the winter chills more bearable. At times the air
that comes in from the hinterland is so cold that a thin layer of ice
covers the urine in the majolica chamber pots. The news spreads
across the concubines' floors and all of them, even those grown
most angelic, on the uppermost floors, pack up their few possessions. They whisper among themselves, already arguing over spots
in the caravan.

Over the next few days the palace visibly revives; it's been ages since it saw so much commotion. Which is why our ruler is surprised everything seems to go unnoticed by the Scarlet Turban or the Miserable Beard.

He thinks they're dumber than he even realized.

Meanwhile they are thinking the exact same thing—that their ruler has turned out to be more stupid than they'd ever even noticed. They'll feel less sorry for him because of it. For already from the West a great army is arriving, by ship and over land—they whisper among themselves. It is said they come in hordes. It is said they have declared a holy war upon the world. That they intend to conquer us, the young ruler's advisers whisper. They care most about Jerusalem, where the remains of their prophet lie. There is nothing that can be done about them—they are insatiable and capable of anything. They will plunder our homes, rape our women, set our houses on fire, desecrate our mosques. They will violate all treaties and agreements, they are greedy and erratic. It is clear—there is no question of a tomb here, we would give them all our tombs, just let them take them, we have plenty here. If what interests them are cemeteries, let them take them. But it has become very apparent this is just a pretext; they want to take the living, not the dead. Just as soon as their ships have moored on our continent, they'll raise their cry of battle in their hoarse and obstreperous language—they cannot speak a proper language, nor read a proper alphabet—and, bleached by the sun from their long journey, faded by the sea salt that covers their skin in the finest layer of silver, they will overrun our cities, unhinging the doors of our houses, shattering pitchers of oil, plundering our larders, and even reaching—heaven help us—the *shalwar* of our women. They are unable to answer any greeting we can offer, they gaze at us dully, and their light-colored irises appear rinsed out, thoughtless. Someone's said they are a tribe born at the bottom of the sea, reared by waves and silver fish, and indeed its members do look like bits of wood spit out upon the shore, their skin is the color of bones the sea has played with for too long. But others insist it isn't true—how, then, could their ruler, the man with the red beard, have drowned in the depths of the river Self?

So they whisper, in earnest, then get to grumbling. This ruler of ours has failed us. His father, of course, he was good, he would have immediately prepared a thousand horsemen for the battle, fortified the enclave, provisioned us with water and grain in case of siege. But this . . . Someone spits after pronouncing his name, then falls silent, afraid of what might come out of his own mouth.

There is a long silence. One man rubs his beard, another stares into the complex pattern on the floor, where bits of colorful pottery compose a labyrinth. Still another rubs the scabbard of his knife, elaborately encrusted with turquoise. His finger strokes the little bulges, back and forth. Today nothing will be determined by these brave advisers and ministers. Already outside the guards are posted. The palace army.

That night in the quiet of their minds ideas germinate, grow like plants, mature in the blink of an eye—soon they will flower and bear fruit. In the morning a messenger sets out on horseback with a humble plea to the sultan to recall this small kingdom no one ever remembers; the council of the elders has risen up, for the good of the righteous, those devoted to Allah, to rid themselves of their current inept ruler—the image of the plunging sword has crystallized— and requests armed support against the heathens on their way from the West, numerous as the grains of sand in the desert.

And that same night the ruler's mother digs him out from under leathers and carpets, from among the bodies of the children he sleeps in bed with; she shakes him out of his slumber and tells him to get dressed.

"Everything is ready, the camels are waiting, two of your steeds have been saddled, and to their saddles rolled-up tents are bound."

Her son moans, groans—how will he get by in the desert without bowls and plates, without coal stoves, without carpets to lie down on with the little ones? Without his toilet, without the view from the window onto the square and the fountains with their crystal-clear water.

"You will be killed," whispers his mother, and a vertical wrinkle slices like a dagger down her forehead. Her whisper is reptilian—the hiss of a sage snake at the well.

"Get up!"

From behind a few of the walls now you can hear tripping steps, his wives having already packed their possessions—the younger ones more, the older ones less, not to give any reason for displeasure. Just modest bundles, only valuable scarves, necklaces, bracelets. Now they squat at the door, outside the curtain, waiting to be sent for, and since it's taking too long, they look with impatience out the window, where to the east over the desert a pink moon is already rising. They do not see the enormity of the desert, which licks with rough tongue the stairs to the palace, since their windows look only onto the inner courtyard. "The branch on which your ancestors pitched their tent was the axis of the world. Its center. Wherever you pitch your tent will become your kingdom," says his mother, pushing him toward the exit. She would never have dared to touch him in such a way before, but now with this gesture she indicates to him that in just these past few hours he has ceased to be the ruler of this saffron state.

"Which wives will you take with you?" she asks, and for a long time he does not give a reply, just pulling the children in—boys and girls, angel cubs, their naked skinny bodies covered by the night; the oldest boy can't be more than ten years old, the youngest girl, four.

Wives? There will be no wives, not the older ones, nor the younger ones; they were fine for the palace. He never particularly needed them, he slept with them for the same reason he forced himself to look upon the bearded mugs of his advisers every morning. Penetrating their ample haunches, their fleshy nooks, never brought him too much pleasure. He was disgusted by their hairy armpits and the bulge of their breasts. Which is why he always took care not to spill even a single drop of his precious seed into those miserable receptacles, so that not a single drop of life would be wasted.

He was, however, certain that by withholding all his fluids, and thanks to the little bodies of the children he drew strength from as he slept, thanks to their sweet breaths on his face, he would someday be immortal.

"We will take the children, my little ones, these dozen angels, let's get them dressed. You help them," he says to his mother.

"You fool," she snarls, "you want to take the children? We won't last even a day with them in the desert. Can't you hear the rustles and whispers approaching? We don't have a moment to lose. You will take other children in the place where we end up, more of them. Leave these, they will be fine."

But seeing his determination, she lets out a furious sob and stands in the doorway with her arms outstretched. Her son goes over to her; now they evaluate each other with their eyes. The children have them surrounded in a semicircle, some holding on to the bottom of his kaftan. Their gaze is calm, indifferent.

"It's them or me," his mother blurts, and when these words emerge from between her lips, when she sees them from the outside, she tries to snatch them back, with her tongue, but it's too late. She cannot catch them.

In one fell swoop her son has struck a fist into her stomach, in the place that years before was his first home, that soft chamber, lined with red and crimson. In his fist he holds a knife. The woman lurches forward, and from the wrinkle in her forehead darkness pours across her face.

There's no time to lose. Gog and Magog load the children onto the camels, the smaller ones in baskets, like birds. They attach the valuables, precious materials rolled up in coarse linen, to disguise them, and as the tiniest sliver of the sun first grazes the horizon, they are on the road. At first the desert lavishes them with lengthy shadows slipping from dune to dune, leaving a trail visible only to the initiated eye. In time this shade will be reduced until finally it disappears completely, when the caravan is able to attain the immortality it seeks.

## ANOTHER OF MENCHU'S TALES

A certain nomadic tribe lived for years in the desert between Christian and Muslim settlements, so they learned a lot. In times of famine, drought, or threat they were obliged to seek refuge among their settled neighbors. First they would send a messenger who would observe the customs of the settlement from behind the brushwood and, based on the sounds, smells, and costumes, determine whether the village was Muslim or Christian. The messenger would return with this information to his tribe, and then they would take out of their panniers the requisite props and head out into the oases, posing as fellow believers. They were never refused help.

Menchu swore that she was telling me the truth.

## CLEOPATRAS

I rode a bus along with about a dozen fully veiled women. Through the slits in their garments you could see only their eyes—and I was astounded by the care and beauty of their makeup. They were the eyes of Cleopatras. The women gracefully drank bottled water with the aid of straws; the straws would disappear into the folds of the black material and find, somewhere within it, the women's hypothetical lips. They'd just put on a movie up front, intended to improve our commute—on the screen was Lara Croft. Now all of us women looked on in fascination as that lithe girl with the gleaming arms and thighs felled soldiers who were all armed to the teeth.

## A VERY LONG QUARTER OF AN HOUR

On the plane between 8:45 and 9:00 a.m. To my mind, it took an hour, or even longer.

## APULEIUS THE DONKEY

A donkey breeder confided his story to me.

The deal with donkeys is that they are a rather costly investment, returns are slow, and it takes a lot of work. Outside high season, when there are no tourists, you have to be able to finance their food and take care of their coats—they have to be kept neat. This dark brown one is a male, the father of a whole family. His name is Apuleius—that's what one tourist lady called him. That one over there is called Jean-Jacques, although it's a female, and that lightest one is Jean-Paul. I have a few more on the other side of the house. Now, in the off-season, only two are working. But when the morning traffic starts I bring them out here, before the tour buses arrive.

The worst are the Americans—most of them are overweight. Oftentimes they're too heavy even for Apuleius. They weigh twice as much as other people. The donkey is an intelligent animal, it can evaluate weight right away, and it will often start to get upset just seeing them come off their tour bus, all overheated, big sweat stains on their shirts, and those trousers they wear that only reach their knees. I get the sense the donkeys can tell them apart by their smell. So they've got problems with them even when their dimensions turn out to be all right. The donkey will start kicking and making a fuss, blatantly trying to get out of working.

But my donkeys are good, I brought them up myself. It's important to us that our clients leave here with fond memories. I'm not a Christian myself, but I understand that for them this is the pinnacle of their excursion. They come here to get on my donkeys to tour the place where a gentleman named John baptized their prophet with water from the river. How do they know it was this spot here? Apparently it's written down that way in their holy book.

## MEDIA PRESENTERS

There was an attack this morning. One person was killed and several wounded. The body has since been removed. The police surrounded the place with red-and-white plastic tape past which you could see enormous bloodstains on the ground; flies circled above them. A motorcycle lay on the ground, and near it a pool of gasoline turning opalescent; beside it a plastic bag of fruit, tangerines tossed out, dirty, grimy; farther on, some rags, a sandal, a baseball cap of indeterminate color, part of a mobile phone—where the screen had been now gaped a hole.

People clustered over the tape and looked on in horror. They spoke infrequently, in half whispers.

The police waited on giving site clearance because a journalist from one of the important stations was supposed to come and do a story. Supposedly he particularly wanted to get those bloodstains on camera. Supposedly he was already on his way.

## ATATÜRK'S REFORMS

One day, in the evening, when I was already lying in bed after a whole day of walking around, looking and listening, I remembered Aleksandra and her reports. I suddenly began to miss her. I imagined that she might be in the same city, that she was sleeping with her bag beside her bed, in the silver halo of her hair. The Fair Apostle, Aleksandra the Just. I found her address in my backpack and wrote her an Infamy that I had learned of here.

When Atatürk was carrying out his intrepid reforms, in the 1920s, Istanbul was a city filled with half-wild stray dogs. A specific breed of them even developed—a midsized dog, with short hair, a light-colored coat, white or cream-colored or a patchy blend of those two colors. The dogs lived around the docks, between the cafés and restaurants, on the streets and squares. By night they went hunting in the city; they scrabbled, they dug through the trash. Unwanted, they returned to their old natural behaviors—they grouped together in packs, electing leaders like wolves and jackals.

But it was very important to Atatürk that Turkey be made a civilized country. Over the course of a couple of days, special forces caught thousands of the dogs, which were transported to nearby islands that were uninhabited, without flora. They were set free. Denied fresh water and any kind of food, they fed on one another for three or four weeks while the residents of Istanbul, especially owners of homes with balconies overlooking the Bosphorus, or people going to the fish restaurants along the waterfront, heard the howling from out there, and were then tormented by the waves of the disgusting stench.

During the night more and more proofs of human wrongdoing came to my mind, until I was drenched in sweat. For example, that puppy that froze to death because it had been given an overturned tin bathtub for a kennel.

## KALI YUGA

"The world is getting darker and darker," the two men sitting next to me agreed. As far as I had understood, they were flying to Montreal for a conference that would be attended by oceanographers and geophysicists. Apparently since the sixties incident solar radiation has fallen by 4 percent. The average rate of light on the planet going out is around 1.4 percent per decade. The phenomenon is not pronounced enough for us to be able to detect it ourselves, but it has been noted by radiometers. Radiometers have shown, for example, that the amount of incident radiation reaching the USSR from 1960 to 1987 actually decreased by one-fifth.

What is the reason for the darkening? It isn't known exactly. It is supposed that it has to do with air pollution, soot, and aerosols.

I fell asleep and saw a frightening vision: an enormous cloud appearing from beyond the horizon—evidence of a great, eternal war taking place in the distance, ruthless and cruel; destroying the world. But it's okay, we are on—for now—a fortunate island: azure sea and clear blue sky. Beneath our feet warm sand and the protruding cubes of shells.

But this is the island of Bikini. Everything will die soon, be burned, be lost, in the best-case scenario undergo a monstrous mutation. Those who survive will give birth to child monsters, twins conjoined at the head, one brain in a double body, two hearts in one rib cage. Additional senses will appear: the feeling of lack, the taste of absence, the ability for particular precognition. Knowing what won't happen. Being able to smell what doesn't exist.

The dark red glow grows, the sky turns brown, it gets darker and darker.

## WAX MODEL COLLECTIONS

Each of my pilgrimages aims at some other pilgrim. This time in wax.

Vienna, the Josephinum: a collection of anatomical wax figures, recently renovated. On this rainy summer day another traveler besides me had wound up here—a middle-aged man, wearing wire-rimmed glasses, his hair completely gray—but he was interested in only one model, to which he dedicated a quarter of an hour, then disappeared, a mysterious smile on his lips.

I myself was planning to stay longer. I'd equipped myself with a notebook and a camera—I even had caffeinated sweets in my pockets, and a chocolate bar.

Slowly, so as not to miss out on any of the exhibition, I took tiny steps among the glass cabinets.

Model 59. A six-and-a-half-foot-tall man. Skinned. His body pleasingly woven out of muscles and tendons. Openwork. The first glance brings a shock, no doubt a reflex—the sight of a body missing its skin is in itself painful, it stings, burns, as in childhood when live flesh came peeking out from behind a skinned knee. The model has one arm back, while the right, raised over his head in the graceful motion of an antique sculpture, shields his eyes—as though he were looking into the sun in the distance. We know this gesture from paintings—this is how one looks into the future. Model 59 could also be displayed at the nearby Museum of Art; in fact, I don't know why it's been sentenced to live out its days in a humiliating Anatomy Museum. It really should appear in the finest art gallery, because it's doubly a work of art—because of its brilliant execution in wax (this is evidently naturalism's greatest achievement), but also because of the design of the body itself. Who is its creator?

Model 60 also presents muscles and tendons, but our attention is drawn above all to the gentle ribbon of the intestines, given perfect proportions here. Their smooth surface reflects the museum's windows. Only after a moment, stunned, do I realize this is a woman—decked in a strange pendant, a piece of gray fur glued onto the base of the abdomen, containing a somewhat crudely marked oblong slit. Evidently the model's creator wanted to make absolutely certain that the viewer, presumably inexpert in anatomy, understood that he or she was seeing feminine intestines. Here we have the hirsute stamp, the gender trademark, the female logo. Model 60 presents the circulatory and lymphatic systems as an intestinal halo. Most of the blood vessels rest on the muscles, but some of them are shown as a kind of aerial grid; only here can you see the fractal wonder of those red threads.

Next there are arms, legs, stomachs, and hearts. Each of the models is laid out carefully on a piece of silk that glimmers in a pearlescent manner. The kidneys grow out of the bladder like two anemones. "Lower limb and blood vessels," an inscription announces in three languages. The grid of abdominal lymph vessels, lymph nodes, the pins and stars with which an unknown hand has ornamented the monotony of muscles. Lymphatic vessels could be jewelers' models.

In the center of this wax collection rests model 244, the most beautiful of all, the one that so interested the man in the wire-rimmed glasses and that is about to capture my attention, too, for half an hour.

It is a woman lying down, nearly intact; only in one place has her body been interfered with: her opened stomach shows to pilgrims like ourselves the reproductive system, pressed up against the diaphragm, the uterus under its ovarian cap. Here, too, that fur seal of gender, utterly superfluous. There can certainly be no doubt this one is a woman. The pubis meticulously covered with fake hair, and below, done with great care, the opening of the vagina, difficult to spot, only for the persistent who don't hesitate to crouch down next to the small feet with their reddened toes, as that man in glasses did. And I think: It's a good thing he's gone, now it's my turn.

The woman has light-colored hair, worn loose, slightly shut eyes, and half-parted lips—you can just see the tips of her teeth. On her neck a string of pearls. I am struck by the absolute innocence of her lungs, smooth and silky just beneath the pearls; they obviously never drew smoke from a cigarette. They could be the lungs of an angel. The heart, cut transversely, reveals its dual nature, both chambers lined with the velour of red tissue intended for unvaried motion. The liver wraps around the stomach like a big bloody mouth. Also visible are her kidneys and ureters, which look like a mandrake root resting atop her uterus. The uterus is a muscle very pleasing to the eye—slim and shapely; it's hard to imagine it traveling around the body and provoking hysteria, as was once believed. There can be no doubt—the organs are packed painstakingly inside the body, preparations for a major journey. So, too, her vagina, cut lengthwise, reveals its secret, the short tunnel that is actually a dead end and appears utterly useless, since it's not really an entrance into her insides. It ends in a blind chamber.

Exhausted, I sat down by the window on the hard bench, facing the silent crowd of wax models, and let myself feel overwhelmed. What was the muscle that was squeezing my throat so tight? What was its name? Who thought up the human body, and consequently, who holds its eternal copyright?

## DR. BLAU'S TRAVELS (I)

Gray beard and salt-and-pepper hair, he travels to a conference on the preservation of medical specimens, focusing on plastinating human tissues. He sits back in his chair, puts his headphones on, and listens to a Bach cantata.

The girl in the pictures he's developed and is now taking with him has an amusing way of wearing her hair—cut straight across the back, but the strands in the front are longer. Reaching her naked shoulders, they flit flirtatiously over her face so that all you can see underneath them is the distinct, red-brown line of her lips, painted onto the smooth surface of her face. Blau liked that, that mouth, just as he liked her body—petite, taut, breasts compact, nipples punctuating the velvety plane of her chest. Hips slender, though her thighs were quite substantial. Blau has always been attracted to powerful legs. "Strength in the thighs" could be Blau's personal hexagram 65. A woman with powerful thighs is like a nutcracker: To venture between them is to risk being shattered. To venture between them is to disarm a bomb.

This excites him. He is skinny, small. Thus he risks his life.

He was in the grips of excitement as he took these photographs of her. He was naked, too, so that slowly his excitement made itself known, unmistakable, even. But with his face concealed behind the camera, he didn't mind; he was a mechanical minotaur with a photographic face, the single eye of the lens atop a stalk zooming in and out, advancing and retreating like a mechanical trunk.

The girl noticed his state, which lent her confidence. She raised her arms, clasped her hands together at the nape of her neck, so exposing her defenseless armpits, the blind, underdeveloped possibilities of her crotch. Raised, her breasts became almost flat, almost boyish. Blau came closer, on his knees, the camera at his face, and began to photograph her from below. He was trembling. He considered that the tuft of black hair, shaved down to a thin line, which slimmed her hips still further to the eye and allured like an exclamation mark, might be about to scratch his lens. By now his erection was significant. The girl had had a little white wine—a Greek retsina, he thought—and she sat down on the floor now, crossing her legs and hiding the place the doctor was so moved by. He could guess what her position meant: they were edging toward the evening's end.

But that wasn't really what he was after. He retreated to the window, his bare thin buttock touching for a moment the cold sill. He was still taking pictures. Another act, this time a seated one, had now been captured. The lamb-like girl was smiling, proud of the readiness of Dr. Blau's body—for this meant she could work her magic from afar. What power! A few years ago, as a child, she'd played at magic, imagined she could move objects with just her will. Sometimes it seemed to her that some teaspoon or clip really did move a millimeter. But never had any object given in to her will so evidently, so theatrically.

Meanwhile Blau was now faced with the real task at hand. There was no use at this stage in putting off the inevitable. Their bodies drifted together. The girl allowed him to caress her and lay her on her back. With gentle fingers the doctor disarmed the bomb. The hexagram of her thighs opened to all interpretation. The camera snapped.

.   .   .

Blau has a whole collection of these photos, dozens, maybe hundreds by now—women's bodies against blank walls. The walls differ, because the places aren't the same: hotels, pensions, his office at the Academy, occasionally his own apartment. The bodies are fundamentally similar, no mystery there.

But not the vulvas. Those are like fingerprints, in fact they could use those embarrassing organs, which the police have yet to appreciate, for identification—they are absolutely unique. Beautiful as orchids that draw in insects with their shape and color. What a strange thought—that this botanical mechanism has been preserved somehow even into the era of humankind's development. It would be understating it to say it's been effective. It almost seems to him that nature itself so delighted in this petal-based idea that it became determined to take it further, heedless of the fact that man would wind up with a psyche that would slip out of control and conceal what had been so beautifully developed. Hide it in underwear, in insinuations, in silence.

He keeps the pictures of vulvas in cardboard boxes with patterns, boxes purchased at IKEA, changing only their design over the years, depending on the current fashion—starting with the garish, kitschy eighties, through the spare grays and blacks of the nineties, up until today—vintage, pop art, ethno. He doesn't even have to write the dates on them, then—he recognizes them instantly. And yet, the doctor's dream is to create a real collection, not made up of pictures.

Every body part deserves to be remembered. Every human body deserves to last. It is an outrage that it's so fragile, so delicate. It is an outrage that it's permitted to disintegrate underground, or given to the mercy of flames, burned like trash. If it were up to Blau, he would make the world differently: the soul could be mortal—what do we need it for, anyway—but the body would be immortal. We will never learn how diverse the human species is, how unique each individual, if we are so quick to condemn bodies to destruction, he thought. In the past, people understood this—but they lacked the means, the methods to preserve. Only the wealthiest could afford embalming. But today the science of plastination was developing very fast, perpetually perfecting its methods. Anyone who wanted to could save his body now, and share its beauty, its mystery, with others. Here is the wondrous system of my muscles, the sprinter would say, the 100-meter world champion. Look, everyone, at how this works. Here is my brain, the greatest chess player would cry. Ah, these unusual two grooves, let's call them "bishop twists." Here is my stomach, two children emerged from here into the world, the proud mother would say. So Blau imagined it. This was his vision of a just world in which we would not be so quick to destroy what is sacred. He therefore strives toward this vision with everything he does.

Why would anyone have any sort of problem with this notion? We Protestants certainly would not. But even Catholics ought not to raise any alarm about it: after all, we have old evidence, collections of relics, the patron saint of plastination might be Jesus Christ himself, when he shows us his red fleshy heart.

///////

The gentle hum of the engines lent to the choir of voices in Dr. Blau's headphones an unexpected depth. The plane was flying west, so the night didn't end where it ought to, dragging on lamely instead. From time to time he raised the shade to see if somewhere on the horizon in the distance a white glow wasn't visible by now, glimmer of a new day, new possibilities. But there was nothing. The screens were off, the film had ended. Every so often they would show a map, and on it the small shape of the plane as it traversed at a turtle's pace a distance not indicated on the map. And it even seemed that the map had been designed by Zeno the Cartographer—every distance is infinite in itself, each point launching a new space that cannot be surmounted, and of course, any movement an illusion, all of us traveling in place.

Unimaginable cold outside, unimaginable altitude, unimaginable phenomenon of launching a heavy machine into thin air. *"Wir danken dir, Gott,"* sang Dr. Blau's angels in his headphones.

He glanced at the hand of the woman sitting to his left and could barely contain himself from petting it. The woman slept with her head on a man's shoulder. To Blau's right a boy dozing, a slightly plump young man. His arm hung limply off his seat, almost touching the doctor's trousers. He also kept himself from petting those fingers.

He sat squeezed into his chair amidst two hundred people, in the oblong space of the plane, breathing the same air they were breathing. In fact, this was why he liked traveling so much—en route people are forced to be together, physically, close to one another, as though the aim of travel were another traveler.

But each of these beings, to whose presence he'd been sentenced for another—he looked at his watch—four hours, seemed monadic, smooth, and shiny; an orb to play pétanque with. Which is why the only kind of contact activated in Blau's instinctive algorithms was petting; grazing with the tip of his finger, its pad, feeling the cool, even curvature. But his hands at this point have lost all hope of discovering any rift in it, having checked thousands of times on women's bodies: there is no tab or hidden latch that would cautiously permit itself to be released by a nail, inviting him inside, no protrusion, no secret little lever, no button that, when pressed, lets out a burst of something, a small spring that would react and reveal to his eyes the desired complex insides. Or perhaps not complex, perhaps very simple, just the inverse of the surface, just curved inward, a spiral wrapped up in itself. The surface of these monads hides within it vast mysteries, not even remotely hinting at the dazzling richness of these marvelously and cunningly packed structures—not even the cleverest traveler would be able to compose his luggage in this way, distancing from one another the organs, for order, safety, and aesthetics, with peritoneal membranes, lining space with fat tissue, cushioning them. So went Blau's ardent ruminations through his unsound airplane half-sleep.

He was fine. Dr. Blau was happy. What more could he have asked for? Seeing the world from above, its beautiful, peaceful order. An order that was antiseptic. Contained in shells and caves, in grains of sand and in the scheduled flights of giant airplanes, in symmetry— the age-old fit of right to left and left to right—in the eloquent light of the information screens, and in all light. Dr. Blau tugged his blanket up over his slender body, a piece of fleece, property of the airline, and fell asleep for real.

///////////

Blau was a boy when his father—an engineer who, like others from socialist nations in the construction industry, spent years rebuilding

Dresden after the destruction of the war—took him to the Hygiene Museum. There little Blau saw the Glasmensch, a glass man created by Franz Tschakert, to educate. A six-foot-five golem without skin, made of perfect imitation glass organs, arranged around the transparent body, seemingly devoid of secrets. It was in its particular way a monument to nature, designer of this perfection. There was in it a lightness and a thoughtfulness, a spatial sensibility, a tastefulness, a beauty and a play of symmetry. The wondrous human machine with rational, streamlined shapes, often resolved with humor (the structure of the ear), periodically eccentric (the structure of the eye).

The glass man became little Blau's friend, at least in the boy's imagination. Sometimes he would visit him and sit in his room, crossing his legs and letting himself be looked at. Sometimes he would incline politely to enable the boy to grasp some detail, an understanding of how the glass muscle tenderly embraces the bone and where the nerve disappears to. He became his friend and silent glass companion. Many children play, in any case, with imaginary friends.

In his dreams he came to life—although he did so rarely, playing what might be called a minor role. Even as a young man, Blau never particularly cared for living things, perhaps only to a certain degree. And then they would talk in silence all evening, under the covers, when he was told to turn out the light in his room. What about? Blau can't remember anymore. By day he became the boy's guardian angel and accompanied him—unseen—in school scuffles; in the boy's imagination the glass man was always ready to pummel enemies on his behalf, and the class troublemaker on those group field trips to the botanical garden, boring and tiring, consisting largely of waiting for the group to be rounded up again.

The group, as a form of collective socializing, was also not a thing Blau ever cared for.

For Christmas he got from his father a small plastic miniature that couldn't possibly compare with the original, it was more like a statue of a divinity, a painful reminder of the existence of the real thing.

Little Blau had a very developed spatial imagination, which would help him later in anatomy. Thanks to his imagination, he assumed control over the Glasmensch's invisibility. He was able to highlight in his body what seemed worth paying attention to at any given moment, making vanish what seemed irrelevant for that time. Hence the glass figure was sometimes a man made of tendons and muscles, without skin, without a face; simply a weave of muscles, cords pulled completely taut, bulging from the effort. Without even knowing himself when it happened, little Blau learned all there was to know about anatomy. His strict-minded and demanding father looked on proudly, already seeing his son's future in very concrete terms—he would be a doctor, a scientist, a scholar. For his birthday the boy received beautifully colored anatomical plates, and the Easter Bunny brought him a life-sized human skeleton.

In his early years, at university and right afterward, Blau traveled often. He visited almost every available anatomical collection. Like a rock groupie, he followed von Hagens and his satanic exhibition around, until finally he met the master in person. His travels were circular, wending their way back to their point of departure, until it became clear that their aim was not far off, but rather here, on the inside of the body.

He studied medicine but rapidly got bored of it. He wasn't interested in diseases, much less so in curing them. Dead bodies don't get sick. He only really participated in his anatomy classes, where he volunteered for the exercises the frightened, simpering girls never wanted to do. He wrote a paper on the history of anatomy and married a classmate, whose specialization in pediatrics resulted in her spending most of her time at the hospital, which suited Blau just fine. When she got what she'd been angling for and gave birth to a daughter, Blau, now assistant professor at the Academy, started going off to conferences and on residencies, so she found herself a gynecologist and moved with the child into his big house with its clinic in the basement. In this way they managed to bring to fruition a certain complete segment of human procreation.

In the meantime, Blau wrote a terrific dissertation, titled "The Behavior of Pathological Samples Under Silicone Plastination: An Innovative Supplement to the Teaching of Pathological Anatomy." His students nicknamed him Formaldehyde. He researched the history of anatomical samples and the preservation of tissues. He visited dozens of museums in search of material for his work, finally settling down in Berlin, where he got a good job cataloging the collections of the Medizinhistorisches Museum, newly being created.

He arranged his personal life neatly, unproblematically. He felt decidedly better living alone; he quelled his sexual urges with his students, whom he would first feel out by inviting them for coffee. He knew it wasn't allowed, but he was operating on the sociobiological premise that the university was his natural hunting ground, and that these women were, in the end, adults who knew what they were doing. He looked good—he was handsome, clean-cut, clean-shaven (from time to time he let his beard grow out, keeping it neat, of course)—and they were curious as magpies. It didn't seem he was cut out for romance. He always used protection, and his needs were modest, since the vast majority of his drive underwent a kind of spontaneous sublimation. Thus with this realm of his life there was no problem, no dark side, no guilt.

At first he thought of his new job at the museum as a respite from the teaching he had done before. When he would walk into the courtyard of the Charité complex, among the manicured lawns, the fancifully trimmed trees, he would feel that he had found himself in a place that was in some sense outside time. He was in the very center of a huge city, but no noise, no rush, could reach in here. He would feel relaxed, and he would whistle.

He'd spend his free time mainly in the massive basement of the museum, which was connected underground to other buildings belonging to the hospital. Those passageways tended to be cluttered with shelves, old dusty display cabinets, armored cupboards that once held God knows what and that had wound up here, empty, who knew when. But some of the corridors were traversable, and after a while, after making copies of a few keys, he learned to move through them through the whole complex. This was how he traveled daily to the cafeteria.

His work consisted of dusting off jars of samples or exhibits otherwise preserved from the murky depths of the museum's stores, and in their expert identification. He was greatly aided in this task by old Mr. Kampa, who had long since reached retirement age, but whose contract got extended year after year because there was no one else who would have been able to navigate those massive stores.

They put shelf by shelf in order. Mr. Kampa would first carefully clean the tops of the jars, making sure not to damage their labels. They learned to decipher together the beautiful old sloping handwriting. Usually the label included the Latin name for the part of the body or the disease, as well as the initials, sex, and age of the original owner of the organs the sample was presenting. Sometimes an occupation was given. Thus they learned that this magnificent intestinal tumor had been in the belly of a seamstress, A.W., age fifty-four. Often, though, the information was imprecise, the labels largely worn away. In many cases, air entered through the chipped sealant applied to the lids of samples in alcohol, and the liquid clouded, and it enveloped the specimen inside in a dense fog—in those cases the specimens had to be destroyed. A committee made up of Blau, Kampa, and two of the people who worked upstairs in the museum would meet and establish this in writing. Then Mr. Kampa would take these pieces of human bodies, extracted from their jars, ruined, to the hospital crematorium.

Some of the specimens required special care (when their container had been damaged). Then Blau would take it to his little laboratory and there, with the utmost care, transfer it to a cleansing bath. Then, after careful examination, and after taking samples (which he would freeze), he would place it in a new container of the finest quality, in a modern solution that he prepared himself. And so although he could not provide the specimens with immortality, he was at least able to lend them a much longer life.

Of course it wasn't only specimens in jars here. There were also drawers full of undocumented pieces of bones, kidney stones, some fossils; there was a mummified armadillo and other animals, in very poor condition. A small collection of shrunken Maori heads, masks made out of human skin—two extremely disturbing examples of these had also wound up in the crematorium.

Blau and Kampa dug out a couple of real archaeological rarities here, too. They came upon, for example, four specimens from Ruysch's renowned collection from the late seventeenth and early eighteenth centuries, a collection that had been dispersed, its fate unknown. Unfortunately, one of them, *Acardius hemisomus*, which could have been the gem of any teratological collection, had to be sent to the crematorium because of a crack in its glass receptacle— there was no way of saving it. The committee, seeing the specimen in its state of considerably advanced decay, did consider briefly whether in such cases there ought not to be some type of funeral arranged.

Blau was overjoyed at this discovery because it enabled him to run a number of tests on the famous preservation concoction of Frederik Ruysch, the Dutch anatomist of the late seventeenth century. This solution was exceedingly effective for its time—it managed to maintain the natural color of the specimen, as well as keeping it from swelling, which was otherwise the bane of that era's fluid preservation. Blau found that in addition to brandy from Nantes and black pepper, it also contained ginger root extract. He wrote an article and joined in the old debate on the ingredients of "Ruysch's solution," that Stygian liquid intended to ensure immortality through immersion, at least for the body. From that time forward Kampa started calling their underground collections "pickles."

He and Kampa—who brought him the specimen one morning— discovered something remarkable, on which Blau then worked for several months, in order to precisely understand the makeup and the workings of the conserving liquid. Namely, an arm. Male, powerful (the circumference of the biceps was fifty-four centimeters), forty-seven centimeters long, cut clean with the clear aim of show-

ing the tattoo—multicolored, representing with great sensitivity
to proportions a whale emerging from the waves of the sea
(white crests captured with Baroque grace and precision), blowing a
fountain into the sky. The drawing was perfectly executed, especially the sky, which from the outside of the arm seemed intensely
blue—though the closer you got to the armpit, the darker it became. The play of hues had been perfectly preserved in the translu-
cent liquid.

The specimen had no label. The jar was reminiscent of those
made in the Netherlands in the seventeenth century, meaning it had
a cylindrical shape—they didn't know at that time how to make
cuboid forms from glass, in any case. The specimen, attached to the
slate cap by horsehair, appeared to float in the fluid. But the strangest thing was the fluid itself . . . It wasn't alcohol, although at first
glance Blau had thought this came from the beginning of the seventeenth century, and from the Netherlands. It was a mixture of water
and formaldehyde with a small amount of glycerin. Its composition
could be said to be very modern, quite similar to the Kaiserling III
mixture still used today. The container no longer had to be hermeti-
cally sealed, because the mixture didn't vaporize like alcohol. In the
wax that was used to seal the lid haphazardly in place he found
fingerprints, which moved him, deeply. He imagined that those tiny
little wavy lines, that natural stamp in the shape of a labyrinth, had
belonged to someone just like him.

He took care of that arm and its artwork with something that
might have been termed love. He wasn't going to find out now
whom it had belonged to, nor who had dispatched this arm with its
tattoo on its travels through time.

He and Kampa shared a moment of terror—which Blau recounted later to a female first-year student, observing with satisfaction how her eyes became wide with surprise as her pupils turned a dark matte, which according to sociobiologists was a sign of erotic interest.

In the wooden boxes in one of the corridors that led to a dead end, they found some stuffed mummies in very poor condition. The skin was completely blackened, dry, torn, seagrass spilling out through the seams, which had split apart in places. The bodies were shriveled, dried up, and to top it all off they were dressed in what must have once been considered lavish garments—now all the lace and the collars had taken on the same color as the dust. Their decorations, folds, and flounces had lost their distinguishing characteristics, become a ball of rotted material from which, here and there, some little button, made of pearl, stood out. From the stretched-out mouth, forced open by desiccation, grass emerged.

They found two mummies like this, small, that looked like children, but on close examination Blau realized they were—thank God—stuffed chimpanzees, very poorly preserved, completely unprofessionally; the sale and purchase of ones like these was quite widespread in the eighteenth and nineteenth centuries. Of course their suspicions could have been confirmed; human mummies had also been bought and sold, and quite ample collections created out of them. Collectors were especially interested in acquiring what was different and exceptional, people of other races, the spectacularly crippled, the diseased.

"Stuffing corpses is the simplest way of preserving them," mused Blau, guiding around the makeshift cellar collection two more female students who had enthusiastically accepted his invitation, much to Kampa's disapproval and dismay. Blau was counting on at least one of them letting him invite her out for wine, adding a new photograph to his collection. "In so doing," he continued now, "they only really leave the skin, which means this isn't, in the full sense of the word, a body. It's just a section of a body, the external form stretched out over a dummy made of hay. Mummification is quite a pathetic way of conserving a body. It only gives the illusion that we have the whole thing here before us. In reality, it is an obvious fraud. A circus trick, since only its shape and external covering have been preserved. And in fact the body has been destroyed, in other words, the ideological opposition to preservation. Barbarity."

Yes, they had breathed a sigh of relief that these were not human mummies. That would have brought them headaches, since the law clearly forbids keeping in state museums whole human corpses (if they are not ancient mummies, and even with that people start to object and cause trouble). If they had been people—children, as they thought in the beginning—they would have faced a complicated bureaucratic procedure and lots of issues. Many times he had heard about these uncomfortable discoveries when collections at medical academies or at universities were put in order.

Emperor Joseph II had created such a collection in Vienna. In his cabinet of curiosities he had decided to collect everything that was particular, every manifestation of the aberration of the world, every instance of matter forgetting itself. One of his successors, Francis I, had not hesitated to stuff his black-skinned courtier, one Angelo Soliman, after his death, at which point his mummy, wearing only a grass band, was displayed for the viewing pleasure of all the monarch's guests.

# JOSEFINE SOLIMAN'S FIRST LETTER TO
# FRANCIS I, EMPEROR OF AUSTRIA

It is with a profound sense of sorrow and of shame that I come to Your Majesty, though also in the hopes that there has somehow been some sort of terrible mistake. Angel Soliman, my father, that unflinchingly faithful servant to Your Majesty's uncle Emperor Joseph (that vastly magnanimous lord to us all), has since his death (may he rest in peace) become victim to a truly reprehensible iniquity that must now be put to rights.

Your Majesty knows well the story of my father's life, and I am also aware that Your Majesty knew my father personally, too, and esteemed him for his long-standing devotion and work, particularly as a faithful servant and chess master, and, like Your Majesty's uncle Emperor Joseph (may he rest in peace) and like many others, You once consistently treated him with distinction and respect. He had many wonderful friends who appreciated his qualities of mind and spirit, his great sense of humor and kindness of heart. He was in close contact for many years with Herr Mozart, from whom Your Majesty's uncle was so gracious as to commission an opera. He also joined the diplomatic ranks and was widely famed on account of his prudence, his foresight, and his wisdom.

I shall now permit myself a brief harkening back to my father's history, thereby to restore his person to Your Majesty's gracious memory. What makes us most human is the possession of a unique and irreproducible story, that we take place over time and leave behind our traces. And yet, even if we did absolutely nothing for others—not for our ruler nor for our state—we would still have the right to be buried with dignity, for burial is merely the act of returning to our Creator His creation, the human body.

My father was born around 1720 in northern Africa, though the early years of his life are shrouded in mystery. He often commented that he could not remember clearly the period of his earliest childhood. His memory reached just back to the time when as a young child he was sold into slavery. With horror he would tell us what he did remember: the long sea voyage in the dark hold of some ship or other, scenes taken straight out of Dante's inferno that had played out before the eyes of that small child following his separation from his mother and his other close blood relatives. His parents most likely ended up in the New World, while he was passed around as a sort of black pet, like a Maltese puppy or a Siamese cat. Why did he speak of it so rarely? Ought he not have done the opposite and spoken up about it all the time once he had obtained his position? I believe that his silence was brought about by a terrible conviction, a conviction he may himself have been unaware of: the faster painful events are erased from memory, the faster they will lose their power over us. They will cease to haunt us. The world will become better. As long as people don't find out how awful and abominable man can be to fellow man, their innocence will be left intact. What happened to my father's body after his death, however, is a testament to the wrongheadedness of that conviction.

After a seemingly endless series of trials, tribulations, and tragedies, my father was bought out of slavery on Corsica by the Prince of Liechtenstein's kindhearted wife and presented at court. This was how he wound up in Vienna, where Her Majesty the Princess developed a great affection for the child, and perhaps even, if I may, love. Thanks to her, he was raised and educated in a meticulous manner. That education seems to have replaced in his memory his distant exotic origins. As his only daughter, I never heard him speak about his roots. Never even did I see him seem nostalgic. His heart was always fully in the service of Your Majesty's uncle.

He became known, of course, as a distinguished politician, an intelligent envoy, and an endearing man. He was always surrounded by friends. He was loved and respected. He also enjoyed one special privilege: the friendship of Emperor Joseph, known as the Second—Your Majesty's uncle, who entrusted to my father on a number of occasions missions requiring tremendous intelligence.

In 1768 he married my mother, Magdalena Christiani, the widow of a Dutch general, with whom he lived in domestic bliss for fourteen years, until her death in 1782. I am the sole fruit of that union. After many years of useful contributions, he undertook the decision to retire from the service of the Prince of Liechtenstein, his benefactor, though he always maintained his relationship with the court and always continued to serve the Emperor.

I know how much my father owed to human kindness, and to the human tendency to help. Many people whose stories began as unhappily as my father's did were simply lost, dissolving into the chaos of the world. Few black-skinned slave children had the opportunity to attain as high and important a position as my father. But this is precisely the reason why his case is so significant—it shows that as beings created by the hand of God, we are all His children, and we are brothers and sisters to one another.

A number of my dear departed father's friends have already written to Your Majesty regarding this matter. I join them here in requesting that Your Majesty release my father's body and allow him to have the Christian burial he deserves.

Hopefully,

Josefine Soliman von Feuchtersleben

## AMONG THE MAORI

The heads of deceased family members are mummified and conserved as objects of mourning. Stages of mummification include steaming, smoking, and coating in oil. Through such treatments, the heads may be maintained in good condition, with their hair, skin, and teeth.

## DR. BLAU'S TRAVELS (II)

He was emerging now from the body of the plane, down long tunnels, following the arrows and illuminated notices that gently divided passengers between those who had reached their destinations and those who were still en route. The streams of people in the large airport swelled and then dispersed again. This painless selection process led him to the escalators, and then a long, broad hallway, where fluidity was hastened by a moving walkway. Those in a hurry took advantage of technology's advances and now leaped into another rate of time—at a leisurely pace they passed by others. Blau passed the glassed-in smoking area where nicotine fanatics, having fasted during extended flights, now gave in to their addictions with evident bliss. To Blau they seemed a separate species, living in an element that wasn't air, but rather a mixture of carbon dioxide and smoke. He watched them through the glass with vague astonishment, as though watching animals in a terrarium—on the plane they'd seemed so like him, but here their distinct biological makeup had been revealed.

He handed over his passport, and the officer sized him up with a quick, professional glance, comparing both faces—the one on the photo and the one on the other side of the pane. Apparently he didn't raise suspicions, because without delay they let him onto the terrain of this foreign nation.

The taxi pulled into the train station, where he showed his electronic ticket at the window. Since he still had over two hours he went to a bar. It reeked of stale grease, and as he waited for his fish, he examined those sitting around him.

The station didn't have any particular characteristics to set it apart. The large screen over the departures board showed all the same ads, for shampoo and credit cards. A familiar logo made this foreign world feel safe. He was hungry. The artificial airplane food had left no trace he was aware of in his body. It was as though it had contained no substance—only shape and smell—which was apparently the food they'd serve in paradise. Food for hungry souls. But now the piece of fried fish served with salad, the piece of white meat fried golden, fortified the doctor's compact body. He also ordered wine, here served in a handy little bottle, its contents equal to one generous glass.

On the train, he fell asleep. He didn't miss much—the train slogged through the city, through some tunnels and the suburbs, confusingly similar to other suburbs, with the same graffitied patterns repeated on the viaducts and the garages they went past. When he came to, he saw the sea, a thin bright belt between the cranes at the port and some ugly warehouse buildings and the shipyards.

"My dear sir," she had written him. "Your questions and their formulations have instilled within me, I must confess, complete and profound trust. A person who knows what he's asking is someone who can expect an answer soon. Perhaps what you need is that pro-verbial pinch that tips the scales."

He wondered what sort of pinch she had in mind. He checked the dictionary thoroughly. He didn't know any proverbs that had to do with scales and pinches. She had taken her husband's last name, but her first name was fairly exotic—Taina. Which might suggest she came from some distant land and equally exotic language, in which both pinch and scale worked perfectly fine as proverb. "Needless to say, it would be best for us to meet. I'll try to examine your dossier and all your articles in the meantime. Please come and see me. This is where my husband worked right up until the end, and his presence is still felt here. This will no doubt aid us in our conversations."

It was a small seaside village stretching down the shore, belted by a straight asphalt highway. The taxi pulled off just before the last sign with the village's name on it, heading downhill, toward the sea, and now they passed wood houses, pleasant to look at, with ter-races and balconies. The house he was looking for turned out to be big, and the most elegant along this gravel road. It was surrounded by a wall of medium height thickly covered with some local vine. The gate was kept open, but he asked the driver to stop on the road and, taking out his wheeled suitcase, he went up the gravel-strewn driveway on foot. The focal point of the neat yard was a magnifi-cent tree, clearly coniferous, but with a deciduous aspect, like an oak with leaves that had somehow been stunted into needles. He'd never seen such a tree, its almost-white bark looked like an elephant's skin.

No one responded to his knocking, so for a moment he stood there on the wooden porch, unable to make up his mind; he summoned his courage and turned the handle. The door opened, admitting him into a bright, spacious living room. The window opposite was completely taken up by the sea. A big orange cat came up to his feet, meowed, and slipped outside, completely ignoring the houseguest. The doctor was sure there was no one home, so he set down his suitcase and went out on the porch to wait for his hostess. He stood there for a quarter of an hour or so, examining that mighty tree, and then he slowly started to go around the house, which was encircled, like the others in this area, by a wooden terrace, on which (as in every other place in the world) stood lightweight furniture with throw pillows. In the back he found a garden with a meticulously mown lawn, densely planted with flowering bushes. In one of them he recognized a fragrant honeysuckle, and guided by a path lined with smooth, round rocks, he discovered a passage he thought must lead straight to the sea. He hesitated for a moment. Then he set forth.

The sand on the beach seemed almost white; diminutive, clean, dotted here and there with white shells. The doctor wondered whether he should remove his shoes, because he realized that it might be rude to walk onto a private beach with shoes on.

In the distance he saw a figure emerging from the water in silhouette—the sun, already low, was still intense. The woman was wearing a dark one-piece bathing suit. On the shore she reached out for a towel and wrapped herself in it. With one end of it she rubbed her hair. Then she picked up her sandals and began approaching the startled doctor. He didn't know what to do now. Whether to turn around and leave or to in fact walk toward her. He would have preferred to meet her in the calm of an office, in a more official setting. But she was already upon him. She held out her hand by way of greeting and said his last name in an interrogative tone. She was of average height and must have been getting close to sixty; cruel wrinkles shot across her face—you could tell she didn't skimp on sun. Had it not been for that, she would probably have looked younger. Her short, light-colored hair stuck to her face and neck. The towel she had around her reached her knees, below which were her evenly tanned legs, and her feet, marred by bunions.

"Let's go inside," she said.

She told him to take a seat in the living room and disappeared for a few minutes. The doctor flushed out of anxiety—he felt as though he had caught her in the bathroom, as though he'd walked in on her cutting her nails. This encounter with her nearly naked old body, with her feet, her wet hair—it threw him off completely. But she didn't seem to be bothered by it at all. She came back after a while in light-colored trousers and a T-shirt, a fine-boned woman, with flabby arm muscles, her skin teeming with moles and birthmarks, ruffling her still-damp hair with her hand. This wasn't how he had imagined her. He'd thought the wife of someone like Mole would be different. Different how? Taller, more modest, distinguished. In a silk blouse with a jabot and a carved cameo at her neck. Someone who didn't swim in the sea.

She sat down across from him, rolled up her trouser legs, and slid a bowl of chocolates toward him. She took one, too, and as she ate she sucked in her cheeks. He looked at her, she had bags under her eyes, hypothyroidism or perhaps just a flabbiness in the *musculus orbicularis oculi.*

"So it's you," she said. "Could you please remind me exactly what you do?"

He hurriedly swallowed his chocolate whole—it didn't matter, he'd grab another one. He told her who he was again and talked a little bit about his work and publications. He reminded her of his *History of Conservation*, which had been published recently and which he had included in the dossier he'd sent her. He praised her husband. He said that Professor Mole had engineered a veritable revolution in the field of anatomy. She watched him attentively with her blue eyes, with a slight, content smile, which he might have taken as friendly or as ironic. Despite her first name, there was nothing exotic about her. He suddenly thought that maybe this wasn't her, that maybe he was speaking with the cook, or the maid. As he finished with his background, he wrung his hands nervously, although he would have liked to keep himself from displaying such obvious evidence of nerves; he felt bedraggled in the shirt he'd worn to travel, and she leaped up, as though reading his mind.

"I'll show you your room. It's this way."

She guided him up the stairs onto the dark second floor and pointed to a door. She went in first and pulled back the red curtains. The windows gave onto the sea, the sun lit the room up orange.

"You can get settled in while I make us something to eat. You must be tired. Are you tired? How was your flight?"

He gave an offhanded answer.

"I'll be downstairs," she said, and left.

He wasn't quite sure how it had happened—this woman of average height in her light-colored trousers and stretched-out T-shirt had with some imperceptible gesture, perhaps just by her eyebrows, arranged anew the whole space and all the doctor's expectations and fantasies. She had rid him of the whole of his long and tiring journey and prepared speeches, possible scenarios. She had introduced something of her own. She was the one who dictated the conditions. The doctor gave in to it without batting an eyelash. Resigned, he took a quick shower, changed his clothes, and went downstairs.

For dinner she served a salad with croutons made of dark bread and baked vegetables. So she was a vegetarian. It was a good thing he'd had that fish at the station. She sat opposite him with her elbows on the table, crumbling what was left of the croutons with her fingertips, and she talked about healthy food, about the harmfulness of flour and sugar, about the nearby organic farms where she bought her vegetables, milk, and maple syrup, which she used instead of sugar. But the wine was good. Blau, unused to alcohol and tired, felt drunk after two glasses. Each subsequent sentence would form in his head, but she always got there first. By the end of the bottle she had told him the story of her husband's death. A motorboat collision.

"He was only sixty-seven years old. There was nothing they could do about the body. Completely mutilated."

He thought she would burst into tears now, but she just took another crouton and crumbled it onto the scant remains of her salad.

"He was not prepared for death, but who is?" she mused. "But I know that he would want a successor who was worthy of him, someone who is not merely competent, but also works with passion, like him. He was a loner, you know that, I'm sure. He left no will, gave no instructions. Should I donate his specimens to a museum? Several museums have already inquired. Do you know of any respectable institution? There's so much bad energy around plastinates now, but of course today, in order to do something, it's not as though you have to cut down the bodies off the gallows," she sighed, and shaped a few leaves of her salad into a slender roll, which she slipped into her mouth. "But I know he would want a successor. Some of his projects are only barely begun; I try to keep them going myself, but I don't have as much energy and enthusiasm as he did . . . Did you know I am a botanist by training? There is, for example, a problem . . ." she started, hesitated. "It doesn't matter, we'll have time to discuss that later."

He nodded, suppressing his curiosity.

"But you deal primarily with historical specimens, is that right?"

Blau waited until the echo of her words had petered out, then dashed upstairs and raced back with his laptop.

They pushed back their plates, and after a moment the screen lit up with a cool glow. The doctor panicked for a moment, wondering what he had on his desktop—if he hadn't left any erotic icons—but he had just cleaned it up recently. He hoped she had read what he had sent her about himself, that she had looked over his books. Now they both leaned into the screen.

As they looked over his work, it seemed to him that she was giving him admiring glances. He noted this to himself—twice. He made a mental note of what had inspired her admiration. She knew her stuff, posing professional questions. The doctor hadn't expected her to know quite so much. Her skin gave off a slight fragrance of the kind of lotion older women put on their bodies, nice, powdery, innocent. The index finger of her right hand—the one with which she touched the screen—was adorned with a strange ring with the shape of a human eye as its stone. The skin of her hand was already being covered by dark liver spots. Her hands were as ruined by the sun as her face. He thought for a second about what method might help stop the effects of the sun on this thin, corrugated skin.

Then they moved to armchairs, she brought half a bottle of port from the kitchen and poured out two glasses.

He asked: "Will I get to see the lab?"

She didn't answer right away. Perhaps because she had port in her mouth, as she had had the chocolate before. Finally she said: "It's a ways from here."

She got up and started clearing the table.

"You can barely keep your eyes open," she said.

He helped her put the plates into the dishwasher, and then with relief he went upstairs, muttering an indistinct "Good night" over his shoulder. He sat on the edge of his made bed and then immediately lay down on his side, not having the strength to take off his clothing. He heard her calling the cat on the terrace.

The next morning he did everything very methodically: he took a long shower, folded up his dirty underwear into a cube and put it inside a bag, unpacked his things and laid them out on a shelf, hanging up his shirts. He shaved, moisturized his face, rubbed his favorite deodorant under his arms, reinforced his graying hair with a little gel. His only hesitation was whether to wear sandals, but he thought it would be better if he continued with his laced-up loafers. Then, in silence (though he wasn't sure why), he went downstairs.

She must have gotten up before him, because on the kitchen counter a toaster was out, and a few crumbs from the bread for toast. As well as a jar of marmalade, a bowl of honey, and butter. His breakfast. There was coffee in the French press. He ate some toast standing out on the terrace, looking at the sea, supposing she must have gone to swim again, so she would undoubtedly come from out there. He wanted to see her first, before she saw him. He was the one who kept an eye on others.

He wondered whether she would agree to take him to the lab. He was very curious. Even if she told him nothing about what was in there, he'd be able to figure out quite a bit from what he'd see.

Mole's techniques were a mystery. Blau had come up with a few theories, of course, and might even have been close to solving it. He had seen his specimens in Mainz and then at the University of Florence on the occasion of the International Conference on Tissue Preservation. He could guess how Mole conserved bodies, but he didn't know the chemical makeup of the fixatives, wasn't sure how you operated on the tissues with them. Whether you needed to prepare them somehow, give them a pre-treatment. When and how were the chemicals dispensed, what was used in place of the blood?

How were the internal tissues plastinated?

However Mole did it (and his wife—of her involvement Blau was more and more certain), his specimens were excellent. The tissues kept their natural color and a certain plasticity. They were soft, but also sufficiently stiff to lend the body the appropriate shape. In addition they were easy to separate, which had an unlikely pedagogical result—you could take them apart and put them back together. Endless possibilities in terms of travels within the body of the preserved organism. From the perspective of the history of conservation of the body, Mole's discovery was revolutionary, it had no equal. Von Hagens's plastination had been the first step in this direction, but at this point it seemed less relevant.

Again she came out in a towel, this time a pink one, and she was coming not from the sea, but from the bathroom. She shook her wet hair and stood in the kitchen, at the stove, where she was heating milk up for coffee in a metal mug. She moved the netted plunger up and down, slowly, until the milky foam poured out onto the heated ceramic surface with a hiss.

"How did you sleep, Doctor? Coffee?"

Oh, yes, coffee. He accepted his mug gratefully and let her add some foamy milk to it. He listened with feigned interest to her story about the orange cat, who one day, the day their previous orange cat had died, had come to their house—who knew where from—and sat down on the sofa as though he'd always lived here, and then stayed. So they had barely even noticed the difference.

"That's the strength of life," she sighed. "As soon as one person departs, another being fills the void."

Poor Blau—he would have preferred to get right to the matter at hand. He had never been good at small talk, he was bored by topics pronounced for the sake of maintaining a soothing social hum. He simply wanted to finish his coffee and get into the library, and to see where Mole had worked and what he'd read. Did he have Blau's *History of Conservation* on his shelves? What routes had taken him to his remarkable discoveries?

"It's interesting that he, like you, started out by researching Ruysch's work."

Blau knew this, obviously, but he didn't want to interrupt her.

"In his first published article he demonstrated that Ruysch was trying to conserve whole bodies, by eliminating their natural fluids, if only that had been possible in those days, and replacing them with a mixture of liquid wax, talcum, and animal tallow. Then bodies, prepared in this way, just like specimens of parts, would be immersed in a 'Stygian water.' It seems the idea never came to fruition because of a lack of glass vessels that would be big enough."

She gave him a hurried glance.

"I'll show you that research," she said, and moved briskly to wrestle with the sliding door because of the coffee she held in her hand. He helped her while she held his mug.

Behind the door was the library—a beautiful spacious room lined with bookshelves from floor to ceiling. With perfect aim she reached out to one of them and took down a moderately sized bound booklet. Blau leafed through it, giving her to understand that he already knew this text well. In any case, he had never been particularly interested in techniques involving liquids—that was a dead end. The example of the English man, William Berkeley, the fleet admiral Ruysch had embalmed with liquid, interested him only insofar as it concerned the problem of rigor mortis. For this was the mystery of the marvelous appearance of that body, described with such delight by his contemporaries. Ruysch had managed to give him a very relaxed aspect, even though he had received the body he was to treat several days after its death, completely stiffened. Apparently he had hired special servants to massage the body patiently, and in so doing, to overcome its rigor mortis.

But something else entirely grabbed his attention. He handed her back the booklet without moving his gaze away from it.

By the window there was a big desk, and on the other side of it some glass display cabinets. Specimens! Blau was unable to control his excitement and found himself standing before them without realizing he'd reached them. She seemed annoyed he hadn't given her time for a slow, museum-like preparation for what he was about to see. He'd gotten away from her.

"This you might not be so familiar with," she said, somewhat grumpily, pointing to the orange cat. It was looking at them peacefully, sitting in a position that suggested an acceptance of existence in this form. The other, live cat followed them into the room now and, as though looking at its reflection in a mirror, gazed at its predecessor.

"Touch him, pick it up," the woman in the pink towel encouraged the doctor.

His fingers trembling, he opened the display case and touched the specimen. It was cold, but not hard. Its coat gave a little bit under Blau's fingertip. Blau picked it up carefully, holding its chest in one hand and its stomach in the other, as you pick up live cats—and it felt very odd indeed. Because the cat had the same weight as a live cat, and like a live cat, its body reacted to the doctor's grasp. The impression was almost impossible to believe. He looked at her with an expression on his face that made her laugh, and again she shook her drying hair.

"You see," she said, coming to stand next to him, as though the secret of the specimen brought them together, rendered them close. "Lay it down and turn it over."

He did this carefully, and she reached out and laid her hand on the cat's stomach.

Under its own weight the cat's body stretched out and for a moment lay before them on its back, in a position no live cat would ever assume. Blau touched its soft fur and thought it felt warm, although he knew that was impossible. He noted that its eyes had not been replaced by glass ones, as was usual in such cases; instead, Mole had in some magical way left its real eyes in; they seemed only slightly turbid. He touched an eyelid—it was soft and gave under his finger.

"Some sort of gel," he said, more to himself than to her, but she was already pointing him to the slit on the cat's stomach, which split open after a slight tug and revealed the cat's whole insides.

Gently, as though touching the most fragile piece of origami, with just his fingertips he pried apart the abdominal walls of the animal and got into the peritoneum, which also let itself be opened, as though the cat were a book made out of precious, exotic material for which there is no name yet. He saw the sight that had since childhood given him a feeling of happiness and fulfillment—the organs perfectly placed in relation to one another, packed into a divine harmony, their natural colors providing absolute verisimilitude, completing the illusion that here the insides of a living body were opening up, that one was participating in its secret.

"Go ahead and open the rib cage," she said, taking a small step back but still hovering over his shoulder. He could smell her breath: coffee and something sweet, stale.

He went ahead and the fine ribs gave way under the pressure of his fingers. He was actually expecting to see a beating heart, so perfect was the illusion. Instead there was a click, something lit up red, and out came a screeching melody, which Dr. Blau later identified as the famous hit by the band Queen, "I Want to Live Forever." He jumped back, frightened, with a blend of fear and disgust, as though he had inadvertently harmed this animal outstretched before him. He held his hands up and out. The woman clapped her hands together and laughed outright now, joyously, pleased with the joke, but Blau must have had an overly stern expression on his face, because she regained control and put her hand on his back.

"I'm sorry, don't worry, it's just his little joke. We didn't want it to be too sad," she said, now fully serious, although her blue eyes were still laughing. "I'm sorry."

The doctor reciprocated her smile with difficulty, and watched fascinated as the tissues of the specimen slowly, almost imperceptibly, returned to their initial layout.

She did take him to the lab. They took the car down the gravel road along the beach and went up into some stone buildings. Once there had been a fish processing plant here, back when the port still functioned as such; now they'd been converted into a few large rooms with clean, tiled walls, and doors that opened with the touch of a remote, like garages. They had no windows. She turned on the light and Blau saw two large tables covered in sheet metal as well as several glass cases filled with jars and instruments. Shelves filled with flasks of Jena glass.

"Papain," he read on one of them, and was surprised.

What had Mole used that enzyme for, what had he used it to break down? "Catalase." Syringes of enormous dimensions for infusing and ordinary small ones, like those used to give people injections. He noted this to himself, not daring to ask. Not yet. A metal bath, a drain in the floor, an interior reminiscent simultaneously of a surgeon's office and a slaughterhouse. She tightened the dripping tap.

"Are you happy?" she asked.

He slid his open palm down the sheet metal of the table and went up to the desk, which still offered up some printouts with a graph of some curve.

"I haven't touched anything," she said encouragingly, as though she were the owner of a home put up for sale. "I just threw out the unfinished specimens, because they were starting to go bad."

He felt her hand on his back and cast a startled glance at her, then immediately lowered his eyes. She moved closer to him, standing so that her breasts were touching his shirt. He felt a panicked rush of adrenaline and just managed to prevent his body from jerking back against his will. But he found a pretext; the table, which he bumped into, swayed, and some small glass ampoules almost rolled onto the floor. He caught them at the last moment; thus he freed himself from that uncomfortable closeness of their bodies. He was certain it had happened naturally enough, as though she'd accidentally leaned on him. At the same time, he felt like a little boy, and suddenly the difference in their ages loomed so large.

She lost a bit of her interest in showing and explaining the details to him; she took out her phone and called someone. She was discussing some rental fee, making plans for Saturday. While this was going on he looked around voraciously, examined every detail and called upon himself to remember all of it. Record in his mind on a map all the equipment in the lab, every little bottle, the location of each of the tools.

After lunch, during which she talked to him about Mole, his daily schedule and little eccentricities (he listened attentively, sensing he was receiving an extraordinary privilege), she talked Blau into swimming in the sea. He wasn't happy, he would have preferred to sit quietly in the library and examine the cat and the room itself once more. But he didn't have the courage to say no to her. He made a last vague attempt to get out of it by pointing out he didn't have a bathing suit.

"Oh, come on," she said, not accepting the excuse. "It's my private beach, there won't be anyone. You can swim naked."

But she was still going in a bathing suit. So Dr. Blau took off his boxers underneath his towel and got into the water as quickly as he could. The cold of it took his breath away. He wasn't a good swimmer—he'd somehow never had an opportunity to learn. In general he didn't like exercise, being in motion. He uncertainly hopped around in the water, taking care to be able to feel the bottom under his feet. Meanwhile she swam out to sea in a beautiful crawl and then returned. She splashed water on him. Blau, surprised, shut his eyes.

"Well, what are you waiting for, swim!" she cried.

He readied himself for a moment for the plunge into the cold water, ultimately doing it in desperation, submissively, like a child not wanting to disappoint a parent. He swam a little distance and turned back. Then she slapped her hand against the surface of the water, hard, and kept going by herself.

He waited for her on the shore, shivering. As she walked toward him, dripping, he looked down.

"Why didn't you swim?" she asked, in a high-pitched, amused voice.

"Cold," was all he said.

She burst out laughing, throwing back her head and shamelessly exposing her palate.

In his room he dozed off briefly, before taking some meticulous notes. He even sketched the layout of Mole's lab, feeling a little bit like James Bond. With relief he washed off the salt water, shaved, and put on a clean shirt. When he went downstairs, she was nowhere to be seen. The door to the library was closed, and the key in the door had been turned, so he wasn't brave enough to go in . . . He went out in front of the house and played with the cat until the cat ignored him. Finally he heard some sounds coming from the kitchen and went toward it from the yard.

Mrs. Mole was standing by the counter and going through green lettuce leaves.

"Salad with croutons and some cheeses. What do you think?"

He nodded eagerly, although he wasn't at all convinced that would fill him up. She poured him a glass of white wine and, without conviction, he brought it to his lips.

She told him in detail about the accident, about the search for the body in the sea, which lasted for a long time, several days, and finally about how it had looked when they finally found it. He lost all desire to eat. She said that she had been able to preserve a piece of the least destroyed tissue. She was wearing a long, airy gray dress with slits down the sides, with a deep-cut neckline that revealed her freckled body. Again he thought she might cry.

The salad and the cheeses they ate almost in silence. Then she took his hand, and he froze.

He put his arm around her, cleverly hiding from her. She kissed his neck.

"Not like this," he blurted.

She didn't understand. "How, then? What do you want me to do?"

But he had slipped out of her embrace, stood up from the sofa, and, red in the face, was looking helplessly around the room.

"How do you want it to happen? Tell me."

In despair, he realized he couldn't pretend anymore, that he didn't have the strength, that there were too many things going on at once, and turning his back to her, he whispered: "I can't. It's too soon for me."

"It's because I'm older than you, right?" she murmured, standing up.

He protested uncertainly. He wanted her to comfort him but without touching him.

"It's not like there's a massive difference in our ages," he said as he listened to her clear the table. "I'm with someone," he lied.

In a certain sense this was true, and truth is always true in a certain sense; he was with someone. He had already been wedded, married, connected by blood. With the Glasmensch and the wax woman with the open stomach, with Soliman, Fragonard, Vesalius, von Hagens, and Mole, for God's sake, who else could there be? Why should he bore into this living, aging warm body, drill into it with his? With what aim? He felt like he would have to leave, maybe even right away. He ran his hand through his hair and buttoned up his shirt.

She sighed deeply.

"So?" she asked.

He didn't know what to say.

A quarter of an hour later he was standing with his suitcase in the living room, ready to go.

"Can I call a taxi?"

She was sitting on the couch. Reading.

"But of course," she said. She removed her glasses and pointed to the phone, and then returned to her reading.

But since he didn't know the number, he thought it would be better if he just went on foot to the bus stop; there had to be one somewhere nearby.

And so he arrived at the conference sooner than he'd planned. After a long debate with hotel reception he managed to finagle a room. He spent the whole evening in the bar. He drank a bottle of wine at the hotel restaurant, and then in bed he began to cry like a little child.

Over the next few days he heard lots of papers and gave his: "The Preservation of Pathology Specimens Through Silicone Plastination: An Innovative Supplement to the Teaching of Pathological Anatomy"—an excerpt from his dissertation.

His talk was enthusiastically received. On the final evening of the conference at the banquet he met a nice, handsome teratologist from Hungary who confided in him that he was about to go to Mrs. Mole's house, at her invitation.

"To her seaside home"—he emphasized the word "seaside." "I figured I'd combine the two trips, it's not really very far from here," he said. "Everything her husband left is in her hands now. If I managed to get a glimpse of his laboratory . . . You know, I have my theory as to the chemical composition. Apparently she is in talks with some museum in the States, sooner or later she'll give all of it away, along with all the documentation. But if I could get access to his papers here and now . . ." he went on dreamily. "My habilitation would be guaranteed, perhaps even my professorship."

Fuckwit, thought Blau. This man would be the last person to whom he would admit he'd gotten there first. And then he looked at him with her eyes, for just a second. He saw his dark hair, gleaming with some sort of gel, and the little sweat stains under his arms on the blue material of his shirt. His already slightly protruding but still-slim belly, his narrow hips, his fresh pale skin with the shadow of dense facial hair. His eyes already blurring from the wine and shining with the glory of impending triumph.

## PLANE OF PROFLIGATES

Reddened northern faces surprised by sudden sun. Faded by salt water, and that hair after several hours daily at the beach. Bags filled with dirty, sweated-in clothes. In their carry-ons last-minute purchases from the airport: souvenirs for loved ones, bottles of strong alcohol from the duty-free shop. Just men; they occupy the same part of the plane now in a sort of tacit pact. They settle into their seats, buckle their seat belts—they will sleep. They will make up for those nights without sleep. Their skin still gives off a smell of alcohol, their bodies have not yet managed to fully digest that two-week dosage—after several hours in the air this smell will have saturated the whole plane. In addition to a stench of sweat mixed with remnants of arousal. A good criminologist would uncover more evidence—a single long dark hair snagged on the button of a shirt; trace amounts of organic matter under index and middle fingernails—human, someone else's DNA; in the cotton fibers of their underwear, microscopic skin flakes; in navels, microquantities of sperm.

Before takeoff they get in a word or two with neighbors to their left and right. Reservedly they express their satisfaction with their recent stay—it wouldn't do to say more, and in any case, it's understood. Just a few, those most incorrigible, ask last questions about the prices and the range of services, and then—content— they doze off. It all turned out to be so cheap.

## PILGRIM'S MAKEUP

An old friend of mine once told me how he hated traveling alone. His gripe was: When he sees something out of the ordinary, some-thing new and beautiful, he so wants to share it with someone that he becomes deeply unhappy if there's no one around.

I doubt he would make a good pilgrim.

## JOSEFINE SOLIMAN'S SECOND LETTER TO FRANCIS I, EMPEROR OF AUSTRIA

Since I have not received any response to my letter, I will ask to be allowed to write to Your Majesty once more, this time in terms much bolder, though I would not wish them to be taken as excessive familiarity: Dear Brother. Because has not God, whomever He may be, made us to be brothers and sisters? Has He not divided dili-gently among us our obligations so that we would carry them all out always with dignity and devotion, tending to His works? He entrusted to us the lands and the seas, and to some He gave indus-try, and to some He gave governance. Some He made highborn, healthy, and attractive, while others He made of lower birth and of lesser physical blessings. With our human limitations, we cannot explain why. All that remains us is to trust that there is His wisdom within it, and that in this way we all form a part of His complex architecture, parts whose purpose we are incapable of divining, but—we *must* believe this—without which this world's great mechanism would simply stop working.

Just a few weeks ago, I gave birth to a baby boy, whom my husband and I named Edward. My great maternal joy is marred, however, by the fact that my little son's grandfather has not yet attained his final resting place. That his unburied body has been exhibited by Your Majesty to curious onlookers at the Prince's Wunderkammer.

We have been so fortunate as to have been born in an age of reason, in an exceptional era that has been able to clearly express to what extent the mind is the most perfect of God's gifts. The power of the mind is such that it may cleanse the world now of superstitions and injustices and make all the world's inhabitants rejoice. My father was fully dedicated to that idea. It was his deeply held belief that human reason is the greatest power we as people can achieve and wield. And I, brought up in all my father's love, believe that, too: reason is the very best thing God could have given us.

In my father's papers, which I put in order after his death, there is a letter from His Majesty the Emperor Joseph, Your Majesty's predecessor and uncle, a letter written in His Majesty's own hand and containing the following passage, which I shall permit myself to repeat here: "All people are equal at birth. From our parents we inherit only animal life, and in this—we know well—there is not the slightest difference between king, prince, merchant, or peasant. There is no law in existence, divine or natural, that could counter that equality."

How am I to believe this passage now?

I am no longer asking but *imploring* Your Majesty for the return to my family of my father's body, which has been stripped of all honor and all dignity, chemically treated and stuffed, and exhibited to human curiosity in the proximity of dead wild animals. I write to You, too, on behalf of the other stuffed human beings contained within that Cabinet of Natural Curiosities of His Royal Highness, since, as far as I know, they have no one of their own to stand up for them, not even family—here I refer to that anonymous little girl, and to one Joseph Hammer and to Pietro Michaele Angiola. I don't even know who these people are, and I would not be able to tell even the most abbreviated version of the stories of their unhappy lives, but nonetheless I feel it is my duty to them as the daughter of Angel Soliman to perform this Christian deed of asking. It is my duty, too, as of now, as the mother of a human being.

Josefine Soliman von Feuchtersleben

## SARIRA

A beautiful bald-headed nun in robes the color of bone bends over a tiny reliquary where, on a little satin cushion, there rests what is left of the burned body of an enlightened being. I stand beside her, both of us just looking at that speck. We are aided in this endeavor by the magnifying glass that is a permanent fixture of the room. That whole enlightened essence takes the form of this tiny crystal, a little bitty stone barely bigger than a grain of sand. The body of this nun, no doubt, will also be transformed into a grain of sand, in some years; mine—no, mine will be lost: I was never practicing.

But none of this should make me sad, given the number of sandy deserts and beaches in the world. What if they're entirely made up of the posthumous essences of the bodies of enlightened beings?

## THE BODHI TREE

I met a person from China. He was telling me about the first time he flew to India on business; he had lots and lots of important individual and group meetings. His company produced quite complicated electronic devices allowing blood to be conserved longer-term, and allowing organs to be safely transported, and now he was negotiating to open up new markets and start some Indian subsidiaries.

On his final evening there he mentioned to his Indian contractor that he had dreamed since childhood of seeing the tree under which the Buddha had attained enlightenment—the Bodhi tree. He came from a Buddhist family, although at that time there could be no public mention of religion in the People's China. But later, once they could avow whatever faith they wished, his parents unexpectedly converted to Christianity, a Far Eastern variety of Protestantism. They felt that the Christian God might come in handier to His followers, that He would be, let's be honest, more effective, and it would be easier with Him to get some money and get set up. But this man did not share that view and kept the Buddhist faith of his ancestors.

The Indian contractor understood the man's desire. He nodded and topped off his Chinese colleague's drink.

In the end they all got pleasantly inebriated, getting out all the tension of signing contracts and negotiations. With the last of their strength, wobbling on swaying legs, they went into the hotel sauna to sober up, since in the morning they still had work to do.

The following morning a message was delivered to his room—a little note with just one word: "Surprise." Clipped to it the business card of his contractor. In front of the hotel stood a taxi, which now conveyed him to a waiting helicopter. After a flight of less than an hour the man found himself in the sacred spot where, beneath a great fig tree, the Buddha had attained enlightenment.

His elegant suit and white shirt vanished into the crowd of pilgrims. His body still preserved the bitter memory of alcohol, the heat of the sauna, and a rustle of papers signed in silence on the glass surface of the modern table. A scraping of a pen that left behind his name. Here, however, he felt lost, and helpless as a child. Women who came up to his shoulder, colorful as parrots, pushed past him in the direction this wide human stream was flowing. Suddenly the man was frightened by the thing that he repeated as a Buddhist several times a day, when he had time—the vow. That he would try to bring with his prayers and actions all sentient beings to enlightenment. Suddenly this struck him as utterly hopeless.

When he saw the tree, he was—to tell the truth—disappointed. He had not a thought in his head, nor any prayers. He paid the place its due homage, kneeling many times, making substantial offerings, and about two hours later, he returned to the helicopter. By afternoon he was back in his hotel.

Under a stream of water in the shower that washed from his body the sweat, dust, and strange sweetish smell of the crowd, the stalls, the bodies, the ubiquitous incense, and the curry people ate with their hands off paper trays, it occurred to him that every day he was witness to what had shaken Prince Gautama so: illness, old age, death. And it was no big deal. It produced no change in him; by now, to tell the truth, he'd grown inured to it. And then, drying himself off with a fluffy white towel, he thought that he wasn't even sure he truly wished to be enlightened. If he really wanted to see, in one split second, the whole truth. To peer inside the world as though by X-ray, to glimpse in it the skeletal structure of a void.

But of course—as he assured his generous friend that same evening—he was extremely grateful for this present. Then from the pocket of his suit coat he carefully extracted a crumbled leaf, which both men inclined over in rapt, pious attention.

## HOME IS MY HOTEL

I look around and take each thing in again. I look at it from scratch, like I've never been here before. I discover details. I am particularly struck by the hotel owners' attention to the flowers—they're so big and pretty, with their luminous leaves, and their appropriately moist dirt, and that tetrastigma: impressive.

What a big bedroom, although the sheets could be better quality, white and well-starched linen. Instead they're the color of faded bark, such that they require neither pressing nor ironing. The library downstairs, though, is actually terrific—it's exactly the kind of stuff I like, and it has everything I would need if I ever had to live here. In fact, I may end up staying longer just because of those books.

And by some strange coincidence I find some clothes in the closet that fit me perfectly, mostly dark colors, which is what I like to wear. They fit me perfectly—that black hoodie, so soft and so comfortable. And—and this is now beginning to be truly incredible—there on the nightstand are my vitamins and the earplugs I always buy. This is really too much. I also like that you never see any of your hosts, that there is no housekeeping staff here in the mornings pounding down your door. That there isn't anybody wandering around. There's no reception. I even make my own coffee in the mornings myself, just the way I like it. On the espresso machine, with steamed milk.

Indeed, it is a good hotel with good rates, this one, perhaps a little bit in the middle of nowhere, and some distance from the main road, which in the winter gets buried in snow, but if one is traveling by car, it doesn't really matter. You have to get off the motorway at the town of S. and go a few kilometers more along a regular road and then turn at G. onto a chestnut-lined avenue that leads to a gravel road. In the winter you have to leave your car by the last hydrant and walk the rest of the way.

## TRAVEL PSYCHOLOGY: LECTIO BREVIS II

"Ladies and gentlemen," began the woman, this time quite young, wearing army boots, her hair pinned up in a way I found amusing; she must have been fresh out of her master's program. "As we have said in previous lectures—which perhaps you have had a chance to listen to at one of the airports or train stations participating in this project—we experience time and space in a manner that is primarily unconscious. These are not categories we could call objective, or external. Our sense of space results from our ability to move. Our sense of time, meanwhile, is due to being biological individuals undergoing distinct and changing states. Time is thus nothing other than the flow of changes.

"Place as an aspect of space pauses time. It is the momentary detainment of our perception on a configuration of objects. It is, in contradistinction to time, a static notion.

"Understood thus, human time is divided into stages, as move-

ment through space is broken up by place-pauses. Such pauses anchor us within the flow of time. A person who is sleeping and loses
any sense of the place in which he or she currently is also loses all
sense of time. The more pauses in space, and the more places we
experience therefore, the more time elapses subjectively. We often
refer to separate stages of time as episodes. They have no consequences, interrupting time without becoming part of it. They
are self-contained occurrences, each starting from scratch; each
beginning and each end is absolute. Not a single episode is to be
continued, you might say."

By now there was some movement in the first row, as in the murmuring of the announcements about passengers urgently requested
someone here had recognized their name and was hurrying to
gather carry-ons and duty-free sacks, jostling past their neighbors
in that scramble. In a panic I checked my own boarding pass again,
losing the thread of the lecture; it was a struggle to get back into
this woman's disquisition as she now embarked upon travel psychology's practical side. She must have sensed we'd had enough of
the strange and complicated theory.

"Practical travel psychology investigates the metaphorical meaning of places. Just take a look at those screens with destinations on
them. Have you ever stopped to think about what 'Iceland' means?
And what are the 'United States'? What sort of response do you find
within yourself when you pronounce those names? Asking yourself
this type of question is particularly helpful in topographical psychoanalysis, where getting to the deeper meaning of places leads to de-
ciphering the so-called itinerarium—the particular route of the
traveler, that is, the deeper reason for his journey.

"Topographical or travel psychoanalysis does not, despite surface similarities, pose the same question as immigration officials: What did you come here for? Our question raises issues of sense and meaning. In essence, one becomes what one participates in. In other words, I am what I look at.

"And this was of course the reason behind the ancient pilgrimages. Striving toward—and reaching—a holy place would bestow holiness upon us, cleanse us of our sins. Does the same thing happen when we travel to unholy, sinful places? To sad and vacant places? Joyful, fruitful places?

"And is it not so . . ." continued the woman, but behind me two middle-aged couples were chatting in hushed voices, which for a moment seemed more interesting to me than the reflections of our lecturer.

I worked out quickly that it was two married couples exchanging impressions from their travels, one couple urging the other:

"You have to go to Cuba—but the Cuba they've got now, under Fidel. When he dies, Cuba's going to be the same as everywhere. But if you go right now you'll see some incredible poverty—the kinds of cars they drive! You really have to get on it, though—apparently Fidel is pretty ill."

## COMPATRIOTS

The woman had finished the practical component of her lecture, meanwhile, and travelers were starting to pose timid questions, though they weren't asking what they should have been. At least that's how it felt to me. I didn't have the courage to say anything myself, though, so I went over to a nearby restaurant to have some coffee. Congregated at its entrance was a group of people who turned out to be talking to one another in my language. I looked them up and down suspiciously—they looked so like me. Yes, those women could have been my sisters. So I found myself a seat that was as far away from them as possible, then ordered coffee.

I was far from pleased to be encountering compatriots in foreign lands. I pretended not to understand the sounds of my own language. I preferred to be anonymous. I watched them out of the corner of my eye and relished their unawareness of being understood. I observed them furtively, then disappeared.

A tired British man wistfully confessed to me he felt the same ("I'm far from pleased when I encounter my compatriots in foreign lands") as he drank yet another beer, watching clientele coming into the restaurant. I chatted with him for a bit, but we didn't really have that much to say to one another.

I finished my coffee and returned to where the lecture was, pretending I had to go soon, which I didn't. I arrived in time for the last few discussions, as the determined lecturer woman was explaining something to the three listeners, those most enduring, gathered around her.

## TRAVEL PSYCHOLOGY: CONCLUSION

"We have seen, ladies and gentlemen, how selfhood has grown and gained a foothold, become increasingly distinct and affecting. Previously barely marked, prone to being blurred, subjugated to the collective. Imprisoned in the stays of roles, conventions, flattened in the press of traditions, subjugated to demands. Now it swells and annexes the world.

"Once the gods were external, unavailable, from another world, and their apparent emissaries were angels and demons. But the human ego burst forth and swept the gods up and inside, furnished them a place somewhere between the hippocampus and the brain stem, between the pineal gland and Broca's area. Only in this way can the gods survive—in the dark, quiet nooks of the human body, in the crevices of the brain, in the empty space between the synapses. This fascinating phenomenon is beginning to be studied by the fledgling discipline of travel psychotheology.

"This growing process is more and more powerful—influencing reality is equally what we have invented and what we have not. Who else moves in the real? We know people who travel to Morocco through Bertolucci's film, to Dublin through Joyce, to Tibet through a film about the Dalai Lama.

"There is a certain well-known syndrome named after Stendhal in which one arrives in a place known from literature or art and experiences it so intensely that one grows weak or faints. There are those who boast they have discovered places totally unknown, and then we envy them for experiencing the truest reality even very fleetingly before that place, like all the rest, is absorbed by our minds.

"Which is why we must ask, once more, insistently, the same question: Where are they going, to what countries, to what places? Other countries have become an external complex, a knot of significations that a good topographical psychologist can unravel just like that, interpret on the spot.

"Our task is to bring to you the idea of practical travel psychology and to encourage you to take advantage of our services. Don't be afraid, ladies and gentlemen, of those quiet corners by the coffee machines, around the duty-free shops, those ad hoc offices where analysis takes place quickly, discreetly, only occasionally disrupted, perhaps, by departure announcements. It's just two chairs behind a screen with maps on it.

"'So, you're going to Peru?' the topographical psychoanalyst might ask you. It would be easy to confuse him with a cashier or the person working check-in. 'So, Peru?'

"And he'll do a short associative test with you, attentively watching which of the words turns out to be the end of the thread. It's a short-term analysis, without any superfluous dragging out of the topic, without invoking that old holy grail of the mothers and fathers to blame. Over a single session we ought to be able to get it.

"Peru, but to what end?"

## THE TONGUE IS THE STRONGEST MUSCLE

There are countries out there where people speak English. But not like us—we have our own languages hidden in our carry-on luggage, in our cosmetics bags, only ever using English when we travel, and then only in foreign countries, to foreign people. It's hard to imagine, but English is their real language! Oftentimes their only language. They don't have anything to fall back on or to turn to in moments of doubt.

How lost they must feel in the world, where all instructions, all the lyrics of all the stupidest possible songs, all the menus, all the excruciating pamphlets and brochures—even the buttons in the elevator!—are in their private language. They may be understood by anyone at any moment, whenever they open their mouths. They must have to write things down in special codes. Wherever they are, people have unlimited access to them—they are accessible to everyone and everything! I heard there are plans in the works to get them some little language of their own, one of those dead ones no one else is using anyway, just so that for once they can have something just for themselves.


## SPEAK! SPEAK!

Inside and out, to oneself and to others, narrating every situation, naming every state; search for words, try them on, that shoe that will magically transform Cinderella into a princess. Move words around like the chips you place on numbers in roulette. Perhaps this will be the time? Perhaps we'll win this one?

Speak, grab people's sleeves, have them sit down across from us and listen. Then turn yourself into the listener for their "speak, speak." Hasn't it been said that I speak, therefore I am? One speaks, therefore one is?

Use all possible means for this, metaphors, parables, wavers, unfinished sentences; don't be put off by the sentence breaking off halfway through, as though past the verb there suddenly yawned an abyss.

Do not leave any unexplained, unnarrated situations, any closed doors; kick them down with a curse, even the ones that lead to embarrassing and shameful hallways you would prefer to forget. Don't be ashamed of any fall, of any sin. The narrated sin will be forgiven. The narrated life, saved. Is it not this that Saints Sigismund, Charles, and James have taught us? He who has not mastered the art of speaking shall remain forever caught in a trap.

## FROG AND BIRD

There are two points of view in the world: the frog's perspective and bird's-eye view. Any point in between just leads to chaos.

Take the airport maps so beautifully drawn on airline brochures. Their meaning becomes clear only once one sees them from above, like the monumental Nazca Lines, created with flying creatures in mind—the modern airport in Sydney is shaped like an airplane, for example. A somewhat uninteresting, I find, concept—your plane landing on a plane. The way becomes the goal, and the instrument the result. The airport in Tokyo, on the other hand, in the shape of an enormous hieroglyphic, is perplexing. What sort of letter is it? We haven't mastered the Japanese alphabet, we won't know what our arrival means, with what word they greet us here. What do they stamp into our passport? A big question mark?

Similarly, Chinese airports bring to mind the local alphabet, you have to learn them, put them in order, create an anagram out of them—then perhaps they will reveal some unexpected wisdom of the journey. Or treat them like those sixty-four hexagrams from *I Ching* and then every landing will be a fortune. Hexagram 40: *Xiè*, Deliverance. Hexagram 36: *Míng yí*, Darkening of the Light. Hexagram 10: *Lǚ*, Treading. 17: *Suí*, Following. 24: *Fù*. Return. 30: *Lí*, Clinging.

But let's give it a rest with this convoluted Eastern metaphysics, for which, apparently, we have a soft spot. Let us look at the airport in San Francisco, and now we have something familiar, something that inspires confidence, that makes us feel right at home: here we have a cross section of the spine. The round center of the airport is the spinal cord, locked in a hard safe shell of individual ribs, and here, radiating out, the nerve roots from which depart the numbered gates, each complete with a sleeve leading to the plane.

And Frankfurt? That great air-travel hub, that state within a state? What do you associate that with? Yes, yes, the spitting image of a chip, a computer chip, a razor-thin plate. Here there can be no doubts—they tell us what we are, dear travelers. We are the individual nerve impulses of the world, fractions of an instant, barely that part of it that permits the change from plus to minus, or maybe the other way around, and keeps everything in constant flux.

## LINES, PLANES, AND BODIES

I often dreamed of watching without being seen. Of spying. Of being the perfect observer. Like that camera obscura I once made out of a shoebox. It photographed for me a part of the world through a black closed space with a microscopic pupil through which light sneaks inside. I was training.

The best place for this kind of training is Holland, where people, convinced of their utter innocence, do not use curtains. After dusk the windows turn into little stages on which actors act out their evenings. Sequences of images bathed in yellow, warm light are the individual acts of the same production titled *Life*. Dutch painting. Moving lives.

Here at the door appears a man, in his hand he has a tray, he puts it on the table; two children and a woman sit down around it. They take their time eating, in silence, because the audio in this theater doesn't work. Then they move to the couch, watch a glowing screen attentively, but for me, standing on the street, it isn't clear what has

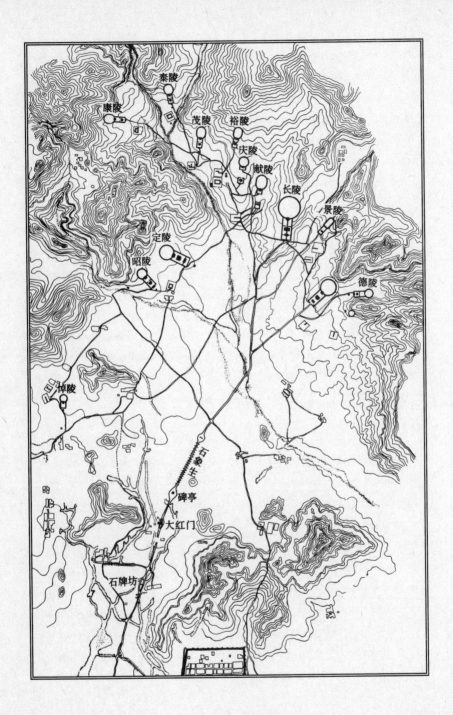

泰陵

康陵

茂陵　裕陵

庆陵

献陵

长陵

景陵

定陵

昭陵

德陵

悼陵

石象生

碑亭

大红门

石牌坊

absorbed them so—I see only flickers, flutterings of light, tiny pictures, too brief and distant to be intelligible. Someone's face, a
mouth moving intensely, a landscape, another face . . . Some say
that this is a boring play and that nothing happens in it. But I like
it—for example, the movement of a foot playing unconsciously with
a slipper, or the whole astonishing act of yawning. Or a hand that
seeks upon a plush surface a remote control and—having found it—
is calmed, withers.

Standing off to one side. Seeing only the world in fragments,
there won't be any other one. Moments, crumbs, fleeting configurations—no sooner have they come into existence than they
fall to pieces. Life? There's no such thing; I see lines, planes, and
bodies, and their transformations in time. Time, meanwhile, seems
a simple instrument for the measurement of tiny changes, a school
ruler with a simplified scale—it's just three points: was, is, and
will be.

## THE ACHILLES TENDON

The year 1542 was the dawn of a new era, although unfortunately
no one so much as noticed. It wasn't a big year, nor the end of a
century—from the perspective of numerology, there was nothing
there, just the number three. And yet that year the first chapters of
Copernicus's *De revolutionibus orbium coelestium* and the entirety
of *De humani corporis fabrica* by Vesalius appeared.

Needless to say, neither book contained everything—but can
anything ever contain everything? Copernicus was missing the rest
of the solar system, planets like Uranus, which was still waiting for
the right time to be discovered, on the eve of the French Revolution.

Vesalius, meanwhile, lacked a number of specific mechanical solutions in the human body, spans, joints, connections—such as, to give just one example, the tendon that joins the calf to the heel.

But maps of the world, of this internal and that external world, had already been drawn up, and that order, once glimpsed, irradiated the mind, etching into it the primary—the fundamental—lines and planes.

Let's say it is the warm November of 1689, sometime in the afternoon. Philip Verheyen is doing what he usually does, sitting at the table, in the pool of light that flows in through the window, as though specially projected for this very purpose. He examines tissues arrayed over the table's surface. Pins driven into the wood keep gray nerves in place. With his right hand, without looking at the paper, he sketches what he sees.

Seeing, after all, means knowing.

But now there's someone banging on the door, and the dog's barking ferociously, and Philip must get up. He is reluctant. His body has already adopted its favorite position, his head inclined over the specimen; now he must lean on his intact leg and drag out from beneath the table the leg that exists as a wooden peg. Limping, he goes to the door, where he manages to calm the dog down. At the door stands a young man whom Verheyen recognizes—but only after a considerable pause—as his student Willem van Horssen. He's hardly pleased by these visits, though no visit would please him, but still he takes a step backward, his wooden leg tapping at the stone slabs of the entrance, and he invites his guest inside.

Van Horssen is tall, with lush, curly hair and a joyful face. He bones and skulls, fine and delicate, and any attentive observer would certainly make out of them still more little fetuses.

"It's beautiful, isn't it?" asks the guest, looking over the host's shoulder.

"What about it?" Philip Verheyen answers offhandedly. "Human bones."

"It's art."

But Philip can't be dragged into discussion, bears no resemblance to that Philip Verheyen whom van Horssen knew from the university. The conversation doesn't exactly flow, and you might get the impression that the host is absorbed by something else, perhaps solitude has stretched out his thoughts into long strands, and accustomed him to internal dialogues.

"Do you still have it, Philip?" asks his old student after a long interlude.

Verheyen's laboratory is located in a small outbuilding, reached through a door in the entrance. He is not at all surprised by the sight inside, more reminiscent of an engraver's workshop, full of plates, etching basins, chiseling sets hanging on the wall, ready prints drying everywhere, and tangles of tow scattered across the floor. The guest unintentionally walks up to the printed sheets of paper—all of them show muscles and blood vessels, tendons and nerves. Carefully marked, absolutely transparent, perfect. There is also a microscope here, first-rate, an instrument that would be the envy of many, with lenses ground by Benedictus Spinoza, through which Philip observes the bundles of blood vessels.

Under the single, but large, south window there stands a clean broad table, and on it, the same specimen that has been there for goes over to the kitchen table and sets down the things he bought en route: a wheel of cheese, a loaf of bread, apples, and wine. He talks loudly, brags about tickets—this is the reason for his having come today. Philip has to make an effort not to let his face betray his irritation with the grimace of a person who's just landed in the middle of some horrendous clamor. He guesses that the reason for the arrival of this fellow—a nice fellow, at that—is explained in the letter that lies uncut in the entrance on the little table. As the guest lays out the victuals, the host cleverly hides the letter, and will henceforth pretend he knows its contents.

He will also pretend he hasn't been able to find a hostess, although he hasn't actually sought one out at all. He will pretend that he recognizes all the names his visitor will mention, although in reality his memory isn't good. He is a rector at the University of Leuven, but since the summer he has been holed up in the countryside, complaining of his health.

Together they kindle a fire and sit down to eat. The host eats reluctantly, but then it's clear that each bite further awakens his appetite. The wine goes well with the cheese and meat. Van Horssen shows him the tickets. They look at them in silence, and then Philip goes up to the window and sets the lenses of his glasses so as to better see the intricate drawing and lettering. Because even the ticket itself is a work of art—below the text at the top there is a beautiful illustration by Master Ruysch, a tableau of skeletons of human fetuses. Two of them sit around a composition consisting of rocks and dried branches, holding in their hands some musical instruments, one of which looks like a trumpet, another like a harp. Looking carefully at the tangle of lines, one can see there are even more years. Next to it you can see a jar containing nothing but straw-colored fluid that fills it two-thirds full.

"If we're to go to Amsterdam tomorrow, help me tidy this all up," says Philip, adding reproachfully: "I've been working."

He begins with his long fingers to delicately detach the tissues and vessels stretched out with the aid of tiny pins. His hands are as fast and as light as the hands of a butterfly-catcher, rather than an anatomist, or an engraver gouging grooves into hard metal that acid will later turn into a negative of an engraving. Van Horssen merely holds a jar of tincture in which parts of the specimen drown in a transparent, lightly brown liquid, as though returning home.

"Do you know what this is?" says Philip, and points with the nail of his pinky finger to the lighter substance above the bone. "Touch it."

The guest's finger extends to the dead tissue but doesn't reach it, remaining suspended in midair. The skin was cut in such a way as to reveal this place in a completely unexpected manner. No, he doesn't know what it is, but he makes a guess:

"It's the *musculus soleus*, a component of it."

His host looks at him for quite a while, as though looking for words.

"From now on it is the Achilles Cord," he says.

Van Horssen repeats after Verheyen, as though memorizing these two words.

"The Achilles tendon."

His hands, which he's wiped off with a rag, now take out from under the files of papers a diagram sketched out from four perspectives, incredibly accurate: the lower leg and foot make up a single whole, and it is already hard to believe that once they were not so put together, that in this place there was nothing at all, just some blurred image, now completely forgotten; everything had remained separate, and now it is together. How could this tendon never have been noticed? It's hard to believe that parts of one's own body are discovered as though one were forging one's way upriver in search of sources. In the same way one follows with a scalpel along some blood vessel and establishes its start. White patches get covered with the network of a drawing.

One discovers, and names. Conquers and civilizes. A piece of white cartilage will from now on be subject to our laws, we'll do with it what we will now.

But the thing that strikes young van Horssen most is the name. He's a poet, in fact, and despite his medical training, he would prefer to be writing verses. It is the name that opens up fairy-tale images in his mind, as though he were looking at Italian canvases peopled by full-blooded nymphs and gods. Could this part of the body be named any better, this part by which the goddess Thetis grabbed on to little Achilles to bathe him in the Styx and immunize him from death for all eternity?

Maybe Philip Verheyen has happened on the trail of a hidden order—maybe in our bodies there's a whole world of mythology? Maybe there exists some sort of reflection of the great and the small, the human body joining within itself everything with everything—stories and heroes, gods and animals, the order of plants and the harmony of minerals? Maybe we ought to take our names in that direction—the Artemis Muscle, the Athens Aorta, Hephaestus's Malleus and Incus, Mercury Spirals.

The men go to bed two hours after nightfall, both in one bed,

a double bed that must have been left here by the previous owners—
Philip has never had a wife. The night is cold, so they have to pile on
a few sheepskins, which with the damp prevailing throughout the
house give off a smell of sheep's fat and pens.

"You have to return to Leiden, to the university. We need you
there," begins van Horssen.

Philip Verheyen detaches the leather straps and sets his wooden
leg to one side.

"It hurts," he says.

Van Horssen understands he's talking about the stump set out on
the nightstand, but Philip Verheyen points beyond it, at the now
nonexistent part of his body, at empty space.

"The scars hurt?" the younger man asks. Whatever it is that
hurts, it doesn't lessen his great sympathy for this slender, fragile man.

"My leg hurts. I feel pain along the bone, and my feet drive me
mad. My big toe and its joint. They're swollen and inflamed, the
skin itches. Right here," he says, leaning down and indicating a
small crease in the sheets.

Willem is silent. What is he supposed to say? Then they both
lie down on their backs and pull the covers up to their necks. The
host blows out the candle and disappears, then says out of the
darkness:

"We must research our pain."


It is understandable that the ambulations of a man moving atop a
wooden orb cannot be too spry, but Philip is brave and were it not
for a slight limp and the clatter of his prosthesis down the bone-dry
way, it would be difficult to realize that this man is missing one leg.

The slower tempo also means there's time to talk. A crisp morning, the streets are lively, sunrise, the sun's disk scraped up by slender poplars—it's a pleasant walk. Halfway there they manage to stop a cart carrying vegetables to the Leiden market, thanks to which they have more time for a real breakfast at the Emperor's Inn.

Then from the harbor at the channel they get on a boat pulled overland by massive horses; they choose cheap places on deck under a tent that shields them from the sun, and because the weather is nice, the trip becomes pure pleasure.

And so I shall leave them—heading on a barge to Amsterdam, in a shadow-stain passing across the water cast by the covering of the tent over their heads. Both of them are dressed in black, wearing white starched batiste collars; van Horssen is more lavish, neater, which means just that he has a wife who takes care of his clothing, or that he can afford a servant—probably nothing more. Philip is sitting with his back to their direction of travel, comfortably leaning, with his healthy leg bent, his black leather slipper crowned by a dark purple tattered ribbon. The wooden orb leans on a knot in the boards of the barge. They both see each other against a backdrop of fleeting landscape: fields bordered with willows, drainage ditches, the piers of small harbors, and wooden houses covered in reeds. Goose down floats like tiny watercraft along the shore. A light warm breeze moves the feathers in their hats.

I will only add that in contrast to his master, van Horssen has no talent for drawing. He is an anatomist, and for each autopsy he hires a professional draftsman. His working method consists in precise notes, so precise that when he rereads them everything comes right back before his eyes. For this, too, is a way. Writing.

Moreover, as an anatomist, he tries to earnestly fulfill the recommendation of Mr. Spinoza, whose teachings were feverishly studied here until they were forbidden—to look at people as at lines, planes, and bodies.

## THE HISTORY OF PHILIP VERHEYEN, WRITTEN BY HIS STUDENT AND CONFIDANT WILLEM VAN HORSSEN

My teacher and master was born in 1648 in Flanders. His parents' home looked like any other Flemish home. It was built of wood and covered by a roof of reeds cut evenly just like young Philip's bangs. The flooring had been very recently done with clay bricks, and now members of the family declared their presence to one another with the clatter of their clogs. On Sunday the clogs were sometimes exchanged for leather shoes, and down the long straight road lined with poplars the three Verheyens would head out for church in Verrebroek. There they would take their places and await the pastor. Their work-worn hands would reach in gratitude for the prayer books; the thin sheets and tiny letters would strengthen their belief that they were more enduring than the fragile life of man. The Verrebroek pastor always began his sermon with the words "*Vanitas vanitatum.*" It could be taken as a greeting, and in fact, that is how little Philip always understood it.

Philip was a peaceful, quiet boy. He helped his father on the farm, but it soon became clear that he would not follow in his footsteps. He would not pour milk out every morning and mix it with the powder from calves' stomachs in order to shape giant wheels of cheese, nor rake out the hay into even piles. He would not observe in early spring whether in the furrows of plowed earth there hadn't collected any water. The pastor of Verrebroek made his parents understand that Philip was gifted enough that it would be worth educating him further after he completed his studies at the church school. And thus the fourteen-year-old boy began his education at the Heilige Drievuldigheid lyceum, where he demonstrated his outstanding ability at drawing.

If it is true that there are people who see the small things, and those who see only big things, then I am certain that Verheyen belonged to that first group. I even think that his body from the beginning felt best in that particular position—inclined over a table, with his legs resting on the bars of his chair, his spine curved into a bow, and his hands furnished with a feather pen that took not even the slightest interest in far-reaching goals, aiming close, within the kingdom of detail, the cosmos of little details, dashes and points, where the image is born. Etching and mezzotint—leaving in metal little traces, signs, the drawing of the smooth indifferent surface of a metal sheet, aging it till it became wise. He told me that the obverse always took him by surprise and confirmed his conviction that left and right are two completely different dimensions: their existence ought in fact to show us the suspect nature of what we naively take to be reality.

And although he was so adept at drawing, so occupied with engraving and etching, dyeing and printing, in his twenties Verheyen set out for Leiden to study theology and, like the pastor from Verrebroek, his mentor, become a pastor.

But even earlier—as he told me in connection with that excellent microscope that stood on his table—every so often that pastor would take him on short expeditions, a few miles down battered roads, to see a particular grinder of lenses, a brash Jew cursed out by his own, as he called them. This man rented out rooms in a stone house and seemed so exceptional that each such expedition was for Verheyen a great event, though he was too young to take part in any conversations, which he could only barely understand. The grinder apparently comported himself in a rather exotic, somewhat eccentric manner. He had a long gown, and on his head a tall stiff cap, which he never removed. He looked like a line, like a vertical pointer—so Philip told me and joked that if you were to put that oddball in a field he might serve the people as a sundial. Different people gathered at his house, merchants, students, and professors, who would sit around the wooden table beneath a large willow tree and have endless discussions. From time to time the host or one of the guests would give a lecture merely in order to get the discussion to flare up again. Philip recalled that the host spoke as though he were reading, fluidly, without mumbling. He'd build long sentences, the meaning of which would immediately escape the little boy, but the speaker governed them perfectly. The pastor and Philip would always bring something to eat. Their host would supply them with wine, which he lavishly diluted with water. This was as much as Verheyen remembered from these meetings, and Spinoza remained for all time his master, whom he would read and battle fervently. Perhaps it was these meetings with this ordered mind, with his power of thought and need to understand, that prompted young Philip to study theology in Leiden.

I am certain that we cannot recognize the fate grooved into the other side of life for us by the divine Engravers. They must appear to us only once they've taken a form intelligible to mankind, in black and white. God writes with his left hand and in mirror writing.

During his second year at university, in 1676, on a May evening, Philip, going up the narrow stairs to the little floor he rented from a certain widow, tore his trousers on a nail, also—as he saw only the following day—harmlessly injuring his calf. A red mark was left on his skin, drawn by the sharp part of the nail, a dash of a few centimeters adorned by drops of blood in little points; the careless movement of the Engraver on the delicate human body. After a few days a fever had begun to consume him.

When the widow finally called the medic, it turned out that the little wound had already been infected; its edges kindled to red and had swollen. The medic prescribed poultices and broth for strength, but already by the next evening it had become clear that there would be no way to stop the process, and that the leg would have to be cut off just below the knee.

"Not a week goes by that I don't have to amputate something off someone. You still have another leg," the medic apparently said to cheer up Philip. The medic would later become his friend, and he was my uncle, Dirk Kerkrinck, for whom Philip executed quite recently several anatomical engravings. "You'll have a wooden crutch made, and at worst you'll just be a bit noisier than you have been until now."

Kerkrinck had been a student of Frederik Ruysch, the best anatomist in the Netherlands, and perhaps the world, so the amputation was an exemplary one and came off perfectly. The part was divided from the whole smoothly, the bone sawed evenly, the blood vessels closed, cauterized precisely with a glowing-hot rod. Before the operation, the patient grabbed his future friend by the sleeve and begged him to preserve the removed leg. He had always been very religious, and he must have taken it literally that in our resurrected bodies we would rise from the grave in our physical form, with Christ's coming. He told me later that at the time he was very fearful that his leg might rise on its own; he wanted his body to be buried, when the time came, as a whole. Had it been an ordinary medic and not my uncle—had it been someone off the street, an ordinary barber-surgeon, the kind who cuts off warts and pulls out teeth—he would not, of course, have fulfilled this bizarre request. Ordinarily the severed limb would travel, shrouded in cloth, to the cemetery, where with solemnity, though with no religious formalities, it would be placed in a small hole, which they wouldn't even mark out. But my uncle, while the patient slept, knocked out by rectified spirit, took meticulous care of the leg. Above all with the aid of an injection of a substance, the composition of which his master had kept a secret, he removed from the blood and lymphatic vessels all the contaminated blood and infiltrations of gangrene. When the limb had been thus drained, he placed it in a glass vessel filled with a balm of Nantes brandy and black pepper, which was to permanently protect it from destruction. When Philip awoke from his alcoholized anesthesia, his friend showed him the leg drowned in brandy, just as mothers are shown newborns after giving birth.

Verheyen recuperated slowly, in the attic of a little house down one of the small streets of Leiden, where he was boarding with the widow. It was she who took care of him. Who knows how this would all have ended had she not been there. The patient became quite depressed, as a matter of fact; it's hard to say whether it was because of the ceaseless pain of the healing wound, or just because of his new situation. At the age of twenty-eight he had, after all, become an invalid, and his theological studies had thus ceased to make sense—without his leg, he could not be a pastor. He did not allow anyone to notify his parents, overwhelmed by shame at disappointing them. Dirk would pay him visits, as well as two colleagues drawn—it seems—less by the suffering of the patient than they were by the presence on his headboard of the amputated limb. It appeared this scrap of the human body was now living its own life as a specimen, submerged in alcohol, in a perpetual haze, dreaming its own dreams of running, of wet morning grass, of warm sand on the beach. A few fellow theology students also came to see him, and to them Philip ultimately confessed that he would not be returning to his studies.

When the guests would leave, the owner of the house, the widow, Mrs. Fleur—whom I later met and consider an angel—would appear in Philip's room. Philip lived in her home for quite a few more years, until he bought a house in Rijnsburg and settled down there for good. She'd bring with her a basin and a tin jug filled with hot water. Although the patient no longer had a fever, and no blood seeped out from his wound now, the woman would delicately wash off his leg and help the student bathe. She would then dress him in a clean shirt and trousers. The left legs of his trousers she had already sewn for him, and everything she touched with her clever hands looked natural, in order, as though that were precisely how God had created it, as though Philip Verheyen had been born without his left leg. When he had to get up to use the chamber pot, he would lean on the strong shoulder of the widow, which at first was exceedingly awkward, but then became natural, like everything connected with her. After several weeks she moved him downstairs, where he ate with her and her two children at the heavy wood kitchen table. She was tall and sturdy. She had wild, curly blond hair, like many Flemish women, which she concealed beneath a linen cap, though there was always one lock of it that escaped onto her back or over her forehead. I suspect that at night, as the children slept their innocent sleep, she would go to him as she did when with the chamber pot, and get into his bed. And I don't see anything wrong in it, for I believe that people ought to support each other in any way they can.

In the autumn, when the wound had healed completely, and upon the stump there remained only a reddish trace, Philip Verheyen, tapping his peg over the uneven paving stones of Leiden, went every morning to lectures at the university medical center, where he began his studies of anatomy.

He soon became one of the most respected students, for he was able to make use of his drawing talent like no one else in order to transfer onto paper what at first glance to the inexperienced eye looked like a chaos of tissues in the human body—tendons, blood vessels, and nerves. He also copied Vesalius's famous hundred-year-old atlas and acquitted himself very nicely of this exercise. It was the best introduction to his own work, the result of which would make him famous. To many of his students, among whom I, too, numbered, he had a paternal relationship—full of love, but also stern. Under his supervision we carried out autopsies, and then his attentive eye and expert hand would lead us down the paths of that most complicated labyrinth. Students valued his firmness and detailed knowledge. They watched the swift movements of his tracer as though witnessing a miracle. Drawing is never reproducing—in order to see, you have to know how to look, and you have to know what you're looking at.

He had always been rather taciturn, and today with the perspective of time I can say that he was also somehow absent, absorbed in himself. Gradually he gave up his lectures, shifting over fully to lonely work in his workshop. I would visit him often in his home in Rijnsburg. I was pleased to bring him news from the city, gossip and sensational stories from the university, but I was unsettled to notice that he had become increasingly obsessed with a single topic. His leg, dismantled into parts, investigated in as much detail as possible, always stood in its jar on his headboard or stretched scarily out on the table. When I realized that I was the only person he had any contact with, I also understood that Philip had crossed over an invisible boundary, a point of no return.

On that day in November our barge moored at Herengracht in Amsterdam in the early afternoon, and we went straight from the harbor to our destination. Since it was already the start of winter, the canals did not stink as mercilessly as in summer, and it was pleasant to walk in the warm milky fog, which before our eyes floated upward, revealing a serene autumn sky. We turned onto one of the narrow side streets of the Jewish neighborhood and wanted to stop somewhere for a beer. It was a good thing we had had a bountiful breakfast in Leiden, because all the inns we passed were overflowing with people, and we would have waited a long time to be served.

At the market, among the stalls, there is the Measures Building, where unloaded goods are weighed. In one of the towers enterprising Ruysch has arranged this theatrum, and this is where we arrived somewhat earlier than the hour printed on our tickets. Though none of the eager participants had yet been admitted inside, several little groups of viewers had gathered nonetheless at the entrance. I looked them over with interest, for the appearance and garments of many of them were testament to Professor Ruysch's fame having long since crossed the borders of the Netherlands. I heard conversations in foreign languages, saw French wigs on people's heads and English lace cuffs protruding from the sleeves of doublets. Many students had also come; they must have had cheaper, unassigned seats, because they were already crowding around the entrance, wanting to secure the best positions.

People we knew from when Philip was more active at the university—high-ranking members of the municipal council or the surgeons' guild, interested in what Ruysch was about to show us, what he'd come up with—approached us constantly. Then my uncle, the imprimatur of the tickets, arrived, dressed immaculately in black, and greeted Philip effusively.

The place looked like an amphitheater with benches set all around, all the way up, almost to the ceiling. It was well lit and carefully prepared for the spectacle. Along the walls down the entrance and the room itself were placed the skeletons of animals, bones connected by wires supported by discreet structures, giving the impression that the skeletons might at any moment come back to life. There were also two human skeletons—one on his knees, with his hands raised in prayer, and the other in a pensive pose, head resting on knees, the little bones of which were meticulously connected by wires.

When the audience, whispering and shuffling their shoes, entered the room and one by one took the seats indicated for them by their tickets, they also passed by Ruysch's famous compositions exhibited in display cabinets, elegant sculptures. "Death does not spare even youth," I read on the sign beneath one of them—it represented two fetus skeletons playing together: delicate cream-colored little bones, blistery little skulls planted around an elevation built from the equally delicate bones of small hands, rib cages. And symmetrically to them another tableau had been arranged, little human skeletons around four months old standing on an elevation of (as far as I could tell) gallstones covered in prepared and dried blood vessels (on the thickest such branch sat a stuffed canary). The skeleton on the left side held a miniature sickle while the other, in a forlorn pose, brought to its empty eye sockets a handkerchief made out of some sort of dried tissue, maybe lung? Someone's sensitive hand had decorated the whole in salmon lace and summed it up in elegant lettering on a silk ribbon: "Why would we miss the things of this world?" which meant it would have been difficult to be overcome by the sight. I was moved by the presentation before it had even begun, because it seemed to me I was seeing the tender evidence not of death, but of some death in miniature. How could they have truly died without ever having been born?

We took our places in the first row along with the other distinguished guests.

On the central table, amidst nervous calling whispers, lay the body already, ready for dissection, still covered in a piece of light-colored shiny fabric that barely gave a sense of its shape. It had already been announced on our tickets, like a delicious dish, *spécialité de la maison*: "Body prepared thanks to the scientific talent of Dr. Ruysch for preserving and reproducing the natural color and consistency, such that it may seem fresh and almost living." Ruysch kept the components of this extraordinary tincture in strict secret; no doubt that substance was an elaboration of the one that was still conserving Philip Verheyen's leg.

Soon every place had been occupied. Finally those in charge admitted a few dozen students; most of them were foreign, and they stood now around the walls among the skeletons in a strange sort of complicity with them, stretching out their necks just to see anything at all. Shortly before the performance, in the first row, the best places were taken by several elegant men dressed in foreign attire.

Ruysch came out with two helpers. It was they who, after a short introduction by the professor, simultaneously lifted the covering on both sides and revealed the body.

No surprise that from all sides we heard a gasp.

It was the body of a slender young woman; as far as I know, only the second such to be presented for a public dissection. Until now, anatomy lessons were permitted only on male bodies. My uncle whispered to us that this was some Italian whore who had killed her newborn child. Her swarthy, smooth, perfect skin looked from here, from the first row, from barely a meter away, flushed and fresh. The lobes of her ears and the toes on her feet were lightly red, as though she'd lain too long in a cold room and frozen. She was no doubt covered in some sort of oil, or perhaps this was part of Ruysch's preservation treatments, because she was glowing. From the ribs down, her stomach fell, and over this petite olive-skinned body rose the mound of Venus, as though the most important, most significant bone in the system. Even for me, used as I was to dissection, it was a moving sight. Normally dissections were performed upon the bodies of convicts who had not taken care of themselves, playing with their lives and health. What was shocking was the perfection of this body, and here I truly had to appreciate Ruysch's care and foresight for having managed to get it in such a good state and prepare it so well.

Ruysch commenced the lesson, addressing those gathered, thoughtfully mentioning the title of all the attending doctors of medicine, professors of anatomy, surgeons, and officials.

"Greetings, gentlemen, and I thank you for coming in such numbers. Thanks to the generosity of our magistrate, I reveal to your eyes what nature has hidden in our bodies. And not at all out of a desire to unload bad feelings on this poor body, nor from a need to punish it for the act it committed, but rather so that we might discover ourselves, and the way in which we were made by the hand of the Creator."

He told us that the body was two years old already, which means that during that time it had lain in the morgue, and that thanks to the method he invented, he had been able to preserve it fresh until today. When I looked this way at the naked, defenseless, beautiful body, my throat tightened, and after all I am not someone on whom the sight of human corpses makes any impression. But it made me think that we could have anything, be anyone, if—as they say—we wanted it badly enough; for man stands at the very center of creation, and our world is the human world, not the divine world nor anyone else's. There is only one thing we cannot have—eternal life, and, by God, whence did that concept come into our heads, that idea of being immortal?

. . .

He introduced the first cut expertly along the abdominal wall; somewhere on the right side of the auditorium someone apparently fell ill, because for a moment there was a murmur in the audience.

"This young woman was hung," said Ruysch, and he raised the body to show us the neck; indeed, you could see a horizontal trace, barely a dash, hard to believe it might have been the reason for her death.

At first he focused on the organs in the abdominal cavity. He discussed in detail the digestive system, but before he moved on to the heart, he let us look into everything below, where from beneath the mount shone the uterus, enlarged after giving birth, and everything he did, even to us, his colleagues, belonging to the same guild, looked like a magic show. The movements of his bright, slender hands were circular, fluid, like on those fairground wizards. Our eyes followed him, fascinated.

That small body opened up before the audience, revealed its secrets, trustingly, believing that such hands would not do it harm. Ruysch's commentary was brief, coherent, and comprehensible. He even joked, though gracefully, as though without lessening his dignity. Then I also understood the essence of this presentation, its popularity; Ruysch with these round gestures was transforming the human essence into a body and before our eyes undressing it of mystery, breaking it down into prime factors as though taking apart a complicated clock. The threat of death slipped away. There's nothing to be afraid of. We are a mechanism, something like Huygens's clock.

After the show people left in silence and fascination, and what remained of the body was mercifully covered with that same fabric.

But after just a moment, outside, where the sun had completely chased away the clouds, they began to talk more boldly, and the audience—including ourselves—went to the magistrate for the banquet prepared for this occasion.

Philip remained gloomy and silent and did not appear at all interested in the delicious food, wine, and tobacco. To tell the truth, I wasn't in the mood myself. It would be wrong to think that we anatomists approach each dissection as though it were part of our daily order. Sometimes, like today, something is "raised," something I myself call "the truth of the body," an odd conviction that despite the evidence of death, despite the absence of a soul, the body left to itself is a kind of intensive whole. Of course the dead body is not alive; what I mean is more the fact of it remaining in its form. Form is in its way alive.

That lesson of Ruysch's marked the beginning of the winter season, and now at De Waag there would be regular lectures, discussions, demonstrations of vivisections of animals, both for students and for the public. And if circumstances supply fresh bodies, public autopsies performed by other anatomists would also take place. Only Ruysch was able, for now, to prepare a body in advance, even two years in advance, as he'd said today (something I still find hard to believe)—and only he did not have to fear the summer heat.

Were it not for the fact that I accompanied him the next day on his way home—first by boat, then on foot—I would never have found out what it was that Philip Verheyen suffered from. But even so, what I heard from him seems strange and extraordinary to me. As a doctor and anatomist I had already heard several times about this phenomenon, but I had always attributed such pains to oversensitivity of the nerves, an exuberant imagination. Meanwhile I had known Philip for years, and no one could equal his exactitude of mind, nor the reliability of his observations and his judgments. An intellect applying the correct method can attain true and useful knowledge about the tiniest details of the world through the aid of its own distinct and clear ideas—this he taught us at the same university where fifteen years before the mathematician Descartes had lectured. Because God, perfect to the utmost degree, who provided us after all with cognitive faculties, cannot be a deceiver; if we use those faculties correctly, we must reach truth.

The pains came at night, starting a few weeks after the operation, as his body was relaxing and slipping across the uncertain boundary between waking and sleep, filled with traveling unsettling images, the travelers inside the sleeping mind. He would have the impression that his left leg was numb, and that he absolutely had to get it into the right position—he felt his toes tingling, an unpleasant sensation. He fidgeted, half conscious. He wanted to move his toes, but the unperformability of that movement awoke him completely. He would sit on the bed, tear the blanket off himself, and look at the aching place—it was some thirty centimeters below the knee, there over the rumbled sheet. He would close his eyes and try to scratch it, but he touched nothing, his fingers combed the void in despair, giving him no relief.

Once, in a fit of despair, when the pain and itching were driving him mad, he stood and with trembling hands lit a candle. Hopping on one foot, he moved to the table the vessel with the cut-off leg, which Fleur, unable to convince him to transfer it to the attic, had covered with a flowery shawl. He extracted the limb and in the candlelight tried to locate in it the reason for the pain. The leg now seemed somewhat smaller, the skin browned by the brandy, but the toenails remained raised, pearlescent, and Verheyen had the impression they had grown. He sat down on the floor, stretched his legs out before him, and laid the amputated limb on the place just below his left knee. He closed his eyes and groped for the painful place. His hand touched a cold piece of flesh—but could not reach the pain.

Verheyen worked on his own atlas of the human body methodically and persistently.

First the dissection—the careful preparation of a model to draw, the unveiling of some muscle, bundle of nerves, the extension of a blood vessel, the outstretching of the specimen in two-dimensional space, the reduction to four directions: up, down, left, and right. He used minute wooden pins to help himself render the complex more transparent and clear. Only then would he emerge, carefully wash and dry his hands, change his surface clothing, and then return with the paper and graphite graver, in order to make order on paper.

He did the dissections sitting down, trying in vain to control bodily fluids that ruined the clarity and accuracy of the image. He transferred the details to paper in hurried sketches, and then, now in peace, he would revise them carefully, detail by detail, nerve by nerve, tendon by tendon.

Evidently the amputation strained his health, because he often suffered from weakness and melancholy. The pain of his left leg, which troubled him ceaselessly, he termed "phantom," but he was afraid to mention it to anyone, suspecting that he was the victim of some nervous illusion or of madness. He would no doubt have lost his high position at the university had anyone found out about it. Very quickly he began working as a doctor and was accepted into the guild of surgeons. His lack of a leg meant that he was called more often than others for any kind of amputation, as though his personal experience guaranteed the success of the operation, or as though a legless surgeon brought—if it could be called this—good fortune in disease. He published particular works on the anatomy of muscles and tendons. When in 1689 he was offered the position of rector of the university, he moved to Leuven, taking in his luggage the tightly packed vessel with the leg in its rolls of linen.

It was I, Willem van Horssen, who served as messenger, when several years later in 1693 I was sent by the printer to show Verheyen the fat edition of his first book—the great anatomical atlas *Corporis humani anatomia*, still damp from the printer's ink. It contained twenty years' worth of his work. Every etching, perfectly executed, transparent and clear, was supplemented by an explanatory text, so that it seemed that in this volume the human body became some sort of mysterious procedure etched down to its very essence, relieved of easily spoiling blood, lymphs, those suspect fluids, the roar of life, that its perfect order had been revealed in the absolute silence of black and white. *Anatomia* brought him fame, and after a few years the work was revised in an even larger print run and became a textbook.

The last time I went to Philip Verheyen's was in November 1710, called by his servant. I found my friend in a very poor state and it was difficult to communicate with him. He was sitting at the south window, looking through it, but I had no doubt that the only things this man could see were his own internal images. He didn't really

react to my entrance, just looked at me without interest, or any sort
of gesture, then turned back to the window. On the table lay his leg,
or what remained of it, for it had been taken apart into hundreds
or thousands of little pieces, tendons, muscles, and nerves broken
down into their smallest components, all of which covered the whole
surface of the table. His servant, a simple person from the country,
was frightened. He was afraid to even go into his master's room, and
the whole while he gave me signs behind his back, silently comment-
ing on his reactions, moving just his lips. I examined Philip the best
I could, but the diagnosis wasn't good—it seemed that his brain had
stopped working and that he had fallen into some sort of apathy. I
knew, of course, that he suffered attacks of melancholy; now the
black bile had reached the level of his brain—perhaps because of
those, as he called them, phantom pains. The last time I had brought
him maps, for I had heard that nothing cures melancholy like looking at maps. I prescribed him rich foods for strength, and rest.

At the end of January, I learned that he had died and immediately hastened to Rijnsburg. I found his body already prepared for
the funeral, washed and shaved, lying in a coffin. Around his
cleaned-up home were some relatives from Leiden, and when I
asked the servant about his leg, he only shrugged. The great table
by the window had been scrubbed and washed with lye. When I
tried to ask further what had become of that leg, which Philip had
repeated so many times he wanted buried with his body, the family
dismissed me. He was buried without it.

By way of comfort and appeasement I was given a sizable stack
of Verheyen's papers. The funeral took place on the twenty-ninth
day of January in the abbey of Vlierbeek.

## LETTERS TO THE AMPUTATED LEG

The loose pages I received after Verheyen's death put me in confusion. Throughout the last years of his life my teacher recorded his thoughts in the form of letters to a particular correspondent, a circumstance I'm certain anyone would deem sufficient proof of his madness. However, when one carefully reads these hurried notes, which were almost certainly intended as an aide-mémoire rather than for someone else's eyes, one sees in them the record of a kind of journey to an unknown land and an attempt to sketch out its map.

I thought long and hard about what I ought to do with this unexpected inheritance, but I decided against its publication in any form. I, his student and friend, would prefer for him to be remembered as a wonderful anatomist and draftsman, who first identified the Achilles tendon and several previously unnoticed parts of our body. I would prefer for us to remember his beautiful engravings and accept that it is impossible to understand everything of anyone else's life. But to address the rumors that have been spreading after his death in Amsterdam and Leiden—that the master had gone mad—I wish to briefly present several excerpts from his papers here and demonstrate in so doing that he was not mad. I have no doubts, meanwhile, that Philip allowed himself to be overwhelmed by a particular obsession connected with his inexplicable pain. Obsession is, in any case, the premonition of the existence of an individual language, an irreproducible language through the attentive use of which we will be able to uncover the truth. We must follow this premonition into regions that to others might seem absurd and mad. I don't know why this language of truth sounds angelic to some, while to others it changes into mathematical signs or notations. But there are also those to whose whim it speaks in a very strange way.

In *Letters to My Amputated Leg*, Philip attempted to prove coherently and without emotion that since the body and soul are in essence one and the same, since they are two attributes of an infinite, all-encompassing God, there must be between them some sort of proportionality designed by the Creator. *Totam naturam unum esse individuum.* This is in essence what interested him the most: In what way do such distinct substances as the body and the soul connect in the human body and act upon one another? In what way can the body, occupying space, establish causal contact with a soul that occupies no space? How and from whence does pain arise?

He wrote, for example:

What is it that awakens me, when I feel pain and suffering, since my leg has been separated from me and is floating now in alcohol? There is nothing pinching it, no reason for its suffering, no such pain that can be logically justified, and yet it exists. Now I look at it and simultaneously feel in it, in the toes, unbearably hot, as though I were submerging it in hot water, and this experience is so real, so obvious, that if I were to shut my eyes, I would see in my own imagination the bucket of water overly heated and my own foot submerged from toes to ankle. I touch my bodily existing limb in the guise of a lump of preserved flesh—and I don't feel it. I feel, meanwhile, something that does not exist, it is in a physical sense an empty place, there is nothing there that might give any sensation whatsoever. The thing that hurts does not exist. A phantom. Phantom pain.

. . .

The combination of these words initially appeared strange to him, but he soon began to use the phrase readily. He also took detailed notes on the progressive dissection of the leg. He took it more and more apart; after a while he was left with no choice but to proceed with the aid of a microscope.

"The body is something absolutely mysterious," he wrote.

The fact that we so precisely describe it does not at all mean that we know it. It is like an argument from Spinoza, that lens grinder who polishes glass precisely in order that we are able to examine everything more closely, who creates an incredibly difficult language in order to express his thought because it is said: seeing is knowing.

I want to know, and not give in to logic. What do I care about a proof from the outside, framed as a geometric argument? It provides merely a semblance of logical consequence and of an order pleasing to the mind. There's A, and after A comes B, first definitions, then axioms and numbered theorems, some supplementary conclusions— and you might have the impression that such command is reminiscent of a wonderfully sketched etching in an atlas, where with letters particular sections are marked, where everything seems so clear and transparent. But we still don't know how it all works.

Yet he believed in the power of reason. And that it was in its nature to consider things as necessary, not accidental. Otherwise, of course, reason would negate itself. He argued over and over that we had to trust our reason, because it was given us by God, and God is after all perfect, so how could He furnish us with something that would deceive us? God is not a deceiver! If we use the powers of our intellect in the right way, we will ultimately attain truth, learn everything about God and about ourselves, we who are a piece of Him, like everything else.

He insisted that the highest sort of reason is intuitive, not logical. Learning intuitively, we will immediately notice the deterministic necessity of the existence of all things. Everything that is necessary cannot be otherwise. When we really realize this, we will experience great relief and purification. We will no longer be unsettled by the loss of our belongings, by the passage of time, by aging or death. In this way we will gain control over our affects and attain some peace of mind.

We must simply remember the primitive desire to judge what is good and what is bad, just as civilized man must remember primitive drives—revenge, greed, possessiveness. God, which is to say nature, is neither good nor bad; it's an ill-used intellect that stains our emotions. Philip believed that all our knowledge of nature is in reality knowledge of God. This is what frees us from the sorrow, the despair, the envy and anxiety that are our hell.

It's true that Philip addressed the leg as though talking to a living, independent person, I will not deny that. Separated from him, it took on some sort of demonic autonomy, simultaneously maintaining with him a painful relationship. I also confess that these are the most unsettling portions of his letters, but at the same time I have no doubt that this is just a metaphor, a kind of mental shortcut. He was thinking that what once formed a whole but was then broken down into parts is still powerfully connected, in an invisible way that is difficult to investigate. For the nature of this relationship is not clear, and it would no doubt elude the microscope.

It is, however, obvious, of course, that we can trust only physiology and theology. These are the two pillars of knowledge. What lies between them does not count at all.

As we read his notes, it must thus be remembered that Philip Verheyen was a man who suffered ceaselessly and without knowing the reason for his pain. Let us keep that in mind when we read his words:

Why am I in pain? Is it because—as that lens grinder says, and perhaps only in this does he not err—in essence the body and soul are part of something larger and something shared, states of the same substance, like water that can be both liquid and solid? How can what does not exist cause me pain? Why do I feel this lack, sense this absence? Are we perhaps condemned to wholeness, and every fragmentation, every quartering, will only be a pretense, will happen on the surface, underneath which, however, the plan remains intact, unalterable? Does even the smallest fragment still belong to the whole? If the world, like a great glass orb, falls and shatters into a million pieces—doesn't something great, powerful, and infinite remain a whole in this?

Is my pain God?

I've spent my life traveling, into my own body, into my own amputated limb. I've prepared the most accurate maps. I have dismantled the thing under investigation per the best methodology, breaking it down into prime factors. I've counted the muscles, tendons, nerves, and blood vessels. I've used my own eyes for this, but relied, too, on the cleverer vision of the microscope. I believe I have not missed even the smallest part.

Today I can ask myself this question: What have I been looking for?

## TRAVEL TALES

Am I doing the right thing by telling stories? Wouldn't it be better to fasten the mind with a clip, tighten the reins, and express myself not by means of stories and histories, but with the simplicity of a lecture, where in sentence after sentence a single thought gets clarified, and then others are tacked onto it in the succeeding paragraphs? I could use quotes and footnotes, I could in the order of points or chapters reap the consequences of demonstrating step by step what it is I mean; I would verify an aforementioned hypothesis and ultimately be able to carry off my arguments like sheets after a wedding night, in view of the public. I would be the mistress of my own text, I could take an honest per-word payment for it.

As it is I'm taking on the role of midwife, or of the tender of a garden whose only merit is at best sowing seeds and later to fight tediously against weeds.

Tales have a kind of inherent inertia that is never possible to fully control. They require people like me—insecure, indecisive, easily led astray. Naive.

## THREE HUNDRED KILOMETERS

I dreamed that I was looking from above at cities splayed out across valleys and on mountain slopes. From that perspective it was very clear that those cities were the felled trunks of once enormous trees, probably gigantic redwoods and ginkgoes. I wondered how high the trees must have been, since today their trunks contained whole towns. Excited, I tried to calculate their heights, using a simple ratio I remembered from school:

A is to B as

C is to D

---

A x D = C x B

If A is the surface of the cross section of the tree, B its height, C the surface area of a town, and D the height of the town-tree I was trying to figure out, then assuming the average tree had a cross-sectional area of around 1 $m^2$ at its base and a height of 30 m, then the town (or rather small settlement) would be 1 ha (or 10,000 $m^2$):

1—30

10,000—D

---

1 x D = 10,000 x 30

which gives a result of 300 km.

This was the answer I got in that dream. The tree would have been three hundred kilometers high. I fear this slumbering arithmetic can't be taken too seriously.

## 30,000 GUILDERS

"It's not such a great sum, really, in the end. It's the annual income of a merchant trading with the colonies, on the assumption that there is peace in the world and the English aren't arresting Dutch ships, resulting in interminable legal wranglings. It is in fact a reasonable sum. To it must be added the cost of strong and stable wooden crates, and transport."

Peter I, tsar of the Russian Empire, had just paid this sum for the collection of anatomical specimens amassed over the years by Frederik Ruysch.

The tsar was traveling all around Europe with a retinue of two hundred people in 1697. He greedily took in everything, but he was most drawn to the Wunderkammers. Perhaps he, too, had some sort of syndrome. After Louis XIV refused the tsar an audience, he remained for several months in the Netherlands. Several times he came incognito, accompanied by several sturdy-looking fellows, to De Waag, to the Theatrum Anatomicum, where with a look of concentration on his face he watched the fluid movements of the professor as his scalpel opened and displayed to the public the bodies of the condemned. He also initiated a kind of friendship with the master. It could be said that they became close, as Ruysch taught the tsar how to preserve butterflies.

But what he liked the most was Ruysch's collection—hundreds of specimens enclosed in glass jars, swimming in fluid, a panopticon of the human imagination broken down into component parts, a mechanical cosmos of organs. He got chills when he looked at human fetuses, and he couldn't take his eyes off them, so fascinating was the sight. And the dramatic, fanciful arrangements of human bones that got him into a pleasant, contemplative mood. He had to have the collection for himself.

The jars were carefully packed into boxes lined with tow, tied with twine, and taken by horse to the port. Some dozen sailors spent an entire day loading the valued goods belowdecks. The professor himself supervised the loading, cursing and flying into rages because one careless movement had already destroyed a beautiful

example of acephaly, a very rare specimen. Ordinarily he didn't
keep aberrations, preferring to focus on pieces that reflected the
beauty and harmony of the body. Now the glass cover had broken,
his famed conserving mixture pouring out onto the pavement and
soaking in between the paving stones. The specimen, meanwhile,
had rolled down the dirty street, rupturing in two places. On one
shard of glass a label inscribed carefully in the hand of the professor's daughter was visible, with an ornate inscription in a black
frame: "*Monstrum humanum acephalum.*" A rare specimen, extraordinary. A shame. The professor had wrapped it up in a handkerchief and, limping, carried it home. Perhaps something could
still be done with it.

It was a sad sight—rooms now empty after the sale of the collection. Professor Ruysch cast a lingering gaze over them and noted on
the wooden shelves some darker stains—flat projections of the
three-dimensional jars, traces in the ubiquitous dust, barely a width
and length, without a hint of reference to their contents.

He was getting close to eighty now. The collection was the product of his work over the past thirty years, for he had started fairly
early. He can be seen in a painting by someone named Backer,
conducting the best anatomy lessons in town at the age of thirty-
two. The painter managed to capture the particular expression on
young Ruysch's face—self-confidence and mercantile cunning. In
the painting we also see a body prepared for dissection, the corpse
of a young man perspectivally foreshortened, looking fresh. The
body looks alive—the skin color is a milky pink, not at all that of
a corpse; its bent knee brings to mind the movement of a person

lying naked on his back but instinctively about to cover the shameful part of his body before prying eyes. It's the body of hanged convict Joris van Iperen, a thief. The surgeons cloaked in black are to this embarrassed and defenseless dead body an unsettling contrast. It shows what thirty years later made the professor's fortune—that mixture of his creation preserves the freshness of tissues for a very long time. Likely the same composition that Ruysch used to conserve his rare anatomical specimens. Deep down he worries he won't have time to reproduce it now, although he feels exceptionally well.

The professor's daughter, a fifty-year-old woman entirely dedicated to him, with delicate hands hidden in cream-colored lace, is just organizing the girls to clean up. Almost no one remembers what her name is, and she's perfectly content with "Professor Ruysch's daughter" and "Miss," as the cleaning women call her. But we remember—it's Charlotta. She has the right to sign documents on behalf of her father, and the signatures are impossible to tell apart. In spite of her delicate hands, that lace, and her extensive anatomical knowledge, she will not go down in history alongside her father. She will not be immortal like him, in human memory and in textbooks. Even the specimens will outlive her, the same ones she prepared with such enormous dedication, anonymously. All those beautiful tiny little fetuses will outlive her, leading their quiet paradisiacal lives in the golden liquid, in their Stygian elixir. Some of them, the most valuable ones, rare as orchids, have an extra pair of hands or feet, because unlike her father, she is fascinated by what is flawed and imperfect. The microcephaly she managed to track down and bribe midwives for. Or the gargantuan intestines, hypertrophied, she got from surgeons. Medics from the provinces made Professor Ruysch's daughter special offers of particular tumors, calves with five legs, the dead fetuses of twins with conjoined heads. But it is to the city's midwives that she owes the most. She has been a good client, although she knows how to strike a bargain.

Her father will leave the business to her brother, Henrik, who appears in the painting done thirteen years after that first one—Charlotta sees it daily on her way down the stairs. In it her father is now a mature man with a carefully trimmed Spanish beard. He wears a wig; this time his hand, equipped with surgical scissors, is raised over the open body of an infant. The abdominal walls are already spread, revealing the order of the interior. Charlotta associates it with a beloved doll that had a pale little porcelain face and a rag torso stuffed with sawdust.

She never got married, which did not bother her; after all, she has dedicated her life to her father. She'll have no children, unless you count those beautiful pale ones swimming in alcohol.

She always regretted that her sister, Rachel, was given away in marriage. She used to work with her, preparing specimens. But Rachel had always been more interested in art than science. She had never wanted to wet her hands in formalin and felt sick at the smell of blood. But she had decorated the specimen jars with floral motifs. She had also come up with compositions out of the bones, especially those smallest ones, which she then gave fanciful titles. But she moved with her husband to Den Haag, and Charlotta was left alone, because brothers don't count.

She drags her finger along the wooden surface of the shelf, leaving a trace. In a moment it will be wiped away by the cloths of the complying girls. She's so sorry to have lost the collection, to which she's given everything. She turns her head to the window so the servants don't notice her tears, and she sees the ordinary city commotion. She fears that there, in the Far North, the jars won't be appropriately stored or maintained. The lacquer sealing the lids sometimes loses its cohesion under the influence of the vapors of the preserving mixture, and then the alcohol evaporates. She wrote this all out very carefully in a long, detailed missive she included with the collection, in Latin. But can they read Latin there?

She will not sleep tonight. She's as worried as if she'd just seen her own sons off on a journey to a distant university. From experience she knows, however, that the best medicine for worrying is work, work for work's sake, which is its own pleasure and reward. She shushes the frolicking girls, who fear her stern figure. They must think that someone like her will go straight to heaven.

But what is heaven to her? What would she find in a heaven of anatomists? It's dark and boring; they're clustered around motionless, standing over open human bodies, just men in dark clothing that barely stands out from the gloom. On their faces, slightly lit by the glow off their white collars, you can see an expression of satisfaction, or even triumph. She's a loner, she doesn't care about being around people. So neither failure nor success concerns her. She clears her throat loudly now, to give herself courage, and kicking up with the movement of her skirt a cloud of dust, she goes out.

But she doesn't go home; she's drawn in the opposite direction, toward the sea, to the port, and after a while she notices from afar the high slender masts of the ships of the East India Company; they sit in the roadstead as little boats float between them, bringing goods to port. Barrels and crates with the logo "VOC" stamped and nailed onto them. Half naked, glistening with sweat, tanned men bear chests of pepper, cloves, and nutmeg down planks. The smell of the sea, fishy, salty, is flavored with cinnamon here. She goes along the waterfront until she sees from afar the tsar's three-master; she passes it quickly because she doesn't even want to look at it or imagine that the jars are sitting now in some dark hold stinking of fish, dirty, that they are being touched by unknown hands, and that they will have to spend many days there, without light, without human eyes on them.

She quickens her pace and walks all the way up to the docks, where she sees ships getting ready for their voyages; soon they will be sailing Danish and Norwegian seas. These ships are completely different from the ones belonging to the Company: decked out, painted bright, with galleons in the shapes of sirens and mythological figures. These ones are rather simple, crude . . .

She comes upon the scene of a drill. Two officials in black clothing and brown wigs sitting on the waterfront at a spread-out table, and in front of them a sizable group of recruits—these are fishermen from neighboring villages, tattered, unshaven, unwashed since Easter at least, with long skulls.

A crazy thought comes to her mind—that she could dress up in any sort of men's rags, coat her shoulders in stinking oil, use it to darken her face, cut her hair off, and go and join that line. Time mercifully annihilates the differences between man and woman; and she knows she's not beautiful, that with her already somewhat drooping cheeks and her mouth in the parentheses of two wrinkles she could pass as a man. Infants and old people look the same. So what is keeping her? A heavy dress, the abundance of petticoats, an uncomfortable white coronet that holds tight her miserable hair; her old, mad father, his attacks of greed when with a bony finger he pushes in her direction along the wood of the table a coin for the upkeep of the house? Who in his carefully masked madness has already decided they will begin again from scratch—she is to prepare herself. They will reproduce the collection in a few years, pay the midwives to be on their guard and not miss a single stillbirth or miscarriage.

She could embark tomorrow; she has heard they still need sailors at the Company. She could get on one of those ships that would take her to Texel, where a whole fleet is waiting. The Company ships are bulky, with great bellies, squat, so they can fit as much as possible— silk, porcelain, carpets, and spices. She would be quiet as a mouse, no one would even realize; she's quite tall and sturdy, and she would bind her breasts with a band of canvas. And even if it came out, they'd be somewhere on the open seas, on the way to the East Indies—what could they do to her then? At most they'd kick her off in some civilized place, for example in Batavia, where apparently— she's seen this on engravings—monkeys run in packs and sit on the roofs of houses, and all year round fruits grow as in paradise, and it is so warm no one even wears stockings.

So she thinks, so she imagines, but then her attention is drawn by a big, sturdy man and his naked shoulders, his naked torso, tattooed, covered in colorful drawings dominated by ships, sails, half-naked women with darker skin; it is as though this man wore his life story written out on his own body, these drawings must represent his travels and lovers. Charlotta can't take her eyes off him. The man throws over his shoulder bundles sewn up in gray canvas and carries them down the planks onto a medium-sized boat. He must feel her gaze on him, because he looks at her fleetingly, neither smiling nor frowning, because she's no attraction to him. An old maid in black. But she can't take her eyes off his tattoos. She sees on his shoulder a colorful fish, a great whale, and because the sailor's muscles are working, she has the impression that this whale is alive and that it lives with this man in some sort of unprecedented symbiosis, on his skin, glued to it for all time, traveling from his shoulder blade toward his chest. This big, sturdy body makes an enormous impression on her. She feels her legs get slow and heavy, and her body opens up from below, that's how it feels—it opens up, to that shoulder, to that whale.

She clenches her teeth so tight her head roars. She starts to walk along the canal toward him, but in the end she slows and stops. She's overcome by a strange feeling that the water here is overflowing onto the banks. Gently, at first checking with the first waves the place of its expansion, then it grows bolder, pours out onto the paving stones, and in a moment it's reached the first steps of the nearest houses' stairs. Charlotta feels distinctly the weight of the element— her skirts absorb the water, become leaden, she can't move. She feels this flood in every inch of her body and sees the surprised boats battering the trees; always lined up with their bows against the current, now they've lost their direction.

## THE TSAR'S COLLECTION

The next day at dawn the Russian sailboat with the collection carefully arranged in the hold raised its anchor and headed out to sea. It met with good fortune crossing the Danish straits, and after several days it was received by the Baltic. The captain, in a good mood, was contemplating his recent purchase, a beautifully executed tellurion by Dutch artisans. He had always been interested in such things much more than sailing itself, and deep down he would rather have been an astronomer, a cartographer, someone who reaches beyond the space available to our gaze and our ships.

From time to time he went down into the hold and checked to make sure the precious cargo was still in place, but somewhere around Gotland the weather changed—after a not-too-violent storm the wind dropped. The air hovered over the sea, forming a great block of atmospheric amber out of August's final heat. The sails slumped, and this went on for several days. The captain, in order to occupy people somehow, ordered them to roll and unroll the halyards, scrub the deck, and in the evenings he made them go through drills. After dark, his authority lost its outlines somewhat, and he snuck back into the cozy cocoon of his cabin, partly of wariness toward these gruff, primitive sailors, partly on account of his travel journal, which he was writing for his two sons.

On the eighth day of dead calm the sailors began to be stormy themselves, and the vegetables they'd bought in Amsterdam, especially the onions, turned out to be poor quality and in large part moldy. Their supply of vodka was already running out—the captain was actually afraid to look under the deck, where they kept the barrels, but the reports from his first officer certainly did not bode well. The captain felt uneasy as nocturnal clattering on deck reached his ears. At first they were individual steps. But then it was several pairs of legs knocking, and in the end he heard a peaceable trot and a rhythmic shouting (could they be dancing?), which finally transitioned into raucous drunken shouts and uneven choruses sung so pathetically and painfully that it reminded him of the wailing of some marine animals. This happened over several long nights, almost until dawn. By day he saw the sailors' puffy eyes and swollen eyelids and their gazes that avoided him. But both he and his first officer agreed that deepest darkness at stilled sea would hardly favor any behavioral correctives. It wasn't until the tenth day of silence, when the nocturnal excesses could no longer be tolerated, that he went out onto the deck, in full sun so that his epaulets and insignia could be seen, and arrested the ringleader, a man by the name of Kalukin.

Unfortunately, with a trembling heart, he confirmed his suspicions that some of the cargo had been damaged. Some dozen or so of the hundreds of jars they were transporting had been opened, and their liquid contents, a strong brandy, drunk till the last drop.

The specimens themselves were still there, lying around on the floor, submerged in tow and sawdust. He didn't take too close a look at them, out of disgust and fear. The next night he made some men stand with arms in hand to guard the entrance to the hold; a mutiny was close to breaking out. The August heat was driving the men crazy. And the smoothness of the surface of the sea. And the cargo itself.

In the end there was no other way—the captain had the remains that were left sewn up in a cloth bag, and he personally threw them overboard. And as though at the touch of a wizard's wand, the sea, mollified by this morsel, smacked and moved. Somewhere near the Swedish mainland the wind came in and pushed the tsar's sailboat toward home.

When they got back to Petersburg the captain had to write a secret report. Kalukin was convicted and hanged, and the collection itself, though incomplete, was transferred safely to rooms prepared expressly for it.

The captain, meanwhile, for his failure to take care of the transport, was sent along with his family to the Far North, where for the rest of his life he organized little fishing expeditions and contributed to the drawing up of more detailed maps of Nova Zembla.


## IRKUTSK–MOSCOW

Flight from Irkutsk to Moscow. It takes off at 8:00 a.m. and lands in Moscow at the same time—at eight o'clock in the morning on that same day. It turns out to be right at sunrise, which means the whole flight takes place during dawn. Passengers remain in this one moment, a great, peaceful Now, vast as Siberia itself.

So there should be time enough for confessions of whole lifetimes. Time elapses inside the plane but doesn't trickle out of it.


## DARK MATTER

In the third hour of the flight, when the man sitting next to me came back from the bathroom and I had to get up to let him in again, we exchanged a few polite remarks on the weather, the turbulence, and the food. During the fourth hour of the flight, however, we introduced ourselves. He was a physicist. He was returning home after giving a series of lectures. When he took off his shoes, I noticed he had an enormous hole in the heel of his sock. Thus I became aware of the physical presence of the physicist, and from that point forward we spoke in a more ordinary way. He told me stories about whales with great enthusiasm, although his work dealt with something else.

Dark matter—that was what he worked on. It's a thing that we know exists, but without being able to access it, with any instruments. The evidence of its existence arises out of complicated calculations, mathematical results. All signs point to it occupying some three-quarters of the universe. Our matter, clear matter, the matter with which we are familiar and which makes up our cosmos, is inordinately scarcer. Dark matter, meanwhile, is located everywhere, says this man in the sock with the hole in it—right here, all around us. He gazes out the window, indicating with his eyes the blindingly bright clouds beneath us: "It's out there, too. Everywhere. The worst part is we don't know what it is. Or why." I wanted to immediately put him in touch with those climatologists who were flying to their conference in Montreal. I got up and glanced around for them, but then right away I realized, of course, that that was not this flight.

## MOBILITY IS REALITY

At the airport, a big ad on a glass wall all-knowingly asserts:

МОБИЛЬНОСТЬ СТАНОВИТСЯ РЕАЛЬНОСТЮ

Mobility is reality.

Let us stress that it is merely an ad for mobile phones.

## FLIGHTS

Over the world at night hell rises. The first thing that happens is it disfigures space; it makes everything more cramped and more massive and unscalable. Details disappear and objects lose their features, becoming squat and indistinct; how strange that by day they may be spoken of as "beautiful" or "useful"; now they look like shapeless bodies: hard to guess what they'd be for. Everything is hypothetical in hell. All that daytime heterogeneity of form, the presence of colors, shades, reveals itself to be utterly in vain—what purpose could possibly be served by beige upholstery, by floral wallpaper, by tassels? What difference does green make to a dress slung over the back of a chair? It's difficult to understand the covetous gaze that fell upon it as it clung to its hanger in the shop window. There are no buttons or hooks or clasps now; fingers in the dark find only vague bulges, rough patches, lumps of hard matter.

The next thing hell does is drag you out of sleep. You can kick and scream; hell is implacable. Sometimes it provides disturbing images, frightening or mocking—a decapitated head, a beloved body covered in blood, human bones in ashes—yes, yes, hell likes to shock. But more often than not it awakes without standing on ceremony—your eyes open onto darkness, launching a stream of consciousness; your gaze, aimed at nothing, is its advance guard. The nocturnal brain is a Penelope unraveling the cloth of meaning diligently woven during the day. Sometimes it's a single thread, sometimes more; complex designs break down into prime factors—warp and weft; weft falls by the wayside, and only straight parallel lines remain, the bar code of the world.

Then you realize: night gives the world back its natural, original appearance, without sugar-coating it; day is a flight of fancy, light a slight exception, an oversight, a disruption of the order. The world in fact is dark, almost black. Motionless and cold.

. . .

She sits straight up in their bed, tickled by beads of sweat between her breasts. Her nightgown sticks to her body like skin about to be shed. She strains to hear in the darkness and catches the quiet whimpering that comes from Petya's room. For a moment she tries with her feet to find her slippers, but then she gives up. She'll run barefoot to her son. Beside her she sees the murky outline of a person as it budges and sighs.

"What?" murmurs the man, still asleep, falling back into his pillow.

"Nothing. Petya."

She turns on a little lamp in the child's room and right away sees his eyes. They're wide open, looking at her from inside the painstaking black cavities the light carves into his face. She puts her hand to his forehead, instinctively, as always. His forehead isn't hot, but it is sweaty, clammy to the touch. Carefully she pulls the boy up into a sitting position and massages his back. Her son's head falls onto her shoulder; Annushka can smell his sweat, recognizing pain in it, a thing she's learned to do: Petya smells different when he is in pain.

"Can you make it till morning?" she whispers, softly, but then she quickly realizes what a stupid question it is. Why should he suffer until morning? She reaches for the pills on the nightstand, pops one out, and puts it in his mouth. Then a glass of warmish water. The boy drinks, chokes, so a little while later she gives him another sip, with greater caution. The pill will take effect any minute now, so she lays his limp body on its right side, tucking his knees up under his belly, thinking he'll be most comfortable this way. She lies down beside him on the edge of the bed and rests her head against his bony back, listening to the air turn into breath as it enters his

lungs and is released into the night. She waits until this process becomes rhythmic, easy, automatic, and then she rises, gingerly, and
tiptoes back to bed. She'd rather sleep in Petya's room, as she had
until her husband had come back. That had been better, her mind
had been easier, falling asleep and waking up facing her child. Not
folding out that double bed each evening: let it be deserted. But a
husband is a husband.

He'd come back four months earlier, after two years away. He'd
come back in civilian clothes, the same ones he'd been wearing
when he'd left, now out of fashion, though you could tell they'd
barely been worn. She'd smelled them—they hadn't smelled like
anything, maybe very slightly of damp, that smell of stillness, a
shut-up storehouse.

He'd come back different—she'd noticed right away—and so far,
he'd stayed different. That first night she'd made an inspection of
his body—it was also different, harder, bigger, more muscular, but
oddly weak.

She'd felt the scar on his shoulder and his scalp, his hair obviously getting thinner and gray. His hands had become massive, his
fingers thicker, as though from physical labor. She had laid them on
her bare breasts, but they'd remained uncertain. She'd tried her own
hand at persuading him, but he'd continued to lie there so quietly,
breathing so shallowly, that it had made her feel ashamed.

At night he'd wake up with a kind of hoarse, furious groan, sit
up in the dark, and then a moment later get up and go over to the
spirits shelf and pour himself a shot. Then his breath would smell
like fruit, like apples. And then he'd say, "Put your hands on me,
touch me."

"Tell me what it was like there, you'll feel better, tell me," she said, whispering into his ear, tempting with her hot breath.

But he didn't tell her anything.

While she would deal with Petya, he would walk the apartment in his striped pajamas, drinking strong black coffee, looking out the window onto the apartment buildings. Then he'd look in on the boy, crouching down beside him sometimes, trying to make contact. And then he'd turn on the TV and draw the yellow curtains, making the daylight sickly, dense and fevered. He didn't get dressed until around noon, when Petya's nurse was about to come, and even then he didn't always. Sometimes he'd just close the door. The sound of the TV would grow fainter, become a rankling rumbling, a summons to a newly senseless world.

The money came in like clockwork, every month. And in fact it was enough—plenty for Petya's medications, for a better, barely used wheelchair, for a nurse.

Today Annushka will not be dealing with the boy; she has today off. Her mother-in-law will be here soon, though she doesn't know which of them she's really coming to watch, her son or her grandson, which of them she'll fuss the most over. She'll lay her plaid plastic bag down by the door and extract from it her nylon housecoat and her slippers—her home uniform. She'll look in on her son, ask him a question, and he'll respond, without taking his eyes off the TV: yes or no. Nothing else, no point waiting, so she'll go to her grandson. He needs to be washed and fed; his sheets, drenched in sweat and urine, need to be changed; he needs his medications. Then the laundry needs to be put in, and their lunch needs to be made.

Then she'll spend time with the child; if the weather's nice, the boy can be taken out onto the balcony, not that there is much to see from there—just apartment buildings like great gray coral reefs in a dried-up ocean, populated by industrious organisms, their ocean bed the hazy horizon of the gigantic metropolis, Moscow. But the boy always looks up at the sky, hovering over the underbellies of the clouds, following them for a while, until they drift out of view.

Annushka is grateful to her mother-in-law for this one day a week. As she heads out the door she gives her a quick kiss on her soft, velvety cheek. That's all the time they spend together, always at the door, and then she'll rush down the stairs, feeling lighter and lighter the farther she descends. She has the whole day ahead of her. Not that she will spend it on herself, of course. She has many things to take care of. She'll pay the bills, go grocery shopping, pick up Petya's prescriptions, visit the cemetery, and then finally she'll go all the way to the other end of this inhuman city so she can sit in the encroaching darkness and burst into tears. Everything takes forever because there are traffic jams everywhere, and crushed between people she watches through the windowpanes of the bus as the gigantic cars with tinted windows glide effortlessly ahead, invested with some diabolical power, while the rest of them are at a standstill. She looks out at the squares filled with young people, at the mobile bazaars selling cheap Chinese goods. She always transfers at Kievsky Station, where she passes by all sorts of people as they make their way up and out from the underground platforms. But there is no one who attracts her attention, no one who terrifies her like this bizarre figure standing by the exit, against a backdrop of makeshift fences concealing the dug-up foundations of some construction under way, fences pasted over so densely with advertisements that they seem to be screaming.

That woman's orbit is the strip of untamed land between the wall and the just-laid sidewalk; in this way she bears witness to the uninterrupted procession of people, receives that parade of tired and hurrying pedestrians whom she tends to catch still in the middle of their journeys from work to home or vice versa—now they'll switch their modes of transport, change from metro to bus.

She's dressed differently from all of them—she's wearing a plethora of things: trousers, and over them several skirts, but arranged so that each sticks out from below the next, in layers; and the same on top—multiple shirts, sheepskins, vests. And over everything a gray quilted drill coat, the height of refined simplicity, an echo of a distant eastern monastery or a labor camp. Combined, these layers makes some aesthetic sense, and Annushka even likes it; it strikes her that the colors have been carefully selected, though it isn't clear if the selection is a human one or rather the haute couture of entropy—fading colors, fraying and falling apart.

But the strangest thing is the woman's head—tightly wrapped in a scrap of material, pressed together by a warm hat with earflaps—and her hidden face; all you can see is her mouth as it emits a ceaseless stream of curses. The sight of this is so upsetting that Annushka never tries to understand the meanings these curses might contain. And now, too, as she passes by her, Annushka speeds up, fearful that this woman might latch on to her. That in the rush of those furious words, Annushka might even hear her own name.

It's pleasant December weather, the sidewalks are dry, cleared of snow, and her shoes are comfortable. Annushka doesn't get on the bus, instead crossing the bridge and then promenading along the multi-lane highway, feeling like she's walking down the shore of an immense river with no bridges. She enjoys this promenade, won't cry until she gets to her church, in the dark corner where she always kneels and remains in that uncomfortable position until she's lost sensation in her legs, until she's attained the stage that comes after the stiffening and shooting pains—the stage of nothingness. But now she throws her purse over her shoulder and holds on tightly to the plastic bag that holds the plastic flowers for the cemetery. She tries not to think about anything, and least of all about the place she's come from. She's approaching the most elegant neighborhood of the city, so there are things for her to look at—it's full of shops here, where smooth, slender mannequins indifferently exhibit the most expensive clothing. Annushka pauses to look at a purse sewn from a million beads, embellished with tulle and lace: a kind of miracle. Finally she reaches the specialized pharmacy, where she will have to wait. But she'll receive the necessary medications. Futile medications, which only barely relieve her son's symptoms.

At a covered stand she buys a bag of pirozhki and eats them sitting on a bench in the square.

In her little church she finds a lot of tourists. The young priest who normally bustles around the sanctuary like a merchant amidst his wares is busy now, telling the tourists about the history of the building and about iconostasis. In a singsong voice he recites his teachings, the head on his slim, tall body looming over the little crowd, his pretty light beard like an extraordinary halo that's slipped off his head and slid down to his breast. Annushka backs out: How could she possibly pray and cry in the company of all these tourists? She waits and waits, but then the next group comes in, and so Annushka decides to find another site for her tears—a little farther on there is another church, small and old, more often than not closed. She once went in but didn't like it—she'd been repulsed by the chill and the scent of damp wood.

But now she isn't picky, she has to find a place where she can finally cry, a secluded place, but not empty; it has to have the palpable presence of something larger than her, of big outstretched arms trembling with life. Annushka also needs to feel someone's gaze on her, to feel that her crying is witnessed by someone, to feel it isn't just addressing a void. It can be eyes painted on wood, always open, eyes that never tire of anything, eternally calm: let those eyes watch her, unblinking.

She takes three candles and drops a few coins in the tin. The first is for Petya, the second for her reticent husband, the third for her mother-in-law in her non-iron housecoat. She lights them from the other few that burn here and looks around and finds a spot for herself on the right side, in a dark corner, so as not to bother the old women who are praying. She crosses herself sweepingly, commencing in this way the ritual of her tears.

But when she raises her eyes to pray, another face emerges from the gloom—the vast face of the gloomy icon. It's a piece of square board hung high, almost right under the dome of the church, and on it the simple features of Christ, painted in shades of brown and gray. The face is dark, against a dark background, with no halo, no crown; only the eyes glow as they stare straight into her, just like she'd wanted. And yet, it wasn't this type of gaze Annushka had been thinking of—she'd expected gentle eyes filled with love. This gaze, hypnotic, paralyzes her. Under it, Annushka's body shrinks. He was here just for a moment, floats down from the ceiling from afar, from deepest darkness—that's God's place, his hiding spot. He has no need of a body, just the face she must confront now. It's a penetrating gaze, driving painfully into her head, as though with a screwdriver. Drilling a hole into her brain. It might as well be the face not of the Savior, but rather of a drowned man who didn't die, shielding himself against omnipresent death under the water instead, who now, due to mysterious currents, has floated up under the surface, conscious, highly aware, saying: Look, here I am. But she doesn't want to look at him. Annushka lowers her eyes, she doesn't want to know—that God is weak and has lost, that He's been exiled and that He is creeping around the trash heaps of the world, in its fetid depths. There's no sense in crying. This is not the place for tears. This God won't help, or support, or encourage, or purify, or save. The gaze of the drowned man bores into her forehead; she hears a murmur, an underground thunder off in the distance, a vibration below the church's floor.

It must be because she barely slept last night, because she's barely eaten anything today—now she feels faint. The tears won't flow, dry beds where they're supposed to be.

She jumps up and walks out. Stiffly, straight to the metro.

It feels like she has had an experience of some kind, that something's gotten into her, making her tense on the inside like a string on a musical instrument, causing her to make a clean sound, inaudible to anyone. A quiet sound, meant just for her body—a short-lived concert in a brittle acoustical shell. She still listens for it anyway, all her attention turned inward, but in her ears there is only the rush of her own blood.

The stairs go down, and she has the impression that it lasts forever, some people going down, others up. Ordinarily her gaze slips over others' faces, but now Annushka's eyes, struck by that sight in the church, can't manage. Her gaze alights on each and every passerby—and every face is like a slap, hard, stinging. Soon she won't be able to bear it anymore, she'll have to cover her eyes like that crazy woman in front of the station, and just like her she'll begin to shout out curses.

"Have mercy, have mercy," she whispers, and sinks her fingers into the handrail, which moves faster than the stairs; if Annushka doesn't let go she'll fall.

She sees the silent swarm of people going up and down, shoulder to shoulder, packed in. They glide toward their spots as though on tethers, heading somewhere in the suburbs, to a tenth floor, where they can pull the covers over their heads and fall into a sleep made up of scraps of day and night. And in reality in the morning that sleep does not dissolve—those scraps form collages, splotches; some configurations are clever, you could almost say premeditated.

She sees the brittleness of arms, the fragility of eyelids, the unstable line of people's lips, readily contorting into grimace; she sees how weak their hands are, how weak their legs—they will not, cannot, carry them to any destination. She sees their hearts, how they beat in time, some faster, some slower, an ordinary mechanical movement, the lungs' sacs are like dirty plastic bags, you can hear the rustle of exhalations. Their clothes have become transparent, so she watches them wed entropy. Our bodies are poor, dirty, grist—without exception—for the mill.

The escalators take these beings all straight down into the depths, into the abyss; here are the eyes of the Cerberi in the glass booths at the bottom of the stairs, here the fraudulent marble and columns, massive sculptures of demons—some with sickles, others with sheaves of grain. Massive legs like the columns, giants' shoulders. Tractors—infernal machines towing sharp-toothed instruments of torture that deal the earth never-healing wounds. From all sides cramped groups of people, their hands raised pleadingly in panic, their mouths open to scream. The Last Judgment takes place here, in the depths of the metro, lit by crystal chandeliers that cast dead yellow light. The judges are nowhere to be seen, it's true, but everywhere you feel their presence. Annushka wants to retreat, run up against the current, but the escalators won't permit her to, she has to keep going down, she won't be spared. The mouths of the underground trains will open before her with a hiss and suck her into their gloomy tunnels. But of course the abyss is everywhere, even on the upper floors of the city, even on the tenth and sixteenth floors of the high-rise buildings, at the tops of spires, on the tips of antennas. There is no escape from it. Wasn't it maybe this the madwoman was screaming about, in between her curses?

Annushka staggers, leans against a wall. It imprints her wool twill coat with white traces, anointing her.

She has to get off, it's dark already, she gets off slightly at random because you can't see anything out the windows of the bus, frost has already etched silvery twigs across them—but she knows the route by heart, she was right. Just a few courtyards—she takes a shortcut—and she'll be at her building. But she slows, her legs don't want to take her to her destination, they resist, her steps get smaller and smaller. Annushka stops. She looks up and sees the lights on in her apartment. They must be waiting for her—so she starts up again, but a second later she stops again. The cold wind pierces through her coat, blows apart the bottom, seizes her thighs with its icy fingers. Its touch is like razor blades, like broken glass. Tears fly down her cheeks from the cold, which suits the wind, finally providing it a way to sting her face. Annushka rushes on, toward their stairwell, but when she gets to the door she turns, puts up her collar, and as fast as she can she goes back to where she just came from.

It's warm only in the big waiting room at Kievsky Station or in the bathroom. She stands, unable to make her mind up as the patrols pass by her (they always walk with a slow, loose step, moving their legs lightly as though meandering along a seaside boulevard), she pretends to read the timetable; she doesn't even know why she's afraid, after all she's done nothing wrong. And in any case the patrols are interested in something else, unerringly singling out olive-skinned men in leather jackets and women in headscarves from the crowd.

Annushka walks out in front of the station and sees from afar that shrouded woman still scrambling, her voice hoarse from cursing—in fact, neither it nor the curses themselves are really recognizable now. Good then—after a moment's hesitation she approaches her calmly and stands in front of her. This throws the woman off for just a second—she must be able to see Annushka through the material that covers her face. Annushka takes another step closer and now stands so near she can smell the woman's breath—dust and must, old oil. The woman speaks softer and softer until she finally falls silent. Her scrambling turns into rocking, as though she can't stand still. They stand facing each other for a moment as people pass them by, but indifferently; one person just glances over at them, but they're in a hurry, their trains will leave at any moment.

"What are you saying?" asks Annushka.

The shrouded woman freezes, holds her breath, and then starts sideways, spooked, toward the passage through the construction, over the frozen mud. Annushka follows her, does not take her eyes off her, is a few steps behind her, behind her quilted coat, behind her tiny, teetering wool felt boots. She will not let her get away. The woman looks over her shoulder and tries to speed up, almost running, but Annushka is young and strong. She has strong muscles—how many times has she carried both Petya and his carriage all the way down the stairs, how many times has she carried them all the way up, when the elevator wasn't working.

"Hey!" Annushka shouts intermittently, but the woman gives no reaction.

They pass through the courtyards between homes, pass trash heaps and trodden squares. Annushka doesn't feel tired but drops the bag with flowers for the cemetery; it would be a waste of time to go back for it.

Finally the woman squats and pants, unable to catch her breath. Annushka stops a few meters behind her and waits for her to stand back up and turn to her. The woman has lost; now she has to surrender. And sure enough, she looks over her shoulder, and you can see her face, she's pulled the covering off her eyes. She has light blue irises, frightened, looking at Annushka's shoes.

"What do you want from me? Why are you chasing me?"

Annushka doesn't answer, she feels as though she's caught a big animal, a big fish, a whale, and now she doesn't know what to do with it; she doesn't need this trophy. The woman is afraid, clearly in this fear all her curses have escaped her.

"Are you from the police?"

"No," says Annushka.

"Then what?"

"I want to know what you're saying. You've been saying something all this time, I see you every week as I go into town."

To this the woman answers, more boldly:

"I'm not saying anything. Leave me alone."

Annushka leans over and extends her hand to help her stand, but her hand changes course and caresses the woman's cheek. It is warm, nice, soft.

"I didn't want anything bad."

At first the woman freezes, astonished by this touch, but then, seemingly mollified by Annushka's gesture, she scrabbles and gets up.

"I'm hungry," she says. "Let's go, there's a kiosk right here, they have cheap hot sandwiches, you can buy me something to eat."

They walk silently, side by side. At the booth Annushka buys two long rolls with cheese and tomatoes, watching to make sure the woman doesn't run away. She can't eat anything. She holds her roll out in front of her like a flute, about to play a winter melody. They sit on a wall. The woman eats her roll, and then wordlessly she takes Annushka's. She is old, older than Annushka's mother-in-law. Her cheeks are broken up by wrinkles that run diagonally from her forehead to her chin. It's hard for her to eat because she's lost her teeth. The tomato slices slip off of the bread, she grasps at them, saves them at the last minute, and carefully puts them back in place. She tears off big bites with just her lips.

"I can't go home," Annushka says suddenly, and looks down at her feet. She's stunned she said something like this, and only now does she think in terror what it means. The woman murmurs something indistinct in response, but after swallowing her bite, she asks:

"Do you have an address?"

"Yes," says Annushka, and she recites it: "Kuznetskaya forty-six, apartment seventy-eight."

"So just forget it," blurts the woman, with her mouth full.

Vorkuta. She was born there in the late sixties, when the apartment buildings, which now seem age-old, were just going up. She remembers them as new—rough plaster, the smell of concrete and the asbestos used as insulation. The promising smoothness of the PVC tiles. But in a cold climate everything gets older faster; the frost breaks down the consistent structure of the walls, slows electrons in their ceaseless circulation.

She remembers the blinding whiteness of winters. The whiteness and the sharp edges of the light in exile. Such whiteness exists only in order to create a framework for the darkness, of which there is decidedly more.

Her father worked at a massive heating plant, and her mother in a cafeteria, which is how they got by—she always brought something home for them to eat. Now Annushka thinks that everybody there had a kind of weird illness, hidden deep inside the body, under clothing, a great sadness, or perhaps something vaster than sadness, but she can't think of the right word.

They lived on the seventh floor of an eight-floor building, one of many identical buildings, but with time, as she grew up, floor four and up emptied out, people moved away to more amenable locales, usually to Moscow, but anywhere, as far away from there as possible. Those who stayed moved downward, took up residence in the lowest-level apartments they could, where it was warmer, closer to people, to the earth. Living on the eighth floor during the many months of polar winter was like hanging from the concrete vaults of the world in a frozen drop of water, right in the middle of a frozen hell. When she'd last visited her sister and mother, they lived on the ground floor. Her father had died long ago.

It was fortunate that Annushka got into a good teaching school in Moscow; unfortunate she didn't finish the course. If she had, she would be a teacher now, and perhaps she would never have met the man who had become her husband. Their genes would never have blended together in that toxic mix that was to blame for Petya coming into the world suffering from a disease that had no cure.

Many times Annushka had tried to barter with anyone she could, with God, with the Virgin, with Saint Parascheva, with the whole iconostasis, even with the closer, vaguer realm of fate. Take me instead of Petya, I'll take his illness, I'll die, just let him recover. She didn't stop there—she threw in others' lives: that of her reluctant husband (let him get shot) and of her mother-in-law (let her have a stroke). But of course, there was never any answer to her offer.

She buys a ticket and goes downstairs. There is still a crowd, people returning from the city center to their beds, to sleep. Some already falling asleep in their train cars. Their sleepy breaths fog up the glass; you could draw something in those with your finger, anything, it wouldn't matter because regardless it would vanish a moment later. Annushka gets to the final station, Yugo-Zapadnaya, gets off and stands on the platform, only to realize a moment later that the train will go back, the same train. She sits back down in the same seat and from there returns, and then comes back again, until after several rides like this she switches to the Koltsevaya line. This line takes her in a circle, until around midnight she reaches Kievsky Station as though coming home. She sits on the platform until a menacing lady comes along, insisting that she leave, saying they're about to close the metro. Annushka leaves, although she doesn't want to—outside the frost is biting—but then she finds a small pub near the station, with a television up by the ceiling; the tables are peopled by a few lost travelers. She orders tea with lemon, one after another, then borscht, terrible, watery, and with her head propped up against her hand she drifts off briefly. She is happy, because she doesn't have a single thought in her head, a single care, a single expectation or hope. It's a good feeling.

The first train is still empty. Then at each station more and more people get on, until finally the crush is such that Annushka stands squashed between the backs of some kind of giants. Since she can't reach the handles, she's condemned to having anonymous bodies hold her up. Then suddenly the throng thins out, and at the next station the train is empty. Only a couple of people remain. Now Annushka learns that some people don't get off at the end stations. She alone gets off and switches trains. But she sees the others through the windows finding themselves spots at the ends of their cars and setting out around their feet their plastic bags or their backpacks, usually old, made of hemp. They doze off with their eyes half shut or unwrap some food and, excusing themselves over and over, mumbling, chew reverentially.

She changes trains because she's scared someone might spot her, might grab her by the arm and shake her, or—worst of all—might lock her up somewhere. Sometimes she walks over to the other side

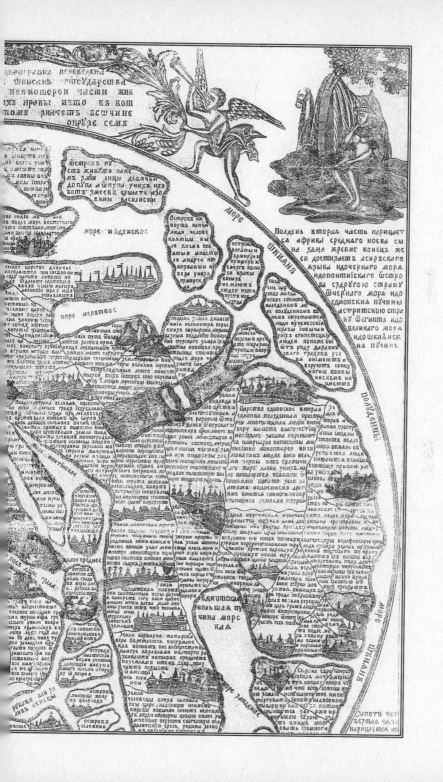

of the platform, and sometimes she changes platforms; then she travels by escalator, by tunnel, but never reading any of the signs, completely free. She goes, for example, to Chistye Prudy, changes from Sokolnicheskaya to Kaluzhsko-Rizhskaya, and goes to Med-vedkovo and then back to the other side of the city. She stops in the toilets to check her appearance, to make sure she looks all right, not because she feels the need to (in truth she does not), but rather to avoid being spotted, due to unkemptness, by one of those Cerberi who from their glass booths guard the escalators. She suspects that they have mastered the art of sleeping with their eyes open. At a kiosk she buys some pads, some soap, the cheapest toothpaste and toothbrush. She sleeps through the afternoon, on the Koltsevaya line. In the evening she emerges from the station by way of the stairs, so as to maybe meet the shrouded woman out front—but no, she isn't there. It's cold, even colder than the day before, so Annushka is relieved to be going back underground.

The next day the shrouded woman is back, swaying on stiff legs and shouting out curses that sound like gibberish. Annushka stands in her line of vision, on the other side of the passageway, but the woman evidently does not see her, lost in her lamentations. Finally Annushka, taking advantage of a momentary lapse in the crowds, goes and stands right in front of her.

"Let's go, I'll buy you a roll."

The woman stops, snapped out of her trance, rubs her gloved hands together, stamps her feet like a saleswoman at a bazaar who is frozen to the bone. They go up to the kiosk together. Annushka is truly happy to see her.

"What's your name?" she asks.

The woman, busy with her roll, merely shrugs. But a moment later she says with her mouth full:

"Galina."

"I'm Annushka."

That's it for conversation. Finally, when the frost drives her back toward the station, Annushka asks another question:

"Galina, where do you sleep?"

The shrouded woman tells her to come back to the kiosk when the metro closes.

All evening Annushka rides the same line and indifferently examines her own face reflected in the window against the dark walls of the underground tunnels. She already recognizes at least two people. She wouldn't dare try to talk to them. She's traveled a few stops now with one of them—there is a tall, thin man, not old, perhaps even young, it's hard to say. His face is covered in a sparse light-colored beard that comes down to his chest. He's wearing a flat cloth cap, a worker's cap, ordinary and threadbare, a long gray overcoat, pockets stuffed with something, and a weathered backpack. Then tall lace-up boots with homemade socks protruding out of them, the legs of his brown trousers tightly tucked in. He seems to not be paying attention to anything, immersed in his own thoughts. With verve he hops out onto the platform, giving the impression that he's heading for some distant but concrete destination. Annushka has also seen him twice from the platform; once he was sleeping on some completely deserted train that seemed to be retiring for the night; the other time he was also dozing, resting his forehead against the glass; his breath conjured up a mist that concealed half his face.

The other one Annushka remembers is an old man. He walks

with difficulty, with a cane, or rather, a walking stick, a thick piece of wood that curves a little at the end. When he gets into a train car he has to hang on to the door with his other hand, and usually somebody helps him then. Once inside people give up their seats for him, reluctantly, but they do it. He looks like a beggar. Him Annushka does try to hunt down, as she hunted down the shrouded woman earlier. But all she manages to do is ride with him for some time in the same car, stand in front of him for more or less half an hour, so that she knows by heart every detail of his face, his clothing. She isn't brave enough to talk to him, however. The man keeps his head down, not paying attention to what's happening around him. Then a crowd of people going home from work sweeps her away. She lets herself be carried by this warm stream of scents and touches. She becomes free of it only after it has carried her through the turnstiles, as though the underground had spit her out like some foreign body. Now she will have to buy a ticket to go back in, and she knows that she will run out of money soon enough.

Why does she remember those two? I suspect because they're constant, somehow, as though they moved differently, more slowly. Everyone else is like a river, a current, water that flows from here to there, creating eddies and waves, but each particular form, being fleeting, disappears, and the river forgets about them. But those two move against the current, which is why they stand out the way they do. And why they aren't bound by the river's rules. I think that this is what attracts Annushka.

When they close the metro she waits in front of the side entrance for the shrouded woman, and just when she gives up, the woman finally appears. Her eyes are covered, and with all those layers of clothing her shape is that of a barrel. She tells Annushka to follow her, and Annushka obeys. She is very tired, to be frank, has no energy at all and would be thrilled to just sit down somewhere, anywhere. They walk along the bridge of boards over the excavation, passing tin fencing pasted over with posters, and then they go down into an underground passageway. For a while they walk down a narrow corridor, where it is pleasingly warm. The woman indicates a place for Annushka on the floor, and Annushka lies down without getting undressed and immediately falls asleep. As she's dozing, just as she has always wanted—deeply, without a thought in her head—the image she just saw walking down the cramped corridor returns for a moment under her eyelids.

A dark room, and in it an open door that leads into another room, bright. Here there is a table, and people sitting around it. Their hands are arranged on the tabletop, and they are sitting up straight. They sit and look at each other in absolute silence and without moving. She could swear that one of those people is the man in the worker's cap.

Annushka sleeps soundly. Nothing wakes her, no rustling, no creaking of the bed, no TV. She sleeps as though she were a piece of rock against which stubborn waves are crashing, or a tree that has fallen and is now being covered by moss and mushroom spawn. Just before waking she has a funny dream—that she's playing with a colorful toiletry bag, with a pattern of little elephants and kittens, which she's turning over in her hands. And then suddenly she lets it go, only the bag doesn't fall, it hangs between her hands, suspended in midair, and Annushka finds that she can play with it without even touching it. That she can move it with the power of her will. It's a very pleasant realization, with a great joy in it that she hasn't felt for a long time, since childhood, in fact. So she wakes up in a good mood, and now sees that this is not some abandoned workers' dormitory at all, as she'd thought yesterday, but rather a common boiler room. That's why it's so warm in here. And she is sleeping on cardboard laid out alongside a pile of coal. On a piece of newspaper lies a quarter loaf of bread, quite stale, and an ample helping of lard mixed with hot pepper. She guesses this is from Galina, but she won't touch the food until she has relieved herself in the disgusting bathroom without doors, and managed to wash her hands.

Oh, how good it feels—how incredibly good—to become part of a crowd that gradually warms up. Overcoats and furs give off the smells of people's homes—grease, detergent, sweet perfumes. Annushka goes through the turnstile and from there allows herself to be carried by the first wave. The Kalininskaya line this time. She stands on the platform, then feels the warm underground air. No sooner do the doors open than Annushka finds herself inside, pressed between bodies, so much so she doesn't need to hold on. When the train curves she gives in to that motion, sways like grass amidst more grass, a blade among other grains. At the next station people still get on, although you really couldn't even squeeze a match in now. Annushka half closes her eyes and feels as though her hands are being held, as though from all sides she is being embraced affectionately and rocked by reassuringly kind hands. Then suddenly they pull into a station where many people get off the train, and one must stand on one's own two feet again.

When the train car almost completely empties out near the final station, she finds a newspaper. At first she stares at it suspiciously— maybe she's forgotten how to read—but then she picks it up and anxiously leafs through it. She reads about a model who's died of anorexia, and how the authorities are thinking about prohibiting overly skinny girls from being displayed on the runways. She also reads about terrorists—yet another plot's been foiled. TNT and detonators found in an apartment. She reads of disoriented whales swimming up onto beaches where they die. Of the police tracking down a ring of pedophiles on the internet. Of the forecast predicting it will get colder. Of mobility becoming reality.

There's something wrong with this paper, which must be falsified somehow—which must be fake. Every sentence she reads is unbearable and hurts. Annushka's eyes fill with tears and brim over, big drops plopping onto the news. The poor-quality paper instantly absorbs them like the barely-there pages of a Bible.

When the train goes aboveground Annushka rests her head against the glass and looks out. The city's every shade of ash, from dirty white through to black. Made up of rectangles and unformed masses, of squares and straight angles. She tracks high-voltage lines and cables, then looks up over the roofs and counts antennas. She shuts her eyes. When she opens them again the world has skipped from place to place. Right at dusk, revisiting the same place once again, she sees, just for a moment, just a few instants, the low sun break through from behind the white-blooming clouds to illuminate the apartment buildings with a red glow, but just their tips, the highest floors, and it looks like giant torches being set alight.

Then she sits on a bench on the platform beneath a large ad. She eats what was left from her breakfast. She washes up in the bathroom and returns to her seat. Rush hour is about to begin. Those who went one way in the morning will now go back the other way. The train that stops in front of her is well lit and almost empty. Just one person in the whole car—that man in the cap. He stands taut as a chord. When the train starts, it jostles him a little; then the train disappears, swallowed up by the black mouth of the underground.

"I'll buy you a roll," Annushka says to the shrouded woman, who stops her rocking for a second, as though able to digest a sentence only if she stays still. Then after a second she sets off toward where the sandwiches are sold.

They lean against the back of the kiosk and eat, after the woman has crossed herself a dozen or so times, and bowed.

Annushka asks her about the people who were sitting in silence in the boiler room the day before, and once more she freezes, this time with a bite of the roll in her mouth. She says something unconnected, something like, "How so?" and then she spits out spitefully, "Get the fuck away from me, little miss."

She leaves. Annushka rides the metro until one o'clock in the morning, and then, when it shuts down and the hellhounds chase everyone away, she circles around the place where she thought the entrance to the warm boiler room was, but she doesn't find it. So she goes to the station and there, scraping up almost all of her remaining money, she spends the night over a series of teas and borschts in small plastic cups, valiantly propped up on her elbows over the laminated tabletop.

The second she hears the grating of the bars being opened, she buys a ticket from the machine and goes downstairs. In the window of the train she sees her hair's become greasy already, that

there's no trace left of her hairstyle, and that the other passengers
are somewhat reluctant to sit beside her now. Periodically she panics at the fleeting thought she might run into someone, but the
people she knows don't take this line; just in case, she finds a
place in the corner, against the wall. Come to think of it, who
does Annushka even know? The postwoman, the woman from the
shop downstairs, the man who lives across from them: she doesn't
even know their names. She feels like covering her face like that
shrouded woman; that's actually a good idea—putting a covering
over your eyes to be as little visible to yourself as you can be, and
to be seen as little as you can. She gets bumped into, but it only
brings her pleasure, to be touched by someone. An older woman
sitting near her takes an apple out of a plastic bag and offers it to
her, smiling. When at the Park Kultury station she stands in front
of the pirozhki kiosk a young guy with close-cropped hair buys a
portion for her. She gleans from this that she must not look her
best. She says thank you, and she doesn't refuse, although she still
has a couple of coins left. She is witness to a number of events:
The police nabbing a guy in a leather jacket. A couple arguing,
voices raised as loud as they will go, both of them drunk. A young
girl, a teenager, who gets on the train at Cherkizovskaya and sobs,
repeating, *Mum, mum,* but no one has the courage to do anything
to help her, and then it's too late, the girl has gotten off at Kom-
somolskaya. She sees someone running away, a short dark man,
knocking into passersby, but he gets stuck in the crowd at the
stairs and gets caught there by two other men, who pry open his
hands. A woman fleetingly bemoaning having just had everything
stolen, everything, but her voice arrives from an ever greater distance, dies down, and finally dies away. And twice today she sees

a stiff old man with absent eyes flitting before her on the brightly lit train. She doesn't even know that it's been dark for a long time now, and that lanterns and lamps are on, seeping yellow light into the icy, thick air; today sunlight has completely escaped Annushka. She goes up to the surface at Kievskaya and heads toward the temporary passageway along the building being built, in the hope of finding the shrouded woman.

She is where she usually is, doing what she usually does—scampering in place, tracing circles of sorts and figures of eight, and snarling out her same old curses, looking like a clump of dampened rags. Annushka stands in front of her for so long that the woman finally notices and stops. Then—although they've made no plans to—they both start hurriedly walking, without so much as a word, as though rushing toward some objective that will vanish for all time if they're not quick enough. At the bridge the wind hits both of them like a kind of lady boxer.

At the kiosk on the Arbat they have delicious blinis, not expensive, dripping with grease and with sour cream on top. The shrouded woman puts some coins on the little glass saucer and gets two warm servings. They find themselves a place on the wall where they can eat this treat. Annushka gazes as though hypnotized at the young people all along the benches despite the cold, playing guitar and drinking beer. Making a ruckus more than singing. Shouting over one another, mucking around. Two young girls ride up on horseback; an unusual sight indeed, the horses are tall, well cared for, evidently straight from the stable; one of these Amazons greets the kids with the guitar, elegantly dismounts, chatting, keeping a tight hold on the bridle. The other girl tries to talk some straggling tourists into giving her some money to feed the horse—or so she tells them—but they deduce the money is really for beer. The animal does not look like it lacks for nourishment.

The shrouded woman elbows her. "Eat," she says.

But Annushka cannot take her eyes off this little scene; she looks greedily at the young people with her blinis steaming in her hand. In all of them she sees her Petya; they're around the same age. Petya comes back into her body, as though she'd never given him up into the world. He's there, curled up, heavy as a stone, painful, swelling inside her, growing—it must be that she has to give birth to him again, this time out of every pore she has in her skin, sweating him out. For now he comes up in her throat, sticking in her lungs, and he won't emerge in any other way besides a sob. No, she won't be able to eat a blini—she's full. Petya's lodged in her throat, when he could have been sitting there and reaching up with a beer can in his hand, giving it to the girl with the horse, leaning into it with his whole body, bursting out laughing. He could have been in motion, could have bent down to his boots and then lifted his arms and placed his foot in the stirrup and swung his other leg over. Sat on the back of that animal, traversing the streets sitting straight up and smiling, a scraggly mustache shading his upper lip. He could have run down the stairs, storming them; after all, he is the same age as these boys, and she, his mother, would have worried about him failing his chemistry class, not getting into university and winding up like his father, worried he'd have trouble finding a job, that she wouldn't like his wife, that they'd have a baby too soon.

This ocean of lead gathers heavily inside her and becomes unbearable and runs into a gesture one of the girls makes, wanting to tame the impatient horse—she jerks his head down by his bridle to force him to be still. And when the horse tries to pull away she cracks a whip over his back and screams, "Stay, goddammit! Hold still!" and now Annushka's blinis with sour cream fall from her hand, and she has launched at the girl fighting the horse, begun attacking her blindly with her fists.

"Leave him alone!" she shrieks, her voice straining in her throat. "Leave him alone!"

It takes a second for the startled kids to react, to try to pull off this woman in the checkered coat, suddenly deranged, but by now another woman is rushing to her aid, some shrouded lunatic all dressed in rags, and both of them are trying to take away the reins from the girl and to push her away. The girl whimpers, shielding her head with her hands—she hadn't expected this furious attack. The horse kicks, whinnies, and gets away from the girl, running down the middle of the Arbat, spooked (it's a good thing the promenade is almost empty at this hour); the clatter of his hooves echoes off the walls of the buildings and brings to mind a street fight, a strike; people's windows open. But now at the end of the street two policemen appear, walking serenely, probably talking about video games—there's nothing happening—but then they see the commotion, swing into action, grabbing their truncheons, taking off at a run.

"Sway," says the shrouded woman. "Move."

They're sitting at the police station awaiting their turn for the flushed and disagreeable policeman to take down their statements.

"Sway." And for these couple of hours she chatters in a kind of frenzy, no doubt scared. Adrenaline has awakened the shrouded woman's tongue. She whispers directly into Annushka's ear so that no one else is privy to their conversation—not the man who was robbed, not the two young dark-skinned whores, not the man with the wounded head holding a bandage in place with one hand. Meanwhile Annushka cries, tears spilling down her cheeks incessantly, though her reserves will run out soon, it's clear.

Then, when their turn comes, the red-faced policeman shouts over his shoulder to someone in the other room:

"It's that runaway woman."

The voice from in there answers:

"That one you can just let go, but write the other one up, for disturbing the peace."

And to the shrouded woman the policeman says:

"Next time we're going to ship you out of town, a hundred kilometers out, got it? We don't want any cult members around here."

Meanwhile he takes Annushka's ID from her, and as though he couldn't read he also has her repeat her first name, patronymic, and last name, and her address, he asks for her address. Annushka touches the tabletop with her fingertips and, partially closing her eyes as though reciting a poem, gives him her information. She repeats her address twice:

"Kuznetskaya forty-six, apartment seventy-eight."

They release them separately, an hour apart, first the shrouded woman, so by the time Annushka gets out, there is no trace of her. Nothing surprising about that, the cold is horrendous. She meanders around the station; her legs urge her on, would carry her down these broad streets off somewhere to the source of all streets, to where they emerge from the hilly outskirts, and past them, to where new and different vistas open up—of the great plain that plays with its breath. But Annushka's bus is arriving; she runs up and gets on it just in time. People are in motion already, the streets overtaken by morning movements even though the sun is not yet out. Annushka's on the bus for a long time, reaching the city's edge, and then she's standing at the base of her apartment building, looking up at her windows, all the way up. They're still dark, but when the sky starts to get lighter she sees that in the kitchen of her apartment there is a light that switches on, and she heads for the entrance.

## WHAT THE SHROUDED RUNAWAY WAS SAYING

Sway, go on, move. That's the only way to get away from him. He who rules the world has no power over movement and knows that our body in motion is holy, and only then can you escape him, once you've taken off. He reigns over all that is still and frozen, everything that's passive and inert.

So go, sway, walk, run, take flight, because the second you forget and stand still, his massive hands will seize you and turn you into just a puppet, you'll be enveloped in his breath, stinking of smoke and fumes and the big trash dumps outside town. He will turn your brightly colored soul into a tiny flat one, cut out of paper, of newspaper, and he will threaten you with fire, disease, and war, he will scare you so you lose your peace of mind and cease to sleep. He will mark you and record you in his records, provide you with the documentation of your fall. He'll occupy your thoughts with unimportant things, what to buy, and what to sell, where things are cheaper and where they're more expensive. From then on you will worry over trifles—the price of gasoline and how that will affect the payments on our loans. You will live every day in pain, as though your life were a sentence. But for what crime? Committed when and by whom? You'll never know.

Once, long ago, the tsar tried to reform the world but he was vanquished, and the world fell right into the hands of the Antichrist. God, the real one, the good one, became an exile from the world, the vessel of divine power shattered, absorbed into the earth, disappearing into its depths. But when he spoke in a whisper from his hiding place, he was heard by one righteous man, a soldier by the name of Yefim, who paid attention to his words. In the night he threw away his rifle, took off his uniform, unwrapped his feet, and slid his boots off. He stood under the sky naked, as God had made him, and then he ran into the forest, and, donning an overcoat, he wandered from village to village, preaching the gloomy news. Flee, get out of your homes, go, run away, for only thus will you avoid the traps of the Antichrist. Any open battle with him will be lost outright. Leave whatever you possess, give up your land, and get on the road.

For anything that has a stable place in this world—every country, church, every human government, everything that has preserved a form in this hell—is at his command. Everything that is defined, that spans from here to there, that fits into a framework, is written down in registers, numbered, testified to, sworn to; everything collected, displayed, labeled. Everything that holds: houses, chairs, beds, families, earth, sowing, planting, verifying growth. Planning, awaiting the results, outlining schedules, protecting order. Rear your children thus, since you had them without understanding, and set out on the road; bury your parents, who brought you into this world without understanding—and go. Get out of here, go far away, beyond the reach of his breath, beyond his cables and wires and antennas and waves, resist the measurements of his sensitive instruments.

Whoever pauses will be petrified; whoever stops, pinned like an insect, his heart pierced by a wooden needle, his hands and feet drilled through and pinned into the threshold and the ceiling.

This is precisely how he died, Yefim, he who rebelled. He was captured and his body nailed to the cross, immobilized like an insect, on display for human and inhuman eyes, but most of all inhuman eyes, which take the most delight in all such spectacles; hardly a surprise that they repeat them every year and celebrate, praying to the corpse.

This is why tyrants of all stripes, infernal servants, have such deep-seated hatred for the nomads—this is why they persecute the Gypsies and the Jews, and why they force all free peoples to settle, assigning the addresses that serve as our sentences.

What they want is to create a frozen order, to falsify time's passage. They want for the days to repeat themselves, unchanging; they want to build a big machine where every creature will be forced to take its place and carry out false actions. Institutions and offices, stamps, newsletters, a hierarchy, and ranks, degrees, applications and rejections, passports, numbers, cards, election results, sales and amassing points, collecting, exchanging some things for others.

What they want is to pin down the world with the aid of bar codes, labeling all things, letting it be known that everything is a commodity, that this is how much it will cost you. Let this new foreign language be illegible to humans, let it be read exclusively by automatons, machines. That way by night, in their great underground shops, they can organize readings of their own bar-coded poetry.

Move. Get going. Blessed is he who leaves.

## JOSEFINE SOLIMAN'S THIRD LETTER TO FRANCIS I, EMPEROR OF AUSTRIA

Your Majesty maintains a silence and is no doubt engaged in important affairs of state. But I will not abandon my efforts, and so I write to Your Majesty once again in order to beg for mercy. My last letter was written over two years ago, yet I have had no response. I repeat, then, this plea.

I am the only child of Angel Soliman, Your Majesty's servant, eminent diplomat for the Empire, an enlightened and widely respected man. I beg for mercy for myself, for I shall never know peace so long as I should have the knowledge that my father, my father's body, has not yet obtained a Christian burial but is instead—stuffed and chemically treated—on view in the Cabinet of Natural Curiosities at the court of Your Majesty.

Since the birth of my son, I have suffered from an illness that continues to get worse. I fear this matter is as hopeless as my own health and now believe that if I am to obtain anything—which I think I shall not—it will be but by the skin of my teeth. The word "skin" fits perfectly here, as—if I may be permitted one more mention of it—my father was skinned when he died, subsequently stuffed, and now serves as an exhibit in Your Majesty's collection.

Your Majesty refused the young mother, but perhaps the same shall not be true of the young mother on her deathbed. I visited that horrible place before leaving Vienna. For I married Your Majesty's servant Herr von Feuchtersleben, military engineer, subsequently transferred to the northern reaches of our country—to Kraków. I was there and saw it. I might say that I went to visit my father in hell, since as a Catholic I believe that without his body he will not be able to be resurrected in the Last Judgment. That faith also suggests that in spite of what some think, the body is our greatest gift—that it is sacred.

When God became man, the human body was forever sanctified, and all the world took on that form of one single individual man. There is no other access to other people or to the world other than by way of the body. Had Christ not taken on a human form, we could never have been saved.

My father was skinned like an animal, stuffed haphazardly with grass, and placed in the company of other stuffed human beings among the remains of unicorns, monstrous toads, two-headed fetuses floating in alcohol, and other similar curiosities. I watched as they crowded in to see Your collection with their own eyes, My Lord, and I saw how their faces flushed as they beheld the skin of my father. I heard them praise You for Your vigor and Your courage.

When You visit Your exhibit, my Lord, go to him. Go to Angel Soliman, Your faithful servant, whose skin serves You even after death. Those hands, which have since been stuffed with grass, once embraced and reassured me; that face, now dried out and caved in, once brushed up against my own. That body loved and was loved, until attacks of rheumatism finally finished my father off.

From this arm, Your own doctor let my father's blood. These remains labeled with my father's name were once a living man. I often wonder—every night it keeps me from falling peacefully asleep—what the real reason is for such cruel treatment of my father's corpse (may he rest in peace).

Can it be that it is simply the color of his skin? Dark? Black?

Would a white-skinned man who wound up in some exotic locale be treated the same—be stuffed and exhibited to the curiosity of passersby? Is it sufficient for another human being to be different, be it outwardly or inwardly and be it in any way, for him to be stripped of the rights and customs ordinarily afforded to man? Were those rights conceived and created merely for people who were identical to one another? But the world is full of diversity. Many miles to the south there are people who are different from those who settled the North. And in the East, there are people who are different from those in the West. What is the point of a law that applies only to some? The law should be observed for everyone without exception, wherever our ships and our money are able to take us. Would Your Majesty stuff a courtier if he were white? A person of the absolute lowest position has the right to a funeral. By refusing my father that right, are You then denying his very humanity?

I think that those who govern us do not aim to govern our souls, as is commonly thought. The "soul" is a concept that is hard to understand or identify with these days. If God is—may I be forgiven this bile—the One who wound up the clock, the Clockmaker, or, in fact, the spirit of nature, appearing in its hazy way and completely impersonal, then the notion of "soul" becomes uncomfortable, embarrassing. What sort of ruler would reign by means of something so ephemeral and indefinite?

What sort of enlightened ruler would wish for power over something whose existence has not been proven in a laboratory? There is no doubt, Your Majesty, that real human power can only affect the human body—and that is precisely how it is exercised. The establishment of countries and of the boundaries between them demands of the human body that it remain in a clearly delineated space; the existence of visas and passports holds in check the body's natural desire to roam and to move around. The ruler who sets up taxes has his sway over what his subjects will eat, what they shall sleep on, and whether they'll wear linen or silk.

You determine, too, which bodies will be important, and which less so. Nourishment shall be divided unevenly by the mother's milk-filled breasts. The child from the palace atop the hill will suckle till it's satiated, while the child from the village in the valley will just lap up what's left. And when You declare war, in so doing You are hurling thousands of human bodies into pools of blood.

To rule over the body is to truly be king of both life and death, which is greater than being the emperor of even the greatest country. So now I write to You accordingly, as to life and death's lessee, as to a tyrant and usurper, and I no longer request but demand. Give me back my father's body, so that I may bury him. I will follow You, my Lord, like a voice from the darkness, even when I die I will never let You be, never cease to whisper.

Josefine Soliman von Feuchtersleben

## THINGS NOT MADE BY HUMAN HANDS

After seeing the sarira relics exhibition I can say that I'm no longer much surprised by things not made by human hands. These include the tomes that appear spontaneously in the damp of mountain caves and let themselves be found every once in a while by righteous humans, who then ceremoniously transfer them to temples. Also, icons with gods' faces. All you have to do is leave a clean wooden board with a primed surface outside and wait. Sometimes in the night a divine face might appear on it, look out from beneath it, flow out of deepest darkness, from the very waterlogged foundations of the world. Because maybe we live in an enormous camera obscura, just enclosed in a dark box, and as soon as a small opening can be made, as soon as some needle makes it through to us, an image from the outside hits with a ray of light and leaves its trace on the inner, light-sensitive surface of the world.

It is said that one particular Buddha statue appeared on its own, perfect, made out of the best metal. It only had to have the soil removed from it. It represents a sitting Buddha resting its head in its hands. This Buddha is smiling a little bit, to himself, with a hint of irony, like someone who's just heard a subtle joke. A joke in which the punch line comes not in the final sentence, but in the breath of the person telling it.

## PURITY OF BLOOD

A certain island-dwelling woman from the other hemisphere, whom I met in a hotel in Prague, told me the following:

People have always slogged around with them millions of bacteria, viruses, and diseases; there's no way to stop it. But we can at least try. After the worldwide panic over mad cow disease some countries introduced new legislation. Any of the residents of her island who went away to Europe could no longer donate blood; it might be said that according to the law they suffered from lifelong contamination. And this would now be her case—she would never be able to give blood now. This was the price of her trip, not included in the cost of the ticket. Lost purity. Lost honor.

I asked her if it was worth it, if it made sense to sacrifice the purity of her blood for the pleasure of looking around a few cities, churches, and museums.

She answered seriously that all things have a price.

## KUNSTKAMMER

Each of my pilgrimages aims at some other pilgrim; this time I immediately recognized the sensitive hand of Charlotta. In the oblong jar, with a lid that looked like a sculpture, there floated a small fetus with closed eyes hanging from two horsehairs. Its little feet touched the dyed-red remains of the bed at the bottom of the jar. On the jar's shale lid a little underwater still life—everything evoking the marine, even the protagonist of this exhibit, the fetus. We all come from water. Which is no doubt why Charlotta adorned this one with seashells, starfish, corals, and sponges, and at its center, a dried-out sea horse—a hippocampus.

One other specimen made an impression on me—conjoined twins preserved in Stygian water, and next to it, their dried skeleton. Proof of great economy of material—two specimens with one double body.

## MANO DI COSTANTINO

The first thing that caught my eye upon arriving in the Eternal City was the beautiful black salesmen of handbags and wallets. I bought a little red coin purse, because my last one had been stolen in Stockholm. The second thing was the stalls laden with postcards—as a matter of fact, you could leave it at that, spending the rest of your time in the shade on the banks of the Tiber, perhaps having a glass of wine later on in one of the expensive little cafés. Postcards of landscapes, panoramas of old ruins, postcards ambitiously prepared so as to show as much as possible on that flat space, are slowly being replaced by photographs focusing on details. This is no doubt a good idea, because they relieve tired minds. There is too much world, so it's better to concentrate on particulars, rather than the whole.

Here is a nice detail of a fountain, a little kitten sitting on a Roman ledge, the genitalia of Michelangelo's *David*, a stone sculpture's gigantic foot, a mutilated torso that instantly makes you wonder what face belonged to that body. An individual window on a wall the color of ochre, and finally—yes—just a hand with its index finger raised up into the sky, monstrous, detached from some incredible whole just here, at the wrist—the hand of the Emperor Constantine.

I was infected by that postcard. You really have to be careful about what you look at when you're first starting out! From that point forward I saw hands pointing something out everywhere; I became a slave to that detail, which possessed me.

The half-naked statue of a warrior, just in a parade helmet and with a pike in one hand; the other pointing out something up above. Two putti with greasy fingers directing others' attention to the fact that there, above their heads—but what? And more, two women tourists bent over with laughter, their fingers, a group of people in front of an elegant hotel—because Richard Gere and Nicole Kidman had just come out of it—and on St. Peter's Square you could see hundreds of those pointing fingers.

At the Campo de' Fiori I saw a woman petrified by the heat next to a tap with water, her finger up against her ear, as though she wanted to remember a melody from her youth and was just beginning to hear the first notes of it.

And then I noticed an old, sick man in a wheelchair being pushed by two girls. The old man was paralyzed; sticking out of his nose were two little transparent plastic tubes that disappeared into a black backpack. An expression of absolute terror was frozen on his face, and his right hand, with a predatory gnarled finger, was pointing at something that must have been just over his left shoulder.

## MAPPING THE VOID

James Cook set out on the southern seas to observe the passage of Venus over the solar disk. Venus revealed to him not only its beauty, but also the land that had already been noticed by the Dutchman Tasman. From his notes the sailors already knew it had to be here somewhere. Every day they looked out for it, and every day they made the same mistakes—taking clouds for land. In the evenings they would talk about the mysterious island—that it would certainly be beautiful, given it was in the custody of Venus, but that it had to also have other superior characteristics, being the land of Venus. Everyone had his own fantasy about it.

The first officer was from Tahiti; he was certain that this land would be like his Hawaii—warm, tropical, sun-drenched, surrounded by long, endless beaches, full of flowers, useful herbs, and beautiful women with bare breasts. The captain himself came from Yorkshire (of which he was very proud), and as a matter of fact he wouldn't have anything against here being like there. He even wondered if maybe lands on the other side of the globe might not be connected by some sort of correspondence, a planetary intimacy, a likeness—if not obvious and trivial, then perhaps manifested in some other, deeper way. The cabin boy, Nils Jung, dreamed of mountains, wanted this land to be mountainous, for them to reach up into the sky and have snow-capped peaks, and between them, for there to be fertile valleys, filled with grazing sheep, and clear streams in which trout swam (he apparently came from Norway).

And it was his eyes that first spotted New Zealand on October 6, 1769.

From then on the *Endeavour* sailed straight ahead, and the sight of land emerged from the clouds, mile by mile. In the evenings an emotional Captain Cook transferred its contours onto paper, drawing maps.

Over several years of this mapping they had many adventures, which have already been colorfully described. When a crew member mused aloud that such an extraordinary land must be inhabited, the next day they saw smoke over the bush. When they began to fear obstacles in securing provisions on land and to imagine it peopled by valiant savages, that same morning those savages appeared on the land—scary and frightening. Those beings had tattooed faces; they stuck out their tongues and shook their spears. To definitively demonstrate their advantage and immediately establish a hierarchy, the newcomers shot several savages—that's when the explorers were attacked.

New Zealand was, it seems, the last land we invented.


## ANOTHER COOK

In 1841, Thomas set out on foot to a meeting of the Temperance Society—for he was a great advocate of the temperate mind—from his native Loughborough to Leicester, eleven miles removed. With him went several other gentlemen. Along the way, which was long and tiring, this Cook had an idea—it now seems so strange that no one had ever thought of it before, but that is of course the famous simplicity of brilliant ideas—namely, to rent a railway car to transport all the travelers together on the next trip.

A month later he managed to ready his first excursion for several hundred people (it is unknown whether all of them were heading to the Temperance Society, however). And so the first travel agency was born.

Thomas Cook and James Cook: two of the chefs who cooked up our reality.

## WHALES, OR: DROWNING IN AIR

In Australia, everyone in the environs would come out onto the seashore when the news was circulated that yet another disoriented whale had run aground. In shifts, people would charitably ladle water over its delicate skin and try to convince it to go home. Older ladies dressed like hippies would maintain that they knew what they were doing. Apparently all you had to do was say, "Go, go, my brother," or, if need be, "sister." And, with your eyes shut tight, transfer some of your energy into it.

All day, little tiny figures would mill about the beach, waiting for high tide: let the water take it back. Attempts would be made to fasten nets to boats and drag it out by force. Yet the great beast would soon become dead weight, a body indifferent to living. It's no surprise people would begin to call it "suicide." A small group of activists would appear in order to argue that animals ought to be allowed to simply die, if they so wished. Why should the act of suicide be the dubious privilege of mankind? Maybe the life of every living being has its own set limits, invisible to the eye, and once those have been crossed, life just runs out, on its own. Let that be taken into consideration for the Declaration of Animal Rights being drafted in Sydney or in Brisbane at just that moment. Dear brothers, we give you the right to choose your death.

Suspicious shamans would come down to the dying whale and perform rituals over it, followed by amateur photographs and thrill-seekers. A teacher from a village school brought her whole classroom, and the children were tasked with drawing "The Whale's Farewell."

Usually it took several days for the whale to die. In that time, the people on the shore became accustomed to the tranquil, magisterial being with its impenetrable will. Someone would name it, usually a human name. The local television station would show up, and the whole country, and the whole world, would take part in the death, thanks to satellite TV. The problem of this individual on the beach would conclude every news broadcast on three continents. Then they'd take the opportunity to talk about global warming and ecology. Scholars would be brought into the studios for debates, and politicians would tack earth-related topics onto their election platforms. Why do whales do this? The ichthyologists and the ecologists all gave different answers.

A collapsed echolocation system. Water pollution. A thermonuclear bomb at the bottom of the sea that no country would admit to setting off. Could it not be a decision, the kind elephants make? Old age? Disenchantment? As was recently discovered, after all, little distinguishes the whale's brain from the human's; a whale's brain even contains certain areas *Homo sapiens* lack, in the best, the most developed, portion of the frontal lobe.

In the end, the whale would finish dying, and its body would need to be removed from the beach. The crowds would have dispersed by this time—in fact, no one would be left, except the service people in bright green jackets who would cut the corpse up and load it onto trailers to haul it off somewhere. If there was a cemetery for whales, that's definitely where they were headed.

Billy, an orca, drowned in air.

Everyone inconsolable in their grief.

Although there have been instances of people managing to save the whales. In response to the great and dedicated efforts of dozens of volunteers, these whales would take deep breaths and head back into the open sea. Their famous fountains could be seen springing joyfully up toward the sky, and then they would dive down into the depths of the ocean. The crowd would break into applause.

A few weeks later they'd be caught off the coast of Japan, and their gentle, pretty bodies would be turned into dog food.


## GODZONE

She's been packing for days. Her things lie in piles on the rug in their room. To get to the bed she steps between them, wading in among the stacks of shirts and underwear and balled-up socks, trousers folded neatly along the crease, and a couple of books for the road, the novels everyone's been talking about that she has not had time to read. And then a heavy sweater and a pair of winter boots, which she's purchased just for this—she's about to venture, after all, into the heart of winter.

They're just things—soft, inscrutable skins that can be shed time and time again, protective cases for a brittle body in its fifties, to shield from ultraviolet rays and prying gazes. Indispensable on her long voyage, as well as when she gets there, for her weeks at the ends of the earth. She has set everything out on the floor, guided by a list she spent days making, working on it in rare free moments, knowing already she'd need to go. Once you give your word, you have to keep it.

As she carefully fills her red suitcase, she acknowledges she doesn't really need much. With each passing year she's discovered she needs less. Thus far she's eliminated skirts, mousse, nail polish and anything else having to do with her nails, earrings, her portable iron. Cigarettes. Just this year she'd discovered she no longer needed pads.

"You don't have to take me," she says to the man who now turns his face to her, still basically asleep. "I'll take a taxi."

With the backs of her fingers she brushes his delicate pale eyelids, and she kisses him on the cheek.

"Call me when you get there or I'll worry sick," he mumbles, and then his head drops back down into the pillow. He'd had the night shift at the hospital. There had been some kind of accident; the patient had died.

She puts on a pair of black trousers and a black linen tunic. She pulls on her boots and slings her purse over her shoulder. Now she's standing motionless in the hall without even knowing why herself.

In her family they used to say that you always had to sit for a minute before heading off on any kind of trip—an old provincial Polish habit—but this little entrance has no place to sit on, no chair. So she stands there and sets her internal clock, her inner chronometer, so to speak, speaking cosmopolitan, that flesh-and-blood timer ticking dully to the rhythm of her human breath. And suddenly she collects herself, grabs the handle of her suitcase in her hand, like a child that got distracted, and she flings open the door. It's time to go. So she gets going.

A cabdriver with darker skin carefully arranges her bag in the trunk. Several of his gestures strike her as unnecessary, and overly intimate: as he lays down her suitcase, for instance, she thinks she sees him giving it a tender caress.

"Going on a trip, are we?" he says, smiling, revealing his big white teeth.

She confirms that she is. He smiles even wider, via the discreet intermediary of the rearview mirror.

"To Europe," she adds, and the taxi driver expresses his awe with a sound that is half exclamation and half sigh.

They go along the bay; the tide is just going out, and the water slowly discloses its stony, mussel-strewn bottom. The sun is blinding, and very hot. You had to be careful of your skin. Now she thinks forlornly of her plants in the garden and wonders if her husband will really water them like he said he would; she thinks of her mandarin oranges and wonders if they'll make it to when she gets back—if so, she'll make marmalade—and she thinks of her figs that have just begun to ripen and of her herbs that have been exiled to the driest place in the garden, where the soil is almost rock, though they seem to like it there, because this year the tarragon has attained unprecedented proportions. Even the clothes she hangs to dry above the garden return suffused with its brisk, tart scent.

"Ten," the taxi driver says. She pays him.

In that local airport, she shows her ticket at the counter and takes her luggage up to customs. She's left with just her backpack, and she heads straight for her plane; sleepy people are already being loaded onto it, with children, with dogs, with plastic bags brimming over with provisions.

As the little plane that will transport her to the main airport becomes aloft she sees a view so beautiful that for a moment she is overwhelmed by a kind of elation.

"Elation," a funny, lofty word, originally meaning "to be raised up," and now here she is literally being lifted up into the clouds. These islands, the sandy beaches are as much a part of her as her own hands and feet; the sea that winds up into foaming coils at the shores, scraps of ships and boats, the gentle, undulating shoreline, the green insides of the islands all belong to her. Godzone, that's what the island's inhabitants call it. It's where God came to settle down, bringing with Him all the beauty in the world. Now He gives that beauty out, for free, to everybody on the island, requesting nothing in return.

At the big airport she goes to the toilet to wash her face. She watches the edgy little line to use the free computer for a while. Travelers pause here for a moment to let people near and far know they are here. It occurred to her that even she might go up to one of those screens, type in the name of her service provider, and then her address and password, and check who might have written to her, too—but she knows what she will find: nothing of note. Something about the project she's working on now, jokes from a friend in Australia, perhaps a rare e-mail from one of her kids. The sender of the messages that had given rise to this expedition had been silent for some time.

She's surprised by all the safety rites; she hasn't flown for quite a while. They scan both her and her backpack. They confiscate her nail clippers, and she laments the loss, because she'd liked them, and had been using them for years. The airport officials attempt to evaluate, with their expert gaze, who among the passengers might be armed with an explosive, gazing particularly at those with darker skin and at the girls wearing headscarves, who are chipper and twittering. It would seem that the world where she is heading, standing right on the border of it now, just behind the yellow line, is governed by a different set of rules, and that its grim and angry rumbles reach all the way here.

After passport control she makes incidental purchases at the duty-free shop. She finds her gate—nine—and sits down facing it and tries to read.

The plane takes off painlessly, on time; so once more the miracle has happened, of a machine as big as a building slipping gracefully out of earth's grasp, soaring gently up and up.

After the plastic airplane food everyone begins to get ready for bed. Just a few with headphones over their ears are watching a movie about the fantastic voyage of several brave scientists reduced in some sort of "accelerator" to the size of bacteria, now headed into a patient's body. She watches the screen without headphones, loves the spectacular photography—settings that resemble the bottom of the ocean, the crimson corridors of blood vessels, the pulse of constricting arteries, and inside these the bellicose lymphocytes like visitors from outer space, and the gentle, concave blood cells, innocent little sheep. A flight attendant passes discreetly down the aisle with water, a single slice of lemon for the whole jug. She drinks a cup.

When it rained it flooded the park paths, washing them out and collecting the fine light sand; you could write on them with the end of a stick—these undulating bands cried out for inscription. You could draw squares on them for hopscotch and princesses in hoop skirts with tiny waists, and then a few years later riddles and confessions and the romantic algebra of all those M + B = GLs, which meant that a Marek or a Maciek loved a Basia or a Bożena, while GL stood for "Great Love." This always happens when she flies: she gets a bird's-eye view of her whole life, of particular moments that you'd think on the ground had been completely forgotten. The banal mechanism of the flashback, mechanical reminiscence.

When she first got the e-mail, she couldn't figure out who it could be from, who was hiding behind that name and how come they addressed her so informally. This amnesia lasted several seconds— she ought to be ashamed. On the surface, as she later realized, it was just a Christmas greeting. It arrived in the middle of December, as the season's first heat waves were just rolling in. But it clearly went beyond the ordinary phrases people say at the holidays. It struck her as a kind of crying out on the other side of a speaking tube, far-off, muffled, indistinct. She didn't understand all of it, and some sentences unsettled her, like the one about how "life seems like a disgusting habit we lost control over a long time ago."

"Did you ever give up smoking?" he'd added. Yes, she'd given it up. And it had been hard.

For a good couple of days she mulled over that strange letter from a person she'd known more than thirty years ago, and whom she hadn't seen once since then, whom she had completely forgotten by now, but whom she had, after all, once loved, for two intense years in her youth. She responded politely, in a totally different tone, and from that point forward she got letters back from him on a daily basis.

These e-mails took away her peace of mind. They evidently awoke that dormant section of her brain where those years had been stored, parceled up into images, scraps of dialogue, shreds of smells. Now, on a daily basis, when she drove to work, as soon as she turned on the engine these tapes came on, too, these recordings filmed with whatever camera had been at hand, with faded colors or even black-and-white, generic scenes, moments, with no logic to them, scattered, out of order, and she had no idea what to do with them. That for instance they walk outside the city limits—the limits of the little town, more like—into the hills, to where the high-voltage line runs, and from then on their words are accompanied ceaselessly by a buzzing, like a chord to underscore the significance of this walk, a low monotone, a tension that neither increases nor decreases. They hold hands; this is the era of first kisses, which couldn't possibly be called anything other than strange.

Their secondary school was a chilly old building where on two floors classrooms multiplied inside the broad hallways. They all looked more or less the same—three rows of benches, and opposite these, the teacher's desk. Boards covered in dark green rubber that could be moved up and down. One of the kids would be put in charge of moistening the sponge before each class. On the walls hung black-and-white portraits of men—it was only in the physics department that you could find the single female face in the whole school, Madame Maria Skłodowska Curie's, the sole indication of the equality of the sexes. These rows of faces hanging over the students' heads were no doubt supposed to remind them that by some miracle the school remained within that great family of knowledge and learning, that in spite of its provincialism it was heir to the finest tradition, and it belonged to a world in which everything could be described, explained, proved, demonstrated by examples.

In her first year there she began to be interested in biology. She'd found an article—maybe her dad had given it to her—on mitochondria. It said that most likely in the remotest past, in the primeval ocean, mitochondria were creatures in their own right before they were intercepted by other single-cell organisms and forced, for the remainder of history, into laboring on behalf of their hosts. Evolution had sanctioned this slavery—and that was how we'd turned out the way we had. That was how it had been described, in those terms: "seized," "forced," "slavery." In truth, she had never been able to come to terms with this. With the hypothesis that in the beginning there'd been violence.

So she'd already known at school that she wanted to become a biologist, which was why she had studied biology and chemistry with such zeal. In Russian she'd written notes filled with gossip that had been dutifully passed by her classmates beneath the benches to her best friends. In Polish she'd been bored to death, until in year six she had fallen in love with a kid her same age but with a different homeroom, a kid who had the same name as the author of these e-mails, and whose face she strove so hard now to call forth. He must have been the reason she'd learned so little about positivism and Young Poland.

Her daily commute is a pendular voyage along an elegantly curved arc, eight kilometers of coast, there and back, from home to work and vice versa. The sea is ever-present in this journey, and one could say without hesitation that hers is a maritime voyage.

At work, she'd stop thinking about his e-mails. She was herself again, and anyway there was no place for hazy recollections here. As soon as she'd pulled out of the driveway at home and merged onto the highway, she was always kind of excited at all the things that awaited her in the lab and in her office. And then the familiar solidity of that low, glassy building would readjust her consciousness, and her brain began to work more efficiently, as focused as a well-oiled engine, reliable, the kind that always gets you to your destination.

She was taking part in a massive program aimed at eliminating pests like weasels and opossums, which—imprudently introduced into the region by humans—now wreaked havoc among the endemic bird species, feeding mostly off their eggs.

She worked on a team that tested poisons on these small animals. The poison was injected into the eggs, which were then distributed as bait in special wooden cages throughout forests and in the bush; it had to be fast, humane, and also highly biodegradable, so that the fallen animals didn't poison insect populations, as well. A crystal-clear poison, completely safe for the world, aimed only at the pest, at one chosen organism type, self-neutralizing after completing its mission. The James Bond of ecology.

This was what she did. She created just this sort of substance, had been working on it for seven whole years.

Somehow he knew. He must have found it on the internet—everything's on there somewhere. If you're not on the internet, it's almost as though you don't exist at all. You have to have at least one little mention, even if it's just in a list of school alumni. And it would have been easy for him to track her down since she never changed her name. So he must have just put her name into Google, and up came several pages: her articles, the courses she taught, and her environmental activism. At first she thought that that was what interested him. And so she innocently let herself be pulled into the exchange.

It is hard to sleep on this great, transcontinental airplane. Her ankles swell, and her feet go numb. She dozes off in short spurts, which disorients her even further in terms of time. Can the night really be so long? wonders the lost human body estranged from earth, from its place, where the sun rises and sets, and the pineal gland, that hidden third eye, conscientiously registers its movement in the sky. Finally it starts to get light out, and the plane's engines change their tone. From the tenor to which the ear had grown accustomed to lower registers, baritones and basses; finally, faster than she'd expected, the great machine makes its landing, deft and smooth. On the jet bridge as she heads into the airport she can feel how hot the air is here, squeezing in through the cracks, sticky, damp—the lungs rear up, trying to take it in. But fortunately she won't have to deal with it. Her next flight leaves in almost six hours, and she plans to spend that time here in the airport, napping and nodding off, trying to get her bearings in time. Another twelve-hour flight awaits her next.

She thought often of the man who had unexpectedly sent her that e-mail. And then more e-mails, so forming a correspondence brimming with hints and surmises. Such things aren't written out, but to those with whom you once had an intimate physical relationship a certain kind of loyalty remains in effect, in the end—so she understood. Was that why he had come to her? It was obvious. Losing your virginity is a singular and irreversible event that can never be done over; by virtue of this it somehow becomes momentous, whether you want it to be or not, regardless of whatever ideology. She remembers exactly what it was like: the brief, piercing pain, an incision, a scarification—how astonishing that it had been effected by such a mild, blunt instrument.

She also recalls the beige-gray buildings around the university, the gloomy pharmacy that always kept the light on, in any weather, in all seasons, and the old brown jars with their contents painstakingly spelled out on the label. The little yellow packages of pills for headaches, six in each, held together with a rubber band. She recalls the pleasant ovoid shape of those telephones, molded out of hard rubber, most often black or mahogany—they didn't even have a rotary dial, just a little crank, and their sound was like a little tornado wound up deep within the cable tunnels in order to bring about the voice desired.

She's surprised she can see it all so clearly—for the first time in her life. She must be starting to get old, because it seems like it's in old age that you begin to hear from those little nooks in the brain that have the records of everything that ever happened. She'd never had time before to really think about those types of things, from days gone by; the past was like a smudged streak. Now the movie slows and reveals details—capacious is the human brain. Hers had preserved even her little brown purse, prewar, which had originally belonged to her mother, with soft sides made out of rubber-lined material, with a beautiful metal clasp that looked like a jewel. On the inside it was smooth and cool to the touch; when you reached inside, it seemed like a dead offshoot of time had gotten stuck there.

The next plane, the one to Europe, is even larger, with different stories. It flies well-rested, suntanned tourists. They try to stuff their eccentric souvenirs into the overhead bins—a high drum covered in an ethnic pattern, a straw hat, a wooden Buddha. She sits crammed in between two women, in the very center of the row, in a very uncomfortable place. She rests her head back on her seat, but she knows she won't be able to sleep.

They came to do their studies from the same small town, he specializing in philosophy, she biology. They met up every day after classes, both a little frightened of the big city, a little lost. Sometimes they'd smuggle one another into their different dorms; once—now she remembers—he even climbed up to the second floor of hers along the drainpipe. She remembers her room number, too: 321. But university and the city lasted for only a year. She managed to get through end-of-year exams, and then they left. Her father sold his clinic for a song, lock, stock, and barrel: that dentist's chair, the metal and glass cabinets, the autoclaves and instruments. By the by, now she wonders, where did all of that end up? In the trash heap?

Was the off-white paint still peeling off it? Her mother sold the furniture. There was no sadness, no despair—just an unease about getting rid of everything, because after all it meant starting over.
They'd both been younger than she was now (though then they'd
seemed absolutely elderly to her), and they'd been ready to embark
on a new adventure, anywhere'd be fine: Sweden, Australia, maybe
Madagascar—anywhere, just as far as they could get away from
their rotten, claustrophobic northern life in that absurd, unfriendly
communist country of the late sixties. Her father said it was not a
country suited to human beings, though then he spent the rest of his
life pining away for it. And she wanted to go, she really wanted it,
like any nineteen-year-old—wanted to set out into the world.

It was not a country suited to human beings, but rather to small
mammals, to insects, moths. She's asleep. The plane is suspended in
this clear, frosty air that kills bacteria. Every flight disinfects us.
Every night cleanses us completely. She sees a print, though she
doesn't know its title—she remembers it from her childhood: a
young woman touches the eyelids of an old man kneeling before
her. It's a print from her father's study, and she knows where the
book was kept, on the bottom right shelf, with the other art books.
Now she could shut her eyes and enter that room with the bay windows where you could stand and see the garden. To the right, at eye
level, there was the black hard rubber outlet with the little cylinder
you had to take between your index finger and your thumb and dial
around. It would always put up some resistance before it gave way.
The light came on in the chandelier with the five glass shades like
calyces, which in turn formed a kind of circling wheel. But that

light from the ceiling was faint, and too high up, and she didn't like it. She preferred to turn on the floor lamp with the yellow shade, which had—although who knew how—blades of grass inside it, and she'd sit beside it in that tattered old chair. As a child she thought *boboki* lived inside it, those horrible, not-quite-defined creatures. The book she would now open over her lap was—she remembers—a book of Malczewski. She opens it to the page where the pretty young woman with a scythe is calmly and lovingly shutting the eyes of the old man who kneels before her.

Her terrace looks out over vast meadows, and past these the azure waters of the bay; the rising tide plays with colors, mixes them, varnishes the waves with a silver sheen. She always goes out onto the terrace in the evenings after dinner—a hangover from when she used to smoke. She stands there and watches people engaged in all manner of pleasure and delight. If you painted it, it would look like a joyful, sunny, and perhaps slightly childish Bruegel. A southern Bruegel. People flew kites—one was in the shape of a big, bright fish, whose long, slender fins floated in the air with the grace of a veiltail. Another was a panda bear, an enormous oval that rose high above the people's tiny little figures. Another is a white sail that pulls its owner's short cart along the ground. Think of all the uses you can get out of a kite! Think how helpful the wind is. How good.

People play with dogs, throwing them colorful little balls. The dogs retrieve them with boundless enthusiasm. Itsy-bitsy figures run and ride bikes and roller-skate and play volleyball and badminton and practice yoga. Along the nearby highway glide cars with trailers, and on them boats, catamarans, bicycles, mobile homes. There is a light breeze, the sun is shining, little birds scuffle over some forgotten crumbs beneath a tree.

This is how she understands it: life on this planet gets developed by some powerful force contained in every atom of organic matter. It's a force there is no physical evidence of, for the time being—you can't catch it on even the most precise microscopic images, nor in photographs of the atomic spectrum. It's a thing that consists in bursting open, thrusting forward, in constantly going beyond what it is. That is the engine that drives changes, a blind and powerful energy. To ascribe goals or intentions to it is to misunderstand. Darwin read this energy as well as he could, but he still read it wrong. Competition shmompetition. The more experienced a biologist you become, the longer and harder you look at the complex structures and connections in the biosystem, the stronger your hunch that all animate things cooperate in this growth and bursting, supporting one another. Living organisms give themselves to one another, permit one another to make use of them. If rivalry exists, it is a localized phenomenon, an upsetting of the balance. It is true that tree branches jostle one another out of the way to reach the light, their roots collide in the race to a water source, animals eat each other, but there is in all this a kind of accord, it's just an accord that men find frightening. It might appear that we are actors in a great bodily theater, as though those wars we wage were merely civil wars. This—what other word to use?—lives, has a million traits and qualities, so that everything is contained within it, and there is nothing that might lie outside of it, all death is part of life, and in some sense there is no death. There are no errors. There are no guilty parties and no innocents, either, no merits, no sins, no good or evil; whoever thought up those notions led humankind astray.

She went back into the bedroom and read his letter, which had just arrived, announced by an electronic ping, and suddenly she recalls all the despair this person, this letter-writer had provoked in her, long, long ago. Despair at leaving while he stayed. He came to the train station back then, but she doesn't remember him standing on the platform, although she knows she'd carefully preserved that image once—but all she can remember now is the movement of the train and the flashes of a wintry Warsaw as they slipped faster and faster away, and the words "never again," and the conviction they had triggered. Now it sounds so sentimental, and to tell the truth, she can't understand that pain. It was a good pain, like menstrual pain. A thing reaches completion, an internal process is finalized, eliminating all that is unnecessary. That's why it hurts, but it's just the pain of purging.

For some time they wrote letters to one another; his letters came in light blue envelopes with stamps the color of whole-wheat bread. Their plan, of course, was for him to someday make it to where she was. But, of course, he never made it; how could she ever have believed he would? There were reasons, all of which seem vague now, and even incomprehensible—no passport, politics, the abyss of the winters, which you could get stuck in as though you'd fallen into a crevasse and couldn't move again.

Just before she'd come here she'd suddenly been battered by waves of a strange nostalgia. Strange because it had to do with things that were too trivial to really be missed: the water that collects in puddles in the holes in the sidewalks, the shades of neon left in that water by stray drops of gasoline; the heavy, creaky old doors to the dark stairwells. She also missed the glazed earthenware plates with the brown band with the Społem co-op logo on it that they used at the cafeteria to serve lazy pierogi with melted butter and sugar sprinkled on top. But then with time that nostalgia had seeped into the new land like spilled milk, not leaving any trace. She graduated, and she got a fellowship. She traveled around the world, and she got married to the man she's still with now. They had twins, who will soon have their own children. So it would appear that memory is a drawer stuffed with papers—some of them are totally useless, those one-time documents like dry-cleaning tickets and the proofs of purchase of winter boots or a toaster long since gone. But then there are other reusable ones, testaments not to events but to whole processes: a child's vaccination booklet, her student ID like a tiny passport, its pages half filled with stamps from each term, her school diploma, a certificate of completion from a dressmaking course.

In the next letter she got from him, he wrote that although he was in the hospital now, they'd said they'd let him out for Christmas, and he wouldn't go back after that. They'd already done everything they could, scanned everything they could, diagnosed it all. So now he'd be at home, and he lived outside of Warsaw, in the country, and there was snow, and severe cold all over Europe, with people even freezing to death. He also gave her the name of his illness, but in Polish, so she had no idea what it was, because she just didn't know the Polish name for it. "Do you remember our promise?" he wrote.

"Do you remember that last night before you left? We were sitting in the park, on the grass, it was very hot, it was June, we'd already aced all our exams, and the city, after being heated all day long, now gave off a warmth mixed with the scent of concrete, like it was sweating. Do you remember? You'd brought a bottle of vodka, but we couldn't finish it. We promised we would see each other. That no matter what happened, we would meet again. And there was one other thing. Do you remember?"

She remembered, of course.

He'd had a little pocketknife with a bone handle that had the corkscrew he'd just used to open the bottle (because back then vodka bottles had corks, too, and wax seals), and now with the sharp part of the corkscrew he dug into his hand—if she remembered right, it had been a long cut between his index finger and his thumb—and she had taken that curly metal blade from him and done the same to herself. Then they touched these bloodstains together, applying one scratch to another. This youthful romantic gesture was called blood brotherhood, and it must have come from some movie that had been popular then, or maybe a book, maybe one of Karl May's series on the Apache chief.

Now she inspected her palms, the left and then the right, because she couldn't remember which one it was, but of course she turned up nothing. Time commemorated other kinds of wounds.

Of course she remembered that June night—with age, memory starts to slowly open its holographic chasms, one day pulling out the next, easily, as though on a string, and from days to hours, minutes. Immobile images move, first slowly, repeating over and over those same moments, and it's like extracting ancient skeletons from sand: at first you see a single bone, but a brush soon uncovers more, until finally the whole complex structure is on display, the joints and articulations that make up the construction that supports the body of time.

From Poland they'd gone to Sweden first. It was 1970, and she was nineteen. Within two years they'd realized that Sweden was too close, that the Baltic Sea brought in certain fluids, nostalgias, miasmas, a kind of unpleasant air. Her father was a good dentist, and her mother a dental hygienist—the kinds of people needed all around the world. Just multiply the population count by the number of teeth they'd have, then you'd know your chances. And the farther away the better.

She'd responded to this message, too, reaffirming in surprise that strange promise. And by the next morning she'd already received his reply, as though he'd been waiting impatiently all along, the contents of his next message saved somewhere on his desktop, ready to copy and paste.

"Imagine, if you can, constant pain and progressive paralysis that goes one step further every single day. But even that could be borne, if not for the knowledge that past that pain there is nothing, no redress due, and that every hour will be worse than the one before it, which means you're headed into truly unfathomable depths, into a kind of hell made up of hallucinations, with ten circles of suffering. And you don't get anyone to guide you through it, nobody to take you by the hand and explain what's going on—because there is no explanation, no set of punishments or rewards."

And the next letter, where he complained that it was horrendously difficult for him to write even just clichés: "You know that here there can be no question of anything of the kind. Our tradition's not conducive to that line of thought, and that's exacerbated further by the innate disinclination to any type of reflection on the part of my (could they still be yours, too?) compatriots. It's typically attributed to our painful history, for history was always unkind to us—as soon as things started to go well, they'd always come crashing down again, and so it became sort of established that we'd be wary of the world, and scared, that we'd have faith in the saving power of ironclad rules but also want to break the very rules we came up with.

"My situation is as follows: I'm divorced, and I'm not in any contact with my wife—my sister's taking care of me, but she would never carry out my request. I don't have children, which I greatly regret—it's precisely for these types of things you have to have them, if for nothing else. I am, unfortunately, a public figure, and an unpopular one at that. No doctor would dare to help me. During one of the many political skirmishes in which I was involved I got discredited, and I don't have what you would call a good name now, I know that, and I couldn't care less. I'd get the occasional visitor in the hospital from time to time, but I suspect it wasn't out of any real desire to see me, or out of sympathy (this is what I think), but rather—even if they weren't fully aware of it—to get some closure. So this is what's become of him! And they'd shake their heads by my bedside. I get that, it's a human emotion. I myself am certainly not particularly pure of heart. I messed up a lot of things in my life. I've only really got one thing going for me, which is that I've always been organized. And I'd like to take full advantage of that now."

She had trouble understanding his Polish—she'd forgotten a lot of words completely. She didn't know, for example, what *osoba publiczna* meant, she'd had to think about it, though then she'd figured out it must be "public figure." But what did he mean by "messed up"? That he'd made a mess out of things? That he'd harmed himself?

She tried to picture him writing that letter, if he was sitting up or lying down, and what he looked like, if he was in pajamas, but his image in her head stayed just an outline, not filled in, an empty shape she could look through and see the way out to the meadows and the bay. After this long letter she took out the cardboard box where she kept her old pictures from Poland, and in the end she found him—a young boy, his hairstyle proper, the shadow of his youthful facial hair, in funny-looking glasses and some sort of high-lander's stretched-out sweater, with a hand up around his face—he must have been saying something when this black-and-white picture was taken.

An instance of synchronicity: a few hours later she got a letter with a picture attached. "Writing is harder and harder on me. Please hurry. This is how I look. You should know—although this was taken a year ago." A massive man, the gray hair on his head shaved short, his face smooth, his features soft, a little blurred, sitting in some room where the shelves are loaded down with papers— publishing? There was no resemblance between the two photo-graphs; you could be excused for thinking they were two completely different people.

She didn't know what kind of illness it was. She entered its Polish name into Google, and she found out. Aha. In the evening she asked her husband about it. He explained in detail the mechanism of the illness, its incurability, the progressive degeneration and paralysis.

"Why do you ask?" he said finally.

"Just curious. A friend of a friend has it," she responded evasively, and then, as though in passing, surprising even herself, she brought up a conference in Europe, a last-minute emergency, that she would need to attend.

At only an hour long, from London to Warsaw, the last flight doesn't even really count. She almost doesn't notice it. A lot of young people going home from work. What an odd feeling— everyone speaking Polish so naturally. At first she's as taken aback as though she'd happened on a bunch of Ancient Greeks. They are all dressed warmly: hats, gloves, scarves, down jackets like the ones you wear when you go skiing—and it is only now that it really sinks in that she'll be landing in the heart of winter.

A beleaguered body, reminiscent of a single tendon, stretched out on the bed. He doesn't recognize her when she enters the room, of course. He examines her attentively, knowing it must be her, but he doesn't really recognize her, or at least that's what it looks like.

"Greetings," she says.

And he smiles faintly and closes his eyes for a while.

"You're amazing," he says.

The woman at his bedside, who must be the sister he'd mentioned, makes room for her so she can put her hand on top of his. His hand is bony and ashen; now his blood bears ash, not fire.

"Well, would you looky here," says his sister to him. "Somebody has a visitor! Look who came to see you." And then to her: "Would you like to sit?"

His room looks out onto a snow-covered yard and four enormous pines; at the back there is a fence and a road, and farther down, real villas; she is stunned by the glamour of their architecture. She remembered it differently. There are columns, verandas, lighted driveways. She hears the wheezing of an engine as a neighbor tries in vain to start his car. There is a slight scent in the air of fire, of the smoke given off by coniferous wood.

He glances at her and smiles, but only with his lips, whose corners curl up a little while his eyes stay serious. There's a stand with an IV drip to the left of the bed; his IV protrudes from a blue, swollen vein that seems to be near collapse.

When his sister leaves, he says, "Is it you?"

She smiles.

"Would you look at that, I came," she says: a simple sentence she'd been practicing in her head for some time now. And it turns out fine.

"Thank you," he says. "I didn't think—" And he swallows like he's about to cry.

She's afraid she'll be subjected to some uncomfortable scene. "Don't be silly," she says. "I didn't hesitate for one second."

"You look lovely. Young. Although you did dye your hair," he says, trying to lighten things up.

His lips are cracked. She spots a drinking glass on his bedside table with a straw wrapped in gauze sticking out of it.

"Would you like some water?"

He nods.

She wets the gauze in the glass and leans over this prostrate man; he smells sickeningly sweet. His eyes flutter shut as she delicately moistens his lips.

They try to have a conversation, but they can't quite pull it off. He keeps shutting his eyes for a few seconds, and she can never tell if he's still there or if he's drifted off somewhere. She tries some-thing along the lines of "Remember when . . . ," but it doesn't take. When she falls silent he touches her hand and says, "Please tell me a story. Please talk."

"How much longer . . ." She tries to find the words. "Will this last?"

He says it could be within weeks.

"What's that?" she asks, glancing at the drip.

He smiles again.

"Super-value meal," he says. "Breakfast, lunch, and dinner. Pork chops and cabbage, apple pie and beer for dessert."

Quietly she repeats after him the word for "cabbage," *kapusta*, a word she had all but forgotten, and it is enough to make her hungry. She takes his hand and rubs his cold fingers carefully. A stranger's hands, a stranger—there is nothing in him that she knows now. A stranger's body, a stranger's voice. She might just as easily be in someone else's room.

"Do you really recognize me?" she asks him.

"Of course I do. You haven't changed that much."

But she can tell this isn't true. She knows he doesn't recognize her at all. Maybe if they could spend more time together, time for all these different faces, gestures, habits of movement to properly unfold . . . But what would be the point? She thinks he's drifted off again for a while now—he's shut his eyes as though he's sleeping. She doesn't dis-turb him. She watches his ashen face and sunken eyes, his nails that are so white they look like they are made of wax, but carelessly, be-cause the line between them and the skin of his fingers is blurred.

After a while he comes to again, looking at her as though only a second has passed.

"I found you online a long time ago. I read your articles, although I couldn't really follow most of them." He smiles wanly.
"All those complicated terms."

"Did you really read them?" she asks in surprise.

"You seem good," he says. "You look good."

"I am," she says.

"How was your trip? How many hours is it?"

She tells him about her layovers, about the airports. She tries
to figure out the hours, but nothing works out right: time apparently expanded when you flew from east to west. She describes her
home to him, and the view of the bay. She tells him about the opossums, and about her son going to Guatemala for a year to teach
English in a rural school. About her parents, who had died in quick
succession, fulfilled, gray-haired, telling secrets to each other in
Polish. About her husband, who performs complicated neurological
operations.

"You kill animals, don't you?" he asks suddenly.

She is startled. She looks at him. And then she understands.

"It's hard," she says, "but it has to be done. Water?"

He shakes his head.

"Why?" he says.

She makes a vague gesture with her hand. Of impatience. It's
obvious why. Because people had introduced domesticated animals
to the island that were previously unknown to the native ecosystem.
Some had been brought in out of carelessness, a long time ago, over
two hundred years ago, while others seemed to have come ashore
through no fault of anyone, just by escaping rabbits. Opossums and
weasels farmed for their fur. Plants had slipped out of people's

gardens—just recently she'd seen clumps of bloodred geraniums on the side of the road. Garlic had gotten away and turned feral in the wilderness. Its flowers had faded somewhat—who knew, maybe after thousands of years it was making some sort of local mutation of its own here. People like her worked hard to keep the island from being contaminated by the rest of the world; to keep random seeds from sneaking out from random pockets and landing in the island's soil; to keep foreign fungi from banana peels brought in from knocking down the whole ecosystem. And on their shoes, on the soles of their hiking boots, to keep any other undesirable immigrants from getting through—bacteria, insects, algae. It's a battle that must be waged, though of course it's been doomed from the start. You have to make peace with the fact that in the end there won't be individual ecosystems. The world all sloshed together in a single sludge.

But you have to enforce customs regulations. You're not allowed to bring any biological substances onto the island; seeds require a special permit.

She notices he is listening attentively. But is this topic appropriate to this type of encounter? she thinks, and then gets quiet.

"Tell me, tell me," he says.

She straightens his pajamas, which have fallen open at his chest, revealing a blanched section of skin with a couple of gray hairs.

"Look, this is my husband. These are my kids," she said, reaching for her purse, pulling out her wallet, where in a transparent compartment she keeps her pictures. She shows him her children. He can't move his head, so she raises it slightly for him. He smiles.

"Had you been here before?"

She shakes her head.

"But I've been in Europe, for different conferences. Well, three."

"And you didn't feel like coming back?"

She thinks for a moment.

"I had so much going on in my life, you know, with school, and then the kids, and then work. We built this house on the ocean," she starts to say, but in her mind she hears the voice of her father, saying how the country was suited only to small mammals and insects, moths. "I guess I just forgot about it," she concludes.

"Do you know how to do it?" he asks after a longer pause.

"I do," she says.

"When?"

"Whenever you want."

With evident strain he turns to face the window.

"As soon as possible," he says. "Tomorrow?"

"Okay," she says. "Tomorrow."

"Thank you," he says, and he looks at her as though he's just told her he loves her.

As she leaves an old, overfed dog comes up and sniffs her. His sister is standing in the snow, on the porch, smoking a cigarette.

"Smoke?" she says.

She knows this is an invitation to talk, and to her own surprise, she accepts a cigarette. It's very slender, mentholated. She is staggered by her first drag.

"He's on morphine patches, that's why he's not fully conscious," says the woman. "Was it a long trip for you?"

And she realizes that he hasn't told his sister. So she doesn't know what to say.

"No, no. We worked together for a while," she says without

hesitation; she'd never had the slightest suspicion she was capable of lying. "I'm a foreign correspondent," she adds quickly, wanting to come up with something to explain her accent, which sounds foreign after all this time.

"God is unjust, unjust and cruel. To torment him," says his sister, with a fierce determination on her face. "It's good you came. He's so alone. There's a nurse who comes from the clinic in the mornings. She says it would be better to put him back in hospice care, but he doesn't want that."

They extinguish their cigarettes in the snow simultaneously. They don't so much as hiss as they go out.

"I'll be back tomorrow," she says. "To say good-bye, because I've got to go already."

"Tomorrow? So soon? He was so happy you were coming . . . and you only came for a few days." The woman makes a movement like she wants to grab her hand, as though she wants to add: Please don't leave us.

She has to rebook her tickets—she hadn't thought it would go so quickly. The most important flight, the one from Europe home, can't be changed now, so as it turns out she has a week to kill. But she decides not to stay here—it'd be better to just go already, and besides, she feels out of place in this snow and this darkness. There are seats available to Amsterdam and London for the following afternoon; she chooses Amsterdam. She'll be a tourist there for a week.

She eats dinner by herself, and then she takes a walk down the main street of the Old Town. She looks in the windows of the little shops, which mostly sell souvenirs and amber jewelry she doesn't care for. And the city itself seems impenetrable, too big and too cold. People move around it all bundled up, their faces half hidden by their collars and their scarves, their lips emitting little clouds of steam. Piles of frozen snow lie on the sidewalks. She gives up on the idea of visiting the halls where she'd once lived. In fact, everything here repels her. Suddenly she's utterly baffled by this phenomenon of people actually choosing, of their own free will, to go back and visit the different places of their youths. What is it they think they're going to find? What is it they have to have validation of—just the fact that they had been there? Or that they'd done the right thing in leaving? Or perhaps they were urged on by some hope that recollecting more precisely these lost places would work with the lightning speed of a zipper to unite the past and future, creating a single stable surface, tooth to tooth, a metal suture.

And clearly she repels the locals, too, who don't so much as look at her, overlooking her as they pass. It is as though her childhood dreams of being invisible have all come true. A fairy-tale gadget: the hat of invisibility you put on your head to temporarily vanish from everyone else's view.

In the last few years she has realized that all you have to do to become invisible is be a woman of a certain age, without any outstanding features: it's automatic. Not only invisible to men, but also to women, who no longer treat her as competition in anything. It is a new and surprising sensation, how people's eyes just sort of float right over her face, her cheeks and her nose, not even skimming the surface. They look straight through her, no doubt looking past her at ads and landscapes and schedules. Yes, yes, all signs point to her having become invisible, though now she thinks, too, of all the opportunities that this invisibility might afford—she simply has to learn how she can take them. For example, if something crazy were to happen, nobody on the scene would even remember her having been there, or if they did, all they'd say would be, "Some woman," or "Somebody else was over there . . ." Men are more ruthless here than women, who sometimes still paid her compliments on things like earrings, if she wore them, while men don't even try to hide anything, never looking at her longer than a second. Just occasionally some child would fixate on her for some unknown reason, making a meticulous and dispassionate examination of her face until finally turning away, toward the future.

She spends the evening in the sauna at the hotel, and then she falls asleep, too fast, exhausted from jet lag, like a lone card taken out of its deck and shuffled into some other, strange one. She wakes up too early in the morning, seized by fear. She is lying on her back; it's still dark, and she thinks about her husband saying good-bye to her almost in his sleep. What if she never sees him again? And she pictures leaving her purse on the steps and taking off her clothes and lying down with him the way he likes her to, pressing up against his bare back, her nose against the nape of his neck. She calls. It's evening there, and he's just come home from the hospital. She tells him a little bit about the conference. And the weather, how cold it is, how she suspects he wouldn't make it. She reminds him to water the flowers in the garden, especially the tarragon in the rocky patch. She asks if she's gotten any phone calls from her work. Then she takes a shower, makes herself up, and heads down to breakfast, where she is the first to arrive.

In the little bag with her makeup there is also a vial that looks like a perfume sample. She takes it with her today, picking up a syringe at a pharmacy on her way. It's actually kind of funny because she can't remember the bizarre word for syringe, *strzykawka*, so instead she says the word for injection, *zastrzyk*. They sound so similar.

As her taxi crosses the city, it slowly dawns on her what the source of her sense of not belonging was: it's a different city now, in no way reminiscent of the one she'd had still in her head; there's nothing here for her memory to grab on to. Nothing looks familiar. The houses are too stocky, too squat, the streets too wide, the doors too solid; it's different cars driving down different streets, plus in the opposite direction of what she's used to now. Which is why she can't quite shake the feeling that she's ended up on the other side of a mirror in some fictional land, where everything is unreal, which somehow also makes everything allowed. There is no one who could grab her hand, no one who could detain her. She moves along these frozen streets like a visitor from another dimension, like some higher being; she has to sort of contract inside herself to even be able to fit. And her only task here is this one mission, obvious and aseptic, a mission of love.

The cabdriver gets a little lost once they get to that little town with the villas, which also have a fairy-tale name: Zalesie Górne, meaning over the hills, and through the woods. She asks him to stop around the corner, at a little bar, and she pays.

She walks several dozen meters quickly, and then she struggles through all the uncleared snow on the familiar path from the gate to the house. As she opens the gate she knocks off its snowy cap, revealing the address underneath: *One*.

His sister lets her in again. Her eyes are red from crying.

"He's expecting you," she says, and then she disappears, saying, "He even asked for a shave."

He is lying in fresh bedding, conscious, facing the door—he really has been expecting her. When she sits down on the bed beside him and takes his hands, she notices there is something strange about them: they're dripping with sweat, even the backs of them. She smiles at him.

"So how's it going?" she says.

"Okay," he says.

He is lying: it is not going okay.

"Stick that patch on me," he says, and he glances over at a flat box lying on his bedside table. "I'm in pain. We have to wait until it starts to work. I wasn't sure when you'd get here, and I wanted to be conscious when you came. I might not have recognized you otherwise. I might think that maybe it wasn't you. You're so young and beautiful."

She strokes the hollow at his temple. The patch adheres like a second skin, a mercy skin, just above where his kidneys are. She is shaken by the sight of a section of his body, so battered and beleaguered. She bites her lip.

"Will I feel it somehow?" he asks, but she assures him he doesn't need to worry about that.

"Tell me what you'd like. Would you like to be alone for a minute?"

He shakes his head. His forehead is dry as parchment paper.

"I don't want to do confession," he says. "Just hold my face in your hands." He smiles weakly; there is mischief in his smile.

She does it without hesitation. She feels his thin skin and delicate bones, the cavities of his eyeballs. She feels him pulsing underneath her fingers, trembling, as though tense. The skull, that delicate latticework structure of bone, perfectly solid and strong yet fragile at the same time. Her throat tightens, and it is the first and last time she is close to tears. She knows this contact brings him relief; she can feel it soothing the tremor beneath his skin. Finally she removes her hands, but he stays still, with his eyes closed. Slowly she leans in over him and kisses his forehead.

"I was a good person," he whispers, digging into her now with his eyes.

She assents.

"Tell me a story about something," he says.

Stumped, she clears her throat.

He prompts her: "Tell me what it's like where you are." So she starts:

"It's the middle of summer, the lemons on the trees are ripe now . . ."

He interrupts: "Can you see the ocean from your window?"

"Yes," she says. "When the tide goes out, the water leaves seashells in its wake."

But this is a ruse: he hadn't planned to listen, and for a moment his gaze clouds over, but then its former sharpness is restored. Then he looks out at her from very far away, and then she knows that he is no longer a part of the world where she is. She could not have identified exactly what it was she saw in him—whether fear and panic or precisely the opposite: relief. Faintly he conveys—clumsily, and in a whisper—his gratitude, or something like it, and then he goes to sleep. Then she takes the vial from her purse and fills the syringe up with its contents. She removes the drip from the IV and slowly injects all the droplets of the liquid she has brought. Nothing happens aside from the fact that his breathing stops, suddenly, naturally, as though the movement of his rib cage from before had been an odd anomaly. She runs her hand over his face, reinserts the drip into his IV, and smooths out the place on the sheets where she'd been sitting. Then she leaves.

His sister is standing on the porch again, smoking.

"Cigarette?" she says.

This time she says no.

"Do you think you'll be able to visit him again?" asks the woman. "It's been so important to him that you come."

"I'm leaving today," she says, and as she goes down the stairs, she adds, "You take care of yourself."

When the plane takes off it switches off her mind. She does not give it a further thought. All those memories now disappear. She spends several days in Amsterdam, which at this time of year is windy and cold and could essentially be reduced to combinations of three colors, white, gray, and black, wandering around museums and spending the evenings at her hotel. As she walks along the main street, she comes upon an anatomy exhibit, with human specimens. Intrigued, she goes inside and spends two hours there, taking in the human body in all its possible permutations, perfectly preserved using the latest techniques. But since she's in a strange state of mind and very tired, she sees it through a kind of fog, inattentively, just the outlines. She sees nerve endings and the vas deferens that look like exotic plants that had escaped the control of their gardener, bulbs, orchids, lace, embroidery of tissues, meshwork of neuration, slate shards, stamens, antennae and whiskers, racemes, streams, folds, waves, dunes, craters, elevations, mountains, valleys, plateaus, winding blood vessels . . .

In the air, over the ocean, she finds the colored leaflet for the exhibit in her purse, featuring a human body, without skin, posed like in the sculpture by Rodin: head resting on hand resting on arm resting on knee, body troubled, almost thinking, and although it's missing its skin and its face (the face turns out to be one of the most superficial characteristics of the whole human form), you can still see that the eyes are oblique, exotic. Then, half asleep, submerged in the dark, discreet rumble of the plane's engines, she imagines that soon enough, when the technology becomes more affordable, plastination will be available to all. You'll be able to put up the bodies of your loved ones instead of putting up tombstones, with labels like "So-and-so traveled in this very body for a few years. Then he left it at such-and-such an age." As the plane prepares for its descent, she is suddenly seized by fear and panic. And she grips the armrests, hard.

When finally, exhausted, she gets back to her own country, back onto that beautiful island, the customs officer asks her several routine questions: had she come into contact with any animals where she'd been, had she been in rural areas, might she have been exposed to biological contaminants.

She pictures herself on that porch, shaking the snow off her boots, pictures that overfed dog running up the stairs and rubbing up against her legs. And she pictures her hands as they opened the vial that looked like a perfume sample. So she says, peacefully, yes.

The customs official requests that she step aside. And there her heavy winter boots are washed down with a disinfecting agent.

## FEAR NOT

I gave a ride to a young Serb in the Czech Republic named Nebojša. The whole way he told me stories about the war, to the point that I began to regret that I'd picked him up.

He said that death marks places like a dog marking its territory. Some people can sense it right away, while others simply start to feel uncomfortable after a time. Every stay in any place betrays the quiet ubiquitousness of the dead. As he said:

"At first you always see what's alive and vibrant. You're delighted by nature, by the local church painted in different colors, by the smells and all that. But the longer you're in a place, the more the charm of those things fades. You wonder who lived here before you came to this home and this room, whose things these are, who scratched the wall above the bed and what tree the sills were cut from. Whose hands built the elaborately decorated fireplace, paved the courtyard? And where are they now? In what form? Whose idea led to these paths around the pond and who had the idea of planting a willow out the window? All the houses, avenues, parks, gardens, and streets are permeated with the deaths of others. Once you start feeling this, something starts to pull you elsewhere, you start to think it's time to move on."

He added that when we are in motion, there's no time for such idle meditations. Which is why to people on trips everything seems new and clean, virginal, and, in some sense, immortal.

And when he got out at Mikulec, I repeated to myself his strange-sounding name. Ne-boy-sha. It sounded exactly like the Polish *Nie bój się*: do not be afraid.

## DAY OF THE DEAD

The guidebook maintains that this holiday lasts for three days. When it falls in the middle of the week, the government rounds out the length of the holiday's duration, and schools and public offices get a whole week off. Radio stations broadcast without interruption the music of Chopin, since it is thought that this favors concentration and serious reflection. It is expected that every inhabitant of the country will visit in this time the graves of their dead. Since the country has over the course of the last twenty years gone through an unprecedented boom and industrialization, this means that almost all the residents of several of the large modern cities set out for distant provinces. All the flights and trains and buses have been reserved for months. Those who weren't quick enough before will now be forced to drive to the graves of their ancestors in their own cars. On the eve of the holiday the roads out of the cities are already congested. Because the holiday is in August, sitting in a traffic jam in high temperatures is not much fun. Therefore people, anticipating all sorts of inconveniences, come equipped with small portable plasma TVs and coolers. If you close the tinted windows and turn on the AC, you can get through those few hours, particularly in the pleasant company of family or friends, with a traveling buffet. This is a time people make phone calls. Thanks to the fact that mobile phones are being used everywhere for video connections, you can make up the distances in social contacts. You can even, sitting in a traffic jam this way, connect with your friends through video-conferences, gossip and make plans to meet up after everyone gets back home.

To ancestral spirits one brings gifts: cookies baked especially for this purpose, fruit, prayers written on pieces of material.

Those who remain in the cities experience very strange sensations: the giant shopping centers are closed and even the huge screens with advertisements are turned off for this period. The number of metros is reduced, and some stations are completely shut down (for example, University and Stock Exchange). Fast-food restaurants and nightclubs are closed. The city is so empty that this year the authorities decided to stop the electronically controlled system of city fountains, which is expected to bring massive savings.

## RUTH

After his wife died, he made a list of all the places that had the same name as her: Ruth.

He found quite a few of them, not only towns, but also streams, little settlements, hills—even an island. He said he was doing it for her sake, and besides, it gave him strength to see that in some indefinable way she still existed in the world, even if only in name. And that furthermore, whenever he would stand at the foot of a hill called Ruth, he would get the sense she hadn't died at all, that she was right there, just differently.

Her life insurance was able to cover the costs of his travels.

## RECEPTION AREAS AT LARGE FANCY HOTELS

In a rush I enter and am greeted by the polite smile of the porter. I look around as though I'm busy, as though I've come to meet someone. I put on an act. I glance impatiently at my watch, and then I collapse into one of the chairs and light a cigarette.

Reception areas are better than cafés. You don't have to order anything, you don't have to get into any disputes with the waiters, or eat anything. The hotel extends before me its rhythms, it's a whirlpool, and its center is the revolving door. The flowing stream of people pauses, turns in place for a night or two, then continues.

Whoever was supposed to come won't come, but does that undermine the ethos of my waiting? It's an activity similar to meditation—time flows and brings little in the way of novelty, situations repeat (a taxi drives up, a new guest gets out of it, the porter takes their suitcase out of the trunk, they walk up to reception, with the key to the elevator). Sometimes situations double up (two taxis arrive symmetrically from two opposing directions, and two guests get out of them, two porters take out two suitcases from the two trunks) or multiply, it gets crowded, the situation gets tense, chaos looms, but it's just a complicated figure, hard to see at first its complex harmony. At other times the hall becomes unexpectedly empty, and then the porter flirts with the receptionist, but only absentmindedly, halfheartedly, remaining at full hotel readiness.

I sit like this for about an hour, no longer. I see those coming out of the elevator and rushing off to a meeting, late by nature, sometimes in their rush they spin around in the revolving door as though in a mill that will grind them into dust in a moment. I see those who shamble along, dragging their feet, as though forcing themselves to put one foot in front of the other, lingering before every movement. Women waiting for men, men waiting for women. The women wear fresh makeup that the coming evening will wipe off completely, and over them a cloud of perfume, a sacred halo. The men act out complete freedom, but in reality they're tense, living somewhere in the lower floors of their bodies today, in their lower abdomens.

This waiting periodically brings lovely presents—here a man is escorting a woman to a taxi. They get out of the elevator. She is small, petite, dark-haired, dressed in a tight short skirt, but she doesn't look vulgar. An elegant prostitute. He walks behind her, tall, graying, in a gray suit, with his hands in his trouser pockets. They don't talk, and they keep a distance; it's hard to believe that just a moment ago their mucus membranes were rubbing against each other, that he was thoroughly investigating the insides of her mouth with his tongue. They walk side by side now, but he lets her go first again into the mill of the revolving door. The taxi is waiting, notified. The woman gets in without a word, at most just a slight smile. There is no "See you later" or "This was nice," nothing of the kind. He leans into the window just a little, but I don't think he says anything. Maybe a completely superfluous "good-bye," perhaps still bound by habit. And she's driven off. He comes back, meanwhile, with his hands in his pockets, light and content, there's even the hint of a smile on his face. He's already starting to come up with plans for the evening, has already remembered e-mail and phones, but he won't go to them just yet, he'll keep enjoying this lightness for a bit, perhaps he'll just go out for a drink.

## POINT

Passing through these cities, I do know that at some point I will have to stay in one of them for longer, maybe even settle down. I weigh them in my mind, compare and evaluate, and it always seems to me that each of them is too far, or too near.

Which means there must be some fixed point around which all of my perambulations revolve. Too far from what, too near to what?

## CROSS SECTION AS LEARNING METHOD

Learning by layers; each layer is only vaguely reminiscent of the next or of the previous; usually it's a variation, a modified version, each contributes to the order of the whole, though you wouldn't know it looking at each one on its own, cut off from the whole.

Each slice is a part of the whole, but it's governed by its own rules. The three-dimensional order, reduced and imprisoned in a two-dimensional layer, seems abstract. You might even think that there was no whole, that there never had been.

## CHOPIN'S HEART

It is widely known that Chopin died at two o'clock in the morning (*"aux petites heures de la nuit,"* as French Wikipedia tells us) on October 17, 1849. By his deathbed were several of his closest friends, among them his sister Ludwika, who attended to him munificently until the very end, as well as Father Aleksander Jełowicki, who, shaken by the quiet, animal deceasing of a thoroughly ruined body, by the drawn-out battle that was every gulp of air, first fainted in the stairwell and then, under the rubric of some rebellion he wasn't altogether conscious of, thought up a better version of the virtuoso's death in his memoirs. He wrote, among other things, that the last words of Fryderyk Chopin had been, "I am already at the source of all happiness," which was a very obvious lie, although certainly beautiful and moving. In fact, as Ludwika recalled it, her brother said nothing; in fact, he had been unconscious for a few hours. What actually escaped his lips in the very end was a stream of dark, thick blood.

Now Ludwika, freezing and exhausted, is driving off in a stagecoach. She's nearing Leipzig. It's a wet winter, and heavy clouds with black bellies are coming up on them from the west; it will most likely snow. Many months have passed since the funeral, but yet another funeral, in Poland, awaits Ludwika now. Fryderyk Chopin had always said he wanted to be buried in his native land, and because he knew perfectly well that he was dying, he had planned his death quite carefully. And his funerals, too.

No sooner had he died than Solange's husband had arrived. He arrived so promptly it was as if he had been waiting in his overcoat and his boots for a knock on his door. He appeared with all his equipment in a leather bag. First he coated the lifeless hand of the deceased in fat, placed it deliberately and respectfully upon a small wooden trough, and poured plaster over it. Then with Ludwika's help, he made a death mask—they had to do it before the lines of his face had stiffened unduly, before death had intervened in them, for death renders all faces similar.

Quietly, with no fuss, Fryderyk Chopin's next wish was fulfilled.

The second day after his death a doctor recommended by Countess Potocka asked that the body be undressed to the waist and then, having laid an armful of sheets around the body's bare rib cage, opened it with his scalpel in a single swift movement. Ludwika, who was there for this, felt that the body had trembled, and had even let out a sort of sigh. Later, when the sheets were almost black with blood clots, she turned to face the wall.

The doctor rinsed the heart in a basin, and Ludwika was surprised at how big, shapeless, colorless it was. It barely fit into the jar filled with alcohol, so the doctor advised they get a bigger one. The muscular tissue must not be compressed nor touch the walls of the jar.

Ludwika dozes off now, rocked by the regular clatter of the carriage, and in the seat opposite her, next to her traveling companion, Aniela, a lady appears, someone she doesn't know, but someone she might have known a long time ago, back in Poland, wearing a dusty mourning dress like the widows of the 1830 uprisings, with an ostentatious cross on her breast. Her face is swollen, made ashen by Siberian frosts; her hands, in worn-out gray gloves, keep the jar. Ludwika awakes with a moan and checks the contents of her basket. Everything is fine. She pushes her hat back up; it had slid down onto her forehead. She curses in French: her neck is so stiff. Aniela wakes up, too, and draws the shades. The flat winter landscape is strikingly sad. In the distance there are some hamlets, human settlements bathed in a wet gray. Ludwika imagines herself crawling along a large table, like an insect under the attentive gaze of some monstrous entomologist. She shudders and asks Aniela for an apple.

"Where are we?" she asks, looking out the window.

"We have a few hours left," says Aniela soothingly. She hands her companion one of last year's wrinkled apples.

The funeral was supposed to take place at La Madeleine. They had already arranged the mass, but in the meantime the body was displayed in the Place Vendôme, where hordes of friends and acquaintances kept coming to pay their respects. Despite the covered windows, the sun kept trying to sneak in to play with the warm colors of the autumn flowers: purple asters, honey-toned chrysanthemum. Inside the candles had exclusive sovereignty, giving the impression that the color of the flowers was profound and succulent, and the face of the deceased not so pale as in daylight.

As it turned out, it was going to be difficult to fulfill Fryderyk's wish that Mozart's *Requiem* be played at his funeral. His friends had managed, through their numerous contacts, to assemble the finest musicians and singers, including the best bass singer in Europe, Luigi Lablache—an amusing Italian who could impersonate whomever he wished in a manner found impressive by all. And in fact, on one of the evenings when everyone was awaiting the funeral, he had done such a perfect impersonation of Chopin that the whole company had roared with laughter, not really knowing if they ought to—for the deceased was not yet even underground. But in the end someone said that after all it was really a proof of love and remembrance. And that in that way he would remain with the living for longer. Everyone remembered how Fryderyk could so proficiently and maliciously parody others. One thing was certain: he had been a man of many talents.

In essence, everything got complicated. Women weren't allowed to perform solos—or even to perform in the choir—at La Madeleine. Such was their age-old tradition: no women. Only men's voices, at the most the voices of eunuchs (to the Church even a man with no balls is better than a woman, as the situation was summarized by the woman in charge of the sopranos, an Italian singer, Miss Graziella Panini), where were they going to find eunuchs in that day and age, in 1849? How could they sing "Tuba mirum," then, without the soprano and alto parts? The parish priest at La Madeleine told them that the rules could not be changed, not even for Chopin.

"How long are we supposed to keep the body? Are we going to have to turn, for the love of God, to Rome for an answer?" cried Ludwika, who had been driven to despair.

Because October was quite warm that year, the body was transferred to a chilly morgue. It was overlain with flowers, and it was practically invisible underneath them. It lay in semidarkness, slight, gaunt, heartless; a snow-white shirt concealed the set of not particularly painstaking stitches with which the rib cage had been resealed.

In the meantime the rehearsals continued for *Requiem*, as well-placed friends of the deceased negotiated delicately with the parish priest. In the end it was decided that the women, the soloists as well as the members of the choir, would stand behind a heavy black curtain, invisible to churchgoers. Only Graziella complained, no one else, but in the end it was decided that in this particular situation such a resolution was still better than none.

While waiting for the funeral, Fryderyk's close friends came every evening to his sister's or to George Sand's to remember him. They would dine together and exchange the latest society gossip.

Those days were strangely peaceful, as though not belonging to the ordinary calendar.

Graziella, petite and dark-complexioned, with a tempest of curly hair, was a friend of Delfina Potocka, and both women had come to visit Ludwika on several occasions. Graziella, sipping liqueur, mocked the baritone and the conductor but was quite happy to speak about herself. As artists always are. She limped with one leg because she had been mauled the previous year in Vienna during the street fighting. The crowd had overturned her carriage, no doubt in the conviction that it contained some wealthy aristocrat rather than an actress. Graziella had a weakness for pricy carriages and an elegant toilette, probably because she came from a family of cobblers in Lombardy.

"Can an actress not travel in a sumptuous carriage? Is it wrong, when one has attained successes, to allow oneself a little pleasure?" she said in her Italian accent, which made it sound like she was stuttering slightly.

Graziella's misfortune had been to find herself in the wrong place at the wrong time. The crowd, with its revolutionary inclinations, not daring to attack the emperor's palace, which was surrounded by guards, began to ransack his collections. Graziella watched them drag out everything that could be equated, in the mind of the people, with aristocratic decadence, luxury, and cruelty. The raving crowd threw armchairs out of windows, ripped apart settees, tore the high-priced paneling off the walls. With a crash they broke the beautiful crystal mirrors. They destroyed, too, the glass cases containing archaeological treasures. Hurling fossils out onto the sidewalk, they shattered the windowpanes. In no time they had plundered the semiprecious stones; they then took to the skeletons and the stuffed animals. Some sort of spokesman of the people called for all the stuffed humans and other mummies to be given a proper Christian funeral, or at the very least for these proofs of the authorities' usurpation of the human body to be destroyed. A great pyre was built; they burned everything they came across.

The carriage landed in such an unfortunate position that the wires of the crinoline wounded her leg and obviously severed nerves, because the limb was left somewhat lifeless. As she was recounting these dramatic events, she raised her skirt and showed the other ladies her leg, immobilized by a leather sleeve with whalebone, held in place by the hoops that also held up her dress.

"Here's what crinoline's good for," said the singer.

It was the singer's gesture—whose voice and performance were much appreciated at the funeral mass—that gave Ludwika the idea. That gesture: lifting up the bell-shaped dress and revealing the mystery of the complicated dome that extended along whalebone and the wires of a parasol.

Several thousand people came to the funeral. They had to redirect cab traffic from the route of the procession. All of Paris came to a stop because of the funeral. When they began the "Introitus," prepared with such diligence, and the voices in the choir struck the vault of the church, people began to cry. The "Requiem aeternam" was very powerful, and everyone was very moved by it, but Ludwika could no longer feel any sadness, having cried it all out already—but she did feel anger. Because what kind of miserable, pathetic world was this, where you die so young—where you die at all? And why him? Why that way? She raised a handkerchief to her eyes, but not to wipe tears, just to be able to clamp down on something as hard as she could, and to cover her eyes, which contained not water, but fire.

*Tuba mirum spargens sonum*
*Per sepulcra regionum,*
*Coget omnes ante thronum*

began the bass, Luigi Lablache, so warmly, so plaintively, that her anger abated. Then the tenor came in, and the alto from behind the curtains:

*Mors stupebit et natura,*
*Cum resurget creatura,*
*Judicanti responsura.*
*Liber scriptus proferetur,*
*In quo totum continetur,*
*Unde mundus judicetur.*
*Judex ergo cum sedebit*
*Quidquid latet apparebit:*
*Nil inultum remanebit.*

Until finally she heard the pure voice of Graziella shooting up like fireworks, like the revelation of her crippled leg, of the naked truth. Graziella sang the best, that was clear, and her voice was only slightly muffled by the curtain; Ludwika imagined the little Italian girl straining, intent, head raised, the veins of her neck swollen—Ludwika had seen her in rehearsals—as she belted out the lyrics in that extraordinary voice of hers, crystal clear, diamond clear, in spite of the heavy curtain, in spite of her leg, to hell with the whole damn world:

> *Quid sum miser tunc dicturus,*
> *Quem patronum rogaturus . . .*

A half hour or so before the border with the Grand Duchy of Poznań, the stagecoach stopped at an inn. There the travelers first freshened up and had a small meal—a little cold baked meat, bread, and fruit—and then they went off and disappeared, much like the other passengers, into the thicket by the side of the road. For a little while they just enjoyed the buttercups in bloom; then Ludwika took from her basket an ample jar with a brown piece of muscle and tucked it away into a cleverly woven leather pouch. Aniela meticulously tied the ends of the leather straps to the scaffolding of the crinoline level with the pubic mound. When the dress fell into place, it would be impossible to tell that such a treasure lay concealed under the surface. Ludwika turned away several times, covered herself up with her dress, and headed back to the carriage.

"I wouldn't get far with this," she said to her companion. "It's bashing against my legs."

But she didn't have to get far. She returned to her seat and sat straight up, perhaps somewhat stiffly, but she was a lady, the sister of Fryderyk Szopen. She was a Pole.

When the Prussian gendarmerie at the border ordered them to get out of the carriage, when they carefully inspected it to make

sure the women weren't trying to slip something into Congress Poland that might encourage some ridiculous independent inclinations of the Poles, they naturally found nothing.

On the other side of the border, in Kalisz, a carriage sent from
the capital was awaiting them, along with several friends. Friends
and witnesses to that sad ceremony. In their tailcoats and their top
hats, they formed a kind of hedgerow, their faces pale and mournful, their heads turning devotedly toward each package as it was
unloaded. But Ludwika, with the help of Aniela, who had been let
in on the secret, managed to get away for a moment and extricate
the jar from the warm insides of her dress. Aniela, rummaging
around in lace, drew out the jar safely and handed it to Ludwika
with the gesture of someone handing a mother her newborn child.
And then Ludwika burst into tears.

Escorted by several carriages, Chopin's heart did ultimately
make it back to Warsaw.


## DRY SPECIMENS

Each of my pilgrimages aims at some other pilgrim. This time in the
details draped over oak shelves crowned with a beautifully calli-
graphed inscription:

> Eminet in Minimus
> Maximus Ille Deus

Here the so-called dry specimens of internal organs are collected.
They are done in such a way that a given body part or organ is

cleansed and then stuffed with cotton wool and dried. After drying, the surface of the specimen is coated in a varnish, the same kind used to conserve the surfaces of paintings. Several layers are applied. After the cotton wool is removed, the inside of the specimen is also coated in the varnish.

Unfortunately, the varnish is unable to keep the tissues from aging, so that with time all dry specimens acquire a similar brownish shade.

Here, for example, we have a splendidly preserved human stomach, enlarged, balloon-like, the lining thin as though made of parchment; meanwhile the intestines, thick and thin—I wonder what goods of the world were consumed by this digestive system, how many animals passed through it, how many seeds slipped through, how many fruits rolled through.

Next to it, as a bonus, there's also a turtle penis and the kidney of a dolphin.

## NETWORK STATE

I am a citizen of a network state. Occupied with moving around in various directions, I've lost my orientation in the political matters of my country in recent times. Conversations have gone on, negotiations, conferences, sessions, summits. Great maps have roamed over tables where flags have marked conquered positions, vectors drawn to show the directions of the next conquests.

Just a few years ago on the screen of my phone at the inadvertent crossing of some now totally invisible or conventional border, the exotic names of foreign networks would register, ones no one remembers today. We didn't notice the nighttime coups, the contents of the capitulation treaties were never released to the public. Of the movements of imperial armies made up of polite, obliging officials the public was not informed.

My phone, equally polite, immediately informs me as soon as I get off a plane which province of the network state I now find myself in. It also gives necessary information, offers help should anything happen to me. It has emergency numbers, and from time to time for Valentine's Day or Christmas it encourages me to take part in promotions and contests. This disarms me, and my anarchist moods melt in an instant.

With mixed emotions I recollect one distant journey when I found myself out of range of any network. My phone in a panic first sought some sort of way back in, but couldn't find it. Its messages seemed increasingly hysterical. "No network found," it repeated. Then it gave up and looked at me blankly with its square pupil, lo and behold, just a useless gadget now, a piece of plastic.

I was vividly reminded of an old engraving of a wanderer who had reached the edge of the world. Excited, he threw out his traveling bundle and was now looking out, beyond the Network. That traveler from the engraving can consider himself a fortunate man: he sees the stars and planets, spread out evenly across the firmament of the sky. And he hears the music of the spheres.

We've been denied that gift at the end of our travels. Beyond the Network there is silence.

## SWASTIKAS

In a city in South Asia the vegetarian restaurants are generally indicated with red swastikas, ancient signs of the Sun and life force. This makes vegetarians' lives much easier in a foreign city—all you have to do is look up and follow that symbol. There they serve vegetable curry (the vegetables vary greatly), pakoras, samosas and kormas, pilafs, little cutlets, as well as my favorite rice sticks wrapped in dried seaweed sheets.

After a few days I'm conditioned like one of Pavlov's dogs—I drool at the sight of a swastika.


## VENDORS OF NAMES

I saw on the street some tiny shops where names are sold for children who will be coming into the world soon. You have to go in early and place your order. You have to give them the exact date of conception, as well as a copy of the ultrasound—because the sex of the child is extremely important when choosing a name. The salesperson records this information and tells you to come back in a few days. During this time they prepare the future child's horoscope and dedicate themselves to meditation. Sometimes the name comes easily, materializing at the tip of their tongue in two or three sounds stuck together by saliva into syllables, which the expert hand of the master subsequently turns into red symbols on paper. Other times the name is resistant, unclear, in outline; it puts up a fight. It's hard to enclose it in words. Then helping techniques are deployed that will, however, remain the secret of every name vendor.

You can see them through the open doors of the shops covered in rice paper, Buddha figurines and hand-painted prayer texts, drudging away with a brush in their hand aimed at the paper. Sometimes the name just falls from the sky like a blot—surprising, clear, perfect.

In such circumstances nothing can be done. It does happen that the parents aren't pleased, would prefer a gentle name filled with optimism, like Moon Glow or Good River, for girls, or for boys, for example, Always Going Forward, Fearless, or He Who Has Achieved His Aim. The explanations of the vendor that the Buddha himself named his son Fetter are for naught. The clients leave unsatisfied, and, huffing and puffing, head to the competition.

## DRAMA AND ACTION

Far from home, at a video rental shop, rummaging around the shelves, I swear in Polish. And suddenly an average-sized woman who looks to be about fifty years old stops beside me and awkwardly says in my language:

"Is that Polish? Do you speak Polish? Hello."

Here, alas, her stock of Polish sentences is at an end.

And now she tells me in English that she came here when she was seventeen, with her parents; here she shows off with the Polish word for "mommy." Much to my dismay she then begins to cry, indicating her arm, her forearm, and talks about blood, that this is where her whole soul is, that her blood is Polish. This hapless gesture reminds me of an addict's gesture—her index finger showing veins, the place to stick a needle in. She says she married a Hungarian and forgot her Polish. She squeezes my shoulder and leaves, disappearing between shelves labeled "Drama" and "Action."

It's hard for me to believe that you could forget the language thanks to which the maps of the world were drawn. She must have simply mislaid it somewhere. Maybe it lies wadded up and dusty in a drawer of bras and panties, squeezed into a corner like sexy thongs acquired once in a fit of enthusiasm that there was never really an occasion to wear.

## EVIDENCE

I met some ichthyologists who were not at all bothered in their work by the fact that they were creationists. We were eating vegetable curries at the same table and we had a lot of time before our next flight. So we moved from the table to the bar, where a young man with Eastern features and a ponytail was playing Eric Clapton's hits on his guitar.

They were talking about how it was God who created their beautiful fish—all those trout, pike, turbot, and flounder, along with all the evidence of their phylogenetic development. To complete the set of fish, which He called into existence on the third day, He also prepared their excavatable skeletons, their bold imprints in sandstone, their fossils.

"To what end?" I asked. "Why create this false evidence?"

They were ready for my doubts, so one of them answered:

"Describing God and his intentions is like a fish trying to describe the water it swims in."

Another added after a moment:

"And its ichthyologist."

## NINE

In a cheap little hotel above a restaurant, in the town of X, I was assigned to room number nine. The porter, handing me the key (made of ordinary patent silver, with the number attached on a ring), said:

"Please be careful with the key. Nine gets lost the most."

I froze with the pen raised over the form I was filling in. "What does that mean?" I asked in a state of internal alert. He couldn't have aimed better, this man behind the counter—me, a homegrown detective, a private investigator of signs and coincidences.

He evidently noticed my unease, because he explained sooth-ingly, almost amicably—it means nothing. Simply by the eternal laws of coincidence the key to room number nine gets lost most of-ten by distracted travelers. He knows this for sure because every year he replenishes the stocks of keys and remembers that he has to order the largest quantity of nine. Even the locksmith was surprised.

I was careful with the key during my entire four-day stay in the town of X. When I'd return to the hotel, I would always put it in some visible place, and when I would leave, I handed it over to the safe hands of the receptionists. When once I unintentionally took it with me, I placed it in the safest pocket and made sure it was there with my fingers over the course of the day.

I wonder what law governed the number nine key, what cause and what effect. Or maybe the receptionist's spontaneous intuition was right—that it was a coincidence. Or maybe it was the opposite—it was his fault; he was choosing without realizing it for room num-ber nine particularly distracted guests, untrustworthy, susceptible to suggestion.

After a rather hurried departure from X because of a sudden sched-ule change, several days later, I was shaken to find the key in the pocket of my trousers—meaning I had inadvertently taken it with me. I thought of sending it back, but, to tell the truth, I no longer remembered the address of the hotel. My only consolation was that there were others like me—a small group of people leaving the town of X with a nine in their pockets. Perhaps even unconsciously we create a kind of community, the aim of which we cannot guess yet. Perhaps in the future it will be explained. The porter's prophecy, however, did come true—he would once again have to order the key to number nine, to the unceasing astonishment of the locksmith.

## ATTEMPTS AT TRAVEL STEREOMETRY

A man awakens from an uneasy sleep on a big intercontinental plane and puts his face to the window. He sees below a massive dark land. Only here and there do weak groups of lights make their way out of that darkness—those are big cities. Thanks to the map illuminated on the screens, he figures out that this is Russia, somewhere in central Siberia. He wraps himself up in his blanket and falls back asleep.

Down below, in one of those dark spots, another man is just walking out of his wooden home and raising his eyes to the sky, checking the weather for tomorrow.

If we were to pull a hypothetical straight line out of the center of the earth, it might turn out that for a fraction of a second both of these people found themselves on that radius. Perhaps for just a second their gazes fell on it together, this beam perhaps linking their eyes.

For a brief moment these men were vertical neighbors; what is, after all, eleven thousand meters? Barely more than ten kilometers. That's a lot less than the nearest settlement for that man on earth. It's less than the distance dividing the neighborhoods of a big city.


## EVEN

Driving, I pass billboards that announce in black and white, in English, "Jesus loves even you." I feel uplifted by the unexpected encouragement; I'm only slightly alarmed by that "even."


## ŚWIEBODZIN

After several hours of walking along the steep banks of the ocean among the sharp leaves of yuccas, in the blotches of shade we go down onto the rocky coast. There is a small shelter there with a fresh water intake. In this great wilderness stands a roof atop three walls. Inside it are benches to sit and sleep on. On one of them— strangely—lies a notebook in a black plastic cover and a yellow Bic pen. It's a guestbook. I throw down my backpack and maps and read it greedily, from the beginning. Columns, styles of handwriting, foreign words, the laconic basics of all those who by some twist of inscrutable fate have found themselves here before me. Number, date, first and last name, the Three Pilgrimage Questions: country of origin, last place visited, place of destination. It turns out I am the 156th to come here. Before me were Norwegians, Irish, Americans, two Koreans, Australians, Germans, but there are Swiss people here, too, and even—would you look at that—Slovakians. Then my gaze stops at one name: Szymon Polakowski, Świebodzin, Poland. I gaze hypnotized at that unhurried entry. I say the name out loud,

*Świebodzin,* and from then on I have the impression that over the ocean, yuccas, and steep path someone has placed a milky film. That funny, difficult name, against which the undisciplined tongue rebels, that soft, perverse *ś* that immediately brings a vague sensation, something like cold oilcloth spread over the kitchen table, a basket of freshly plucked tomatoes from the country garden, the smell of the fumes from the gas stove. It all combines to make Świebodzin the only real thing. There's nothing else. The rest of the day hangs over the ocean—a great fata morgana. And although I've never been in that small town, I see somewhat indistinctly its streets, bus stops, butcher shops, church tower. At night I am overwhelmed by a wave of nostalgia, unpleasant, like a contraction of the intestines, and half asleep I see a stranger's lips flawlessly arranging themselves in that astonishing *św.*

## KUNICKI: EARTH

Summer's closed its door to Kunicki. Slammed its door. He is just settling in now, switching his sandals for slippers, his shorts for long trousers, sharpening the pencils on his desk, putting receipts in order. The past has ceased to exist, becoming just life's scraps—no sense in regrets now. So what he feels must be a phantom pain, unreal, the pain of every incomplete, jagged form that by its nature longs for wholeness. There is no other explanation.

Lately he can't sleep. Or rather—he falls asleep in the evenings, is exhausted to dropping, but he wakes up around three or four in the morning, as he did years ago, after the flood. But back then he knew where the insomnia was coming from—he'd been terrified of the disaster. Now it's different. There is no catastrophe. And yet a kind of hole has opened up, a rupture. Kunicki knows that words would mend it; if he were to find the appropriate quantity of sensible, correct words to explain what had happened, the hole could be patched up, there wouldn't be a trace of it, and he would sleep till eight. Sometimes, rarely, he thinks he hears a voice, one or two words, piercing, resounding. Words ripped from both the sleepless night and the frenetic day. Something sparking off between his neurons, unidentifiable impulses that leap from place to place. Is this not exactly how thought happens?

The phantoms are fully assembled now, standing at the gates of reason, factory-made. They're not really scary, it's no biblical deluge, they include no Dantean scenes. Just the terrible inevitability of water, its omnipresence. The walls of his apartment soak it up. Kunicki checks the sick soggy plaster with his finger, the wet paint leaving a mark on his skin. The stains on the walls make maps of countries he can't recognize, he can't name. Drops seep through the window frames, wash away the carpet. You hammer a nail through the wall, and a little streamlet springs out; you open a drawer and water burbles out of it. You raise a stone and I will be there, murmurs the water. Whole rivulets pour onto computer keyboards, the screen splutters out underwater. Kunicki runs out in front of his apartment building and sees the sandpits and flower beds have disappeared, the low hedges have ceased to exist. He goes with water up to his ankles to the car, he'll try to drive it out of their neighborhood and onto higher ground, but he won't make it now. It turns out they are surrounded, in a trap.

Just be glad it all turned out okay, he tells himself, getting up in the dark to go to the bathroom. Of course I'm glad, he answers himself. But he isn't glad. He lies back down on the warmed-up sheets and stays there with his eyes open till morning. His legs are unsettled, they keep heading off somewhere, taking a pretend walk of their own accord under the folds of the blanket, itching from within. Sometimes he dozes off for a little bit, and then his own snoring wakes him up. He lies there and sees it getting lighter and lighter out the window, listens to the trash collectors start to raise their ruckus, the first buses, trams set forth from the depot. In the morning the elevator starts up, you can hear its despairing squeaks, the squeaks of a creature caught in two-dimensional space, up and down, never diagonally or sideways. The world moves forward, with that irreparable hole in it, crippled. It limps.

Kunicki limps along with it to the bathroom, then he drinks his coffee standing up, at the kitchen counter. He awakens his wife. She sleepily, wordlessly, vanishes into the bathroom.

He has found one advantage to not sleeping—he can hear what she says in her sleep. In this way the greatest mysteries give themselves away. They escape like wisps of smoke, of their own accord, and immediately vanish, you have to catch them right there at the lips. So he lies there, thinking, and eavesdrops. She sleeps quietly, on her stomach, you almost can't hear her even breathing. Sometimes she sighs, but there aren't any words in her sighing. When she turns over from one side to the other, her hand seeks out another body, on its own, tries to hold it, her leg travels over his hip. Then for a moment he stiffens, because what the hell would that mean? Then he realizes that it's a mechanical movement, and he lets her get away with it.

It is as though nothing has changed, except that her hair has gotten brighter in the sun, and a couple of freckles came out on her nose. But when he touched her, when he slid his hand over her naked back, he thought he figured something out. He doesn't even know himself. That skin puts up resistance now, it's harder, more inert, like tarpaulin.

He can't permit himself any further searching, he's afraid, he draws back his hand. Half asleep, he imagines that his hand encounters some sort of foreign territory, something he'd overlooked for seven years of their marriage, something shameful, some defect, a strip of hairy skin, a fish scale, some bird down, an unusual structure, an anomaly.

He scoots over to the edge of the bed and from there looks at the shape that is his wife. In the pale light of the development that flows through the window her face is just a faint outline. He falls asleep gazing into that spot, and when she wakes up, it's starting to get light in their bedroom. The light of dawn is metallic, it ashens colors. For a moment he has the frightening impression that she is dead—he sees her corpse, her empty dried-out body left a while ago now by its soul. He's not afraid, exactly, just surprised, and quickly, in order to chase away this image, he touches her cheek. She sighs and turns to him, putting her arm on his chest, her soul returning. From now on her breathing is steady, but he doesn't dare move. He waits for the alarm clock to release him from this awkward situation.

He's unsettled by his own inaction. Shouldn't he make a note of all these changes, in order not to overlook something? Get up quietly and slip out of bed and divide a piece of paper in half at the kitchen table and write: before and now. What would he write? Her skin is rougher—maybe she's just aging, or maybe it's an effect of the sun. T-shirt instead of pajamas? Maybe the heaters are on higher than they used to be. Her smell? She's switched lotions.

He recalls the lipstick she had on the island. Now she has a different one! That one was a light, creamy, gentle one, the color of her lips. This one is red, crimson, he doesn't know how to define color, he was never good at that, he never knew what the difference was between crimson and red, let alone purple.

Carefully he slides out of bed, touches down his bare feet on the floor, and blindly, so as not to wake her, he goes to the bathroom. Only once he gets inside does he let himself be blinded by turning on the bright light. On the shelf under the mirror lies her cosmetics bag, embroidered with beads. He opens it carefully, in order to make sure of his suppositions. The lipstick is different.

In the morning he's able to act it all out perfectly, that's what he thinks: perfectly. That he's forgotten something else and has to stay five minutes more at home.

"Go on ahead, don't wait for me."

He pretends he's in a hurry, that he's looking for some papers. She puts her jacket on in front of the mirror, wraps a red scarf around herself, and takes the boy by the hand. They slam the door. He hears them going down the stairs. He freezes over his papers and the echo of the slamming doors reverberates a few more times in his head like a ball—boom, boom, boom, until there's silence. Then he takes a deep breath and stands up straight. Silence. He feels it wrap him up, and now he moves slowly and precisely. He goes to the closet, pulls back the glass door, and stands facing her clothes. He stretches his hand out to a light-colored blouse, she's never worn it, it's too formal. He palpates it and then runs his whole hand over it, gets his hand tangled in the folds of silk. But this blouse tells him nothing, so he keeps going; he recognizes the cashmere suit, which she also rarely wears, and her summer dresses, and a few shirts, one after the next; a winter sweater still wrapped up from the cleaners, and a long black coat. He hasn't seen her much in that one, either. Then it occurs to him that this clothing is hanging here to throw him off, to trick him, to lead him astray.

They're standing next to each other in the kitchen. Kunicki is dicing up parsley. He doesn't really want to get into it again, but he can't restrain himself. He can feel the words swelling up in his throat, and he can't quite swallow them back down. Meaning the old "Well then, what did happen?" yet again.

She says in a tired voice, pointing out in a tone of I'm-reciting-this-*yet*-again that he's being boring, that he's making things difficult, "Here you go, one more time: I didn't feel well, I think I had food poisoning, I told you." But he doesn't give up so easily. "You didn't feel sick when you went off," he says.

"Right, but then I got sick, I got sick," she repeats, with pleasure. "And I guess I passed out for a minute, and then the child started crying, and that brought me to again. He was scared, and I was scared, too. We started toward the car, but just because of everything we ended up going the wrong way."

"Which way? Into town? Toward Vis?"

"Yes, toward Vis. No, I mean, I don't know, whether toward Vis or not, how was I supposed to know, if I had known, I would have come *back*, I've told you this a thousand times." She raises her voice. "When I figured out I had gotten us lost, we just sat down in this little grove, and the child fell asleep. I was still feeling weak . . ."

Kunicki knows she's lying. He dices the parsley up and says in a sepulchral voice, not raising his eyes from the cutting board, "There was no grove."

She just about screams, "Of course there was!"

"No, there wasn't. All there was were individual olive trees and vineyards. What grove?"

There's a silence, and then she suddenly says with deadly seriousness, "Okay. You've cracked it. Good job. We were carried off by a flying saucer. They did experiments on us. They implanted chips in us, here," and she lifts up her hair to reveal the nape of her neck. Her gaze is icy.

Kunicki ignores her sarcasm. "All right, all right, continue."

"I found a little stone house. We fell asleep, it got dark . . ."

"Just like that? It got dark? What happened to the whole day? What were you doing all day?"

She presses on. "We had a nice morning. I thought that you might worry about us a little bit and actually remember that we exist. Like shock therapy. We ate grapes all the time and kept going swimming . . ."

"You're telling me you didn't eat for three days?"

"Like I say, we ate grapes all the time."

"What did you drink?" Kunicki urges.

Here she grimaces. "Water from the sea."

"Why don't you just tell me the truth?"

"That is the truth."

Kunicki severs meticulously the fleshy little stems. "Okay, and then what?"

"Nothing. We went back to the road and flagged down a car that took us to—"

"After three days!"

"So what?"

He throws the knife down into the parsley. The cutting board crashes to the floor. "Do you have any idea how much trouble you caused? There was a helicopter out looking for you! The whole is-land was mobilized!"

"Well, they shouldn't have been. It just happens that people dis-appear for a little while, you know? There was no need for anybody to panic. We can just still say that I wasn't feeling well, and that then I got better."

"What the fuck is wrong with you? What is going on? How can you explain it all?"

"There's nothing that requires an explanation. I'm telling you the truth, you're just not listening."

She's screaming, but here she lowers her voice. "Just what do you think, you tell me, what do you think happened?"

But he doesn't answer her now. This conversation has already repeated itself multiple times. It seems both of them have lost the strength for it.

Sometimes she leans back against the wall and glares at him and taunts him: "A bus full of pimps drove by and took me off to a brothel. They kept the child on the balcony, on bread and water. I had sixty clients over the course of those three days."

When she does that he slams his fist into the table to not hit her.

He never thought or worried about it—that he can't remember indi-vidual days. He doesn't know what he did on a given Monday, or not even a given, but last Monday, Monday before last. He doesn't know what he did the day before yesterday. He tries to remember the Thursday before they left Vis—and nothing comes to mind. But when he focuses it returns to him, that they walked down the path, that the dried-out bushes of herbs crackled beneath their shoes, and the grass was so dry that it scattered into dust under their shoes. And he remembers the low stone wall, although probably only because they saw a snake there, which ran away from them. She told him to take the boy's hand. Then he picked him up, and she tore off the little leaves of some plant and rubbed it between her fingers. "Rue," she said. Then he realized that everything smelled like it here, like this herb, even raki, they put whole branches of it in the bottles. But he can't know now how they got back and what happened to the evening of that day. And he doesn't remember the other evenings. He doesn't remember anything, he's missed it all. And when you don't remember it means it never happened.

Details, the weight of details: he used to not take them seriously. Now he's sure that when he arranges them in a tightly made chain—cause plus effect—everything will be explained. He should sit quietly in his office, lay out a piece of paper, best if it's large-format, the largest he can find, he has some like that from the paper that books are wrapped in, and plot it all out in points. After all, that's the truth.

So, okay. He slices through the plastic tape on a package of books and takes out the stack of them without even looking at them. That's one of those bestsellers, who cares. He picks up the sheet of gray paper and straightens it out on the desk. This extended gray space, slightly creased, confuses him. With a black marker he writes: border. They fought there. But maybe he should go back to before they left? No, he'll start there, at the border. He must have held out his passport through the car window. That was between Slovenia and Croatia. Then he recalls them going down the asphalt highway through empty villages. Stone homes without roofs, bearing traces of fire or bombs. Clear signs of war. Overgrown fields, dry, barren land lacking care. Its owners in exile. Dead paths. Gritted teeth. Nothing, nothing wrong, they're in purgatory. They're in the car and looking out in silence at those haunting landscapes. But her he can't remember, she was sitting too close to him, next to him. He doesn't remember if they stopped anywhere or not. Yes, they got gasoline at some little station. He thinks they bought some ice cream. And the weather, that it was stifling. Milk in the sky.

Kunicki has a good job. At work he's a free man. He works as a sales representative for a big Warsaw publisher—representative, meaning he peddles books. He has several spots in town he has to stop by every so often to tout his wares; he always brings them the latest stuff and makes them special offers.

He drives up to a little shop on the outskirts of town and gets the order he's fulfilling out of the trunk of his car. The shop is called Book and School Supplies Shop, it's too small to give itself such airs as a specific name, and anyway, most of what it sells are simply notebooks and textbooks.

The order fits into a plastic box: guidebooks, two copies of the sixth volume of the encyclopedia, the memoirs of a famous actor, and the latest bestseller with the unrevealing title of *Constellations*—a whopping three copies of this. Kunicki promises himself he's going to read it. They serve him coffee and a slice of cake. They like him. Washing down mouthfuls of cake with the coffee, he shows them the new catalog. This sells well, he says, and this right here gets ordered all the time. Such is Kunicki's job. As he's leaving he purchases a calendar that's on clearance.

In the evening in his tiny office he fills in the publisher's corporate forms with the orders he's received; he sends the forms by e-mail. He'll receive the books in the morning.

He takes deep, relieved breaths, inhaling the smoke from his cigarette: the workday is done. He's been waiting for this moment since morning so he can look through the pictures in peace. He hooks up the camera to the computer.

There are sixty-four of them. He doesn't delete any. They come up automatically, for ten to twelve seconds each. The pictures are boring. Their one merit is that they fix instants that would otherwise have vanished completely. But would it be worth it to copy them? Even so, Kunicki copies them to a CD, turns off the computer, and sets off for home.

All his actions he performs automatically: he turns the key in the ignition, turns off the alarm, fastens his seat belt, flips on the radio, puts the car in first gear. It immediately rolls along from the parking lot into the busy street, in second gear. They're doing the weather on the radio. They're saying it's going to rain. And sure enough it starts to rain, as if all the drops of rain had just been waiting to be conjured up by the radio; the windshield wipers come on.

And suddenly something changes. It's not the weather, not the rain, not the view from the car, but somehow, in a single moment, he sees everything differently. It's as if he's taken off his sunglasses, or as if the windshield wipers have scraped off more than their usual skimming of urban grunge. He feels hot and steps on the gas in spite of himself. People are honking at him. He pulls himself together and tries to catch up with the black Volkswagen. His hands start to sweat. He would happily pull over, but there's nowhere to pull over to, he has to keep going.

He sees with terrible clarity that the road, so familiar to him, is suffused entirely with lurid signs. These signs are messages for him alone. The one-legged circles, the yellow triangles, the blue squares, the green and white markers, the arrows, the indicators. The lights. The lines painted on the asphalt, the motorway markers, warnings, reminders. The smile on the billboard, not immaterial, either. He saw them this morning, but he didn't understand them then, this morning he could ignore them, but now, now there is no way for him to do that. Now they are all communicating with him, quietly, categorically, there are so many more of them, in fact there is no space they do not inhabit. The names of shops, the ads, the post office symbol, the pharmacies, the bank, the lifted STOP paddle of the nursery school teacher overseeing the children crossing the road, sign goes through sign, across sign, sign indicating another sign—a little farther on, a sign taken up by another sign, passed farther along, a conspiracy of signs, a network of signs, an understanding between signs behind his back. Nothing is innocent, and nothing is insignificant, it's all a big endless puzzle.

In a panic he looks for a place to park: he has to shut his eyes or he'll go crazy. What is wrong with him? He starts to shake. Relieved, he finds the bus stop and pulls over. He begins to be able to control himself. It occurs to him that he might have had a stroke. He's afraid to look around. Maybe he has discovered a way of viewing things, or another Point of View, capitalized, all of it capitalized.

His breathing returns after a little while to normal, although his hands are still shaking. He lights a cigarette, that's it, let it pollute his lungs with a little nicotine, stupefy him with smoke, evict the demons. But he knows now that he can't go any farther, that he wouldn't be able to handle this new knowledge that now overwhelms him. He gasps for breath with his head on the steering wheel.

He positions the car on the sidewalk, he's sure they'll give him a ticket, and carefully he walks away. The asphalt surface of the road seems viscous now.

"Mr. Untouchable," she says.

Provocatively, Kunicki doesn't respond. She slams the cabinet door after pulling out a packet of tea, waiting out the duration she's given him to react.

"What's going on with you?" she asks. Aggressively now. Kunicki knows that if he doesn't answer now she'll launch a full-blown attack, so he says calmly:

"Nothing. What would be going on?"

She snorts and says in a monotone:

"You don't say anything, you don't let me touch you, you scoot over to the very edge of the bed, you're not sleeping, you're not watching TV, you come home late, smelling of alcohol . . ."

Kunicki contemplates how he should behave. He knows that whatever he does will be wrong. So he stops. He stiffens in the chair, looks at the table. He's as uncomfortable as if he'd swallowed something that won't go down his throat. He feels a menacing movement of air in the kitchen. He tries one last time:

"We have to call things by their name . . ." he starts, but she interrupts him.

"I mean, yeah, if only we knew what their name was."

"Fine. You didn't tell me what really . . ."

But he doesn't finish, because she throws the tea on the floor and runs out of the kitchen. After a second the door slams.

Kunicki thinks she's a great actress. She could have been a great actress.

He's always known what he wanted. Now he doesn't know. He doesn't know anything, he doesn't even know what it is he ought to know. He pulls out trays of catalogs and inattentively looks over boxes impaled on skewers. He doesn't know how to search or what to search for.

He sat up the whole previous night on the internet. And what did he find? An inexact map of Vis, the official Croatian tourism page, the ferry schedule. When he typed in the name Vis, dozens of pages came up. Only a few about the island. Hotel prices, attractions. Also Visible Imagine System, in English, with satellite photos, as far as he could tell. And Vaccine Information Statements, Victorian Institute of Sport. And System for Verification and Synthesis.

The internet itself led him from one word to the next, giving links, pointing out. When it didn't know something it tactfully kept quiet or stubbornly showed him the same pages, ad nauseam. Then Kunicki had the impression that he had just landed at the border of the known world, at the wall, at the membrane of the heavenly firmament. There wasn't any way to break through it with his head and look through.

The internet is a fraud. It promises so much—that it will execute your every command, that it will find you what you're looking for; execution, fulfillment, reward. But in essence that promise is a kind of bait, because you immediately fall into a trance, into hypnosis. The paths quickly diverge, double and multiply, and you go down them, still chasing an aim that will now get blurry and undergo some transformations. You lose the ground beneath your feet, the place where you started from just gets forgotten, and your aim finally vanishes from sight, disappears in the passage of more and more pages, businesses that always promise more than they can give, shamelessly pretending that under the flat plane of the screen there is some cosmos. But nothing could be more deceptive, dear Kunicki. What are you, Kunicki, looking for? What are you aiming at? You feel like spreading out your arms and plunging into it, into that abyss, but there is nothing more deceptive: the landscape turns out to be a wallpaper, you can't go any farther.

His office is small, it's a single room he rents for cheap on the fourth floor of a dilapidated office building. Next door there's a real estate agency, and farther down, a tattoo parlor. What fits in here is a desk and a computer. On the floor lie packages of books. On the windowsill an electric kettle and a jar of coffee.

He cranks up the computer and waits for it to wake back up. Then he lights his first cigarette. He looks at the pictures again, but this time he carefully studies each one, for a long time, until he gets to the ones he took at the end—the contents of her purse laid out on the table, and that ticket with the inscription "Kairos," yes, he's even memorized that word: καιρός. Yes, that word will explain everything to him.

So he has found something he hadn't noticed before. He has to light a cigarette, he's so excited. He looks at that mysterious word, it will guide him now, he'll let it up with the wind like a kite and follow it. "Kairos," Kunicki reads, "Kairos," repeating it, unsure how it's pronounced. It has to be Greek, he thinks happily, Greek, and he dives into his bookshelves, but there's no Greek dictionary there, only *Useful Latin Phrases*, a book he's never even opened. Now he knows he's on the right track. Now he can't stop. He lays out the pictures of the contents of her purse, good thing he thought to take them. He places them next to one another like in solitaire, in even rows. He lights another cigarette and walks around the desk like he's some kind of detective. He stops, inhales some smoke, examines the photographed lipstick and pen.

Suddenly he realizes: there are different kinds of looking. One kind of looking allows you to simply see objects, useful human things, honest and concrete, which you know right away how to use and what for. And then there's panoramic viewing, a more general view, thanks to which you notice links between objects, their network of reflections. Things cease to be things, the fact that they serve a purpose is insignificant, just a surface. Now they're signs, indicating something that isn't in the photographs, referring beyond the frames of the pictures. You have to really concentrate to be able to maintain that gaze, at its essence it's a gift, grace. Kunicki's heart starts beating faster. This red pen with "Hotel Mercure" written on it is obscuring some dark unknowable, impenetrable thing.

He knows this place, the last time he was here was when the water was going back down, just after the flood. The library, the respectable Ossolineum, sits by the river, faces it, a fatal error. Books should be kept in elevated places.

He remembers that view, when the sun showed itself again and the water was subsiding. The flood brought in sludge and mud, but some places had been cleared, and the library workers were laying out books there to dry. They set them out, open, on the floor, there were hundreds of them, thousands. In that position, unnatural for them, they looked like live creatures, a cross between a bird and an anemone. Hands in thin latex gloves patiently unsticking wet pages, in order for individual sentences and words to dry. Unfortunately, the pages withered, darkened from the sludge and water, warping. People were walking between them carefully, women in white aprons, as at a hospital, opening volumes to the sun, letting the sun read. But in fact it was a terrifying sight, something like a meeting of the elements. Kunicki stood and looked on in horror, and then, animated by the example of some other passerby, joined in enthusiastically to help.

Today at the library in the city center, beautifully renovated after the flood, tucked away in buildings arranged around the well in the courtyard, he feels uneasy. When he goes into the great reading room he sees tables placed in even rows at discreet distances from one another. At almost every single one sits someone's back— leaning over, hunched. Trees over a grave. A cemetery.

The books set on the shelves show only their spines to people, and it's as though, thinks Kunicki, you could see people only in profile. They don't tempt you with their colorful covers, don't boast with banners on which every word is a superlative; as though being punished, like recruits, they present only their most basic facts: title and author, nothing more.

Instead of folders, posters, and commercials there are catalogs. The egalitarian quality of those little cards stuffed into drawers inspires respect. Only a little information, numbers, a short description, no showing off.

He's never been here. When he was at university he used only the modern library. He wrote out a title and author on a card and turned it in and after a quarter of an hour received the book. But even there he didn't go too often, in truth he went only exceptionally, since most of the texts he needed he got Xeroxed. That was a new generation of literature—text without spine, fleeting copy, something like the Kleenex that took the helm after the abdication of cloth handkerchiefs. Kleenexes led a modest revolution, eliminating class differences. After using them once you just threw them away.

He has three dictionaries in front of him. *Greek-Polish Dictionary*. Edited by Zygmunt Węclewski, Lwów 1929. Samuel Bodek Bookstore, Batory Street 20. *Little Greek-Polish Dictionary*. Eds. Teresa Kambureli, Thanasis Kamburelis. Published by Wiedza Powszechna, Warsaw, 1999. And the four volumes of *Greek-Polish Dictionary* edited by Zofia Abramowiczówna, 1962. Published by PWN. There, with difficulty, using the tabular alphabet, he deciphers the word: καιρός.

He reads only what's written in Polish, in the Latin alphabet. "1. (On measure.) Due measure, appropriateness, moderation; difference; meaning. 2. (On place.) A vital, sensitive place in the body. 3. (On time.) Critical moment, right time, appropriateness, opportunity, nick of time, the propitious time is fleeting; those who turned up unexpectedly; miss the moment; when the right time comes, help in the event of a storm, on time, when the opportunity arises, prematurely, critical moments, periodic states, the chronological sequence of facts, situation, state of things, placement, ultimate danger, benefit, use, to what aim?, what will help you?, where would be convenient?"

That's one dictionary. The next, older—Kunicki goes over the tiny entries with his eyes, passing over the Greek words and stumbling over old spellings: "in good measure, moderation, correct relations, attain an aim, overmuch, the appropriate moment, a suitable time, a nice moment, a convenient occasion, just here, time,

hour, and in plural, circumstances, relations, times, cases, inci-
dents, decisive moments of the revolution, dangers; the occasion is
convenient, the occasion suits, it comes in time. It is also said: something happens at the appropriate time." In the newest dictionary
they finally give the pronunciation in brackets: "[kieros]." And:
"weather, time, season, what's the weather?, now is grape season,
wasting time, from time to time, one time, how long?, this was
needed long ago."

Kunicki looks around the reading room in despair. He sees the
tops of heads leaned over books. He returns to the dictionaries,
reads the previous entry, which looks similar, different by only one
letter: καιριος. And here there's still more: "done in time, purpose-
ful, effective, lethal, fatal, question solved and: a dangerous place
on the body where wounds are effective, what is always on time,
what always has to happen."

Kunicki gathers his things and heads home. At night he finds on
Wikipedia a page about Kairos, from which he simply learns that
it's a god, of little importance, forgotten, Hellenic. And that this
god was discovered in Trogir. That museum has its image, so she
wrote down the word. Nothing more.


When his son was still a baby, when he was an infant, Kunicki never
thought of him as a person. And that was fine, because then they
were close. People are always far away. He figured out how to
change his diapers as efficiently as possible, he could do it in just a
couple of swift motions, almost imperceptibly, but for the sound of
diapers. He would submerge his little body in the bath, wash his
belly, and then carry him still wrapped up in his towel into his
room, where he would put him in his pajamas. That was easy. When

you have a little kid, you never have to think about anything, everything is obvious and natural. Attaching child to breast, and his
weight; his smell—familiar and heartwarming. But children aren't
people. Children become people when they wriggle out of your
arms and say "no."

Kunicki is unnerved now by the silence. What was the child doing? He stands in the doorway and sees the child on the floor, surrounded by blocks. He sits down next to him and picks up one of
his little plastic cars. He moves it along the painted road. He doesn't
know if he's supposed to start off with a story: once upon a time
there was a little car that got lost. He's getting his mouth ready to
speak when the boy rips the toy from his hands and gives him something else—a wooden truck carrying blocks in the back.

"We're going to build," says the child.

"What are we going to build?" improvises Kunicki.

"A little house."

All right then, a little house. They position the blocks in a square.
The truck brings the materials.

"Hey, what if we build an island?" says Kunicki.

"No, a house," says the child as he plops the blocks down willy-
nilly, one on top of the other. Kunicki delicately rearranges, so that
the whole house doesn't come crashing down.

"But do you remember the sea?" says Kunicki.

The child assents, and the truck empties out a new supply. Now
Kunicki has no idea what to say or what to ask. He might point to
the rug and say, this rug is the island, and we are on the island,
but the boy is lost on the island, and Daddy is worried, because
where could his little son be? Which is what he says, but it doesn't
really work.

"No," insists the boy. "Let's build a little house."

"Do you remember when you and Mommy got lost?"

"No!" screams the child, gleefully tossing blocks onto the little house.

"Have you ever gotten lost?" Kunicki asks again.

"No," says the child, and the truck crashes into the newly constructed house at full speed. The walls fall down. "Boom! Boom!" laughs the boy.

Kunicki begins patiently to build it back up again.

When she comes home, Kunicki first sees her from the floor, just like the child. She's large, flushed from the cold, suspiciously excited. Her lips are red. She tosses a red (or maybe mauve, maybe plum) shawl onto the arm of a chair and hugs the child. "Are you guys hungry?" she asks. Kunicki feels as though a wind has come with her into the room, the cold, blustery wind that comes off the sea. He would like to say, "Where were you?" but he can't afford to.

In the morning he has an erection and has to turn away from her; he has to hide these inconvenient notions the body sometimes gets, so that she won't read them as encouragement, attempts at reconciliation, any type of attachment. He turns to face the wall and celebrates the erection, that purposeless readiness, that state of alert, that adherent, taut extremity; he has it all to himself.

The tip of his penis rises like a vector, pointing out the window, toward the world.

Legs. Feet. Even when he stops, when he sits down, they seem to keep going, they can't restrain themselves, they cross a given space in small, hurried steps. When he wants to restrain them, they rebel. Kunicki is afraid his legs will break out into a run, whisk him off, take him a way he would never agree to, will leap up into the air like they're folk dancing, against his will, or they'll go into the gloomy courtyards of moldy old stone buildings, work their way up someone else's stairs, pull him up through hatches and onto steep, slippery roofs and make him walk along the scaly roofing tiles, like they would a sleepwalker.

It must be because of his restless legs that Kunicki can't sleep: from the waist up he's calm, relaxed, and sleepy; from the waist down—insuperable. He's obviously made up of two people. His upper person wants calm and justice; his downward person is transgressive and ignores all principles. His upper person has a name, an address, a social security number; there's not really anything his downward person can say for himself, in fact he's had it up to here with himself.

He'd like to quiet his legs, rub a soothing ointment into them; as a matter of fact, this internal tickling sensation is painful. He finally takes a sleeping pill. He restores his legs to order.

Kunicki tries to control his own extremities. He invents a way of doing so: he lets them be in constant motion, even just his toes in his shoes, while the rest of his body is at rest. And when he sits down— he releases them then, too: lets them be uneasy. He peers down at the toes of his shoes and sees the delicate movement of the leather as his feet begin their obsessive marching in place. But he also takes frequent walks around town. He thinks that this time he will have crossed all the possible bridges over the Odra and the canals. That he will not have missed a single one.

. . .

The third week of September is rainy and windy. They have to get their autumn things out of storage, jackets and rubber boots for the child. He picks him up from nursery school; they walk quickly to the car. The boy jumps into a puddle and splashes water everywhere. Kunicki doesn't notice, he's thinking about what to say, stringing together sentences. Such as, "I'm concerned the child may have had a kind of shock," or, with more self-confidence, "I believe my son has experienced a shock." Now he remembers the word "trauma." "To experience trauma."

They drive across the wet city, the windshield wipers working as hard as they can to clear off the water from the windshield, baring for just a second at a time the world plunged in rain, the smeared world.

It's his day, Thursday. Thursdays he picks up his son from nursery school. She's busy because she works all afternoon, she has some workshops or something, she won't be back until late, so Kunicki has the child to himself.

They pull up to a big renovated brick building in the very center of the city and look for a little while for a parking place.

"Where are we going?" asks the child, and because Kunicki doesn't answer, the boy begins to repeat the question over and over: "Wherewegoing wherewegoing?"

"Be quiet," says the father, but then, a moment later, he explains, "To see a lady."

The child doesn't protest. He must be intrigued.

There's no one in the waiting room; a towering woman around the age of fifty appears almost immediately and ushers them into her office. The room is bright and pleasant—in the middle of it there's a large, soft, colorful rug with toys and blocks on top. Then there's a couch and two armchairs, a desk and an office chair. The child sits down cautiously on the edge of the couch, but his eyes wander over to the toys. The woman smiles and offers Kunicki her hand, greeting the boy, too. She talks to the child like she wants to make it very clear she's not paying attention to the father. So he speaks first, preempting whatever questions she might ask.

"My son has had trouble sleeping for some time," he lies. "He's become anxious and—"

The woman doesn't let him finish. "First let's play," she says. This sounds ridiculous, and Kunicki wonders if she's going to be playing around with him, too. In his surprise he stands stock-still.

"How old are you?" the woman asks the child. The child holds up three fingers.

"He turned three in April," says Kunicki.

She sits down on the rug, near the boy, and hands him some blocks; she says, "Your dad's going to go sit out there for a little while and read, and we're going to play, like this."

"No!" says the child, jumping up and running over to the father. Kunicki gets it. He convinces the child to stay.

"The door can stay open," the woman assures him.

He presses gently on the door without shutting it all the way. Kunicki sits in the waiting room and listens to their voices, but they're hard to hear, he can't tell what they're saying. He had been expecting a lot of questions, he had even brought the little booklet with the child's records, which he reads to himself now: birth at full term, spontaneous labor, Apgar score of 10, vaccinations, weight 3,750 grams (8.3 pounds), length 57 centimeters (22.4 inches). We speak of grown-ups being "tall," but a child is "long." He takes a glossy magazine from the table and opens it mechanically, happening immediately upon ads for new books. He goes through the titles and compares prices. He feels a pleasant rush of adrenaline: his are cheaper.

"Can you clarify what's wrong, please? What you're talking about?" says the woman.

Kunicki feels embarrassed. What's he supposed to say, that his wife and child just up and disappeared, that they weren't there for three days, for forty-nine hours—he knows exactly how long it was. And he doesn't know where they were. He's always known everything there was to know about them, and now the most important thing is unknown to him. And then, for a split second, he imagines he says, "Please, you have to help me. Please just hypnotize him and get access to those forty-nine hours, minute by minute. I have to know."

And she—that towering woman, standing straight as an arrow—comes up so close to him that he can smell the antiseptic scent of her sweater—that's what nurses smelled of in his childhood—and takes his hand in her big, warm hands and holds him to her breast.

It doesn't happen this way, though. Kunicki lies: "He's just been restless lately, he wakes up in the night, cries. We went on vacation in August, to Croatia, to the island of Vis. I thought maybe something had happened, something we weren't aware of, maybe something had scared him . . ."

He can tell she doesn't believe him. She picks up a ballpoint pen and plays with it. She speaks with an enchanting, warm smile. "You have here a very intelligent child with above-average social skills. Sometimes these things just mean the child is going through a normal developmental phase. Don't let him watch too much TV. But to me there's nothing, absolutely nothing wrong with him."

Then she looks at him with concern, or so he thinks.

As they're walking out, as the child finishes up his bye-byes to the woman, Kunicki begins to consider her a bitch. Her smile strikes him as insincere. She's hiding something, too. She hasn't told him everything. He now realizes he should never have gone to a woman. Don't they have men child psychologists in this city? Or have women established some kind of monopoly on children? Women are never really clear; you can never tell upon first inspection if they're weak or strong, how they're going to behave, what they want; you have to stay on your guard. He thinks of the pen she was holding in her hand. A yellow Bic, just like the one in the picture he got out of the purse.

It's Tuesday, she has the day off. He's been agitated since early, he can't sleep, he pretends he's not watching her morning meandering, from the bedroom to the bathroom, from the kitchen to the entrance and then back to the bathroom. The child emits a quick, impatient cry, probably when she's tying his shoes. The sound of her spraying on her deodorant. The whistle of the kettle.

When they finally go out, he stands at the door and listens to see whether the elevator has come yet. He counts to sixty—the time it will take them to make it downstairs. Fast as he can he slips on his boots and rips the bag off the jacket he's bought used so she won't spot him. He shuts the door quietly behind him. As long as he doesn't have to wait too long for the elevator.

Yep, things couldn't be going smoother. He darts after her, at a safe distance, in a jacket she couldn't recognize. He fixes on her

back, he wonders if she feels somehow uncomfortable, probably
not, because she's walking quickly, briskly, you might even say joyfully. She and the child both leap over puddles, rather than bypass-
ing them, they leap—why? Where did she get all that energy on a
drizzly autumn day like today? Had the coffee kicked in already?
The rest of the world seems slow and sleepy, and she's more vibrant
than usual, her frenetic pink scarf a blot of brilliance against a
background of that day; Kunicki hangs on to it like to a straw.

They finally make it to nursery school. He watches her take leave
of the child, but it doesn't move him in the least. She might be whispering something to him as she embraces him so tenderly, some
word, exactly the word Kunicki has been searching for so franti-
cally. If he knew what it was, he could type it into Wikipedia, and
that cosmic search engine would in the blink of an eye give him a
simple, straightforward answer.

Now he sees her as she pauses before the crosswalk, awaiting the
green light, pulling out her phone and typing in a number. For a
moment Kunicki has some hope that his own phone will begin to
ring in his pocket, he's got a different ringtone for her—a cicada,
yes, he had assigned her the song of the cicada. Tropical insect. But
his pocket remains silent. She crosses the road while she has a brief
conversation with someone; she hangs up. Now he has to wait for
the light to change, which is dangerous, because she's actually going around the corner and out of sight, so he immediately, as soon
as he can, speeds up his pace, already fearing he's lost her, already
beginning to be angry with himself and with those lights. Oh, to
lose her only two hundred meters from home! But there she is; her
scarf is floating into the revolving doors of the shop. It's a big shop,
a shopping center, really; they've just opened it, it's practically

empty, so that Kunicki hesitates, whether to go in after her or not, whether or not he will actually be able to hide in between the different displays. But he has to, because the shop has another exit, onto another street, so he puts his hood on—which is perfectly reasonable, it is raining, after all—and enters the shop. He sees her—she's walking around slowly, as if something were holding her back, and she looks at makeup, at perfume, she stops at a shelf and reaches for something. She holds a bottle of something in her hand. Kunicki rummages through the discounted socks.

When she moves, lost in thought, to the purses display, Kunicki picks up the bottle. Carolina Herrera, he reads. Should this name be retained or discarded from memory? Something tells him he should retain it. Everything means something, we just don't know what, he repeats to himself.

He sees her from a distance—she's standing in front of a mirror with a red purse on her arm, gazing at her reflection from one and then another angle. Then she goes to the checkout, right to Kunicki. He retreats in panic behind the socks shelf, bowing his head. She passes by him. Like a ghost. But then suddenly she turns around like she's forgotten something, and she looks right at him, hunched over, with his hood pulled down to his forehead. He sees that her eyes are wide with astonishment, he feels her gaze, feels it physically: it works its way over his body, it gropes him.

"What are you doing here?" she says. "Do you have any idea what you look like?"

Then her eyes soften, a moment later a kind of haze comes over them, and she blinks. "Jesus," she says, "what is going on with you? What is wrong?"

This is weird, this isn't what Kunicki had expected. He had

expected a fight. And then she wraps her arms around him and holds him to her, nestling her face into his bizarre secondhand jacket. A sigh works its way out of Kunicki, a little round "Oh," he's not sure whether from surprise at her unexpected behavior or because all of a sudden he can see himself bursting into tears into her fragrant down jacket.

It's only when they're in the elevator that she says, "Are you okay?"

Kunicki says he's fine, but he knows that they're headed toward the final confrontation now. Their kitchen will serve as battlefield, and they'll both take up attack positions—he by the table, she with her back to the window, as always. And he knows he shouldn't underestimate this important moment, that this is perhaps the last and only possible moment to find out what happened. What the truth is. But he knows, too, that he is treading on a minefield. Every question will be like a bomb. He's not a coward, and he will not back down in the face of establishing the facts. As the elevator rises, he feels like a terrorist with a bomb under his clothes that will explode the second they open the door to their apartment and scatter everything to dust.

He props the door open with his leg so that he can slide in his shopping bags first, and then he squeezes in past them. In fact, he doesn't really notice anything out of the ordinary, he turns on the lights and sets out the groceries on the kitchen counter. He pours some water into a glass and sticks a fading bunch of parsley into it. This will bring him to, he thinks, parsley.

He passes through his own apartment like a ghost, he feels like he could walk through the walls. The rooms are empty. Kunicki is

an eye that is figuring out one of those "Spot the differences between Picture A and Picture B" puzzles. And Kunicki looks. There's
no doubt they're different, the apartment now and the apartment
from before. This puzzle would work only for the extremely unob-
servant. Her coat is gone from the coatrack, and her shawl, and the
child's jacket, the parade of boots (all that remains are his lone flip-
flops), and the umbrella.

The child's room seems totally deserted; in fact, all that's left is
furniture. A single little toy car lies on the rug, like the bits and
pieces left over after an unimaginable cosmic crash. But Kunicki
has to know for sure—and so with his hand held out before him he
steals into the bedroom, to the wardrobe with the glass in the doors,
which he pulls open; they are heavy, and they open begrudgingly,
with a sad grumbling. All that's left is a silk blouse, too fancy to
wear. It looks lonely there by itself in the wardrobe. The motion of
the doors. Kunicki looks over the empty shelves in the bathroom.
His shaving appliances are still there, in the corner. And his battery-
powered toothbrush.

He needs a lot of time to understand what he is seeing. All evening, all night, and even the next morning.

At around nine he brews himself some potent coffee and then
gathers up some of his shaving things, a few shirts from the wardrobe, some trousers, and puts them in a bag. Before he leaves, as
he's about to go out the door, he checks his wallet: ID, credit cards.
Then he runs down to his car. Snow has fallen in the night, so he
has to scrape off the windshield. He does so sloppily, by hand. He's
counting on being able to get to Zagreb by nightfall, and to Split by
the following day. Meaning tomorrow he sees the sea.

He heads south, straight as an arrow, toward the Czech border.

## ISLAND SYMMETRIES

According to travel psychology, the appearance of similarity between any two places is directly proportional to the distance between them. What is nearest seems absolutely dissimilar, totally foreign. Often the most striking similarities are ones we find—according to travel psychology—clear on the other side of the world.

Particularly interesting is the phenomenon of island symmetries. Unfathomable, unexplained, it is a phenomenon that would seem to merit its own monograph. Gotland and Rhodes, Iceland and New Zealand. Viewed without its partner, each of these islands appears incomplete, imperfect. The naked limestone cliffs on Rhodes are complete only when they meet the moss-coated cliffs of Gotland; the sun's blinding glare is rendered real only in contrast with the golden softness of a northern afternoon. Medieval city walls can take one of two forms: dramatic or melancholic. This is well known to the Swedish tourists on Rhodes, who have established a kind of informal colony, unreported to the UN.

## AIRSICKNESS BAGS

On a plane from Warsaw to Amsterdam, I was playing with a paper bag without realizing it; then I looked and saw it had been written on:

"10/12/2006: Striking out for Ireland. Final destination Belfast. Students of the Rzeszów Institute of Technology."

The inscription, in pen, was visible on the bottom of the bag, in the empty space between the official print, which repeated the same thing in multiple languages:

"air-sickness bag . . . *sac pour mal de l'air . . . Spuckbeutel . . .*
*bolsa de mareo.*" Between these words some human hand had written in those other words with the "1" at the start reinforced, as
though their author hesitated for a moment about whether or not to
leave behind this anonymous expression of anxiety. Did they think
the inscription on the bag would find a reader? That I would in this
way bear witness to someone else's journey?

I was moved by this one-sided act of communication, and I wondered whose hand had written it, how their eyes had looked as they
guided that hand along the line of preprinted text. I wondered if
it was working out for them there, in Belfast, for those students
from Rzeszów. As a matter of fact I wanted on some other plane in
the future to find an answer to my question. I wanted them to write:
"It went fine. We're going back to Poland now." But I know that
writing on bags is something people do only out of anxiety and
uncertainty. Neither defeat nor the greatest success is conducive to
writing.

## THE EARTH'S NIPPLES

These young people—a girl, at most nineteen, studying Scandinavian literature, and her boyfriend, a small blond with dreadlocks,
insisted on hitchhiking from Reykjavík to Ísafjörður. They were
categorically advised against it for two reasons: first, there's not a
lot of traffic in Iceland, and especially up north, so they might get
stuck somewhere along the way; second, the temperature is liable to
plummet out of nowhere. But these young people did not listen.
Both warnings, as it turned out, came true: they got stuck in the
wilderness, where before they got off the road to go to some distant

little village their previous car had left them, and no other car was forthcoming. In the course of an hour the weather changed radically, and snow started to fall. Increasingly worried, they stood by the road, which crossed a plain full of lava rocks from one side to the other, and they kept warm by smoking, hoping that some other car would finally come along. But it didn't. Evidently people had given up on getting to Ísafjörður that evening.

There was nothing to make a fire from—only damp cold moss and sparse bushes the fire wouldn't even put in its mouth, let alone digest. They camped out in sleeping bags between the rocks in the moss, and when the snow clouds disappeared and a starry freezing sky was revealed, they saw faces in the lava stones, and everything started whispering, murmuring, rustling. It turned out that all you had to do was reach under the moss, under the stones, in order to touch the earth, which was warm. Your hand could feel distant, delicate vibrations, some far-off movement, a breath—there could be no doubt: the earth was alive.

Then they learned from the Icelanders that no real ill could have come to them: for lost souls like them the earth is able to bare its warm nipples. You just have to suck at them with gratitude and drink the earth's milk. Apparently it tastes like milk of magnesium— what they sell in pharmacies for hyperacidity and heartburn.

## POGO

Tomorrow is the Sabbath. Young fledgling Hassidim pogo dance on the boardwalk to the rhythm of lively, trendy South American music. "Dance" isn't the right word. These are wild ecstatic leaps, twirling in place, bodies bounding into one another and bouncing back off—it's the dance stamped out by teenagers all over the world at concerts, in front of the stage. Here the music comes from some speakers placed atop a car in which sits a rabbi, supervising everything.

Some entertained Scandinavian tourist girls join in with the boys and awkwardly, holding hands, attempt a cancan. But then they're issued orders by one of the teenagers:

"We ask that if women wish to dance, they do so over to one side."

## WALL

Here there are some who believe that we have reached the end of our journey.

The city is completely white, like bones left in the desert, licked by tongues of heat, polished by the sand. It looks like a calcified coral colony grown up over the hill from the times of the immemorial sea.

It is also said that this city's runway is uneven—difficult for any pilot—a runway from which gods once took off from land. Those who have any idea about those times repeat, unfortunately, contradictory things. No one can agree on any one version of events today.

Beware, all pilgrims, tourists, and wanderers who have made it this far—you sailed up in ships, came on planes, crossed on foot over straits and bridges, military cordons and barbed wire. Many times were your cars and caravans stopped, your passports carefully checked, your eyes looked into. Beware, traverse this labyrinth of little streets according to signs, stations, do not be guided by the index finger of an extended hand, the numbered verses in a book, the Roman numerals painted on the walls of houses. Do not be misled by stalls with beads, carpets, water pipes, coins unearthed (supposedly) from the sands of the desert, spices sprinkled in colorful pyramids; do not be distracted by the colorful crowd of people like you, of all possible types, colors of skin, faces, hair, clothing, hats, and backpacks.

At the center of the labyrinth there's neither treasure nor a minotaur you'll have to fight in battle; the road ends suddenly with a wall—white like the whole city, tall, impossible to climb. Supposedly this is the wall of some invisible temple, but facts are facts—we've reached the end, there's nothing past this now.

And so don't be surprised by the sight of those who stand before the wall in shock, or those who cool their foreheads resting them against the chilly stone, or even those who out of exhaustion and disappointment have sat down and are now snuggling up to the wall like children.

It's time to go back.

## AMPHITHEATER IN SLEEP

On my first night in New York I dreamed that I was wandering the streets of the city at night. I did, however, have a map, and I checked it from time to time, searching for a way out of this grid labyrinth. Suddenly I came to a big square and saw an enormous ancient amphitheater. I stood, completely astonished. Then a couple of Japanese tourists came up and pointed it out to me on my city map. Yes, it really is there, I sighed with relief.

In the thicket of perpendicular and parallel streets that intersect

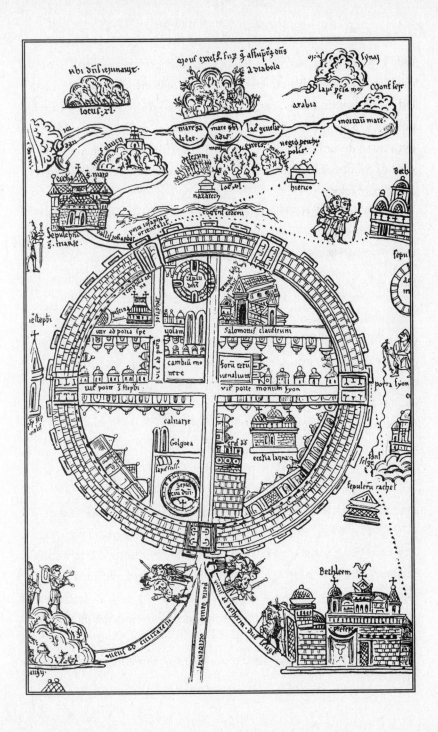

with each other like warp and weft, in the midst of that monotonous network, I saw a great round eye gazing up into the heavens.

## MAP OF GREECE

It's reminiscent of a great Tao—if you look at it closely, you can indeed see a great Tao made of water and earth. But in no place is it as though one element were gaining an advantage over the other— they embrace each other reciprocally: earth and water. A Peloponnesian strait is what the earth gives to the water, and Crete what the water gives to the earth.

I do think that the Peloponnese has the most beautiful shape. It's the shape of a great maternal hand, not a human one, that is dipping into the water to check if the temperature is right for a bath.

## KAIROS

"We are the ones who confront head-on," said the professor, once they were out of the big airport building, waiting for their taxi. He took pleasure in deep breaths of warm, gentle Greek air.

He was eighty-one years old, with a wife twenty years his junior, a woman he had married prudently, as the air was leaking out of his first marriage, his adult children having left the nest. And it was a good thing, because that other wife now needed to be cared for herself, living out her days in a perfectly reasonable retirement home.

He handled the flight well, and a few hours' time difference didn't really make a difference; the rhythm of the professor's sleep had long since come to resemble a cacophonous symphony, random

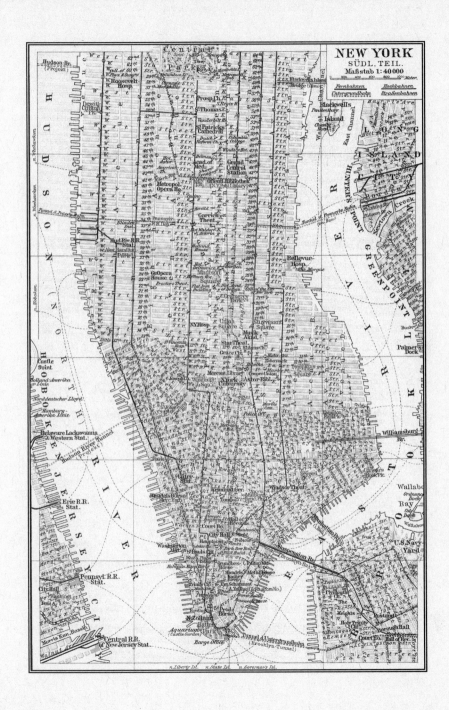

# NEW YORK
## SÜDL. TEIL.
### Maßstab 1:40000

timetables of unexpected sleepiness and dazzling lucidity. The time change merely shifted those chaotic chords of waking and sleep by seven hours.

The air-conditioned taxi took them to their hotel; there, Karen, the professor's younger wife, skillfully oversaw the unloading of their baggage, collected information from the organizers of the cruise at reception, got the keys, and then, accepting help from a solicitous porter—for this was no easy task—took her husband up to the second floor, to their room. There she carefully arranged him in their bed, loosened his scarf, and took his shoes off for him. Instantly he was asleep.

And they were in Athens! She was happy, she went up to the window and struggled for a second with its ingenious latch. Athens in April. Spring at full tilt, leaves feverishly clambering into space. The dust had risen already outside, but it wasn't yet severe; and the noise, of course: ever-present. She shut the window.

In the bathroom Karen tousled her short gray hair and got into the shower. Inside it she felt all her tension washing away with the soap, pooling at her feet, then escaping for all eternity down the drain.

Nothing to get worked up about, she reminded herself, deep down. All of our bodies must conform to the world. There is no other way.

"We're nearing the finish line," she said aloud, standing still under the stream of warm water. And because somehow she couldn't help thinking in images—which, she thought, had almost certainly been a hindrance to her academic career—she saw something like an ancient Greek gymnasium with its characteristic starting block, raised on cables, and its runners, her husband and herself, trotting awkwardly toward the finish line, although they'd only just taken off.

She wrapped a fluffy towel around herself and applied moisturizer, thoroughly, to her face, neck, and chest. The familiar scent of the cream soothed her fully now, so she lay down for a moment on the made bed beside her husband, and fell asleep without realizing.

Over dinner, which they ate downstairs, in the restaurant (sole and broccoli for him, for her a feta salad), the professor asked her if they'd brought his notebooks, books, outlines, until finally among those ordinary questions there came the one that sooner or later had to arrive, revealing the latest situation on the front:

"My dear, where are we right now?"

She reacted calmly. She explained in a few simple sentences.

"Ah, of course," he said happily. "I'm ever so slightly discombobulated."

She ordered herself a bottle of retsina and looked around the restaurant. Mostly wealthy tourists, Americans, Germans, Brits, and also those who had lost—in the free flow of money, which they let guide them—any and all defining traits. They were simply attractive, healthy, moving with unsummoned ease from language to language.

At the table next to theirs, for example, sat a pleasant group, people who might have been a little younger than she was, happy fifty-somethings, hale and flushed. Three men and two women in fits of laughter, the waiter bringing them another bottle of Greek wine—Karen had no doubt she would have fit in. It occurred to her that she could leave her husband, who just then was scraping apart the pale corpse of his fish with a trembling fork. She could grab her retsina and as naturally as a dandelion seed fall onto a chair at that next table, catching on to the final chords of those people's laughter, chiming in with her own smooth alto.

Of course she did not do so. She got to gathering up the broccoli from the placemat, which had jumped ship from the professor's plate, offended at his incompetence.

"Gods in heaven," she snapped, calling over the waiter to request some herbal tea. Then, turning back to him: "Can I help you?"

"I draw the line at being fed," he said, and with redoubled strength went back to hacking at his fish.

Often she got mad at him. The man was utterly dependent on her, and yet he acted as though it were the reverse. She thought to herself that men, or at least the cleverest among them, must be prompted by some self-preservation instinct in clinging to much younger women, not realizing it, near desperation—but not at all for the reasons sociobiologists ascribed them. Since no, it was in no way connected to reproduction, to genes, to stuffing their DNA into the tiny little tubes of matter through which time coursed. It has to do instead with the presentiment men have at every moment of their lives, a foreboding adamantly hushed and hidden—that left to their own devices, in the dull, quiet company of passing time, they would atrophy faster. As though they'd been designed for a brief spurt of intensity, a high-stakes race, a triumph and, immediately afterward, exhaustion. That what kept them alive was excitement, a costly life strategy; energy reserves eventually ran out, and then life would be lived in overdraft.

. . .

They had met, fifteen years earlier, at a reception in the home of a mutual friend who was just finishing up his two-year appointment at their university. The professor brought her a glass of wine, and when he handed it to her, she noticed how his totally outmoded woolen vest was coming apart at the seams, how at the professor's hip fluttered a long, dark thread. She had just arrived to take the place of a professor who was retiring, taking on all his students; she was just furnishing her rented home and stocking up after her divorce, which would have been more painful had they had children. Her husband, after fifteen years of marriage, had left her for another woman. Karen was over forty, already a professor, with several books to her name. She specialized in lesser-known ancient cults of the Greek islands. Religious studies was her field.

It took a few years, after that meeting, before they got married. The professor's first wife was seriously ill, which made it more difficult for him to get divorced. But even his children were on their side.

She often reflected on how her life had turned out, and she was coming to the conclusion that the truth was simple: men needed women more than women needed men. In fact, thought Karen, women could get along perfectly fine without men altogether. They tolerated solitude well, took care of their health and cultivated friendships, lasted longer—as she tried to think of other qualities, she realized she was imagining women as a highly useful breed of dog. With a certain satisfaction she began to expand this list of canine traits: they learned quickly, they liked children, they were sociable, they kept at home. It was easy to awaken in them—particularly when they were young—that mysterious, all-encompassing instinct that only sometimes was connected with the possession of offspring. But it was something decidedly greater—an encompassing of the world; the tamping into place of trails; the unfurling, then tucking in of days and nights; the establishment of soothing rituals. Rousing this instinct with little exercises in helplessness wasn't hard. Then they'd be blinded, the algorithm would kick in, at which point it would be possible to pitch a tent, settle down in their nests, tossing everything else out of them, and the women wouldn't even notice that the chick was a monster, and someone else's castoff.

The professor had retired five years earlier, receiving awards and distinctions when he took his leave, inclusion in the registry of the most meritorious academics, a commemorative publication with articles by his students; several receptions were given in his honor. One of these was attended by a comedian well-known from TV, which, truth be known, was the thing that most cheered and revived the professor.

Then they settled down permanently in a modest but comfortable home in their university town; there he occupied himself with "putting his papers in order."

In the morning Karen would brew him tea and make a light breakfast. She'd go through his correspondence, responding to letters and invitations, a task that hinged primarily upon declining politely. In the mornings she tried to match his early rising, sleepily preparing herself some coffee as she made his oatmeal. She'd lay out clean clothing for him. At around noon the home help would come, so Karen had a few hours to herself, as he gave in to his daily nap. In the afternoon another mug of tea, this time herbal, and then she'd see him off on the walk he took in the early evenings on his own.

Reading Ovid aloud, dinner, and the nightly preparations for bed. All this interspersed with the meting out of pills and drops. Each year, for these five peaceful years, there had been only one invitation to which she'd said yes—the luxury cruises every summer around the Greek islands, where the professor gave daily lectures to the passengers, not counting Saturdays and Sundays. It was ten lectures in all, on the topics that most fascinated the professor; there was no fixed list of subjects.

The ship was called *Poseidon* (its black Greek letters stood in stark relief against the white hull: ΠΟΣΕΙΔΩΝ), and it contained two decks, restaurants, a billiards room, little cafés, a massage parlor, a solarium, and comfortable cabins. For several years they'd occupied the same one, with a queen-sized bed, a bathroom, a table with two armchairs, and a microscopic desk. On the floor a soft coffee-colored carpet, and Karen, as she looked at it, still held out hope that in its long fibers she might still find the earring she lost here, four years before. The cabin led directly out onto the first-class deck, and in the evenings, once the professor was already asleep, Karen liked to take advantage of this amenity and stand at the railing to smoke her one daily cigarette, gazing out at the lights in the distance they had passed. The deck, heated by the sun during the day, now, too, gave off a warmth, while a dark, cool air flowed out over the water, and it seemed to Karen that her body marked the boundary between day and night.

"For you are the savior of ships, the tamer of warsteeds, blessed art thou, O Poseidon, wielding the earth, raven-haired and fortunate, show mercy upon the sailors," she'd say under her breath, and then she'd throw her barely started cigarette to the god, her daily allocation—an act of pure extravagance.

The ship's trajectory hadn't changed in five years. From Piraeus it went to Eleusis, then to Corinth, and from there back south, to the island of Poros, so that the passengers could see the ruins of Poseidon's temple and meander around the little town. Then their route took them to the Cyclades—it was all supposed to be unhurried, even lazy, so that everyone could bask in sun and sea, in the views of the towns arrayed along the islands, towns with white walls and orange roofs, scented by lemon groves. High season hadn't started yet, so there wouldn't be hordes of tourists—these the professor was always disparaging, unable to conceal his impatience. He felt that they looked without seeing, their gazes sliding over everything, alighting only on whatever their mass-produced guidebooks pointed out to them specifically—the print equivalent of a McDonald's. Next they stopped on Delos, where they would study the temple of Apollo, and then finally they'd head for the Dodecanese island of Rhodes, completing their excursion there and flying home from the local airport.

Karen was fond of the afternoons when they docked at little ports, and, dressed for walking—the professor with the scarf he simply had to have around his neck—they'd go into the town. Bigger boats would also moor at these ports, and when they did the local merchants would immediately open up their little shops to offer visitors towels with the name of the island, sets of shells, sponges, mixes of dried herbs in tasteful baskets, ouzo or just ice cream.

The professor walked valiantly, indicating landmarks with his cane—gates, fountains, ruins encircled by frail barriers, and he'd tell stories his listeners would never be able to find even in the best guidebooks. These walks were not included in his contract, though. It stated just a single lecture every day.

. . .

He would begin: "I'm of the belief that human beings need, to live their lives, more or less the same climatic conditions as lemons."

He'd raise his gaze to the ceiling dotted with little round lights and let it stay there for a moment longer than was strictly permissible.

Karen would clench her hands until her knuckles went white, but she thought she managed to contain the intrigued, lightly provocative smile—raised eyebrows, irony across her face.

"This is our point of departure," continued her husband. "It is not by chance that the range of Greek civilization coincides, roughly speaking, with the incidence of citrus. Beyond this sun-drenched, life-giving realm, everything undergoes a slow, but inevitable, decline."

It was like an unrushed, protracted takeoff. Karen saw the same picture each time: the professor's plane would stagger, its wheels dipping down into a rut, maybe even running off the runway—so he would take off from the grass. But in the end the engine would kick in, tossing from side to side, rocking, and by then it would be clear the plane would fly. And Karen would let out a discreet, relieved sigh.

She knew the topics of the lectures, knew their outlines from the index cards covered over in the professor's minuscule handwriting, and from his notes that she would use to help him if something were indeed to happen—she could stand up from her seat in the first row and latch on to any of his sentences halfway through and just proceed, along the path he'd beaten. But it was true she wouldn't speak with the same eloquence, nor would she permit herself the little quirks with which he held his audience's attention, without even always being aware of them. Karen would await the moment when the professor would stand up and start pacing, which meant—returning to her picture—that his plane had reached its cruising altitude, that everything was fine, that she could now simply walk out onto the upper deck and extend her gaze in joy over the surface of the water, letting it linger on the masts of the yachts they had passed, on the just-traced mountain peaks in the light white mist.

She looked at the listeners—they were sitting in a semicircle; those in the first row had notebooks before them on their small folded-out tables, eagerly jotting down the professor's words. Those in the last rows, around the windows, lounging, ostentatiously indifferent, were also listening. Karen knew it was these rows that produced the most inquisitive among them, the ones who would later exhaust the professor with questions, calling her into the service of shielding her husband from all additional—now unpaid—consultations.

She was amazed by this man, her own husband. It seemed to her that he knew everything there was to know about Greece, everything that had been written, excavated, ever said. His knowledge wasn't so much enormous as monstrous; it was made up of texts, quotes, references, citations, painstakingly deciphered words on chipped vases, drawings not entirely intelligible, dig sites, paraphrases in later writings, ashes, correspondences and concordances. There was something inhuman in all this—to be able to fit all that knowledge in himself, the professor must have needed to perform some special biological procedure, permitting it to grow into his tissues, opening his body to it and becoming a hybrid. Otherwise, it would have been impossible.

It was clear that such an enormous stock of knowledge could not be put in order; it had instead the form of a sponge, of deep-sea corals growing over years until they started to create the most fantastic forms. This was knowledge that had already attained critical mass and had since crossed over into some other state—it appeared to reproduce, to multiply, to organize in complex and binary forms. Associations traveled down unusual routes, likenesses were found in the least expected versions—like kinship in Brazilian soap operas, where anyone could turn out to be the child or husband or sister of anybody else. Well-trodden paths turned out to be worth nothing, while those thought untraversable proved convenient routes. Something that meant nothing for years suddenly—in the professor's mind—became the departure point for some great revelation, a real paradigm shift. She had an unshakable awareness of being the wife of a great man.

As he was speaking, his face changed, as though his words washed it clean of old age and exhaustion. A different face emerged: now his eyes shone, his cheeks lifted and tightened. The unpleasant impression of a mask that face had made only moments earlier now faded. It was as much of a change as if he had been given drugs, a small dose of amphetamines. She knew that when that drug wore off—whatever kind of drug it was—his face would freeze back, his eyes go matte, his body would slump into the nearest armchair, taking back on that appearance of helplessness she knew so well. And she would need to lift that body carefully, by its armpits, prod it ever so slightly, lead it dragging its feet and swaying to a nap in their cabin—it would have expended too much energy.

She knew the course of the lectures well. But each time it brought her pleasure to observe him, like putting a desert rose in water, as though he were recounting his own history rather than that of Greece. All the figures he mentioned were him, that was obvious. All the political problems were his problems, personal as possible. Philosophical concepts—those were what kept him up at night; they belonged to him. The gods he knew intimately, of course; he had lunch with them daily, at a restaurant near their house. Lots of nights they'd stayed up talking, drinking an Aegean Sea of wine. He knew their addresses and phone numbers, could call them up at any time. Athens he knew like the inside of his pocket, though not (needless to say) the city they'd just set sail from—that one, truth be told, did not interest him in the slightest—but rather the old Athens, from the times of, let's say, Pericles, and their map was overlaid onto today's layout, rendering the present one spectral, unreal.

Karen had already done her private survey of her fellow passengers that morning, when they had boarded the ship in Piraeus. Everyone, even the French, spoke English. Taxis had brought them straight from the airport in Athens or from their hotels. They were polite, attractive, intelligent. Here was a couple, in their fifties, slim, probably older than they looked, in fact, in light-colored natural clothing, linen and cotton, him playing with his pen, her sitting up straight and loose, like someone trained in relaxation techniques. Continuing on, a young woman whose eyes were glazed by her contact lenses, taking notes, left-handed, writing in big round letters, drawing figure-eights in the margins. Behind her two gay guys, well dressed, well groomed, one of them wearing funny glasses à la Elton John. By the window a father with his daughter, which they mentioned immediately upon introducing themselves, the man probably afraid of being suspected of an affair with a minor; the girl always wore black and had her head shaved almost bald, with pretty, dark pouting lips that betrayed an expression of irrepressibly swollen disdain. The next couple, harmoniously gray-haired, was Swedish, apparently ichthyologists—Karen had noticed this on the list of lecture participants they had received ahead of time. The Swedes were calm and looked a lot like one another, though not in the way people look like each other from birth—it was instead the kind of resemblance that must be worked at, hard, over the course of many years of marriage. A few younger people, this cruise was their first; they seemed to still be unsure whether this ancient Greek stuff was for them, or whether they wouldn't rather delve into the mysteries of orchids or of turn-of-the-century Middle Eastern decorative arts. Was their rightful place this ship with this old man who commenced lectures by rambling about citrus fruits? Karen took a longer look at the redheaded, fair-skinned man in jeans that hung around his hips, who rubbed the several days' worth of light-blond stubble on his face. She thought he looked German. A handsome German. And a dozen or so others, in focused silence, watching the professor.

Here was a new type of mind, thought Karen, that didn't trust words from books, from the best textbooks, from papers, mono-graphs, encyclopedias—abused over the course of its studies, now it had cerebral hiccups. It had been corrupted by the ease of breaking down any construct—even the most complex—into prime factors. Reducing ad absurdum every ill-considered argumentation, taking on every few years a completely new, fashionable language, which—like the latest advertised version of a pocketknife—could do any-thing with everything: open cans, clean fish, interpret novels, and foresee the evolution of the political situation in central Africa.

A mind for charades, a mind that employed citations and cross-references like knife and fork. A rational and discursive mind, lonely and sterile. A mind that seemed to be aware of everything, even things it didn't really understand, but that moved fast—a quick, intelligent electric impulse without limits, linking everything with everything, convinced that all of it together must mean something, even if we couldn't yet know what.

Now, with verve, the professor began to expound upon the origins of the name Poseidon, and Karen turned her face toward the sea.

After every lecture he needed her assurance that it had gone well. In their cabin, as they dressed for dinner, she would hug him to her, his hair smelling slightly of his chamomile shampoo. Now they were ready to go, him in his lightweight dark-colored jacket and his favorite old-fashioned scarf, her in her green velvet dress, and stood inside their cramped cabin with their faces at the windows. She handed him his little cup of wine, he took a sip and whispered a few words, then dipped his fingers in and sprinkled wine around the cabin, but carefully, so as not to stain the fluffy brownish carpet. The drops sank into the dark upholstery of the chair, wine vanishing into furniture; there would be no trace of it. She did the same.

At dinner, the golden German man joined their table, which they were sharing with the captain, and Karen saw that her husband was none too pleased with this new presence. The man, however, was pleasant, tactful. He introduced himself as a programmer, and said he worked with computers in Bergen, near the Arctic Circle. So he was Norwegian. In the soft lamplight his skin, eyes, and the thin wire frames of his glasses all seemed made of gold. His white linen shirt unnecessarily covering his golden torso.

He was interested in one of the words the professor had used during his lecture, which had in fact been explained with great precision.

"Contuition," repeated the professor, his irritation painstakingly concealed, "is, as I said, a variety of insight that spontaneously reveals the presence of some larger-than-human strength, some unity above heterogeneity. I'll expand tomorrow," he added, with his mouth full.

"Right," responded the man somewhat helplessly. "But what would that mean?"

He did not receive a response, because after ruminating for a moment, evidently searching through the stocks of the abyss of his memory, the professor finally began to trace a series of small circles in the air with his hand, reciting:

"Reject everything, do not look, shut your eyes and change your gaze, awaken another one that almost everyone has, but that few use."

He was so proud of himself he actually blushed.

"Plato."

The captain nodded knowingly, and then raised a toast—this was their fifth shared journey:

"To our happy little anniversary."

It was strange, but just then Karen felt certain this would be their last shared journey.

"May we meet again next year," she said.

The professor, animated now, told the captain and the ginger-haired man, who introduced himself as Ole, about his latest idea.

"A trip that would follow in the footsteps of Odysseus," he said, and then waited, to give them time to be astonished by the thought.

"Approximately, of course. We'd need to think how to organize it, logistically." He looked at Karen, who muttered:

"It did take Odysseus twenty years."

"That doesn't matter," the professor replied merrily. "In today's day and age you could do it in two weeks."

Then Karen's and Ole's eyes met, by accident. It was on that night or the following one that she had an orgasm, just like that, in her sleep. It was somehow connected with the redheaded Norwegian, but it wasn't clear how, because she didn't remember very much of what had gone on there, in her dream. She'd simply known that golden man, profoundly. She woke up with echoes of contractions in her lower abdomen, stunned, amazed, and then embarrassed. Without realizing she was doing it, she started counting them, catching the final four.

The next day, as they were moving along the coast, Karen openly admitted to herself that in many places, at this stage, there was nothing left to see.

The road to Eleusis was an asphalt highway down which cars went speeding; thirty kilometers of ugliness and banality, desiccated hard shoulders, concrete homes, ads, parking lots, and land it wouldn't have made sense to cultivate. Warehouses, loading ramps, a giant dirty port, a heating plant.

Once they were ashore, the professor led the whole group to the ruins of Demeter's temple, which now looked rather sad. The group could not conceal its disappointment, so he called on all of them to imagine turning back time.

"This route from Athens was barely reinforced by stones back

then, and very narrow—look, swarms of people move along it toward Eleusis, walking, kicking up the dust feared by the greatest
rulers of the world. The packed crowd cries out, the sound of hundreds of throats."

The professor stood still, leaned back on his heels, wedging his
cane into the ground, and said:

"It might have sounded something like this," and his voice cut
off for a moment, for him to gather his breath, and then he shouted
out with all the strength of his old throat. And suddenly his voice
was loud and clear. His wailing was carried by the heated air, causing everyone to look up: surprised tourists on their own, making
their way between the rocks, and ice cream vendors, and workers
lining the railings because high season was about to start now, and
a small child poking at a frightened beetle with a stick, and two
donkeys grazing off in the distance, on the other side of the slope.

"Iacchus, Iacchus," cried the professor with his eyes closed.

Even after he had fallen silent again, his shout still hung in the
air, so that everything held its breath for half a minute, for a few
dozen strange seconds. Jarred by this eccentric comportment, his
listeners couldn't bring themselves to even look at one another, and
Karen turned bright red, as though it had been her crying out in
that strange way. She moved off to the side, to cool off from her
embarrassment and from the heat.

But the old man didn't look even remotely chagrined.

". . . and perhaps it is possible," she heard him say, "to look into
the past, cast our glances backward, imagine it as a panopticon of
sorts, or, dear friends, to treat the past as though it still existed, it's
just that it's been shifted over into another dimension. Maybe all we
need to do is change our way of looking, look askance at it all

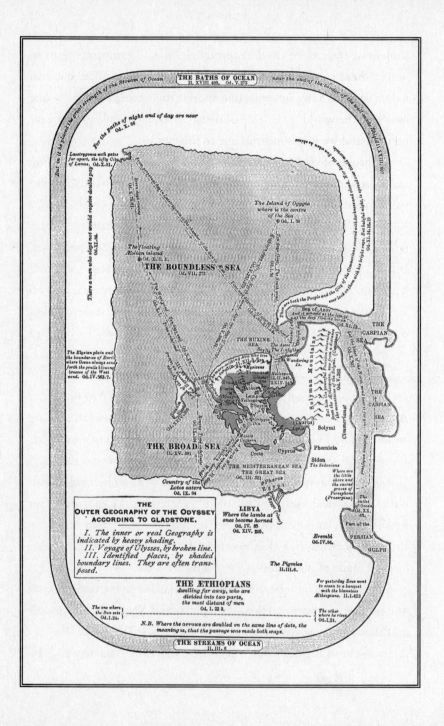

THE BATHS OF OCEAN
II. XVIII 489. Od. V. 275

near the end of the border of the stream of Ocean. Od. XII. 1.

But in it he places the great strength of the Stream of Ocean

For the paths of night and of day are near
Od. X. 86

As soon as the Sun when his bright light Od. XIX. 233.

Laestrygonia with gates far apart, the lofty City of Lamos. Od. X. 81.

There a man who slept not would receive double pay.
Od. XI. 84.

The floating Æolian island
Od. X. 1. 2.

THE BOUNDLESS SEA
Od. VII. 273

The Island of Ogygia where is the centre of the Sea
Od. I. 50

Then are both the People and the City of the Cimmerians covered with darkness and cloud and never look on them with his bright rays. But baleful night, is spread Od. XI. 14, 15, 19

THE CASPIAN SEA

Sea of Azov And it arrived at the limits And the deep flowing ocean
Od. XI. 13.

THE BUXINE SEA

The Elysian plain and the boundaries of Earth where Ocean always sends forth the gentle blowing breezes of the West wind. Od. IV. 563, 7.

The Aune
Scylla. The Lofty
Charybdis
The Wandering Is.
Od. XII. 235
Mycenae

Helleno
II. III. 945.
XXIV. 544

Solyman Mountains

THE CASPIAN SEA

But when the powerful Poseidon afar from the Æthiopians, saw from a distance from the mountains of the Solymi Od. V. 282

Taurus
Lycia

Solymi

Lotos-eating

Lampos
Hellespont
Scylla

Crete

Cyprus

Phœnicia

Sidon
The Sidonians

THE BROAD SEA
II. XV. 381

THE MEDITERRANEAN SEA
THE GREAT SEA
Od. III. 321

Pharos

Where are the little shore and the sacred groves of Persephone (Proserpina)

The outlet of Ocean Od. XX. 65.

Country of the Lotos eaters
Od. IX. 84

LIBYA
Where the lambs at once become horned
Od. IV. 85
Od. XIV. 295.

Part of the PERSIAN GULPH

THE
OUTER GEOGRAPHY OF THE ODYSSEY
ACCORDING TO GLADSTONE.

I. The inner or real Geography is indicated by heavy shading.
II. Voyage of Ulysses, by broken line.
III. Identified places, by shaded boundary lines. They are often transposed.

Erembi
Od. IV. 84.

The Pigmies
II. III. 6.

For yesterday Zeus went to ocean to a banquet with the blameless Æthiopians. II. I. 423

THE ÆTHIOPIANS
dwelling far away, who are divided into two parts, the most distant of men
Od. I. 22 3.

The one where the Sun sets
Od. I. 24.

The other where he rises
Od. I. 24.

N.B. Where the arrows are doubled on the same line of dots, the meaning is, that the passage was made both ways.

THE STREAMS OF OCEAN
II. III. 5

somehow. Because if the future and the past are infinite, then in reality there can be no 'once upon,' no 'back when.' Different moments in time hang in space like sheets, like screens lit up by one moment; the world is made up of these frozen moments, great meta-images, and we just hop from one to the next."

He broke off for a moment to rest, because they were walking uphill, and then Karen heard him squeeze the next words out between his whistling breaths:

"In reality, movement doesn't exist. Like the turtle in Zeno's paradox, we're heading nowhere, if anything we're simply wandering into the interior of a moment, and there is no end, nor any destination. And the same might apply to space—since we are all identically removed from infinity, there can also be no somewhere—nothing is truly anchored on any day, nor in any place."

That evening Karen did a mental breakdown of the costs of that expedition: a burned nose and forehead, a foot injured to bleeding. A sharp stone had gotten under the strap of his sandal, and he hadn't felt it. That must have been a serious symptom of worsening arteriosclerosis, which the professor had had for many years.

She knew this body well, too well—shrunken, sunken, the dried-out skin dappled with brown spots. The remains of gray hairs on his chest, his frail neck that barely held up his trembling head, the thin bones beneath a thin covering of skin, and a skeleton that seemed made of aluminum it was so light, avian.

Sometimes he fell asleep before she had managed to undress him and prepare the bed, and then she had to carefully remove his jacket and shoes and steer him, still slumbering, toward the bed.

Every morning they had the same problem—his shoes. The

professor suffered from an irritating ailment—he had ingrowing toenails. His toes became inflamed, swollen, his nails got raised, boring holes into his socks, scraping painfully against the tops of his shoes. Placing a foot in such pain in its black leather slipper would be a gratuitous act of cruelty. So, for everyday things the professor wore sandals, and covered shoes they ordered from a particular shoemaker near where they lived, and for an incredible sum he would produce for the professor beautiful soft shoes, with a raised top, loose.

That evening, likely from the sun, he had a fever, so Karen gave up on dinner at the table and ordered food to their cabin.

In the morning, as the ship was sailing up to Delos, after brushing their teeth and a laborious shave, they went out together onto the deck with the pastries from the previous day's tea. They crumbled them and threw them into the sea. It was early, everyone else was probably asleep.

But the sun had already lost its redness and was shining, gathering its strength moment by moment. The water had turned a golden honey color, thick, the waves had died down, and the great iron of the sun pressed them without leaving even the finest line. The professor put his arm around Karen's shoulder, and in fact that was the only gesture to be made in the face of such an obvious epiphany.

Looking around where you are once more is like looking at an image in which a million details conceal a hidden shape. Once you see it, you can never forget it's there.

I won't record every day of the trip, or relay each lecture—in any case, Karen might have them published someday. The ship sailed, every evening there was dancing on the deck, the passengers with glasses of wine in their hands, leaning against the railings, having lazy conversations. Others gazed out at the nighttime sea, at the cool, crystal darkness, lit up from time to time by the lights of big ships, bearing thousands of passengers, calling daily at different ports.

I'll mention only one lecture, which happened also to be my favorite. Karen had come up with the idea, to talk about those gods who didn't make it into the pages of the famous, popular books, those not mentioned by Homer, then ignored by Ovid; those who didn't make names for themselves with drama or romance; who weren't terrifying enough, cunning enough, elusive enough, who are known only from fragments of rock, from mentions, from the little extant from burned-down libraries. But thanks to that they've preserved something the well-known gods have lost forever—a divine volatility and ungraspability, a fluidity of form, an uncertainty of genealogy. They emerge from the shadows, from formlessness, then succumb once more to looming darkness. Just take Kairos, who always operates at the intersection of linear, human time and divine time—circular time. And at the intersection between place and time, at that moment that opens up for just a little while, to situate that single, right, unrepeatable possibility. The point where the straight line that runs from nowhere to nowhere makes—for one moment— contact with the circle.

He entered the room with a brisk step, dragging his feet and panting, and stood at his podium—the ordinary little restaurant table— and took a bundle out from under his arm. She knew his methods. The bundle was a towel, right out of their cabin. He knew perfectly well that as soon as he began to unroll it the room would fall silent, and the heads in the last row would incline toward him. People are children. Under the towel there was, first, her red scarf, and then, finally, there shone something white, a piece of marble, which may have looked like some shard of rock. The tension in the room had reached its pinnacle, and he, aware of the interest he was arousing, celebrated it with a slight sly smile, drawing out his gestures like he was acting in a movie. Then he lifted that light, flat piece almost to eye level, extending his arm, parodying Hamlet, and began:

Who is the sculptor, and where does he come from?

From Sicyon.

And his name?

Lysippus.

And who are you?

Kairos the All-Mastering.

Why do you tread on tiptoes?

I ceaselessly circumnavigate the world.

Why do you have wings on both feet?

Because I fly by with the wind.

And in your right hand, why do you carry a razor?

It is a sign to people that I am sharper than any blade.

Why does your hair fall over your eyes?

So that anyone who confronts me head-on can still catch me.

But, by Zeus, why is the back of your head bald?

So that no one I've run over with my winged feet might seize me from behind, for much as he desired to do so.

Why did the sculptor create you?

On account of you, foreigners, and he set me at the
entrance as a lesson.


He began with this lovely epigram by Posidippus—he ought to have
used it as an epitaph. The professor went up to the first seats and
handed the proof of the god's existence over to his audience. The
girl with the swollen, contemptuous lips reached out for the relief
with exaggerated caution, sticking out her tongue slightly from the
exertion. She passed it on, while the professor waited in silence,
until the small god had made it halfway around the room, and then,
with a stony expression on his face, he said:

"Please don't worry, it's a plaster cast from a museum gift shop.
Fifteen euros."

Karen heard a murmur of laughter, the shifting of the listeners'
bodies, the scraping of someone's chair—a clear sign that the tension had been broken. He'd started well. He must be having a good
day today.

She quietly slipped out onto the deck and lit a cigarette, looking
at the island of Rhodes as it got nearer, and the big ferries, the
beaches still mostly empty at this time of year, and the city, which
like some colony of insects climbed up the steep slope toward the
bright sun. She stood there, enveloped in a peace that suddenly
flowered over her, who knew from where.

She saw the island's shores, and its caves. Cloisters and the
naves carved into the rock by the water brought strange temples
to her mind. Something had carefully built them over millions of
years, that same force that now bore their small ship, rocked

them. A thick transparent power, that had its workshops on land as well.

Here were the prototypes of cathedrals, the slender towers and the catacombs, thought Karen. Those evenly stacked layers of rock on the shore, perfectly rounded stones, carefully elaborated over the ages, and grains of sand, and the ovals of caves. The veins of granite in sandstone, their asymmetrical, intriguing pattern, the regular line of the island's shore, the shades of sand on the beaches. Monumental buildings and fine jewelry. What, in the face of this, could those little strings of houses lining the shores ever hope to be? Those little ports, those little ships, those little human shops, where with excessive confidence old ideas—simplified and in miniature—were sold.

Now she recalled the water grotto they'd seen somewhere on the Adriatic. Poseidon's Grotto, where once a day the sun burst through an opening in the top. She remembered she herself had been next to the column of light as it pierced—sharp as a needle—the green water, and for just an instant revealed the sandy bed below. It lasted just a moment before the sun continued on its way.

The cigarette disappeared with a hiss into the great mouth of the sea.


He was sleeping on his side, with a hand under his cheek, his lips parted. His trouser leg had rolled up and now showed his gray cotton sock. She lay down beside him gently, put her arm around his waist, and kissed his back in its woolen vest. It occurred to her that after he was gone she'd have to stay a little longer, even just to tidy all their things up and make room for others. She'd gather all his notes, go through them, probably publish them. She'd arrange things with the publishers—several of his books had already been made into textbooks. And in reality there was no reason not to continue his lectures, although she wasn't sure the university would invite her to do so. But she would definitely want to take over these mobile Poseidon-like seminars on this meandering ship (if they asked her). Then she'd be able to add a lot of her own things. She thought about how no one had taught us to grow old, how we didn't know what it would be like. When we were young we thought of old age as an ailment that affected only other people. While we, for reasons never entirely clear, would remain young. We treated the old as though they were responsible for their condition somehow, as though they'd done something to earn it, like some types of diabetes or arteriosclerosis. And yet this was an ailment that affected the absolute most innocent. And, her eyes closed now, she thought of something else: the fact that her back remained uncovered. Who would hold her?

In the morning the sea was so calm, the weather so pretty, that everyone went out onto the deck. Someone was insisting that with such great weather they ought to be able to see in the distance the Turkish coast of Mount Ararat. But all they saw was a high rocky shore. From the sea the massif looked so powerful, dappled with bright splotches of bare rock resembling bones. The professor stood hunched over with his neck wrapped up in her red scarf, squinting. An image came to Karen's mind: they were sailing underwater, because in reality the water level was high, like in times of flood; they were moving in an illuminated greenish space that slowed their motion and drowned out their words. Her scarf no longer flapped obnoxiously, but rippled, silent, and her husband's dark eyes looked at her so softly, gently, rinsed by omnipresent salty tears. Glistening even more was Ole's red-gold hair, his whole body like a drop of resin in the water that would harden into amber soon. And high above their heads someone's hands were just releasing a bird to scout out the mainland, and soon they'd realize it was known where we were sailing, and just then that same hand was pointing out a mountaintop, a safe spot for a new beginning.

In that same moment she heard screams from up ahead, and instantly a hysterical whistle of warning, and the captain, who'd just been standing nearby, now ran toward the bridge, which, since it was such a violent departure from his usual decorum, frightened Karen. The passengers all started screaming and waving their hands; those leaning against the railings were no longer aiming their wide eyes at the mythical Ararat, but at something down below. Karen felt the ship brake sharply, the deck shifting and shuddering beneath their feet, and at the last possible moment she seized the metal of the railing and quickly tried to catch her husband's hand, but she saw the professor pawing his way backward, taking tiny steps, like she was watching a movie playing in reverse. On his face amusement arising from surprise, but not fear. His eyes said something like: "Catch me." Then she saw him hit his back and head on the iron scaffolding of the stairs, saw him bounce off of them and fall onto his knees. In the same instant from up ahead she heard the bang of a collision and people's shouting, and then the splash of life buoys and the powerful impact in the water of a lifeboat, because—as Karen was able to put together from other people's shouts—they'd rammed into some little yacht.

Around her people were rising from the deck, nobody else injured, and she was kneeling down beside her husband, gently trying to revive him. He was blinking, blinks that were too long, and then he said quite audibly, "Pick me up!" but that couldn't be done now, his body refused to obey, so Karen laid his head on her lap and waited for help to arrive.

The professor's well-selected health insurance meant that that same day he got transferred by helicopter from Rhodes to the hospital in Athens, where he underwent a battery of tests. The CT scan revealed extensive damage to the left hemisphere of his brain; he'd had a massive stroke. There was no way to s.. it. Karen sat by his side to the end, stroking his already limp hand. The right side of his body was completely stiff; his eye stayed shut. Karen had called his children, who must have been en route by now. She sat up next to him all night, whispering into his ear, believing he heard and understood her. She led him down the dusty road among the ads, the warehouses, the ramps, the dirty garages, down the side of the highway, all night.

But the crimson inner ocean of the professor's head rose from the swells of blood-bearing rivers and gradually flooded realm after realm—first the plains of Europe, where he'd been born and raised. Cities disappeared underwater, and the bridges and dams built so methodically by generations of his ancestors. The ocean reached the threshold of their reed-roofed home and boldly stepped inside. It unfurled a red carpet over those stone floors, the floorboards of the kitchen, scrubbed each Saturday, finally putting out the fire in the fireplace, attaining the cupboards and tables. Then it poured into the railway stations and the airports that had sent the professor off into the world. The towns he'd traveled to drowned in it, and in them the streets where he had stayed awhile in rented rooms, the cheap hotels he'd lived in, the restaurants where he'd dined. The shimmering red surface of the water now reached the lowest shelves of his favorite libraries, the books' pages bulging, including those in which his name was on the title page. Its red tongue licked the letters, and the black print melted clean away. The floors were soaked in red, the stairs he'd walked up and down to collect his children's school certificates, the walkway he'd gone down during the ceremony to receive his professorship. Red stains were already collecting on the sheets where he and Karen had first fallen and undone the drawstrings of their older, clumsy bodies. The viscous liquid permanently glued together the compartments of his wallet where he kept his credit cards and plane tickets and the photos of his grandkids. The stream flooded train stations, tracks, airports, and runways—never would another airplane take off from them, never would another train depart for any destination.

The sea level was rising relentlessly, the waters swept up words, ideas, and memories; the streetlights went out under them, lamp bulbs bursting; cables shorted, the whole network of connections transformed into dead spiderweb, a lame and useless game of telephone. Screens were extinguished. And finally that slow, infinite ocean began to come up to the hospital, and Athens itself stood in blood—the temples, the sacred roads and groves, the agora empty at this hour, the bright statue of the goddess and her little olive tree.

She was by his side when they made the decision to unplug the machine that wasn't necessary now, and when the gentle hands of the Greek nurse covered in one deft motion his face with the sheet.

The body was cremated, and Karen and his children scattered the ashes into the Aegean Sea, believing this to be the funeral he would have wanted.

## I'M HERE

I've progressed. At first, when I would wake up someplace new, I'd think I was at home. It would take me a minute to make out the unfamiliar details, now disclosed by daylight. The heavy hotel drapes, the hefty TV set, my messy suitcase, the meticulously folded white towels. As a new place took shape beyond the curtains, wimpled, enigmatic, frequently cream-colored or yellow still from the streetlamps.

But then I entered into a phase that travel psychologists refer to as "I Don't Know Where I Am." I'd wake up totally disoriented. Like an alcoholic coming to, I would try to remember what I'd done the previous evening, where I'd been and how I'd gotten there, going over every detail in an effort to decipher the here and now. And the longer this procedure would take, the more I would panic—an unpleasant state, similar to labyrinthitis, the loss of basic balance, verging on nausea. Where in God's name am I? But the world is merciful in its particularities, which would always steer me back in the right direction in the end. I'm in M. I'm in B. This is a hotel, this is my friend's apartment, the guest room in the home of the N. family. Someone's sofa.

This type of awakening was like getting my ticket stamped for the next part of my journey.

Then came a third phase, which travel psychology refers to as the key phase, the crowning phase. In this phase, whatever your destination might be, you are always heading in that direction. "It Doesn't Matter Where I Am," it makes no difference. I'm here.

## ON THE ORIGIN OF SPECIES

The planet's witnessing the appearance of new creatures now, ones that have already conquered all continents and almost every ecological niche. They travel in packs and are anemophilous, covering large distances without difficulty.

Now I see them from the window of the bus, these airborne anemones, whole packs of them, roaming the desert. Individual specimens cling on tight to brittle little desert plants, fluttering noisily—perhaps this is the way they communicate.

The experts say these plastic bags open up a whole new chapter of earthly existence, breaking nature's age-old habits. They're made up of their surfaces exclusively, empty on the inside, and this historic forgoing of all contents unexpectedly affords them great evolutionary benefits. They are mobile and light; prehensile ears permit them to latch on to objects, or the appendages of other creatures, thus expanding their habitat. They started out in suburbs and trash heaps; it took them several windy seasons to reach the provinces and far-flung wilds. But by now they have occupied vast tracts of the globe— from gigantic highway junctions to winding beaches, from the abandoned lots of grocery shops all the way to the bony slopes of the Himalayas. At first glance they seem delicate, frail, but this is an illusion—they are long-lived, almost indestructible; their fleeting bodies won't decompose for some three hundred more years.

Never before have we been faced with such an aggressive form of being. Some, in a kind of metaphysical rapture, believe it's in the bags' nature to take over the world, to conquer all continents; that they are pure form that seeks contents but immediately tires of

them, throwing themselves to the wind yet again. They maintain that the plastic bag is a wandering eye that belongs to some imaginary "there," a mysterious observer taking part in the panopticon. Oth ers, meanwhile, with their feet more firmly on the ground, asser that these days evolution favors fleeting forms that can flit throug the world while at the same time attaining ubiquitousness.

## FINAL TIMETABLE

Each of my pilgrimages aims at some other pilgrim; today I final arrived. This other pilgrim was embedded in plexiglass or, in t other rooms, plastinated. I had to wait my turn in line to see it, drift along among these exhibits, beautifully lit, bilingually scribed. Arrayed before us, they resembled precious cargo brous from very far away, set out for the eye to feast on.

First I examined the carefully prepared specimens embedded plexiglass, little bits of the body, exhibits of screws and spans, ter pins and soldered joints, of those often unappreciated sma parts we don't even remember exist. The method is sound—noth can get in or out. If a war broke out, the mandible I had in fror me right now would most likely still survive, under the rubbl the ashes. If a volcano erupted, if there was a deluge or a lands the archaeologists of the future would rejoice in such a find.

But this is only the beginning. We pilgrims advanced in sil in single file, those behind nudging those ahead. What do we here, what's next, what part of the body will we be shown no these crafty plastinators, heirs of embalmers, of tanners, of a mists and taxidermists.

A spine extracted from a body and stretched out in a glass case. Retaining its natural curvature, it looked like the Alien—a passenger traveling in a human body toward its destination, an enormous polypod. A Gregor Samsa assembled out of nerves and plexuses, fashioned from a rosary of little bones interwoven with blood vessels. We could say a prayer over it, at least, or lots of prayers, until someone finally took pity and permitted it to rest in peace.

Now there was a whole person—or better said, a corpse—halved lengthwise, revealing the fascinating structure of the internal organs. The kidney, in particular, distinguished itself with its remarkable allure, like a great, lovely bean, blessed grain of the goddess of the underworld.

Farther on, in the next room—a man, a male body, slender, eyes that were slanted even though there were no eyelids, no skin at all so we pilgrims could see the starting and end points of the muscles. Did you know that muscles always start closer to the body's central line, ending more peripherally, farther out? And that dura mater is not the name of some sexy porn star, but rather a covering for the brain? And that muscles have starting points and end points? And that the strongest muscle in the body is the tongue?

Faced with this display made up exclusively of musculature, we pilgrims all involuntarily checked to see if what the description said was true, flexing our skeletal muscles, the muscles that obey our will. Unfortunately, there are also disobedient muscles, over which we hold no sway—there's really nothing whatsoever we can make them do. They settled us in the distant past, and now they govern our reflexes.

Next we learned a lot about the work of the brain, and about

how it's actually the amygdala to which we owe the existence of fragrances, as well as the expression of emotions, and the fight-or-flight impulse. To the hippocampus, meanwhile, that little sea horse, we owe our short-term memory.

The septal area is a tiny little structure in the amygdala that regulates the relationship between pleasure and addiction. This is something we should be aware of when it comes time to deal with our bad habits. We ought to know who we should be praying to for help and support.

The next specimen consisted of a brain and peripheral nerves perfectly arranged on a white surface. You could easily mistake that red design on its white background for a metro map—here's the main station, and extending out from it, the main arterial route, and then the other lines that spread out off to the side. You had to admit—it was well planned.

These modern specimens were multicolored, bright; the blood vessels, veins, and arteries beautifully displayed in fluid so as to make their three-dimensional networks stand out. The solution in which they float peacefully is no doubt Kaiserling III—it turns out that's what keeps the best.

Now we crowded around the Man Made of Blood Vessels. He looked like the anatomical version of a ghost. This was a ghost that haunted brightly lit, tiled places that fell somewhere between slaughterhouses and cosmetics labs. We sighed: we would never have thought we had so many veins in us. It's hardly a surprise we bleed at even a slight infringement on the integrity of our skin.

Seeing is knowing, we had no doubt about that. Most of all we enjoyed all the cross sections.

One such person-body lay before us now, cut up into slices. And this gave us access to altogether unexpected points of view.

## THE POLYMER PRESERVATION
## PROCESS, STEP BY STEP

- First, you prep the body as you normally would for dissection, i.e., by draining the blood;
- during the dissection you expose the parts you want to show—for example, if it's muscle, you have to remove the skin and the fat tissue. At this stage, you position the body as desired;
- next you bathe the specimen in acetone to get rid of any remaining fluids;
- the dehydrated specimen is then immersed in a silicone polymer bath and sealed inside a vacuum chamber;
- in the chamber, the acetone evaporates, and the silicone polymer takes its place, working its way into the tissues' deepest recesses;
- the silicone hardens but stays pliant.

I've touched a kidney and a liver that had been prepared in this way—they were like toys made out of tough rubber, the kinds of balls you throw for a dog to play fetch with. And the line between what is fake and what is real suddenly became very fine. I also had the rather unnerving suspicion that this technique could permanently transform original into copy.

## BOARDING

He takes off his shoes, places his backpack at his feet, and waits now for them to start boarding the plane. He has a few days' worth of facial hair, is almost bald, aged somewhere between forty and fifty. He looks like a guy who discovered not too long ago that he's not really so different from everybody else—thus attaining, in other words, his own enlightenment. Traces of that shock are still visible on his face: the eyes that only look down, around where his shoes are, likely to prevent his gaze from getting tripped up by the sight of other people. No facial expressions or gestures, which he no longer requires. After a while he gets out a notebook, a nice one, hand-sewn, probably from one of those shops that charges a fortune for cheap third-world products; it says "Traveler's Log Book" in English on the recycled-paper cover. It's a third full. He opens it up on his lap, and his black rollerball pen embarks upon a first sentence.

So I also get out my notebook and start to write about this man writing something down. Chances are he's now writing: "Woman writing something down. She's taken off her shoes and placed her backpack at her feet . . ."

Don't be shy, I think to the rest, all waiting for our gate to open—take your notebooks out, too, and write. For in fact there are lots of us who write things down. We don't let on we're looking at each other; we don't take our eyes off our shoes. We will simply write each other down, which is the safest form of communication and of transit; we will reciprocally transform each other into letters and initials, immortalize each other, plastinate each other, submerge each other in formaldehyde phrases and pages.

When we get home we'll put our written-in notebooks with all the rest—there's a box for them behind the wardrobe, or the bottom desk drawer, or the shelf on the nightstand. Here we have chronicled our other journeys already, our preparations, our happy returns. Raptures over sunset on a beach littered with plastic bottles; that evening in that hotel where the heat was on too high. A foreign street where a sick dog begged for food, and we didn't have a thing; the kids who crowded around in the village where the bus stopped to cool off its radiators. There's a recipe for peanut soup that tasted like dirty sock broth; there's the fire-eater with the scorched lips. Here is where we kept careful track of our expenses and attempted in vain to sketch the likeness of the motif that for once captured our attention for one split second on the metro. The strange dream dreamed on the plane and the beauty of the Buddhist nun in her gray robes, standing ahead of us for a little while in line. Everything is in here, even the sailor who tap-danced on the empty pier that once sent ship after ship on its way.

Who will read it?

The gate's about to open. The flight attendants are already closing in on the desk, and passengers plunged until now in lethargy arise and call their hand luggage to order. They search for boarding passes, set aside the papers they haven't finished reading with no visible regret. In their heads they perform mute examinations of conscience: Do they have everything, passport, ticket, and papers, have they exchanged money. And where is it they're going. And what for. And will they find what they are looking for, have they chosen the direction they need.

The flight attendants, beautiful as angels, check to make sure we're fit to travel, and then, with a benevolent motion of the hand, permit us to plunge on into the soft, carpet-lined curves of the tunnel that will lead us aboard our plane and onto a chilly aerial road to new worlds. That smile of theirs holds—or so it strikes us—a kind of promise that perhaps we will be born anew now, this time in the right time and the right place.

# ITINERARIUM

1. Vienna—Pathologisch-anatomisches Bundesmuseum im Narrenturm, Spitalgasse 2
2. Vienna—Josephinum, Sammlungen der Medizinischen Universität Wien, Währingerstrasse 25
3. Dresden—Deutsches Hygiene-Museum, Lingnerplatz 1
4. Berlin—Berliner Medizinhistorisches Museum der Charité, Charitéplatz 1
5. Leiden—Museum Boerhaave, Lange St. Agnietenstraat 10
6. Amsterdam—Vrolik Museum, Academisch Medisch Centrum, Meibergdreef 15
7. Riga—Pauls Stradiņš Museum of the History of Medicine, Antonijas iela 1, and Jēkabs Prīmanis Anatomy Museum, Kronvalda bulvāris 9
8. Saint Petersburg—Museum of Anthropology and Ethnography (Kunstkamera), Universitetskaya Naberezhnaya 3
9. Philadelphia—Mütter Museum of The College of Physicians of Philadelphia, 19 South 22nd Street

# INDEX OF MAPS AND DRAWINGS

The maps and drawings are taken from the *Agile Rabbit Book of Historical and Curious Maps*, © Pepin Press, Amsterdam, 2005.

## TRANSLATOR'S ACKNOWLEDGMENTS

The translator wishes to thank Antonia Lloyd-Jones, the Institute for the Book in Kraków, the National Endowment for the Arts, Esther Allen, and Sean Bye for their help with and support of this project.